TIMBER

A Novel by Greg Scherer

Editing and Proofing: Rebecca Barry

Cover and Interior design: Rick Soldin, book-comp.com

ISBN: 978-0-9849654-1-0

Printed in the United States of America

Contents

Acknowledgement

Thirty years before this book was published we (myself and two cousins) undertook a project to interview as many lumberjacks eighty years and older from northern Minnesota. As a result of this project we compiled three hundred and fifty pages of stories and recollections from thirty-five interviews that were then compiled in the Lumberjack Preservation Project "In Their Own Words." A copy of this project resides in the Minnesota Historical Society.

Their stories are generously sprinkled throughout the book and a sincere thank you is given to them and their marvelous memories, both the facts as well as the delightful exaggerations.

The characters in this book are fictional and are not intended to be reflective of any particular individuals with a few exceptions. Hungry Mike Sullivan was real. He lived in Deer River, Minnesota for most of his life and his larger-than-life portrayal here is not so much larger than his real life. Jack-the-Horse did, in fact, pull a log-laden sleigh off Jack-the Horse-Lake and he was subsequently killed in a bar room shooting. Reverend Amos Houghton lived in Grand Rapids and ministered to the lumberjacks as depicted.

Most of the other characters, Socrates, Tyler, Snoose, Schnapsie, Patty the Pig, the Maine river rats, et al, are products of my imagination into which I inserted both true stories as well as authentic "lumberjack lies." Some are real and I leave it up to the reader's imagination to sort them out.

I am also grateful to Mark Scherer and John Zitur, the afore-mentioned cousins, who so generously agreed to spend a summer prowling the north woods in search of interviews. They found the people they met to be extremely hospitable and anxious to share their yarns. On some occasions they arrived too late. Today, all our interviewed woodsmen are passed on but in these pages they still live.

Tribute Page

A tribute page, actually an additional acknowledgement page, is a good place to honor friends in the hopes that they might someday spring for drinks at the bar. I'll get to them after I pay tribute to some wonderful people who had a hand in the creation of this novel. My wife, of course, for constantly drumming into my head "You're a good writer, so write for God's sake!" and then patiently taking the time to actually read the manuscript. John Zitur and Mark Scherer for spending a summer of their valuable college years locating and interviewing these marvelous old men, literally all of whom are now passed on.

Rebecca Barry, a gifted writer in her own right, for agreeing to be my reader and character critic. She was willing to ask those irritating questions that lead to a better story. Rick Soldin, my editor, who I would quickly recommend to anyone who needs help working through the application minefields of self-publishing.

Carl Whittaker, a local artist, who took time out from painting trees and mushrooms (Pictures of, not the actual things) to do a water-color rendering of the cover picture of Socrates from an old photo.

John Gerche, a brilliant paleo-artist (By all means get his new book SHAPING HUMANITY) who encourages all creative thinking and action and also lets me help build his haunted village each Halloween.

Then there are my kids and their spouses and our grand-children and the dogs Luna, Oscar and Guthrie who just love so unconditionally.

We have a local coffee shop called Gimme! Coffee where anyone can join our little soirée each morning if they are retired or promise not to work more than twenty hours a week or just want to pull up a chair. Around the tables will sit Tony, Jim, Tom, Barry, Al, Christina, Dave, Limi, Gigi, Marilyn, Marion, Denise, Joel, Francis, David, Dan, et al, whose total lack of initiative and inspiration allowed me to find my own way as an author. But seriously, these people are my fondest and dearest friends. A day without them is a day without laughter. I owe them all a drink. Thanks guys for the encouragement.

TIMBER!!

On The Road

Book 1

One

Chicago, November 2, 1915

*T*he old man woke when the body hurtled through the door and lay sprawled across the floor. If the screaming whistle hadn't done it, the jolting of the boxcar over the rough crossing might have but neither quite as brusquely as the sudden appearance of an intruder.

Silently, he pulled off his blanket and reached for the knife concealed in his boot. He drew it out and waited. The other man lay still for a moment, groaned, rolled onto his belly and laboriously stood up. The engineer, now past the crossing, hit the throttle and the surge of the train knocked him down again. He cursed and the old man confirmed not merely his gender but his age as well; a young male, drunk, or sick. If the former, he was possibly dangerous, if the latter, an unneeded nuisance.

Again, the young man struggled to his feet. He stood silhouetted in the moonlight shining through the doorway. His arms were thrust outward as he groped for balance, his open greatcoat lending him a huge and amorphous shape. He looked toward the front of the car where the old man now crouched in the darkness and took a step toward him. Once more the train lurched again upsetting the youth's balance. He staggered back keeping his feet this time by dropping one leg quickly behind the other until he slammed into the boxcar's back wall. He hung there for a moment like wet wallpaper, then peeled off and slid slowly to the floor.

There was a moment of rustling, shoes scrapping and scratching, then stillness. There was the sound of retching. In a few minutes that stopped and there was nothing.

Chuckling softly, the old man got up, slid the door shut against the cold air and returned to sleep.

Two

Bemidji, MN – Two weeks earlier

*E*ven at 5:30 on a chilly fall morning, Hildi's Bemidji Café was bustling. The air was steamy and fragrant with the smell of buttermilk hotcakes, thick black coffee and greasy pork sausage. At the tinkling of the little bell above the door, John Whittier glanced up from his coffee. His eyes rested momentarily on the man in the doorway while many of the other patrons openly stared. The man was big and burly, with a barrel chest supported by a torso and legs unusually thick for his height. Stopping just inside the door, he looked over the early diners, greeting a number of them with a nod of his large, shaggy head. Spotting Whittier he raised a hand big as a bear paw and headed for his table.

"Morning, Mike," said Whittier gesturing to the chair across from him. "Have a seat. And grab a bite to eat. I'm buying." He knew that the "bite" was offered in mild jest as Hungry Mike Sullivan's reputation as an eater was second only to his fame as a logging boss.

"That's a grand idea, Mr. Whittier," answered Sullivan as he lowered his body into the groaning chair.

A waitress made her way to their table.

"So Mary, how are you this fine morning?" Sullivan asked good-naturedly.

The girl smiled amiably. Sullivan's friendly manner was better than a generous tip from anyone else. Mary was a good waitress, and her frugal customers often rewarded her with an extra dime, but most hoarded their pleasantries like fine gold.

"I'm just fine, Mike, and you?"

"Getting by as usual, thanks. There's a bit of a chill in the air this morning coming down from Canada but it's warm and homey in here. And it smells very inviting. That you, Mary?"

She smiled again. "No, Mike, that would be the bacon unless you noticed the Paris perfume I'm wearing under the pancake flour. Now enough of the devilry. What'll you be having this morning?"

"A stack of the flapjacks, please."

"An a slab of ham, maybe."

"That sounds good."

"And home fried potatoes and onions?"

"If you insist."

She nodded in a satisfied way having often watched him eat over the last twenty years, poured him a big mug of coffee, refilled Whittier's cup and disappeared into the kitchen. Whittier watched Sullivan warm his hands on the coffee cup for some time before either spoke.

"She'll be an early winter, I wager," Mike finally volunteered, unbuttoning his red and black checked mackinaw. "I'm still not used to the chill."

"And you'll also wager a cold one?" said Whittier, watching Mike carefully drape his coat over the back of his chair.

"I think so. Lake Bemidji had a raft of bluebills yesterday and this morning they've all taken off for the south. Sure and the snow will be as deep as a man's suspender buttons and cold, if the bear I shot yesterday knew what he was doing. He had three inches of belly fat."

"Glad to hear it. Means prime logging weather. Mike, I just wrapped up a big and tight contract so we'll need a deep frosty winter to cut and high spring water to drive."

"That's what I think too, Mr. Whittier. We'll get 'em both. Deep snow means deep rivers."

Mary brought eight hotcakes, four thick slices of ham and a mound of fried potatoes covered with fried eggs all nested on a huge platter and set it in front of Mike. "And again, Mike?" she asked.

"Again, Mary, please. But give me a couple minutes for the sake of manners." He answered without looking up. He was already focused on the food, holding his utensils as a man would grip a shovel, using the knife to push food onto the fork that was in constant motion between his plate and mouth. John Whittier watched in respectful wonderment. Just as he was mopping up the first platter, Mary brought a second, just slightly smaller one, along with a plate of unordered baking powder biscuits.

"Well, now that is very considerate. Thank you."

Eventually he paused long enough to down another mug of coffee and speak to his boss. "What you got for me this winter, Mr. Whittier?"

"Mike, we're going to put in a new camp up on Pine Island. That's one of the last major stands of prime white pine in the whole state. It's your project if you want it. If not, we'll get you something else to your liking. Your choice."

With a shrug he waved off the suggestion of anything else. "No sir, if it comes down to cutting spruce and balsam fence posts with a scissors or something that two men and a twelve foot crosscut can wrestle with for half a day, that is not much of a choice choice now, is it?"

"Good," said Whittier. "That's my thinking exactly. You're the best I have and this one's special. Now here're all the descriptions." He passed over a thick, brown satchel filled with deeds, titles, surveys, locations of benchmarks and cruiser's reports. "Get yourself a couple dozen wood butchers and jacks and put the camp together. I want a hundred men in there by early November if the weather holds. There's a flatcar of lumber and all the iron and other supplies you'll need leaving for Craig on the Gut and Liver tomorrow morning. It'll be waiting for you."

Mike collected the documents and set them on the table. As Whittier recited his instructions, Sullivan nodded slowly, politely listening to every word however familiar. The two men had done this many times before but both took seriously the gesture to tradition and the transfer of authority from one man to the other.

"If it's all the same to you, I'll see if I can get my boys together today and we'll ride up with the supplies."

"Fine with me," Whittier replied, smiling at the alacrity with which Sullivan jumped into a new assignment. "Who's your choice for cook then, Mike?" Whittier had thirty years of experience with the Itascan Lumber Company, most of it in the woods, and knew that good wages and heavy timber might bring a lumberjack into a camp, but it took good cooking to keep him there.

So did Mike. "I expect I'll find Socrates down in the Duluth Jungle. He makes good grub and he knows my system."

"He's waiting there for you?"

"No. He'll be there by freeze-up. I expect he's moving up from the south about now."

It's crazy in a way, thought Whittier. A man Socrates' age spending summers in Alabama and going to northern Minnesota for the winter. Just another strange idiosyncrasy in the men he knew to be full of them. "Fine. I know you two go way back."

"We've hoisted and toasted our share; more than I care to admit. Mr. Whittier, he's mellowed so much you would never recognize him. Age will do that. I can feel it beginning to creep over me. But, mind you, he can still swing a mean rolling pin in a fracas."

Whittier raised his mug. "To a good camp."

Mike tapped it with his own. "A safe and happy camp," he said with a smile. Whittier's eyes rested on Mike's before he drank, but he said nothing more. Mike stuck around a bit longer for some small talk, a third, short stack of cakes and several more cups of coffee. Finally he mopped his face with the napkin, stood up and reached for his purse, another gesture to tradition. Whittier, doing his part, waved Mike off. Shaking hands with the old walking boss, and thanking him, as always, for the work, Sullivan started out of Hildi's. He stopped one time at a group of men seated by the window, shared a spirited laugh with them, and was gone.

From a table against the back wall, a paunchy drummer encased in a tight gray suit and high starched shirt collar stood up. His checkered napkin hanging from his neck, he came over to Whittier.

"Excuse me," he hesitated extending his hand. "Alfred Tolliver. I sell women's corsets."

"No thank you," replied Whittier. "I'm content with the one I have."

"Of course, sir, of course. Oh, I see, you're making a joke. No, see, I have to ask you a question. That man who was with you ... who was he?"

Whittier looked the salesman over for a moment then judged him harmless and felt more tolerant of his question than his attire. "Him? That, my curious friend, is Michael Sullivan. Hungry Mike Sullivan as he's known around here." He returned to the newspaper he had opened.

"I watched him just now eat twenty pancakes, most of a whole ham, a dozen biscuits, upward of a pound of potatoes, lord knows how many fried eggs and a gallon of coffee. I never saw a man eat so much!"

"Is that so?"

"I ask you, sir, can a man eat so much?"

"Apparently, sir."

The sales man would not be mollified. "Why, he could keep a butcher in business single-handedly."

Whittier was a pretty fair poker player. "Yes, we feel he's good for the local economy."

"But no one can eat that much!"

Whittier stood up and drew on his coat and began to leave without bothering to look at the man. "He might have eaten sixty if he hadn't already had breakfast before he came in."

Three

In route through Wisconsin, November 2, 1915

*T*en hours out of Chicago Tyler Emerson Caldwell opened his eyes. Sleeping on the rough wooden floor had frozen his limbs into a fetal position. The fact that he had passed out and not had to fight for sleep had only been temporary good fortune. With a moan he tenderly rubbed his bruised and bloodshot eyes and looked around. The straw-covered floor, cracked wooden walls, and the steady rhythm of the wheels clicking over the rails told him more than he wanted to know.

He rolled over onto his back, groaned again, and buried his face in his arms. A cleaving pain hacked away at his skull and the rest of his body felt as though it had just and barely survived a severe beating.

"Oh God," he whimpered, remembering. Even as memories of the previous night flooded back, another thought began to intrude on his misery. If he wasn't dead, he deserved to be. "I should have fallen under this train instead of in it," he announced to the unwelcome morning.

With substantial help from the wall, he painstakingly got to his feet. Feeling his way along the side of the car, he made for the shaft of light coming through a two-inch crack in the boxcar door. Forcing his hands into the opening, he slowly worked the door open until he could get his body into the gap. Then, his feet braced against the sill of the door, he pushed. Initially the door didn't budge, then grudgingly. When the roller worked its way over a spot of welding, it abruptly came free. It cost him his balance and nearly threw him out of the doorway before he caught himself, one leg hanging precipitously outside.

The roadbed raced past him in stony blur. He felt a terrifying urge to let go. Reason battled instinct and, whichever won the test of wills, pulled him back. He stepped back to the opening and, bracing himself against the doorjamb, looked out.

The Wisconsin autumn was clicking by at forty miles an hour, the tracks following the course of a small river. At the edge of the roadbed rock ballast the embankment dropped steeply to a rocky gorge. In the river below, the shallow water sparkled in the early sun as it played among the rocks. Up on the far bank of the river and out into the hills beyond, birch and maple were already ablaze with reds and yellows.

A blast of cold, wet air coursed over the young man's face and turned his long, sandy hair into a flowing streamer. His watering eyes kept moving downward, to the embankment, the steep drop and whatever lay below. He shifted his weight away from the door frame and centered his body in the middle of the opening. His hands rested lightly on his hips; his coat, unbuttoned, floated on the wind revealing the dirty and torn tuxedo he was wearing. His knees bent slightly to maintain his balance in the rocking boxcar. He resembled a sailor braced on the quarterdeck on a rolling, storm-tossed sea.

Slowly he bent forward at the waist. He took his hands off his hips and reached forward and outward.

"You 'oughten be doing that, sonny."

Caldwell spun around so quickly that he nearly did leave the car. Fighting to retain his balance, he stared into the dimly lit rear of the boxcar, straining to find a body to match the voice.

The voice came again, low and gravelly. "I said you don't wanna do that. You might fall out. Or maybe you do?" The boy was trying to make out a body, a face. "If you do want to do it, this ain't the right place anyway."

"Who's there?"

No answer "I said, who the hell is back there? You mess with me and I'll straighten you out quick. You hear me?"

Still no answer. Finally, the kid asked, "Right place for what? Who are you?"

"Nobody back here but us rats, Sonny." The voice was a teasing snarl and not friendly.

Caldwell cautiously moved away from the door. "What do you mean, right place?" he demanded again. If he was getting out, it wouldn't be because some dirty tramp pushed him.

"Ta get kilt, of course. Along here, all you're gonna do is break a leg and end up hollering until some deer hunter packs you out of there. Or die of hunger if he don't. No sir, not the right place at all.

Fact is, a fella'd have to be plain nuts to jump here. Or a brainless boob. You ain't a boob, are you, boy?"

His eyes adjusting to the darkness, the young man picked up the shadowy form picking itself off a pile of straw in the corner. Here was someone real to talk back to now.

"I wasn't going to jump!" He knew his voice to too loud, too strident, even for the noise of the moving boxcar. Did the guy believe him? "You're right, a man would have to be crazy," he said in a calmer tone.

The old man casually walked past him and stood in the opening, confident in his spread-legged stance. The kid backed further into the car. "Name's Socrates. Welcome to my home. What's yours and where's yours, sonny?" Then he undid his fly and threw his next words over his shoulder. "Sure, you weren't going to jump, sonny and I ain't gonna pee. We're both just showing off, right? But you know, boy, you opened the door and stood in front of it like a drunken looney. Sure, a door can be just to look through, but normally its best suited for going in or out. Since you were already in, I figured you were headed out. And I gotta tell you, sonny, the way you came in last night, not knocking, no introductions, forgetting to shut the door, I can't say I'd miss you. You were pukin' and moanin' like a cat full of hair-balls. Then you passed out in the kitchen. I keep an orderly boxcar. No poop, no pee, no puke."

Caldwell had backed against the far car door. "You were here then?" He rubbed his face, trying to scour away his confusion over last night.

"Sure, back there in the bedroom. Saw your whole crazy show. You were for certain running from something then, and just now you looked like you were intent on finishing the running for good. But, before you act on your intentions, I suggest you consider this little gem: '*Behold I set before you the way of life and the way of death; that by your own choosing you shall be delivered this day.*' That's from Jeremiah 2:1 you know. And what it means, seems to me, is it's your choice to make. But that don't guarantee that you'll make the right one, does it?"

The young man, so piously and seriously addressed, swallowed hard. "My name is Tyler Caldwell and I am not a boy," he said with all the firmness at his command which he knew wasn't much.

"Well, I can see you ain't a girl. So what might you be?"

"I'm nineteen years old." Indignation put a hard edge on his voice.

Socrates didn't laugh. "Nineteen? You aren't pulling my leg? Still don't make you a girl. Must be a boy; almost a man. I'm a boy, too, you know, an old boy. We're all boys, us males."

Then he read the pain written over Tyler's face. "No, nineteen certainly is not a boy. I was working five years by the time I was nineteen. Times were so hard I don't remember when it happened. You don't look a boy either, least ways not in size. You are a big one. And you say you weren't going to jump?"

"I was not going to jump," Tyler answered, holding to his story. "I was just looking to see where we were. And the door and the wind ..."

"Sure, it gets to you, don't it? It's the magic of train travel. Even more fun if you ain't hungover. Something I gave up a long time ago."

"Where are we?" he asked, as much to change the subject as because he cared.

Socrates moved to the back of the car and began digging among his belongings. He shouted over the noise. "We're right here, of course. And in five hours we'll still be right here. It's the best place to be on a moving train. As to the other, suit yourself, but if you happen to get an itch to squish yourself, wait 'til we cross this here creek about twelve miles down. The trestle's high enough, the bottom's far enough and she's all rock at the bottom. That should do it right. Even at that, I wonder if you'd mind leaving me that big wool coat you're wearing. You wouldn't want to risk breaking your fall with it and where I'm going, I could sure use it."

"You're a sorry old man," Tyler muttered. Socrates stiffened, sensing he had pushed too far, even for him. Tyler moved back to what he felt was his end of the car and sat down.

In a couple of minutes the old man returned to the doorway. "Why'd you get on at all?" he asked.

"What?"

Socrates turned to look at his face. "I said, why'd you jump the train?" Tyler didn't answer him.

"Okay, none of my nosey business, I guess." Socrates shrugged and went on about his housekeeping."

He stood a good eight inches shorter than Tyler's six feet plus and was slightly built. He had a travel-worn face, what was visible of it. Most was covered with a salt and pepper beard, mostly salt, about two inches long. But he was surprisingly hardy. In his right hand he carried a canvas valise like those cement masons used for their tools. In his left, was a corked bottle full of water. He moved confidently about the rocking car, his walk quick and springy. Finally he sat down in the doorway, his legs dangling outside the car.

Opening the valise, he pulled out a smaller cloth bag, dumped out some toiletries and began to clean himself. He brushed his teeth, combed his hair and splashed some water from the bottle over his face. Returning the items to the valise, he went again to the rear of the car, came back with an old potato sack, resumed his seat at the door and turned his eyes to Tyler.

"Think you can force down a little breakfast, Mr. Caldwell?"

The mention of food set Tyler's stomach to rumbling. When had he last eaten? Not since lunch the day before.

"Maybe. Is it any good?"

"'Course not, but don't be bashful with your compliments. Come over here, sonny, and we'll dig into the turkey and see. But don't be too particular or you'll be eating wishes and dreams instead of my grub. Understand?"

Tyler crawled over and watched him pull a small alcohol stove from the sack, draw a kitchen match across his pants, light the stove and place a small pan on it. He filled half the pan with water from his bottle and threw in some coffee grounds. He then produced some biscuits and a small tin of jelly. In five minutes they were drinking hot coffee and chewing quietly on the hard rolls.

"Not bad for hobo grub," said the old man after a bit. He wasn't soliciting an opinion, just rendering his own appraisal. "There's nothing like an egg for the coffee, though, but they're so darn hard to keep on the road. Heck, there's nothing like fresh eggs is there? You get eggs often, sonny?"

Tyler's idea of breakfast was normally three or four eggs lightly scrambled or poached, several glasses of cold milk, and maybe pancakes or French toast sprinkled with powdered sugar and cinnamon and topped with fresh strawberries; and everything served by a maid.

"Yes, whenever I want," he said. Then, recovering a modicum of manners he added, "But these biscuits taste okay." He spoke through a mouthful of the coffee-softened dough.

"Well now, that sounded a might close to a thank you and if it was, you are right welcome." He paused. "I know what you mean, though. About eggs now. I once worked on a chicken ranch. We were runnin' about ten thousand head of chickens. Out on the horses all day long rounding them up for banding and egg picking. Yep. Chickens and eggs everywhere you stepped. Shipped it all to St. Louis. The woman put eggs in everything she cooked. Not that you can't do that, mind you. Eggs are pretty sociable to the stomach. But lordy, I did get sick of 'em. Know what I mean? Where I'm heading now, there's no eggs at all, hardly. But pork! Pork enough to turn you into a lard can! Or turn your can into lard. Get my drift? Been going there for forty years but damn if I can remember the last time I had bacon *and* eggs. Don't that just bust ya, the way life's always dishing up one or the other but hardly ever both?" He laughed at his own joke.

Tyler was just staring at Socrates but not in the least bit deterred, he headed off again. "I don't normally have meal-company when I'm traveling. Folks on the road mostly look out for themselves." He looked at Tyler. "You probably think I'm a bum, don't ya. Don't worry. I don't mind. I'm not but I've met a lot of nice ones. So even if I was one, I'd still not mind." He chuckled, adding, "It's mighty economical, too. Now, I know you're not a bum either, are you?"

"Are you some kind of preacher?" The old man seemed so annoyingly at peace with himself.

"Who me? Lord, no!"

"You know the Bible."

"Sure, but that don't mean I'm in the preaching business, does it? Last I heard they don't keep the good book locked away, do they?"

"I didn't mean that."

"No matter. Fact is, I can quote from every book in the Bible ... except Numbers, of course. There's nothing worth knowing in Numbers. The rest of it, I find it settling during life's little travails." He thought a moment. "But you know sonny, if I was a priest, I'd be a darn good one, 'cept for the cussin,' which I've tried hard to dissuade from my life."

"How did you get the name Socrates? He was Greek. Are you?"

"Nah, I ain't Greek, but that's right, he was. No, Gerald is what they said my folks had named me; the people in the orphanage. But if I was ever called it, I'd swear the poor fool never existed. Hate the name, Gerald. Folks that can stomach me at all call me Socrates. Quite a handle, huh? The reason is on account of I can read. I suppose that's no big deal to a young whip like you. You can read, can't you?"

Tyler nodded disdainfully and Socrates marched on jovially. "Got a little problem speakin' though, right? No matter, it'll pass with the biscuits. I guarantee you will pass something when you eat my biscuits. Could be too much lard. I never know. Anyway, where I come and go, readin's quite a feather in a man's cap. So, onetime, a fella named Sylvester. ... Come to think of it, that feller must of read a bit, too. Suppose mostly old stuff. Me, I like romance novels." Socrates laughed. He had the wide-open laugh of a man who didn't leave any emotions left unsaid.

"Where are you from?" asked Tyler.

"Eh, the boy is getting a mite curious now. Where from? Just about anywhere you can name, I guess. I was born up north, somewhere between there and a long spit over the Canadian border. Between the stumps. My folks both died of a bad winter when I was maybe a year or two old and relatives took me down to Georgia. Times got hard for them so they put me in an orphanage. Down in Charleston, South Carolina. I guess when they couldn't feed me they figured that was better than nothing. Only that's just what that place turned out to be. Nothin'! I ran away six times by the time I was fourteen. God, but they were hard on a lad. Nothing but beatings and backbreaking chores from dawn to dark. I didn't mind the hard work, but a beating is sure no substitute for play. Anyway, I'd run and they'd catch me and I'd run again and they'd come drag me back and so on. It got to be a game. The sixth time I made it out. Got clean away. Maybe they figured I wasn't worth chasing any more. Made it clear back up into the woods. Got a job in a logging camp there. That was way back in '70. The clerk, this Sylvester guy, took it on himself to teach me to read. He claimed to have known my pa. Maybe he owed him something? Dunno. Do know I owe that clerk plenty. A bit of time passed from then and now and here I am, going back again for the umpteenth time.

"Back where."

"To the camps, Tyler; the logging camps. Only fit place to be if you're on the run or looking for a reason to stop running. Up there a man is a man, the boys get sorted out fast. If I were a young man, I'd be up in the tall timber country or in the pulp if I were just a little younger. I'm sixty. Surprised?"

"Excuse me?"

"I said I'm sixty. Don't look it, do I."

Tyler thought he looked all of sixty, maybe seventy. He was a little bent over as he walked and, over the years, his once solid muscles had begun surrendering to gravity.

"Like it or not, and I don't much," Socrates continued placidly. "That's pretty old for a lumberjack, you know."

"You're a lumberjack?" This little man didn't square with his notion of Paul Bunyan.

"Sonny, if a man were lying, he'd take offense at the way you said that. I ought'a know what I am and ain't. I am so what you think don't rub on me much."

"I didn't mean anything. It's just that I thought ... well, I thought lumberjacks were bigger. A whole lot bigger," he flushed.

"I'll tell you, boy, and I never do take personally honest stupidity, to set the record straight, some of us are mighty big. Some of us are every bit as big as the tall tales make us out to be. Some of us are so much bigger than life that even a hefty lie wouldn't do it justice. Then we gotta resort to the truth. And then," he chuckled contentedly, "some of us are a mite smaller. It don't matter what size your pants are once you put them on up there. If you don't belong, the timber sorts you out soon enough. I've been working up there more than forty years now, doing everything from felling to clerking." He paused. "Guess I'm big enough, all right."

"I didn't mean anything by it. I just didn't know, all right? The ... biscuits were good."

Tyler started to stand up, but the old man yanked him down again. "So, where you from, boy?"

Tyler bumped back onto the car floor, rolling from one butt cheek onto the other.

"Chicago. Evanston. My father ..." He stopped as the anger came surging back. "My father is a banker. A wealthy one." He made himself say it even as he gagged on it. His voice caught as if one of Socrates' biscuits were still stuck in his throat. "We are ... he's wealthy." There was an embarrassing pause. "This is all new to me." Glancing around at the car walls, he repeated, "Real new."

"I figured. Not only do you talk good, but only a banker's son would go bumming a ride on a freight train dressed in a monkey suit." Socrates laughed good-naturedly as he pointed at Tyler. Tyler looked down at his tailored evening dress and then at Socrates.

"Oh, God, I forgot I ..." Then he, too, began laughing and a little of the tension seemed to lift off him.

"Putting those duds together with the welts on your face, I'd say you've been doing some exciting living. What are you running from, Sonny? You kill someone?"

The other Socrates had also been an old man who asked hard questions, Tyler remembered. This one's question called for either an acceptable lie or absolute honesty. Tyler felt he was straddling a crevasse neither side of which had any more attraction than the gulf between he and Socrates. But then, he wasn't sophisticated enough to lie.

"I don't know. And, no I did not kill anyone, other than myself, almost." Tyler stared at his hands. "I almost did, I think." Socrates patiently waited. The old man's hospitality confused him; so did his lack of any posturing. It was going to be a long day and Socrates could be a very patient man.

Finally his silence wore the kid down. "Oh, damn, yes I do," he admitted, looking out the car door. Then he was quiet for a long while before he exclaimed, "Oh, my god! God damn it!" Several more moments passed and he turned to Socrates. It was time to let it out, some of it, anyway.

"My father," he began. "No, my family. Graham. Everyone, I guess. I have a brother, Graham. He was in the war. He flew in an outfit called the Escandrille Lafayette ... in France. A month ago, he shot down a German plane and was wounded so they sent him home to convalesce. He was a big hero. That's when everything went bad for me." Tyler tucked his hands under his legs to stop the shaking. "He was always the good son; the favorite son. And all along he'd been writing my girl behind my back. At least I thought she was my girl. When he came home ... it all came out." Breathing hard he described in labored bursts how the last shreds of a fragile brother-hood had come unraveled. How Graham's heroism had stolen the last remnants of his father's love. How he had stolen Ellie Morgan. "There was a party, in Graham's honor, naturally. I got drunk and we fought. I hit him. He was on crutches and I knocked him down and I ... I wanted to kill him. They pulled me off him and held me. He was enraged and hit me and hit me and cursed me." He touched the welt on his face.

"Who? said Socrates. "Graham?"

"No, not Graham, the kid sobbed. "My father. When I got free of them I just ran. I drove off in the family sedan and piled it into a tree. I saw this train and, I don't know why, I crawled on." Exhausted, he lay back on his elbows, and made a serious study of his toes.

It wasn't in Socrates' nature to rush to judgment. Instead he took out his pipe, carefully filled and lit it. As he drew on it he reflected on how the boy had compounded his real problems with others of his own making. And then he ran away from the lot. An old story. Cain and Abel, Jacob and Esau. One favored over the other. Jacob couldn't get his way either so he had to leave home to work things out on his own. What nonsense. Bible or no, it was a boy's way out of trouble, not a man's.

But he was put to mind of another fellow a lot like that, a young kid who also couldn't help but run either. That guy ran from one problem to another only making them worse by the running. Every time he had a chance to settle down and accept the responsibilities that went with manhood he chickened out. Fact was, he did understand how it could happen because it reminded him of himself.

"Why don't you just go home, sonny?" The words were direct and sharp but there was no hardness in them. "Make up with your brother and your pa. Find another girl. You're a good looking kid."

"I can't!" Tyler said.

"Sure you can. Brothers fight all the time. Go on home, boy, and give yourself time to grow up a little before you hit the road again. Your folks are worried about you and likely just as sorry about this cockup as you are."

"No! Don't you hear me? I can't."

"Why in the hell not?" Socrates was shouting too. This kid had no right to yell at him. But then, yelling back wouldn't help much. "Why can't you?" he asked evenly.

Tyler's head was on his chest, rocking back and forth. "I just can't go back there," he whispered hoarsely. "Not now." He was crying again.

Socrates had seen enough broken men to know this one was close. He studied his downcast companion. The kid was not a boy in any physical sense of the word. He'd measure up in size to most of the men Socrates knew. But he was soft, unformed, a baby. He lacked a tough outer layer, and his heart, if he had one, lacked something too. What Socrates saw aroused no sympathy in him. Rarely had he been shown any during his own hard life and it had never come to be a part of his makeup. He was the type of man who, when he saw a bad situation, either tried to change it or walked away, more often the latter. But that was his manner. The world he grew up in usually gave but one chance, seldom two, and never three.

Tyler had a problem all right. Problems. Out of a home, on the road, and without the common sense of a barn fly. The kid wasn't even very likable. It was unnatural for someone that big to be so needy and still carry an air of superiority. And he had that pampered air about him. Why was a kid so physically mature so emotionally backward? He didn't have the manners of a jackass. Besides, he was probably just getting what he deserved. Things generally worked out that way. He had brought his troubles on himself and, rather than go home and face up to them, he had run and wanted to keep on running. The stupid kid had crashed a car and boarded a train in the middle of the night dressed in a darned opera suit bent on ... what? Killing himself in a Wisconsin gorge? No, Socrates saw now he wouldn't have had the guts to do that. No, definitely no temptation to make the boy's troubles any concern of his.

Socrates had read about that fellow Quixote. He didn't think much of that guy, either. An incompetent boob some other fool made into a hero. There was no room in the real world for such mush. In the woods a guy like Quixote would be exposed for a faker right off and run out of camp. Every man looked out for himself; that was Socrates' code. That was the code of the world.

"So," Socrates announced in a very businesslike manner, "where do you plan to go now?"

"I don't know."

"You got any money?"

Tyler eyed him suspiciously, then slowly nodded. "Some. Enough."

"Well then, you're better off than most folks I know," Socrates grunted. He threw the rest of his things together and started back out of the wind.

"Take me with you," a barely audible voice pleaded.

"What did you say?"

Tyler stood and swallowed hard. "I said take me with you. You said you were going to a logging camp. Take me with you."

"Like hell I will."

Tyler grabbed Socrates' sleeve. "Get me a job. I'll work hard."

"You?" Socrates didn't mean to spit out the word but the notion was ridiculous. "Look at you. You ain't worked an honest day in your life. You're too soft for the woods a spoiled kid like you." The boy wouldn't let go of the old man's eyes.

"Look, I don't hire the help. Everyone gets his own job. And if you do luck onto a job, I danged well guarantee you'll work. Harder than you'd ever imagine."

"Then take me along and I'll get my own job!"

"You mind your tongue, sonny. Besides, I travel alone. I don't need no green kid hanging on my suspenders."

But Tyler wouldn't let it go because he had nowhere else to turn. "You're lying, aren't you? There isn't any camp and you are just a bum. I knew it! You're nothing but a little bag of hot air."

Socrates looked down at the boy's hands clenched tightly to the front of his shirt. His grip was hard; scared hard. His eyes were scared, too. He did need help in a fierce way. *But I don't need him.*

Then the boy let go and broke into crying sobs. "He cursed me. He hit me. I don't know how many times; in front of all of them and he cursed me out of his life. I can't go back. Can't you see? You hear me?"

Socrates stepped away from the child and drew on his pipe. It had gone out. It was a sharp, chilly day and likely to stay that way for some time. It was a lousy time to be out on your own. What the hell, it was none of his concern. He tapped the tobacco back into the bottom of the bowl, looked out over the rocky Wisconsin dairy country and very slowly turned back to the youth.

"I think, then," he said through teeth clenched on the pipe stem, "you should come with me to the camps." He never would understand what made the words come out.

"You swear!"

Socrates shook his head. "I never swear, dammit. But remember, you get your own job and you keep your own job. Understand?"

"Yes," breathed Tyler with immeasurable relief. "Just one thing."

"What's that?" Socrates sighed with annoyance as much at himself as at the boy.

"You don't call me 'sonny' or 'boy' or 'kid' anymore."

Their eyes met and held. A trace of a smile crossed Socrates' face. "Sure, sonny, when you earn it."

Four

Pine Island Forest – Koochiching County – Minnesota
November 2, 1915

*F*irst dawn was starting to show beyond the clearing they had slashed in the pine. Growing each day, it was beginning to acquire the shape and features of what it was to become: Itasca Lumber Camp #2.

Mike Sullivan pushed through the tent flap and looked out over the camp in progress. Frost from his night breath encrusted his beard and moustache. Rubbing his hand over his face, he roughly banished it away along with any lingering sleepiness. His practiced eyes surveyed the work.

The bunkhouse walls were nearly complete. Pine logs, twenty inches in diameter and seventy feet long had been wrestled into position and laid four high, ready for fitting the spruce rafter poles. A partition bisecting the building separated the cook shack on the east side from the sleeping quarters. The camp office and the black-smith shop with the long, low, lean-to shelter for the horses were almost ready for service.

Mike looked down at the heavy hoarfrost that covered every-thing in sight and turned the silent forest into a dazzling crystalline wonderland. Two weeks, he thought, then he'd have to be ready. Hell, two at the outside, maybe less.

It was going to be another cold day. Soon they would all be cold and the ground would stiffen hard enough to get the stompers out in the swamps. The Labrador tea and bog cranberries could be beaten down so the swamp would freeze and become an integral part of the road system he and his cruiser had already laid out.

He was anxious to be done so he could begin. There was no profit in camp building. It was just a place to sleep and get chow.

When the loggers came and set the woods alive with the sounds of axe and cross-cut saws, then Mike wouldn't be so anxious.

He leaned over the washtub, thrust his face through the heavy skim of ice covering the water and buried his head in the tub. Then, straightening like a bull moose rising from cropping water plants in a misty bog, he shook his head, blowing the water from his mouth and nose. Morning toilet completed, he turned back to the tent an bellowed to the slumbering crew.

"Dat's all, boys! Let's get at 'er! Time to get this camp up and running!"

He listened for the muted sounds of men awakening, reaching first for consciousness, then for their boots. Satisfied that they were getting up, he started off toward the smell of frying side pork coming from the cook tent.

A whiskey jay, believed by lumberjacks to be the reincarnation of long dead loggers, its feathers silvery-gray like the morning and still fluffed up against the cold, was perched on the peak of the tent pole. At a whistle from Mike, it glided onto his shoulder and together they went in for breakfast.

A day that promised to be both cold and long had begun.

Five

*T*wenty hours out of Chicago the westbound freight pulled into the Minneapolis Great Northern yards close under the towering grain elevators.

They knew the end had come by the lurching of the cars as they humped and bumped against each other's couplings, bucking against their own inertia. Tyler was sleeping beside Socrates and didn't even open his eyes. They had already made a score or more of such stops at small farm towns along the line. But after the final jolt, Socrates whispered a quiet, "That's it." Tyler jerked awake and climbed eagerly to his feet. He stretched lavishly and started for the door.

"No!" Socrates hissed.

The kid stared at him in some confusion. "What? Let's get out of here. I'm freezing." He began to open the car door.

Socrates stopped him with a cuff on the back of the head. "I said no," he spat in a harsh whisper. "Didn't they teach you that word in your fancy school? You go out there now and you might get your head split open by some yard boss or gandy dancer. Mr. Hill doesn't like folks who think they can ride for free. Who's Mr. Hill? He's the son-of-a-buck that built this railroad."

Tyler reluctantly backed away from the door.

They waited until the thin shaft of light coming through the slit in the door began to show yellow, then red and finally nothing but blackness. At Socrates' sign, they quietly worked open the door just enough to peek out.

Socrates listened at the opening, hushing the already quiet Tyler with his hand. Ten minutes went by before he brought his mouth close to Tyler's ear.

"Hear that? No? Someone's out there. He's between this car and the next one down. He's hunkered down, waiting for someone to move."

Socrates went back to the door. Two minutes later, Tyler heard more feet scurrying across the roof, running away from the man on the ground. Then the sound of shoes on gravel came to them again. Socrates reached into one of his pockets, pulled out a small bag and, opening it, poured the contents into his hand. Again he waited.

The man on the roof had reached the end of the car and started climbing down the ladder. They could hear the man on the ground shift his weight on the gravel.

Suddenly the man was moving, coming along the side of the car. He was right alongside the door when Socrates reached out and threw the contents of his hand in the man's face, grabbed his bags and slid open the door.

"Run, Tyler!" he screamed. "Run like your feet are on fire!"

They dropped to the ground. The man on the gravel was doubled up alongside the car, clawing at his eyes and cursing. The man on the roof scampered out and the three of them ran across the railroad yard past the switchman's house and out onto Washington Avenue. The roof-man nodded a quick thank you and disappeared into the residential neighborhood.

Tyler was breathing heavily with excitement. "What happened? What did you do?"

"That was a yard dick," panted Socrates. "Mean as spit. He was carrying a pick handle to bust that hobo's head in if he caught him. Ours too."

"What did you do to him?"

"Pepper. I threw a little pepper in his eyes. You use salt to tame birds, pepper for train detectives. Look at him now."

The guard was staggering off toward the switch house, clawing at his watering eyes and sneezing all the way. The yard settled into silence. Tyler turned to go on, but Socrates put his hand on the boy's sleeve. "Wait a bit, son and watch the cocoons open up.

Car doors were rolling open all along the train. Motionless lumps up on the catwalks began to stand and move quickly to the ladders. Bodies extricated themselves from the girders and framework of the car's underbellies. In the closing dark, close to twenty-five men left the train and ran off in the general direction of downtown Minneapolis.

"Look at 'em," said Socrates. "Like ticks off a dog headed for the washtub." Tyler stared at the little army of indigents, transients, small-time opportunists and just plain poor folk. "Look and remember, boy. Not many ride the rails just for the thrill and adventure of it like you."

Those that passed close to them had a consistent unwashed odor about them. A few of the ripest needed no breeze to carry their smell. Their faces were streaked with grime. Dark eyes nested in deep sockets, like shrews peeking out of their holes. Cheekbones and jaws protruded like the knees on a grasshopper. Their dirty misshapen garments hung on them like shirts on a clothesline.

As the last man disappeared into the dark, Tyler whispered, "Who are they?"

"Them?" Socrates said, starting off down the street. "Just a few of my friends."

"As opposed to Mr. Hill's friends, I suppose?" Tyler was doing his best to hide his amazement that so many men had been sharing the train with them.

"Yes, Mr. Hill," Socrates snarled. "Lots of them boys lost their youth and their backs laying his track and making him rich. Now they can't even afford to ride on his pretty train. To him I bequeath the whole book of Lamentations." He spat and quickened the pace.

"Where are we going?" Tyler asked hurrying after a suddenly talked out Socrates. They were going north on Washington. Darkened grain mills and warehouses lined the right side of the street while on the left and into the city beyond shone the gas street lights of downtown. Tyler's feet began to throb. His stiff patent leather shoes were not designed for hiking. They moved fast for fifteen minutes.

"Goin'?" Socrates suddenly responded, just when Tyler thought he'd drop, as if the question had just been asked. "Well, we're goin' to Widegirth Gertie's. But don't call her that and expect to live long." At the intersection of Washington and Hennepin Avenues, Socrates turned right, away from the center of town. Tyler glanced back over his shoulder at the cars and carriages moving up and down Hennepin, the main thoroughfare of Minneapolis.

"Well, it seems to me there's more lights behind us. That's where the good hotels would be. Are you sure you're looking in the right direction?"

"We're not looking, sonny, we're going to," snapped Socrates. "Gertie's isn't good but it's acceptable and she's got a clean bed for us. Hot water and suds, too. Besides, it's a good place to rendezvous with the old bunch." He elaborately drew out the word 'rendezvous'. "If you thought my boxcar grub was good, and I know you didn't, wait'll you dig into Gertie's cookin'."

"Why did you call her Widegirth?"

"It fits her. In fact, it fits her better every year. You'll see. Her place, it isn't really a hotel, you know, not like you're thinking, anyway. More of a boarding house."

"Boarding house, a place for tramps and cheap salesmen?"

"Take your pick, Tyler, but don't forget, we ain't selling anything." As an afterthought he added, "She was quite a looker in her day. Yep, we both were, Gertrude and me."

They crossed the steel arch bridge, one of the city's engineering marvels. It connected Minneapolis proper on the west bank with Northeast Minneapolis on the east. The bridge didn't cross the Mississippi in one glorious arching span. It crossed half the river at a time because Nicollet Island interrupted its grand sweep. On the east banks of the island, another bridge picked up the traveler, terminating on the Northeast side at the bottom of a little hill crowned by Our Lady of Lourdes church.

They turned off the bridge onto Island Avenue on Nicollet Island and followed the west bank of the island. Five minutes later they took a right turn on Maple Place and then another right a block later on Nicollet Street. Abruptly, Socrates turned off the wooden sidewalk and onto a rough flagstone walkway that led up to the porch of Gertie's, a beat up two-and-a-half story residence. It was part Gothic, part Queen Anne with a blush of Victorian around the edges. A wide veranda fronted the house, wrapped around the corner and headed off down the street, ending only after it had run out of house to embrace. Numerous bowed and bay windows, dormers, saddles, gabled peaks and turreted corners broke up the faded white clapboard siding. A red light glowed in a front window.

"This is Gertie's?"

"Sure is. Quite a handsome edifice, isn't it," Socrates said with admiration.

He smiled broadly, having a habit of ending many of his remarks that way. You save a lot of teeth for really important scraps that way, he'd explain if asked. 'Course, the place needs a little work but all in all it's a real palace."

Tyler caught up to him on the porch. A sign identified the place as offering 'Clean beds, Fair rates, Meals included.' It also went on to state that if he, or she, were not a person of refined tastes, then he or she need not apply his or her hand to the knocker.

"Does this place have women?"

"What are you talking about, now?"

"The red light. It's advertising women for hire."

"Oh, the light!" Socrates broke into another laugh. "I gotta tell Gertie about that. Don't worry, kid, those days are long past for the folks inside this house so don't get yourself in an up roar. The light is just kept lit for old time's sake. Sort of a monument to Gertie's past glories."

"Oh."

"Anyways, I bet you're a virgin, aren't ya? If you are, hang on to it. There's nothing at all wrong with virginity. I started out as one myself. Just never was much good at it. It's a funny thing, virginity. Like a new pair of shoes, pinches and gnaws at a young man and you can't wait to get shed of it. But once you do, you're just a barefoot beggar again. Still, most young men seem to think that sleeping with a girl has something to do with manhood. I'm speaking from a misspent youth now. I say save yourself for the right girl."

"You have advice for almost everything, don't you?"

"I call it wisdom. I've been soaking it up for a lot of years. One thing I have learned, though, a wise man never tries to convince a dumb one he's right. Sometimes it's hard to tell which is which."

"And that means?"

"It means, my lad, that a smart man is smart enough to get smarter by his own wits without another man's badgering."

"So you're telling me to ignore everything you say?"

"Ignore what you want. Ignore everything but the truth," said Socrates. "The truth wears well on dumb and smart alike. The trick is to sift it out of all the lies. Not that I ever lie, mind you."

Tyler barely nodded.

"Just nuggets off the ground, my boy, nuggets off the ground.

When she opened the door, Tyler recognized Gertie immediately. Though she wasn't quite as wide as her name implied, there was plenty of her to fill a chair and then some. Her days of beauty had been gone for some time. There were still lingering traces of it; a sensual attractiveness that once had easily parted heated young men from their money. Her face was small and round with full, lightly rouged cheeks. Her eyes were brown and very soft, the corners tracked with crows-feet, the brow lightly furrowed. Her blonde, going gray, hair was parted in the middle and tied back into carefully braided pigtails. She had on a pale blue dress, frayed around the collar, the product of much wear and many washings. But she beamed like a little girl when her eyes rested on Socrates.

"Socrates, baby!" she cried. She grabbed him by the shoulders, ate him up with a great bearhug, and swept him into the house.

"Gertie! Gertie!" he groaned, danglling in her arms. "Those are ribs, not barrel staves. Go easy, girl!"

"I should break every bone in your worthless carcass, you old cuss. It would serve you right. Not a single line all summer."

Putting him down, she flung him out at arm's length. About an inch taller than Socrates, she outweighed him by at least fifty pounds. "You old buzzard," she whispered fondly. "I thought you had gone on to your glory somewhere. Every time I heard about some big train pile-up, I pictured you squeezed under that wreckage."

"Now, Sugar."

"Don't 'Sugar' me. I was sure you had bought it in that big freight wreck in Nebraska.

"I wasn't in Nebraska."

"Nebraska. Of all places! I just knew you were buried out there on some god-forsaken prairie. Covered over with all that spilled wheat, buzzards digging for your bones. Yuk! Get away from me!"

"Gertie, I wasn't in Nebraska."

"Promise me right now you will never go back to Nebraska again."

"I promise. I promise."

"I figured they just stuffed your skinny carcass down some gopher hole and plugged it up with a cork. For pity's sake!" She began chewing through a long list of diseases and disasters Socrates might have suffered.

"Gertie, dear," Socrates finally interrupted. "You just stop that carrying on. You know I got your address tattooed on my rear with instructions to mail the remains back here if any part of me gets killed."

"Oh, my name's there all right, along with the names of ten or twelve other floozies. I wouldn't be surprised if you're tattooed all the way down to your ankles. Well, no matter, some of the boys came in yesterday early and said they saw you in Illinois so I knew I'd get at least one more look at your handsome face." Gertie smiled, her pleasure genuine.

"It ain't so much to look at," said Socrates, trying to milk yet another compliment.

"No, you're right, it ain't and it won't get any better, but it's mine and age has improved my ability to see the finer things in a man. And, hello, who is this handsome devil you brought in with you?"

"Gertie," introduced Socrates, "meet Tyler Caldwell from Chicago."

"Well," Gertie cooed, exhaling softly, "I swear I haven't seen such fair features on a man since the time that circuit tenor was sniffing after me." She went up and tenderly touched Tyler's face. "Oh, but someone's been hurting you, haven't they, Honey. What you need is a couple day's let up from whoever's been beating on you."

"Ma'am. I'm quite well, thank you."

"Ma'am, huh? Well, Honey, you're either one busy bodyguard for my old man here or a very poor one. But who ever he travels with and what becomes of them is none of my business. I'm surprised to see him traveling with anyone at all, he's such a loner."

"We met on the train," Tyler offered. "I asked to travel on with him."

"And any friend of this old coot is welcome here. Tyler, was it? Don't just stand there like a bumpus, boys. Come into the parlor and warm up. Dinner will be ready in a minute." She took hold of them and led them through a beaded curtain into the large drawing room.

Fifteen men, most of them well past fifty, uniformly shabby of dress and short on grooming, sat around the room on assorted chairs, stools and benches. They reminded Tyler of the men who had just run off the train, beaten down like a field of grain after a storm.

One of them was reading in a halting cadence from the sports section of the *Minneapolis Journal*. Most of the rest were listening. Some were quite animated, leaning forward and hanging on every word. Others had the slow eyes of farm boys trying to comprehend words that were just beyond their grasp. Some of them were sucking noisily on pipes while the rest were feeding spittoons with tobacco juice. The tobacco smell was heavy, coarse and pervasive. Mixed in was, again, the odor of unwashed bodies.

Gertie cleared her throat like a Model A turning over. "Hey, boys," she boomed, "look what the cat dragged in!"

Heads turned. The reader stopped and broke into a broad tooth-less smile of recognition. "Well, I'll be called a fool for saying it, but ain't you a sight for sore eyes?" He pushed himself out of his chair and met Socrates halfway across the room. "You old cuss, I ain't laid eyes on you since last spring break-up. How in God's good name are you?"

Socrates wrapped his arms around his tonsorial twin, hugging him fiercely. "Well, dang, Schnapsie, I ain't necessarily in God's good graces but you still read like a donkey trying to bluff his way into Sunday school."

"You ain't wrong there, buddy," said Schnapsie, joining in the general laughter. "But I don't need your insults, either. I can always go back to teaching speech at the University for the Deaf." More laughter erupted. Suddenly, everyone seemed more animated as they shared in the grand reunion.

"Schnapsie looked past Socrates to Tyler. "Who's the drummer, Soc?"

Before Socrates could introduce him, Tyler said, "Tyler Cauld-well. And I'd guess that if I were selling something, I'd find few here with the money to buy."

The smile left Schnapsie's face. "Pardon me, boy, but you sure did come dressed as one so I just thought.

Tyler looked down at his much out of place attire and turned a deep scarlet and snapped, "This happens to be a hundred dollar evening suit."

The whole room was staring at Tyler now. Not knowing what more to say, he turned and went back to the foyer. The silent men watched him leave and then looked at Gertie, afraid they might have insulted a friend of hers. But it was Socrates who broke the embar-rassed silence.

"Well then, Schnapsie, where have you been keeping yourself?"

"Pennsylvania. I was working in a brickyard. Goldbricking, you might say. But tell us, what, praise God, is His word for this evening?"

"Well, let's see now." Socrates studied the tin ceiling tiles care-fully. "How about this: '*When one greets a man with too loud a voice, a curse will be laid on his charge.*' Proverbs 27."

"Well, good enough, then. A lesson to us all." Schnapsie walked out to Tyler and, taking the boy's hand, shook it roughly as he pulled him back into the drawing room. "Son," he offered gently, "I didn't know you were a friend of my friend. If you are, then you are my friend too. My name is Schnapsie, named after that sweet flowing nectar that guards a man's blood from the winter night."

"Tyler Caldwell," Tyler repeated, his hand limp in the older man's strong grip.

Scattered faces nodded and a few volunteered a smile.

Gertie finished it off. "Well then. If any of you boys want to eat, let's get at it. If not, go take a bath."

As they walked out, Gertie whispered to Socrates, "Since when did you start taking in strays?"

"He's just a kid into a run of bad luck."

"Where is he headed?"

"I don't know. Following his nose like the rest of us." Socrates resented the interrogation.

"Where do you intend to take him? Not to the woods?"

"I'm thinking on it. I didn't want to. He begged."

"Well, maybe you'll be good for each other. You just make sure the woods don't kill him. Or you."

"Mind your own business, woman."

"If I did you'd have died a long time ago."

"Okay, so you're right. But if he don't make it, he wouldn't be the first," replied Socrates. He held Tyler back at the door to the dining room. "Now, kid, I don't like to give advice, you already know that but here's one piece. A few of these guys will be with us in the woods so I suggest you get to be friends with them as wretched as they are. Up there you'll be needing friends." Having said that, he led Tyler in.

Tyler and Socrates took two empty chairs at the end of the long boarding house table. Gertie passed through into the kitchen to help bring out the food.

There was fresh bread on the table and the men were busy spreading apple butter on thick slabs of it. Aside from the sounds of chewing, the room was absolutely silent.

Tyler looked at Socrates and, in an effort to be sociable, asked what he thought would be on the menu. This drew another chorus of looks.

"Lord, what did I say now?" he whispered.

Socrates grinned. "Nothing, sonny. These are old lumberjacks." The quiet manner in which he spoke brought no objection from the men at the table. "In the camps, if you talk at table, you get a cleaver up alongside the head. Or in it. Theirs is the silence of habit. And there is no menu. It's cooks' choice and pure chance."

Tyler obediently joined the ranks of the silent.

The kitchen door opened and Gertie burst in carrying two huge platters of sliced turkey. She set one at each end of the table and the men dived in. Behind her came another woman, a mulatto who, even at what must have been fifty years of age, and despite a long scar on her cheek, still had an enchanting beauty about her. She was wearing an old yellow housedress and white apron but moved with a sensuous grace. Her long, black hair, shaded with gray, reached far down her back. She was carrying a milk pail full of steaming baked potatoes. With a pair of tongs, she placed one on every plate. Most of the men continued eating without acknowledging her presence. When she came to Tyler he quietly thanked her and, in return, she gave him a polite smile before moving on.

Gertie cleared her throat again and everyone put their hands to rest for grace. "Now we thank you, Lord, for this day and for your bounty. Amen. And please wait for the gravy, gentlemen."

Gertie and her helper returned several more times in the course of the meal, carrying bread stuffing, coffee, the gravy and pan apple pie. For such an emaciated looking bunch, the men ate ravenously. In fifteen minutes they were done and, as if on cue, stood up and left the room. By the door was a small table with a basket on it. Into it most of them dropped some money: nickels, and dimes, a few quarters.

Socrates and Tyler finished last and leisurely and, as they walked out, Tyler reached in his pocket. From across the room Gertie stopped him.

"No, sonny," she said curtly. "I said you're a guest. Your money is no good here." She left with a load of dirty dishes.

Tyler ignored the admonition and put a dollar bill in the basket. This elicited a look of weary disapproval from Socrates.

When they got to the parlor, Socrates put on his coat and headed for the door.

"Where are you going?" asked Tyler.

"I generally take a walk after dinner. It helps keep everything moving down there."

"I'll come along," the boy said reaching for his coat.

"Suit yourself," growled Socrates. He went out the door without waiting.

Tyler caught up to him on the sidewalk where Socrates was lighting his pipe. They went down Nicollet Island and Socrates spoke first. "She'll know where the paper money came from. It wasn't the best thing to do but then, it wasn't a bad thing either."

"What are you talking about now? I can't seem to do anything right around you people. It's my money and I can spend it as I please, can't I?"

"Well, don't get in an uproar over it. I just said it wasn't a bad thing."

"Who wouldn't get in an uproar over it? I've never seen such an odd collection of humanity in my life. Dirty, ragged bums. And still, they manage to make me feel like I'm the strange one."

Socrates let silence absorb the kid's frustration and anger. It was Tyler who finally broke it. "Okay, so what did I louse up this time?"

Socrates nodded. "Nothing, kid. Really. I knew Gertie when she was one of the prettiest women in scarlet in all of Grand Rapids. Sure, she was a hooker. I never made much of a moral judgment about her profession though I admit, like a lot of men, I wanted her to myself. I figure we are what we are partly because of what we make of ourselves and partly because of what the world makes of us. I've always let God sort the right from the wrong. It ain't my job, anyway. So, I was a young jack, full of piss and vinegar and when Cupid fires his arrow, well, he doesn't necessarily pair us off by occupation or social standing. In those days, I thought I could take on the world and wrestle it to a draw. I even thought I could take on Gertie and settle down with her just like regular people.

"God, she was a looker in her day. Skinny as a heifer in January! I said something like 'Gertie, my flower, marry me and I'll build you a temple and therein will I worship the thought of you.' Pretty rich, huh? I must of been awful drunk! But she always had an answer for me. 'Bull, Gerald!' she said. Now remember, Gerald is not what you want to call me, kid. But she said, 'Bull Gerald, if I marry you, we'll both starve to death.' And it turns out she was very nearly right. I was drinking that bold-faced whiskey and thinking I was the big bull of the woods. I drowned just about every nickel I ever made. Hell! I guess we were all like that. Many of them still are. Once a man gets out of the woods, if he ain't stone drunk it's only because he's stone broke. Those guys back at the house, if they weren't so beholden to Gertie, they'd all be drunk. Sure, maybe they are bums, Tyler, but at least they're sober bums. And they're my bums."

A shambling figure wove towards them, stopped and stared into their faces, searching for something and, not finding it, pushed on down the street. Socrates became lost in thought drifting back to how it was years ago.

He knew he could be an obnoxious little rat when he drank. He never started that way, but as the sauce got into him and he into it more and more, he changed until he became a stranger to her. He was like that now, stupid drunk, standing in the middle of her bedroom. His shirt was piled up around his waist and the cuffs on his trousers were stretched so low he was standing on them. His haggard, hungry face was smeared with grime and blood. A fresh cut highlighted his left cheek. A large purple welt on the right one nearly closed the eye.

He had been fighting again. She laughed at that. Socrates in a brawl! He had never won a fight in his life, at least without five pounds of club in his hand. He hadn't won this one either.

"I need a drink." She ignored him. This angered him even more than he already was.

"Gertie? I said I need a drink, woman! He was swaying with the roll men get when they are drunk.

She stuck a red-tipped finger in his chest, her words hot. "You need a bath."

He slowly turned so he could get a better look out of his good eye. "Don't ride me, Gertie girl." A bottle standing alongside the bed caught his eye. He bent to pick it up, lost his balance and fell to the floor, bottle in hand. Rolling over on his back, he pulled his legs up under his rear and triumphantly tipped it into his mouth. A few drops trickled onto his face and he moaned. "Aw, crap, Honey, it's empty. Our bottle is empty."

"Poor baby bumpkins, now you get no dumplins," Gertie sang.

He struggled back to his feet and scavenged the room under her wary eye but soon lost patience. "Where's another bottle, Gertie?" He was yelling pretty good, trying to intimidate her.

She needed to scream at him, too, but didn't. You don't need one, little bumpkin," she crooned, not dismissively but with encouragement.

Then he broke down. It was that quick. "Please, Gertie, I gotta have a drink." He stumbled over to her. "I can't sober up all at once. It hurts too much. Let me do it slow. Please?" He had slipped to his knees, his bloodshot eyes pleading with her.

Suddenly he was looking past her, to the floor behind her chair. "Liar! You lying bitch . . . you were holding out on me!" He scurried around her and grabbed for the bottle but Gertie was quicker. She grabbed up the fifth of Old Trapper and backed out of his reach.

Socrates, back on his knees, followed her around the room. "Be nice now, Gert. Be nice." He finally managed to stand up, he eyes locked on the booze. "Be nice and gimme just a little swallow."

"No, Socrates. Not a drop. You hear me?"

"Come on, Girtie. Gertie. Flirtie, Flirtie. I don't wanna hurt you, you hear me?"

"You can't, Honey. But I can hurt you and I swear I will. It's time you grew up and stopped.

He lunged for the bottle. With her empty hand, Gertie slugged him in the mouth. Socrates staggered. Blood oozed out of the corner of his mouth. He screamed, "I'll kill you, woman!" He rushed at her again but Gertie hit him again, harder than the last time. It knocked him down. As he lay whimpering, she went to the window and poured out the whiskey.

He watched her as a drowning man would watch the life buoy drift away in the wind. He was still whimpering; for the whiskey, not for the beating. She went to him then, clucking and cooing and shaking her head. He started to get up, then fell back, twice, a third time. Finally he grabbed her skirts, buried his face in them and began to sob.

"I can't, Gertie. I can't"

"No, you can't, Honey, "she agreed. "You don't have the guts."

"I don't. I don't have the guts."

"You don't have the courage to do anything but kill yourself." She lowered herself beside him and, holding him, began to rock back and forth. "And even then it wouldn't be quick and painless."

He cried. "Gertie. You're all I got, Gertie and I lost you, too."

"No," she laughed finally. "You haven't lost me yet, Socrates. You still got me for a woman and booze for a god. Now, you tell me what you have that's so terrible to lose."

"I'll die, Gertie. I'm a dying man!"

"Well, at least, Soc, you got the courage to admit that. So now we start over, heh?" She kissed him and held him there on the floor, the two of them crying in each other's arms; one because he wanted the drink so badly, the other because she knew that she was no less trapped in it than he.

She put him to bed and stayed with him through all the shaking and vomiting. For three days she nursed him through it. As bad as it got, he never again begged for a drink. He had put himself in her care and drew upon her strength and knowing that, she quietly went about saving his life.

"Socrates?" Tyler touched his shoulder.

"What?" Socrates was still staring at the receding figure of the drunk.

"You know him?"

"Him?" Socrates answered coming back again. "No, I don't know him." He played at lighting his pipe, worked the coals for awhile and then continued. "So, anyway, as I got older it began to get to me. Not just the booze, but the loneliness and all that goes with it. But, then I got lucky. I broke free. Most don't. It was Gertie that saved me. She put me up, fed me; stayed with me through the worst and the nearly as bad. 'Til I was alive again.

"So that's me. Now here's what else you ought to know about Gertie. Some time after she got me straightened out Grand Rapids started cleaning itself up. The old houses had to go. Gertie had been doing well, but she was getting on in age. She didn't want to move on. She did for a while. Went up to Craig where all the action was. But it wasn't the same. Craig didn't have the class. It was just a muddy street with some shacks hung on the sides. Still is for that matter.

"Then she got a little of the luck she deserved. A happy customer died with a smile on his face and in his last breath gave her the house. It wasn't much, just this old house here. No cash. But she made it work and here she is today."

"And the red light?"

Socrates laughed. "Yes, well that's just for old time's sake. She's having some fun with the local authorities, is all.

"So, getting back to your money. See, this was all a long time ago and sure, maybe we both got regrets that we didn't make more of our lives. So we try to make it up to each other in small ways. Now don't ever tell her this, but I try to send her money through other people. Not much, 'cause I don't get much but it helps her get by. Passing the hat after every meal just doesn't make the bills. You see, a man can get by living on the road and by his wits if he's got to, 'cause that's the nature of man. But a woman without a decent home, without dignity, and ... well ... dignity is it. She's just no better in the eyes of society than a tramp dog. I aim to see that Gertie never loses her dignity."

The old man went back to his pipe, compacting the tobacco and burning up a couple of matches on it. Several puffs later it was blowing smoke again. "And she does the same for me, Tyler. She puts me up and just puts up with me. It's all she has left to give, that little bit of hospitality. But you've got to see, when you paid for that meal and she knows no one else in there had that kind of money, you might have taken a little of that away from her. Sort of hurts her pride."

"Sure," Tyler admitted. "She has to have her pride and all, but money is money, right? There's nothing you can't overlook for money."

Socrates stopped walking and stared the young man down. It was Tyler who first broke eye contact.

"Well, that's the way I was brought up. I don't know any other way." He swallowed. "So I don't understand people? That's about the size of it. Maybe I'm messed up more than I think."

"Nothing we can't fix after we grow you up a little, sonny."

"Watch the 'sonny', old man."

They had reached the steel arch bridge and turned to walk back to Gertie's. Presently Tyler asked, "Why would a cook care if someone talks at their table or not? Back home people talk at meals all the time."

"Sure, the same here but its not like in the camps where men are talking five different languages and have to go back out in the cold."

"I don't understand."

"I'll explain what it's like in the camps. See now, what you got is upwards of a hundred or more men; all eating at the same time in the same room. Out in the woods it's cold and tough. In the cook shack it's warm and friendly. Being as it is, a man would likely kill half a day eatin' his meal, drinking coffee and jawing if he could.

You got to get them fed and back to work as quick as you can or you won't get 'em back at all.

"That I understand. Like I said, money is money and time is too."

"In this case you're right. Then too, your jacks and teamsters come from all over the country ... heck, from all over the world except the really warm jungles. They don't all speak English. You got the Finns, Swedes, Russians, Germans, Frogs; that's the Frenchies, Italians to name a few. Let them all start talking at once and it'd make the tower of Babel sound like a ladies' Sunday tea."

"I didn't know that."

"So you credit those that do, right? Not only that but these jacks get ornery. They're tired and cold. Some of them are lice-ridden. Like you already know, a lot of 'em smell bad. Like little boys, they can take a harmless comment sideways sometimes. Even what isn't meant, they hear it that way and want to start thumping heads. Remember, a lot of these folks hated each other in Europe too. So, it's just better if no one says anything. That's why you got your cooks and cookies – those are cook's helpers – all waiting on them so no one has to ask for anything. Eat it up and get 'em out and get started on the next meal."

"But what you said at dinner, about the cleaver. That wasn't true, was it?"

"Not true? Not true? Let me tell you something, Tyler. I was in a camp once, just a young pup like you. I was a cookie; waited table, peeled potatoes, washed dishes. One night these two crabby guys, Swedes they were, started jawing in Swedish, you know, full of 'yah, sure's' and the like. They were talking about who'd been resting on the crosscut that day and who had done the bigger share. One of them knocked over a pitcher of coffee and that old cook, he had enough of that. He never said nothin' either. Just picked up this big meat cleaver and threw it at them. I can't say if he meant to split the pearly gates with it or not. But that steel flew through the air and buried itself in the one guy's neck. Kilt him right where he sat. He just stopped talking and grabbed at the cleaver, trying to pull it out. But it was stuck in some bone and he couldn't and it had cut some big artery in two. Blood was pouring out of the wound and his mouth. Then he looked at the others for help. It was in his eyes. Finally his face dropped right into his plate of chow and that was it.

"Aw, that's a load of garbage."

"I swear to heaven it ain't! I was there, man. Listen, I don't lie, Tyler, less I'm stretching the truth a bit. But I ain't here. Lying's for little boys and Englishmen. No, that cook killed the poor Swede sure as I'm here. You look a little nervous. Sure you want to come along with me?"

"What happened to the cook?"

"Well, nothing of course. He was a damn fine cook. A good cook is the most valuable man in camp. Swede cutters are a dime a dozen. So what they did was wrap the body in rocks and canvas and cut a hole in a nearby lake but not the one we got our camp water from. They sunk the dead Swede in that water. No one but us in the camp ever knew what kilt him and we were sworn by the foreman not to tell. The man was just a no-name drifter with an X for a name." Socrates sucked his pipe. "Was a long time ago."

They were turning on to Gertie's walk.

"Do you think our camp will have cook like that?" Tyler wondered.

"You can bet your life on it! The cook in my camp will be a real butcher. A real mean tyrant."

"How do you know that?"

"Because," laughed Socrates, "I'm the cook!"

"You? A cook?" Tyler's mind rushed back to the food Socrates had served up on the train. "You said you were a lumberjack."

"I am a lumberjack!" retorted Socrates, his hackles rising. "Once a lumberjack, always a lumberjack. But a man can't cut timber forever. It'd put him in his grave before he started shaving. Besides," he added, regaining his composure, "as I get older, the snow gets deeper and the cold drives closer to your heart. I don't have the body for it anymore." Socrates did an inspection of his chest and stomach. "But one thing you will find to be gospel, a camp would just as soon lose its best cutter as a good cook. Good beans bless the men."

There was another question. "The black woman here, who is she?"

"You saw the scar, huh?"

"I couldn't help but see it. What happened to her? Another cook?"

"That was Merletta. Beautiful woman, isn't she."

"I guess."

"Well, back in her best days there was no one like her. She touched a man's soul when she smiled. The scar is a reminder of something that happened a long time ago up in that Craigtown. Gertie helped her out of a tight spot and they've been together ever since. I guess that's all you need to know right now. Some day I'll tell you the rest of the story, but we've talked long enough and I'm cold. Let's get in."

"One last question."

"Make it short."

"If," Tyler hesitated. "If Gertie is so special to you; I mean if she means so much to you, why do you keep leaving her?"

"None of your business," Socrates snapped. "And if you want to go north with me you'll keep it none of your business."

"Okay, man. Sorry. I didn't know it was so sensitive." He was surprised at the old man's reluctance to discuss the matter, especially in view of his propensity to subject Tyler to a full inquisition concerning his own past.

Socrates bet out the ashes from his pipe and inspected it carefully. Then, without looking at Tyler, he said, "Forget it. You didn't mean nothing by it."

"No," agreed Tyler, "I didn't mean anything."

"We all have something we're running from, kid." He said, walking into the house. "Some of us are just getting' too old to outrun it."

Six

*E*ight men slept in a room half the size of the bedroom Tyler had grown up in. The furniture was a museum of styles ranging from simple cots to an Old Queen Anne four-poster that Socrates and Schnapsie shared.

The night had gone poorly for Tyler. He had been relegated to share an old double bed with one of the older men introduced only as Red. The man was totally bald except for a five day growth of gray stubble on his face. Tyler didn't take the trouble to ask Red how he came by his name.

Accepting the arrangement as reluctantly as old Red welcomed him, Tyler undressed quickly and slipped in, hoping to fall asleep quickly. He positioned himself on the outside eighteen inches of the mattress and planned to stay there all night but the mattress had other designs. Years of hard wear had eventually worn a deep canyon down its middle, deep enough that none who rolled in ever rolled out before dawn.

Red was soon snoring away in the bottom of that hole. Within minutes Tyler began to feel the pull of gravity. He wrapped his arm over the edge and slipped his hand between the mattress and the bed frame but every time he dozed off his hand would slip out and he would slide inexorably into the black hole. There he would wedge up against Red who responded with a murmur of contentment.

At six in the morning Socrates found his young companion lying on the bare braid rug in the center of the room. He gave him a gentle nudge on the ribs with his foot.

"That's all, Tyler. Better get up before these nearsighted apes begin to walk all over you."

Tyler slowly opened his eyes to men in red woolen underwear moving soundlessly about the room, washing their faces, drawing on suspenders and going to or returning from the hall bathroom.

He jumped off the floor; embarrassed to be seen in his underwear. Nonplused, Socrates threw him a pair of ragged trousers and a flannel shirt. "Put these on, boy."

"Thanks. I think." The pants were much older than he and remarkably baggy. On Socrates they would have accordioned several folds over his ankles but when Tyler pulled them up, the cuffs hung free, running out of material six inches above his feet. The waist was close to right but the crotch dropped too low by several inches and there was enough room in the butt for another man's butt.

Tyler buttoned up the fly and adjusted the pants as best he could. Looking up, he found the whole room staring back at him, not with curiosity or humor but satisfaction. It dawned on him that this threadbare piece of absurd dress seemed to make everyone else more comfortable. He was, at least in appearance, now one of them.

He walked over to a full-length mirror and inspected himself. He would eventually come to understand the utility of such clothing but the cut and shape was still atrocious. A smile began to creep over his face. Behind him a murmur of approval ran though the room because everyone had been looking for something to like in the boy.

"My god," Tyler said, finally finding words, "Our gardener had better clothes than this. And he was a Mexican."

"Sure," said Schnapsie, "and you look like you've been standing around in his fertilizer sack too long."

Laughter floated around the room. Nobody seemed to be in any hurry after breakfast since most of them were on the dole, having no jobs to go to. Socrates casually announced that he was going downtown to have a steam bath and started to walk out. Halfway down the sidewalk Tyler caught up with him.

"Coming with me?" Socrates asked.

"You said we were going to get a bath today."

"A bath and I suppose we should find you some proper clothes, too. Let's go down on Hennepin Avenue."

Hennepin Avenue was the grandest street in the grandest city west of the Mississippi and east of the Rockies. Halfway down the block, they stepped into Hy's Off-Hennepin Tailors and Men's Clothing Emporium-Established 1867. They left Tyler's heavy coat to be cut down into a more serviceable Mackinaw style work jacket. From the trimmings, Socrates ordered two pair of heavy woolen "chopper" style mittens with flannel linings. After a proper amount of haggling a price was struck and Tyler paid down two dollars in deposit. The finished goods were promised in two days.

Around the corner from Hy's, over on 1st Avenue North, in the basement of a knitting factory, was Stosh's Roman Steam Bath. Men came there to relax, conduct business, chase colds and talk local politics. For twenty-five cents a man could wrap himself in a large Turkish towel or sit naked, as was the local custom and partake in either a dry sauna or a room filled with heavy, live steam vapors. Balsam fir boughs laid over the steam vents gave the room a fragrant, piney aroma.

The steam melted the dirt and sweat from their pores and took the wrinkles out of their boxcar-sore muscles. For another nickel they got their clothes steamed, brushed and pressed, which added almost two inches to Tyler's borrowed trousers.

From Stosh's baths they walked back over to Hennepin and crossing it, turned back to the river. Although it was nearly 10:30 and the sun was well into the clear sky, it was still cold out. Tyler was shivering without his greatcoat; his head drawn into his turned up collar, his hands crammed under his armpits. Suddenly Socrates stopped.

"Whoa.

"What?" Tyler protested.

Socrates took Tyler's arm. "Tyler, I'm not one to beg and borrow but right now I'd like to have a dollar if you can spare it."

"You sure this won't hurt your dignity?"

"Okay, smart guy." Socrates held out his hand and looked at Tyler who plunged into his trousers and produced a wad of wrinkled bills from which he extracted one. Socrates took it, mumbled a thank you and walked over to a figure sitting on the sidewalk, his back against the brick veneer of the Andrews Hotel. The man wore a misshapen brown felt hat. Sweat and oil stains radiated out from under the sweatband. His coat had more patching than original fabric. His feet were clad in worn felt-pack shoes; his hands wrapped in rags. In front of him, between his feet, was a battered old coffeepot.

Socrates bent over and put the money deep into the coffeepot, taking care that the wind not steal it. Slowly, the man looked up at Socrates. The cloud over his face seemed to lift for a moment.

A mummified hand reached out to take the one Socrates extended but they fell short of each other when the rag hand dropped back into the old man's lap.

Socrates reached out farther, touched the old man on the shoulder and walked on.

"Who was he?" asked Tyler when they had gone a pace.

"Who? That was me, Tyler. That could be you, boy."

"But you knew him, didn't you?"

Socrates stopped and faced the youth, wondering if he should or even could explain.

"I'm sorry, kid. That's another little secret I have to keep."

"Then you did know him."

"Later, Tyler, after we come out of the woods. Maybe then I won't have to tell you."

They turned right on Third Street. At Nicollet they walked into The Leader, a general mercantile store. Socrates took them down to the basement, which contained rows of dry goods marked at clearance prices.

From the bins Socrates chose two pair of thirty-ounce wool trousers, two red and black checked woolen shirts, another of flannel, several pair of woolen socks and two sets of full-body woolen underwear.

From a rack they selected a pair of heavy-soled work boots and a pair of felt 'pack' boots similar to the ones the bum on the sidewalk had been wearing.

"For them really cold days," Socrates counseled. "Thirty below or colder, put on two pairs of wool socks and the felt boots. The insulation is so good, the snow won't even stick to the felt."

Tyler put on one set of clothes and the boots and had the rest of the stuff bagged up. When they walked out of The Leader, he was thirty-one dollars and fifty cents poorer.

They grabbed some ribs and sauerkraut at the Forum Cafeteria. An hour later they were walking back towards Nicollet Island. When they neared the river, they saw a large crowd gathered on the bridge. A woman clad in a heavy robe was up on a platform addressing the crowd.

"Look at that, will you," spat Socrates. "Some fool woman out stumping to right the world's wrongs I wager. I'll bet the only wrong that she can cure is the one she's doing to her poor husband."

Before Tyler had a chance to reply, the woman abruptly turned, slipped off her robe to reveal a stunning swimming suit and dove off the bridge into the river thirty feet below. The crowd screamed and rushed to the rail.

"My God," cried Tyler, "she's killing herself."

But instead of dying, the woman executed a nearly perfect somersault and entered the water in a graceful dive. When she surfaced, a great cheer erupted from the crowd.

"Shades of Roman carnage," whispered Socrates. From where he stood he couldn't see the diver hit the water. "They're sacrificing virgins to the gods."

Another woman, older with gray hair climbed the ten-foot ladder and stepped onto the platform. "This is for all the women who fear to experience the new and daring," she cried out. "I'm coming, darling!" She, too, dove off the bridge.

"Well," mused Socrates, "there goes my virgin theory." Already a man in a trench coat and hat was on the platform, hailing the crowd.

"Be sure to read all about the amazing Mrs. Berlo and her beautiful daughter, Lillian, in tomorrow's Minneapolis Journal! All the events of the day printed for your education and edification. Still only five cents"

Lillian and her mother were quickly gathered into a rowboat and taken downstream to the Minneapolis General Electric Plant dock. Most of the crowd hurried to meet them at the landing.

"Well, can you beat that?" Socrates said. "A diving exhibition! By the way, son, can you swim?"

"Sure," Tyler said. "Everyone can."

"Not me. Twenty five years working river drives and I sink like a stone."

"How did you survive twenty-five years without drowning?"

"Didn't."

"Didn't what?"

"I drowned."

"Socrates."

"Honest! I drowned. Twice, in fact."

"That's impossible."

"Not at all. I fell in a river; can't swim a lick, and drowned and then I had to jump in to try to save myself 'cause no one else on that drive could swim either. Drowned then, too. I know, it sounds corny to me too."

After dinner that evening Gertie took Socrates into the kitchen. She was up to her elbows in dishwater. "Sit down, Sugar. There's a cup of Irish coffee there on the table."

Socrates sat and sipped the liquor-laced black coffee. "Mmmm, that's smooth. Wild Turkey?"

"Uhuh."

"Thank you, Miss Gertrude. It's been a while since I've tasted the stuff."

"I bet."

Gertie was quiet for a ling time, methodically washing the dishes. One slipped out of her hand and shattered on the floor. She swore and picked up the pieces, throwing them back into the soapy water. She swore again and wiped her face with her apron, sighed and looked at Socrates.

"The police were here today," she said finally.

"Police? What for? Looking for vagrants?"

"No," she smiled. "Everyone here is a vagrant. No, they don't care about that so long at the men are peaceable." She turned back to her dishes.

"What then?"

She pulled her hands out of the soapy water and took a deep breath. "They said they're looking for some prostitutes."

Socrates frowned. "Prostitution? No. Not you?"

"No, you old coot, not me. Not me, not Merletta. Not anyone. Okay?"

"Sure. Okay. I knew that. Why does it upset you then?"

"Because these men are serious and I don't know where it will end."

"Okay, now I'm confused. Where will what end?" He looked over at Merletta. She was kneading dough for breakfast biscuits and didn't look up.

"There, read it for yourself," Gertie said, nodding toward the paper on the table. It all came out today."

Socrates picked up the Journal. It had been folded to a left-hand column article. The copy fell in a cascade beneath a two-inch banner. He read aloud:

"Police Expose City-wide Sex-For-Play ring. Rowe Indicted. Hotel Inmates can't be found. Three Women Believed to Have Left Town at Same Time as Proprietor."

*"Arthur Rowe, convicted proprietor of the Elroy
Hotel, 21 Nicollet Avenue, was indicted yesterday by the
Hennepin County Grand Jury on a charge of keeping a
house of ill fame at that place. The indictment was voted
late yesterday following the testimony last week and
James Robertson, attorney of Stobbe, who appeared as a
witness against Rowe.*

*"Three women failed to appear. Deputy sheriffs sent
to serve subpoenas were told that they had not been
seen since Thursday, the date Rowe is supposed to have
disappeared.*

*"James Hirsch, clerk at the Elroy Hotel; W.H. Davis,
proprietor of the Saratoga Hotel and Lillian Hoffman,
alleged keeper of the Elroy, were witnesses called by
the grand jurors in their investigation of the Rowe case.
Hirsch testified that he had been employed by Rowe who
was generally regarded as the proprietor of the Elroy as
well as other hotels in and near the Gateway district.*

*"Police claim that girls working as prostitutes were
routinely transferred from one hotel to another in the
Gateway district and that, following rumors of raids, all
the girls in a certain house would be taken to another
place.*

*"W.H. Davis, in a statement, asserted that prostitu-
tion resorts and gambling houses had been encouraged
by police. Police, in a follow-up statement, have denied
these allegations.*

*"Principal testimony along these lines had been
expected to come from the three women who disappeared along with Rowe."*

"Whoooee," Socrates whistled. "I can think of only a hundred
ways they might try to connect you with this mess. You know some
of these folks, I suppose?"

"I knew all of them. I knew the girls. I met Rowe when he came
here with some men."

"When?"

"About three months ago, to talk about setting up my place for
him. I told him to go jump in the river."

"I'll bet that's the nicest thing you told them. What did the police want today?"

"They said they were looking for the girls."

"And Rowe, I suppose."

"No. Now pay attention, dammit! They know where Rowe is. You just read the blasted story!"

Merletta looked up from her kneading and stared at Gertie.

"Look, Gertie," he said, "I don't know what's going on here. It's your business, not mine. Maybe I should get out."

"Sure, get out like you always do! It's about what I expected."

"Gertie . . . I," he stammered.

"I'm sorry I yelled at you. Sit down. Please." She grabbed a towel and dried her hands. Then she went to a sideboard and pulled out the Wild turkey and nodded to Merletta who left the room. "I don't want her mixed up in this."

Gertie got down another cup, poured it half-full and then offered the same to Socrates who waved it off. She sat beside him and put her hand on his arm and spoke in a low voice. "Just so you know. Whatever happens, I want you to know."

"I want to know," Socrates said.

"I know where the girls are. They're in Michigan, not because they don't want to testify. They ran because they want to live."

"What?"

"When Rowe came to the house, the two men with him were police, not in uniform but I recognized them. They wanted to set up a house here and promised there wouldn't be any trouble. Davis knows there are some police involved, not many, but higher ups; a chief maybe. What Rowe says doesn't matter because he's a convicted felon. But with the girls *and* Rowe," she hesitated, "and me to say exactly what's what, their goose would be cooked."

"If they can't get to those women, then it's just you and Rowe against the crooked cops."

She took a big swallow of whiskey. "Rowe is dead. Two guys took him fishing and used him for an anchor."

"God, Gertie! Then it's only you who could put their necks in the noose."

"That's why they came," she nodded. "They said if I ever talk about any of this, they'd shut me down permanent. Burn me out. I told them that I never had anything against the trade. I said what's going on is their business. Socrates, I said anything I could think of to send them away happy."

"Did it?"

She shook her head indecisively. "They said fine, my word was all right with them and they didn't want anyone to get hurt. Let it end right there. They left and that's where it stands now."

She stood and busied herself at the sink again so she wouldn't have to look at him.

Socrates ran his hand through his beard. He wasn't sure where his obligations lay. He had made a promise to Hungry Mike, a promise to the kid, a lifetime of promises broken to Gertie. She was an independent woman and had never asked for help before. She hadn't now. Still, it was the right thing to offer. "Gertie, I'll stay if you want me to."

"God, no, just another mouth to feed." She laughed. Then she came and stood behind him, her hands on his shoulders. "I do appreciate you offering. I know how hard it is. But it's going to be all right, Sugar. I just wanted you to know."

He pulled her hands down around his chest. They stayed like that for a long time.

Seven

*I*t was a late start from the boarding house the next morning. Tyler's clothes wouldn't be ready yet, giving them a day to kill. Four of the old timers were sitting in the parlor smoking and one of them asked Socrates to read the morning paper for them.

"Sure, boys," he answered, "but how about if we let the young college professor here read. Tyler, pick out a story."

Tyler sat in one of the padded chairs, the one Schnapsie usually claimed when he was around. His interest was immediately drawn to a front-page story.

"Say, here's the story on the women that dove from the bridge yesterday."

"I heard about it but I wasn't there," piped in one of the gray-beards. "Read that one."

"Well, you didn't miss nothing," Socrates said.

Tyler began to read. "*Mother and daughter diving team thrilled thousands. . . .*"

"Tousands? Haw! Weren't more than a hundred," chortled Socrates.

"Well, it says 'tousands', I have to read 'tousands'. All right?" *Thousands who lined the river banks and the bridge from shore to shore saw Miss Lillian Berlo do a triple somersault dive from a tower twenty feet above the bridge deck into the chilly Mississippi River nearly sixty feet below yesterday. As Miss Berlo was being helped into a small boat and bundled in blankets, sixty-five year old Elizabeth Berlo, mother of ten children, mounted the platform and dove from the same height. The Berlos, mother and daughter, are appearing at the Gayety Theater. Following her dive, an old fossil named Socrates climbed up on the tower and began to disrobe before being arrested by the police for public indecency.'* And that's all."

"Okay, smarty pants. First, it was a ten-foot tower; second, the river is only thirty feet below and third, I ain't a fossil. I may be a dinosaur but I ain't fossilized yet."

Tyler's eyes brightened. "Say, Socrates, why don't we go to the Gayety tonight?" The Gayety was Minneapolis' finest vaudevillian theatre with the possible exception of the Unique just one block down. But the Gayety, unquestionably, brought in the big name talent.

"I'd like to Tyler but I'm pretty much tapped out. You know that."

"Forget it. I'll pay. I've still got a little left."

"In that case, you're on, little rich kid," Socrates said. "I ain't been to a show for some time."

"Great! Let's ask Gertie, too."

Socrates ran his fingers through his hair. The woman hadn't been off his mind since last night. "That would be wonderful. Thank you, Tyler, lad. That's good of you."

Tyler bought front row seats.

"You don't mind getting wet, do you, Honey?" Gertie asked Socrates.

"Of course not. I take it in my whiskey, don't I?"

"Only when it's raining."

Auto Girls, an opening chorus line of beauties dressed in abbreviated mechanics uniforms, opened the show with a medley of songs evoking an automobile tour of the country. On their last number the uniforms came off to reveal knee-high silk stockings, garters and lacy bloomers. Socrates let out a sigh of gratitude.

Then Elsie Labergese pranced onto the stage wearing many layers of gauzy veils over a lacey negligee. Beneath subdued lighting she performed Salome's Dance of the Seven Veils followed by a series of 'High Art Poses' which weren't particularly inspiring. Gertie was less than impressed.

"What was that all about? The woman pranced around in a cloud of curtains."

"That's what's called art."

"Well, she 'art' to start doing something different to keep me awake, shouldn't she?"

The third act featured a comedian named Charles Robinson playing off a straight man standing in the wings.

"I saw by the papers that they hung an elephant in Tennessee."

"What kind of line was strong enough to hang an elephant?"

"They used a trunk line."

"Why did they hang the poor elephant."

"To kill the big brute, of course."

"Who did she ever hurt?"

"She killed her keeper."

"An accident?"

"Premeditated. She was sick of working for peanuts."

"How did they kill her?"

"Hoisted her on a derrick at the city dump."

"Why there?"

"They didn't want her hanging around the circus any more."

Socrates whispered a little too loud, "They ought to hang Robinson."

An emphatic roll of the drum echoed every punch line.

"I've got the perfect marriage. My wife has a great job and every night she comes home and makes me a great dinner. After dinner she fixes me a nice drink and rubs my shoulders and then we go in the bedroom and make wonderful love together. You should try it."

"I will. What time does your wife get home?"

Finally it was the Berlo's turn. Entering from stage right in front of the velvet curtain, Elizabeth bowed and introduced Lillian. "My beautiful, talented and charming daughter." She devoted considerable time to the athletic exploits of Lillian, always managing to slip in a greater triumph that she had achieved at a similar age.

Abruptly came a momentous drum roll. The curtain opened to a large wooden tank eight feet in diameter but a scant three feet deep. Alongside it stood a ladder that extended up and out of sight into the rigging of the stage.

"And now, ladies and gentlemen," Elizabeth said, priming the audience, "my beautiful, talented and charming daughter, Lillian, is about to astound you with an act requiring incredible courage and skill. She will climb this fragile ladder, this thirty-foot high frail stairway to the heavens far into the nether rafters of this building. She will then step out onto a platform measuring a mere twelve inches square, and from that lofty precipice, she will execute a perfect dive into this pitifully shallow pool. Ladies and gentlemen, you are about to witness the incredible DIVE OF DEATH!"

Elizabeth went over to the tank and, reaching in, splashed out a handful of water onto the stage. "No more than thirty-six inches of water." She collapsed in a pitiful wailing for her doomed daughter.

"What a lot of garbage," Tyler snickered, untouched by her passionate speech.

"Shush! Don't upset her concentration." Gertie was about to die with Lillian and couldn't take her eyes off the stage.

"I know how she does it," Socrates giggled.

"Oh, come on," Tyler said leaning across Gertie. "She won't do it."

"Shut up, you two, she'll do it."

"No, she can't"

"Yes, she will."

"It's impossible."

"I know how she does it," Socrates repeated.

Gertie shut them up. "Another word out of either of you and I'll crack your heads together like a couple of fresh eggs. Now, quiet! And I mean shush."

Lillian helped her mother off the floor. They embraced and then, reluctantly it seemed, Lillian stepped onto the ladder. She made several false starts, each time flexing her shapely legs for the benefit of the audience. She threw a kiss to the crowd and gestured offstage. A drum roll and she began the slow climb eventually disappearing above the proscenium arch of the stage.

Through the eyes and voice of her mother, they followed her progress.

"She is nearing the top of the ladder. Oh, dear! She is stopped! Lillian, darling, don't look back. No!" The ladder was shaking.

"No!" cried the audience.

"Good Lord, she nearly fell."

"Don't fall,' the audience prayed.

"Darling, you must press on."

"Press on," the crowd pleaded.

"Don't come down. That's my child. My baby. Courage, child, courage." So it went as Lillian made her tortured way to her lofty crag. The drum rolled on. Mrs. Berlo raised her arms heavenward again and again, moving her daughter forward by sheer force of will.

At last Mrs. Berlo raised her arms in triumph. "Yes, she is there! She has reached the lofty summit far above where mortals fear to go!"

"Bravo!" screamed the audience.

The drum stopped. A murmur of expectation ran through the crowded theatre.

"Good Lord in heaven, protect her," Gertie prayed, crossing herself.

Time pressed on as Mrs. Berlo paced anxiously back and forth, her eyes fixed on the dizzying heights. Then, a nod from her, and the drum began its ominous tremor. It grew in intensity; stronger and louder. Louder. Louder, then suddenly ending in a crash of cymbals. Mrs. Berlo screamed and covered her face with her hands. A body flashed into view and out again as it entered the tank. A plume of water erupted.

A full minute passed. Elizabeth stood frozen on the stage. A woman in the audience fainted. People began screaming, "Save her! She's drowning!" Men began to rush forward to affect a rescue. And suddenly, she was there.

Sweeping the water from her hair, Lillian Berlo appeared above the tank. Her sobbing mother wrapped a satin robe around the dripping girl as she climbed out.

The audience stood as one, cheering and applauding the momentous dive. Gertie was bawling for joy. Tyler was stunned. Socrates was humming to himself. The Berlos took seven curtain calls.

A closing musical number brought out the Auto Girls, Mr. Robinson, Elsie and the Berlo family. A final bow and it was over.

They stepped out onto the sidewalk and into the chilly, inky night. A fine dusting of snow was being driven down the street by a gusty wind. The streetcars had stopped running so they reluctantly set off on foot. After half a block Gertie couldn't contain herself any longer.

"That was … Oh, my. My heart is still pounding. That was the most amazing show I have ever seen."

"I didn't think it was all that great," Socrates said.

"Socrates, that girl was incredible. You saw it! She could have killed herself."

"I don't think there was much risk of that. The Auto Girls were nice but, Lillian, I don't think it was so much."

Socrates' smugness had aroused Tyler's curiosity. "How do you know so much about their act?"

"I saw it last summer at the World's Fair in San Francisco. I worked backstage at a theater for a month. Not long enough to play Hamlet, but I saw some things."

"Were the Berlo's there?"

"No, but a couple just like them. That's how I learned how they did it."

Gertie was getting a little nervous. "Okay, big shot, I know what I saw. Are you going to tell me what happened?"

"Alright, I'll tell you. But don't hit me if you don't like it."

"I never hit you."

"Mush. Fine. So, Miss Lillian climbed the ladder, right? We all saw that. But the ladder only went about twenty feet up just far enough we couldn't see her get off it and run off on a catwalk. A stagehand keeps shaking the ladder so it looks like she's still there. She climbed down another ladder behind the curtain and ran down under the stage. Then the stagehand drops a dummy dressed like her into the tank. Other stagehands doused her with water and threw up more buckets of it when the dummy lit. Then Lillian pops up through the trapdoor in the empty tank and all the audience goes crazy. Except me."

"That's a crock!" Gertie screamed, hitting him in the chest.

"Ouch! No, that's the truth," he insisted. "One time in 'Frisco the dummy hung up a leg on the side of the tub and the girl had to fake a broken leg. That's hard when you're doing six shows a day. It just goes to show what I always say. Don't believe none of what you hear and only half of what you see."

"Sure," Tyler agreed, putting it together. "Sure, I get it."

They walked for another block. Suddenly Gertie erupted, swinging her purse up against Socrates' head. "You miserable donkey."

"What? What'd I do?" He picked his cap off the ground.

"You spoiled the whole evening is what you did. Now when I think of that poor little girl, I see a carnival hustler. I didn't want to know."

"I'm sorry, Gertie. You asked."

"I didn't want to know is all. Next time ask me before you tell me and if I won't like it then don't ask me."

"I will. And if you ask me to tell you, I still won't tell you."

"I just didn't want to know."

Soon they were crossing the bridge. Tyler, lost in his own thoughts, had drifted about fifty steps behind them. The diving platform was still erected from the publicity stunt and Gertie stopped to look at it.

"You won't tell me this is all phony too, will you?"

"No, ma'am. They weren't acting out here. My heart was bouncing against my Adam's apple." He held his hand to his throat.

"I told Tyler, I thought she was trying to get herself killed. There's no telling what rocks and snags are hidden down in that water. Water can be a real killer."

"Humph. Well, that makes me feel a little better, anyway."

Two men were coming up from the opposite end of the bridge. One was large and bulky like a stevedore. The other, a smaller man, was dressed like a dandy though his clothes were quite worn. A turkey feather stuck out of a ragged derby. They walked as though they intended to pass on by. The shorter one tipped his hat to Gertie. Then, when they had come alongside, they stopped abruptly and turned to Socrates.

"I say, friend," said the short one, eye to eye with Socrates, "Good evening." He went on, not waiting for a response. "This is my friend, Gorilla. It's an interesting name, don't you think? Gorilla and I have found us to be temporarily inconvenienced for lack of funds. We hope, however, to have this situation corrected quite soon."

"What's that to us," Gertie said?

"My good lady, I am counting on your purse and the gentleman's wallet to be the solution to our dilemma."

Gertie laughed. "My Lord. You don't even have the sense to rob the folks that do have money. I bet we're poorer than you are, you dopes."

"Your crude insults are duly noted. Now why don't we all just turn out our pockets and add it up together," replied the small man. As he moved a step closer, Socrates made out his features to resemble that of a wharf rat and began making little squeaking noises at him. Rat-face was undeterred and decided to call on his assistant.

"Gorilla, please assist this old codger with his wallet."

"Wait," said Socrates, holding his hands in the air. "It's in my sock. Take it."

The large man bent down to pull it out while, at the same moment Socrates did the same thing. Their heads cracked together and both men straightened up abruptly. Then they began weaving and bobbing around each other like two chickens working over a pile of scratch.

"Well, for pity's sake," Gertie said, clucking her tongue. The rat-faced gent rolled his eyes heavenward.

"Gorilla, get on with it!"

Tyler had stopped to lean over the rail and was staring at the water. Glancing over at his companions, he caught the end of the chicken dance and saw a sharp rebuke from Rat Face cause Socrates to shoot his arms into the air again. "God, it's a holdup!" He ran down the bridge towards them. By the time he arrived, Gorilla had found the small leather coin purse hidden in Socrates' sock. The giant opened it, turned it upside down and scowled at Socrates.

"It's empty," Gorilla reported.

"I told you that. It's been empty all week."

"Say," Tyler asked, "what's going on here? Are you trying to rob these people?"

Rat Face moved over to Tyler. "Yeah, it's a stickup, Bub. Maybe you'd be the one with the cash on him?"

"Don't mess with my partner," Socrates warned. "He'll kill you. He's an animal. He killed a hundred men already this week and it's only Wednesday."

Thinking there might be some truth in Socrates' prattle, Rat Face pulled out a switchblade, snapped it open and stuck it in Tyler's nostril. He walked the boy back until Tyler's butt was buckling the metal on the bridge railing, his back arched over the river. The knife never lost contact with his nose and a tiny drop of blood ran down the blade.

"Now," the runt repeated. "One last time. Hand over your purse or I will push this blade up through your eyeball."

Socrates was upside down hanging from Gorilla's arms who was literally shaking him down for money. Tyler was about to fall one of two ways, either into the river or into the dirk which his eyes were crossed and severely focused on. Gertie was watching Tyler's predicament and Socrates' ineptitude with curiosity. She eventually lost faith in their ability to get themselves out of it.

"Well, for pity's sake," she shouted. Rat Face heard her voice alongside him and chanced to look at her at the exact instant her roundhouse connected squarely with the tip of his nose.

"Eeeeeeooowww!" screamed the rat, his nose flattened, smeared across his face, and bleeding profusely. He dropped the knife and fell to his knees.

"You vile woman!" he screamed.

Ignoring him, Gertie took a step towards Gorilla. The distraction gave Socrates a chance to stick two fingers deep into the ape's eyes.

"Take that, you two-eyed Cyclops."

Gorilla dropped Socrates and, finding himself alone against them, began to back away. In shock from his harrowing experience,

Tyler sagged against the railing as Gertie turned back to the little ringleader.

"You vile, evil person," he screamed, hoping that by loud talk alone he might deter her. "My nose is pouring blood."

She grabbed him by the seat of his pants. "Then what you should do is put some cold water on it," she said, sweeping him over the railing and into the river below.

"Watch out, Berlos, you've got competition," she roared. Next she turned her attention to Gorilla, still a formidable opponent. He was staring after his departed boss. His leadership gone, the fight drained out of him. He started whimpering,"I can't swim, ma'am. If you make me go down there, I'll drown."

"Drowning would serve you right, you big oaf. Now get on home," she reprimanded him. "And don't hold forth with the likes of that bum again."

Obediently he turned and fled off the bridge, looking back twice to see that she wasn't pursuing him.

Socrates gathered his dignity while Gertie made a feckless attempt to reclaim her femininity.

"My goodness, wasn't that a pickle?" she tittered "I wasn't much help," Tyler said, his voice ringing hollow in the darkness.

"Well, that is certainly not true," Gertie helped. "You did a good job of distracting him with your nose so I could sneak up on him."

"That's right," seconded Socrates. "You did stick your nose right into it. When you got a knife up agin' ya, you're holding a poor hand."

"Yeah, I guess," Tyler closed the subject. They walked the rest of the way home the silence punctuated only once by Socrates.

"Gertie, old girl, you were great. We were great. Just like old times again, heh?."

Eight

*T*he next morning after breakfast several men reported having seen the two louts from the previous night hanging around the island. One old-timer claimed to have been hung by his heels and shaken for loose change.

"And I ain't had that done to me for years," he concluded rather nostalgically.

"Amen," came a chorus of agreement.

Presently Socrates stood up and announced, "Well, I think I'm off to church." He stretched and walked out of the room. It took Tyler a few seconds to realize this was more than a coarse reference to the bathroom. He hurried out when he heard the front door slam and caught up with Socrates at the corner.

"You really are going to church?"

"Yes I am."

"Why?"

"Why?" Socrates repeated.

"Why? No one else seemed interested in it."

"I see it this way. I've never seen God, but I know a whole lot of folks that place a lot of store in him. I figure I'm not smart enough to know everything. So I play the odds. I'm betting that there's a better chance that He is than that He isn't. Besides, a church is a nice, quiet place to reflect on my errant ways."

"But you know the scriptures, too."

"I just know the words in the books; Proverbs, Psalms,Wisdom. Those are good words for anyone to know."

Okay, thought Tyler, a boy raised in an agnostic family. That seemed to fit his personality. They walked on for awhile, then the youth began again.

"So what are you, then?"

"What do you mean, What am I?"

"You know, Catholic, Lutheran, Methodist? What's your religion?"

"Oh, that. It doesn't much matter to me as long as it's about Jesus and the Good Word. I'm not much on some of these Jesus-come-latelies like the Jehovahs or Mormans. I was raised Baptist, of course. Up in the woods we're all Lutherans more or less. I move around. It's always nice to get a second opinion on matters of faith."

"My folks are Presbyterians," Tyler said.

Socrates smiled at him. "You sound like you never gave it much thought. 1 don't suppose that's unusual. Now that's handy, isn't it? Presbyterian. I thought I'd go to a Catholic church today. Not much difference. They're the only ones with a service on a weekday, anyhow. You coming along?"

"Suits me," Tyler agreed. "My folks don't go to church much. But they know the Bishop from the country club. I don't usually get up on Sundays."

"Why am I not surprised? Maybe it scares you."

"My family wasn't churchy. Maybe if it meant more business for the bank and more privileges at the country club. We always sat in the front pew the better to be seen. But scares me? I'm not a believer."

"Sure it scares you,Tyler. The more you learn about God, the closer you come to the flame. The flame gets brighter and burns hotter. A lot of folks nearly burn right up from God. It's a fact and I heard this from a revivalist preacher once. The Fire of Love, he called it. Burns but doesn't destroy. But if you step back from that flame, if you turn away from Him, you're gonna fear for the rest of your life that He's turned from you too.

"Listen, I haven't turned because I was never there."

"That's right, you probably haven't been there yet. You still haven't put yourself in the middle where it's either heaven bound or damnation forever and had to make a choice. You're scared to go near the flame. But one day, son, it'll come to you and then you'll figure it out."

"What are you talking about?"

"The flame, boy, the flame."

"Flame? At least if I stay away from it, I'll never get burned."

"You'll never be warm, either."

"Yeah? Right now that's the least thing on my mind."

Socrates sat in a pew in a side alcove. Genuflecting, he crossed himself, then knelt for a few minutes in prayer. He brushed through another sign of the cross and, pulling out a tattered King James Bible, sat back and began to read.

Tyler sat down from the start and spent his time gawking at the stained glass, high vaulted ceiling and ornate main altar. The church was small, less than a fifth the size of his parent's basilica back home. Nor were the worshippers as prosperous looking as he would have seen at the basilica's society masses.

It was a weekday mass so the attendance was sparse; people who were generally not employed or employable; old widows, retired men and a few young mothers with restless children.

A small bell by the door of the sacristy announced the entrance of the purple-vested priest. Two altar boys in black and white preceded him. They genuflected at the foot of the altar and began the centuries old liturgy.

"Dominus vobiscum" intoned the priest.

"Et cum spiritu tuo," echoed the altar boys.

Tyler heard the same words, coming from Socrates. He knew the responses of the altar boys. There was no sermon; it would have been unusual at a weekday mass. At communion, Socrates rose to go to the altar railing. Tyler, on the outside of the pew, felt a small pressure on his leg, hesitated, and then moved to let him pass.

Thirty minutes later the two men stepped into the open air. Minneapolis spread out before them in the frosty morning; not clean and white like a young city, but gray, smoky and sooty as befitting a mill town, a lumbering town, a coal fired, muscle-flexing city. Every chimney in sight was sending up a plume of smoke and steam. There was no wind to sweep it away; no clear, warm air to carry it like cathedral spires into the stratocumulus. Today the clouds were low and motionless. They trapped the city's breath and spread it like a pall of fog back into the environs that created it.

"Isn't she beautiful?" Socrates breathed.

Socrates spread his arms like a proud papa as he took it all in. "I wasn't born here but this place, as much as any, is where I call home. I think it's been good to me."

"Have you forgotten last night?" Tyler said remembering the attempted robbery on the bridge.

"That? Nothing at all. A couple guys out having some fun, was all. It put a nice cap on the evening, don't you think?"

"Yeah, sure," said a disbelieving Tyler.

Socrates bustled down the steep staircase of Our Lady of Lourdes. "I'm just glad I didn't hurt anyone."

Tyler watched the energetic old man, elfin-like in so many of his mannerisms, sagacious in other ways, perform an Irish jig at the bottom of the stairs.

Socrates planned to hop the freight for Duluth that evening. Tyler still had thirty dollars in his pockets and was adamant about spending some of it for a good coach seat. When Socrates pointed out that it wouldn't be sociable to ride in comfort while their friends "rode the rods" Tyler reluctantly agreed to purchase a ticket for Schnapsie also.

Then, later, when it was determined that Old Toad Shatsweiss and another crony, Snoose were also planning to go, Tyler accepted the inevitable.

He had saved his stake, but at the expense of another blistering boxcar. They killed the rest of the day in the traditional manner of men with more time than treasure.

In the afternoon they picked up their packages from the tailor. The re-made coat hung well on Tyler's broad shoulders and he wore it with a certain embarrassed pride.

The woolen mittens were heavy and warm. They were double stitched with waxed catgut, inspiring the bubbly little tailor to impart a lifetime guarantee on the sewing job. Knowing they were going up to the woods, he even offered to "provide free alterations should an accident cause a change in the shape of your hand." Socrates thought that such a generous offer he promised to bring his own glove business there in the future.

Over on Fifth Street, they had lunch and beer in the Baron Saloon and then went to the city library. They found a bench and claimed it. The beer had made them drowsy. They sat and engaged in quiet conversation for an hour while Socrates shared a few stories of the camps and the men he had known.

"This Old Toad that's coming with us, he's a character. Not as old as you'd think, though. Maybe forty-five, but he's spent his whole life at the end of a double bit axe so he looks pretty used up. He's real short, you see, and drinks a lot. Drinks all night when it's on the cuff. People in bars will buy him drinks just to see him put it away. He just puts his bead back on the bar and they pour it down his throat. Lives in the camps pretty much year 'round; summers as a caretaker up in the brush. He doesn't ever use a pillow, just a chunk of wood. If he doesn't have a chunk, he just lays there with his neck sticking right out straight. Never seems to sleep much anyway.

"His parents died when he was a boy. That's a story in itself. I just remember there was a gruesome sawmill accident. He's got two sisters that go up north and bring him down here and give him a nice bed. He takes one look at it and lays down right on the rug but first chance he gets, he sneaks off and goes back up.

"He's quite a river pig, too. That's a log driver. Never wears corked boots. Those are spikes in the soles to grip the logs. Never uses them. Just an old pair of rubber shoes. He'll like you 'cause he likes everyone. You want to be nice to him, too." Socrates said this in a protecting manner.

"I don't need you giving me advice like that," Tyler said.

Socrates took the rebuke in stride. "Well, maybe I don't know, either. I just thought." He slapped the boy's knee and stood up. "Let's go read the paper."

On page two of the Chicago Tribune ran a small headline, "Search Continues for Caldwell Youth. Society Parents Fear Kidnapping." The story recapitulated the events that led up to Tyler's disappearance. It told of the hunt for Tyler, mentioned the $1,000 reward for his safe return and reported that police suspected he may have been taken out of state, possibly to Madison or Minneapolis. There was no statement from his father, Patrick Caldwell; no mention of their fight.

Tyler showed the story to Socrates. He read it, looked at the boy and said, tongue in cheek, "Well, kid, you were fun, but the money looks good, too."

"God! A thousand dollars! I guess I am worth something." He looked at Socrates with alarm. "You wouldn't really turn me in, would you?"

"It's tempting, but, hey, it's your decision. Think I'm gonna out-muscle a big galloot like you?"

"What should I do?"

"You should go home. Get out of my hair. They want you back, don't they?"

Tyler thought about it for a moment then rejected the idea. "No, I can't do that. They don't really want me back. That reward is just for show. 'Good form', my father would say. I'll not go back. It wouldn't change anything."

"Fair enough," said Socrates."You'd know about that better than me, but you have to write them."

"Why?"

"They're worried. I think they're feeling the same way most folks would feel if they lost a kid. Tell 'em you're okay, they can call off the manhunt, and you'll be home when the time is right. Besides, according to what the paper says, I'd be the one that kidnapped you, wouldn't I?"

Tyler considered that last remark. "I suppose you would at that. Yeah, okay, I'll write. When?"

"How about now?" They composed a simple letter and gave it to the librarian with a penny to mail to Chicago. The article carried a picture of Tyler in evening clothes since that was how he was last seen. He had already changed substantially. Some of the baby look was already gone and nearly a week of not shaving had left a heavy stubble on his face. Dressed as he was now, he would not be recognized except by a clever detective. And soon he would be off the streets for the winter.

Nine

*D*usk. The sun had dropped below the crown of the forest and the creeping cold began to flow out of the shadows. Sullivan and Johnny Quick were just coming in from laying out the last of the sleigh roads for the camp. They ran four miles from the cuttings to the camp and another mile from the camp down to the rollways at the creek. Mike liked the layout because it gave a natural flow to the scheme of things.

The wood butcher and his two assistants were putting in eighteen-hour days making the six wide-bunk sleighs, three horse jammers and the rut cutter. The water tank for the ice roads was ready.

"Johnny, tomorrow I'm going to Duluth to finish the crew up. I think it may take three or four days until I get back. The camp is yours 'til then. You be the straw boss until Rube comes in. Okay?"

"I'll keep everything in line for you, Mike," said Johnny. Quick was a cruiser by trade, not a foreman. His job was to walk the woods and measure the volume of timber, its quality and the best way to get it out. But he had been in camps all his life, had come up through the system, and knew the routine. He was a very short man. In big cruiser boots he only stood a fraction over five feet three inches tall and looked like a dwarf alongside Sullivan.

He got his handle, Johnny Quick not being his baptized name, not because of his pace in the woods, which was prodigious, but because of his speed in a fight. He was impossible to hit. He'd kick a man in the knee and as soon as his opponent reached down to grab him, he'd be up on a table belting the man in the face. He never stood still long enough to have his measure taken.

He wore a red voyageur's cap over his curly black hair and that made him look French. In reality, he was Basque and Irish, his father coming from the rugged Spanish hill country, his mother from a genteel house in Dublin. He bore both their personalities and wore one when sober, the other when not. He knew the work and would keep order for however long it took until Rube, Mike's second-in-command, saw to the delivery of his seventh child, a seventh son if his luck held out and his wife's didn't, and got into camp.

The building was nearly finished. Men were rolling out the heavy black tar paper on the roofs and nailing it down with wooden slats.

The camp was laid out north and south in two parallel rows of buildings. On the west side, the long house contained the cook shack and larder on the north end with the bunkhouse taking up the south half. The ninety-foot long building was windowless. A back door on each half led to the twelve-hole outhouse. A large sauna was immediately south of that. East, across the "street" from the cook shack was the small building housing Mike's quarters, the camp clerk and the camp store. South of that was a long lean-to building containing the stable, blacksmith shop and wood butcher's work area. That building continued on as a tar paper pole barn large enough to keep the forty-five horses the work needed. They used twenty-four on the sleighs, three on the jammers, ten for skidding to the jammers and another eight for replacement as well as running the hay line into Craig each day.

A small lake a hundred feet out beyond the cook shack provided water. It was a tidy camp, not spectacular, but serviceable. Mike had built six such outfits in his career and he was satisfied with this one.

Already he had thirty-five men in camp. Forty more, mostly teamsters, were expected up from Bemidji during the week. He would find another twenty or more in Duluth when he went to fill out their supply list. Ninety men in camp, give or take a few.

The work assignments were already meted out. Twenty-five teamsters each earning a dollar and two bits a day; eighteen swampers–seventy-five cents day; thirty-eight fellers and buckers–a dollar a day; fourteen on the jammers–again a dollar a day except for the top loaders who earned the same as teamsters. Then there were two clerks, two foremen, three smithies, three wood butchers, six cooks and cooks helpers, and two bull cooks, all earning from fifty cents a day up to Mike's own three dollar a day top wage. Ninety men; at least to start.

Mike smelled the air. "More snow coming, Johnny." Already there was four inches on the ground. The cruiser nodded in agreement.

"We'll roll them out at dawn and I'll ride in with the hay run. Keep brushing and bucking the roads and send out some men to stamp the black spruce bogs."

"Yes sir, we'll stay on it."

Two of the roads they laid out ran north and one southeast and looked like a crooked tailed wishbone with the camp at the junction. The sleighs could only run up gentle grades so the cruiser had followed the paths of least resistance. This meant cutting across lakes, bogs and swamps. In the swamps and bogs the men, ten abreast, stomped down the moss and Labrador tea so the cold could penetrate and freeze the black muck beneath. Then the ice roads could be built.

"We'll start icing the road south tomorrow and then, the other ones, Johnny. You'll see to get that going too."

"I will."

"1 know that."

The cook came out and blew the forty-eight inch Gabriel horn signaling the call to dinner.

"We'll eat and turn 'em in quick. It's come time to make wages, now." Mike winked at Johnny and the two of them joined the rush for the cook shack.

Ten

They gathered in the parlor after dinner: Tyler, Socrates, Old Toad, Schnapsie, Snoose and another man they just called Seifert. Each had a heavy sack-Socrates called it a turkey-containing all their worldly possessions.

"Everything a man needs is just what he's got on him," Snoose said, "and that can all fit in his turkey."

"That's right," Toad agreed, "It all goes in your turkey. If it don't fit, you don't need it."

Tyler packed his few belongings with room to spare and waited. He was nervous. Hanging out in a big city was one thing, but to travel two hundred miles into the wilderness and spend an entire winter was something else. Tyler had never been away from home in his life. Worse, he had never had to put such blind trust in another person before leastwise someone who hadn't received a generous tip for performance. It scared him to do so now.

The freight was scheduled to pull out at four a.m. By eight that evening they had all gone to bed in anticipation of the busy night.

Unable to sleep, Tyler saw Socrates leave his bed sometime before midnight. At three Socrates was back in the room getting them up. Gertie, wearing a large flannel nightgown, had coffee waiting for them downstairs. She gave each of them a half dozen hard rolls that they stowed in their turkeys and walked them to the door where she said her good byes with warm yet brusque affection.

When Socrates' turn came, she gathered him in a tight embrace. "Listen, you old futz … " Moisture was glistening in her eyes and she was unable to finish.

"I know, Gertie," he lovingly patted her ample behind. "I know."

"Tyler!" She boomed, pushing her old lover away with a sudden brusqueness, "You learn from this man! You learn well and maybe you can pay him back sometime. And maybe you'll come back sometime."

"Yes, ma'am," Tyler said, "I will. We'll go see the Berlos again." She forced a laugh and shooed them out the door.

They moved quickly down the island and crossed over to the west side.

There, they left the road and went down the bank, working back north on a narrow fisherman's path. The St. Paul and Duluth depot was close by the river, directly opposite the island.

After ten minutes of picking their way, they climbed back up and looked across the wide freight yard. It was full of switch engines building trains from groups of cars. Spotting their train, they waited while Seifert crept across the yard and, picking an empty car, quietly forced the door open. He came back to the others and lay down. Silently they waited for the whistle. At five minutes after four it blew, and the train jolted forward. Single file, separated from each other by five paces, they ran across the tracks and, throwing their turkeys into the boxcar, climbed in. The train picked up speed and soon the street lamps of Minneapolis receded into the blackness.

They were quiet at first, feeling more like adventuresome boys than men, hoping they hadn't been seen. After awhile, they began to relax and move about. It was one hundred and sixty miles to Duluth. A five hour trip.

They were on a 'milk' run. Every day four trains ran between Duluth and Minneapolis. Two daytime express runs hauled both freight and passengers. These were trains of commerce and business. Mining and timber executives rode the plush club cars while steam shovel parts, cables, saws, fittings and every other part and parcel of their industries filled the boxcars.

At night the two milk trains went out, one going to the big city in the evening and the other returning to the Great Lakes port in the early morning. They stopped at all the small towns along the way, picking up local produce and mail and dropping off catalog orders, agricultural parts and more mail. Sleepy passengers rode in cars with straight-back wooden benches, their heads nodding in rhythm to the roll of the train. It was the economy class trip most favored by the drummers, drifters and farmers.

A short whistle blast announced the approach to each town. The stationmasters would pull their feet off their desks and hurry to roll the freight out of the warehouses and onto the loading platforms.

Each town was a verse in a song to the flavor and texture of Minnesota; names like White Bear Lake, Forest Lake, Willow River, Moose Lake Falls, and, most famously, Hinkley.

The Hunter's Moon, cold and metallic, was sliding toward the western horizon. The first graying of the eastern skies began to give a subtle form to the blackness outside their car. The temperature dropped as it often does just before dawn and the men stood up to stretch their arms and beat the circulation back into their legs.

Tyler moved to the open door and looked out expecting to see the start of the great forest Socrates had bragged on. Instead he saw trees with no tops; a forest of poles numbering in the tens of thousands reaching against the sky like the spars on the ships of a vast sailing armada.

"What is this?" He asked no one in particular. "What happened here?"

Socrates came up and stood beside him. "That, boy, is the legacy of the great Hinkley fire. It must be a little more than twenty years ago it happened. I never saw anything like it in my lifetime."

"Were you there?"

"I was. Now, don't give me that look. I know what you're thinking; this old man swears he was everywhere anything ever happened. But it's the truth. Here, let's go back out of this wind and I'll give you the story."

They sat down in the middle of the car, looking out over the desolation that was materializing with the dawn. Brush and scrub pine formed a thick carpet beneath the forest of dead trees.

"It was, let me see now, . .'93. .No, . .'94. Yes. It Was eighteen ninety-four that she burned off. It was a dry one, that summer; hot winds and drought, you know. Farmers everywhere lost their crops, but up here it was worse. Brown. No hay at all. The farmers had to cut down trees so their livestock could eat the leaves. Got so bad the sheep and cattle would see a man with an axe in his hand and they'd start setting up a beller and follow him out. They had to sneak out to the woods so the trees wouldn't drop on the hungry animals."

"How did it start?"

"Who knows? She just started burning somewhere around Mission Creek and blew north. Over four hundred square miles went black. With the wind blowing it covered ground faster than a man could run. Folks jumped in ponds and lakes; even went down their wells. Some bodies were found buried out in the fields. They tried to lie down in a furrow and cover up with dirt and never got out. Buried themselves alive and got baked. Better than four hundred souls lost their lives plus all the crippled and maimed. And thousands of animals. You couldn't get away from it."

"Where were you when it happened?"

"Me? I was a fireman on this train line. Me and a engineer name of James Root. Jim is dead now. But that day, he was a genuine hero. Settle back sonny and I'll learn you all about it.

"I remember we were coming down from Duluth. Everyone knew there was a big fire down there. In Duluth the sky was like midnight at noon. Ashes were floating out of the smoke. It was so thick you could hardly see your hand at the end of your arm. We had to tie our bandannas over our faces to breath. But we had to see if we could get through.

"Our train was the 'No. 4 Limited' of the St. Paul and Duluth line. Nothing special. Just a meat and potatoes train. We got word that there were still folks trapped in Hinkley. One train had already pulled out with some folks but others had stayed on. Some were still coming in from the farms.

"Anyway, we were heading south that day and when he heard about the trouble in Hinkley, Jim didn't lose a whisker. 'Shovel on the coal, Soc,' he said. 'Let's add some sparks of our own to that fire!' We did, too! We were blowing red ash all the way down the line.

"Finally, we got down to about a mile and a half north of Hinkley. We had been blasting the whistle and ringing the bell the whole way because there were a lot of stragglers on the right-of-way. Outside of town, like I say, we were flagged down by a large mob. They were the last of the townies.

"'Get on quick!' Root says. 'Leave your goods and belongings!' Everyone jumped quick like 'cause Root started backing up right away right after he said that.

"You could see the fire coming at us. Red flames shining through the smoke, trees exploding, their juices boiling up. And, Oh, the noise!

Jesus, it sounded like a tornado rushing down on you. It was from the wind! We thought we'd all die out there!"

Socrates stopped to catch his breath. He could smell the smoke all over again. He saw the flames again. The horror was mirrored in his eyes. He waited until he gathered his composure.

"You know," he began again, "they say a big fire makes its own wind, sucks up all the air. I don't know, maybe just because we were so scared, but it was a labor just to draw a breath.

"We were running back down the track. Right away we could tell that we weren't going to beat it. Then the worst happened. I had gone back over the coal car to see to the passengers and the heat got to Jim and he passed out. I saw the train was slowing down and ran back forward. The pressure was less than sixty pounds and Root was lying on the floor. I threw a pail of water on him and brought him around. Then we poured on more coal. We got going again but never made up any ground.

"It was closing in, dropping burning cinders right on top of us. The cars started burning. My coal pile was on fire! Honest to God! The rail ties were smoking. Root was on fire! He kept looking out the cab of the loco to see where we was backing and sparks lit in his hair and back. I had to beat him out with a wet gunnysack.

"By the time we come to Skunk Lake, it was over. Everything was afire! It was passing us by like we were standing still!"

"Root stopped the train and we ran down each side of the tracks screaming, 'Get out! Get in the water!' Most people knew what to do, but some were too scared; they didn't want to leave the cars. We had to drag them out! One man was so frightened he pulled a pistol and threatened to shoot whoever touched him. Another knocked me down with his fist when I grabbed him. One way or another, we got them all in the water.

"They called it Skunk Lake, but was just a slough really. The drought had run the water down so low. So, everyone went out in that muck and laid down in the muddy water with wet rags over their faces."

"I made one last run along the tracks. Good thing, too! I found a little girl, maybe seven years old. Her hair was all burned off and most of her clothes were gone. She was screaming crazy. I grabbed her and ran down the bank. We hit the water just as the fireball went over our heads. We lay there while the fire passed over us. It went fast. It was so hot; it screamed so loud I couldn't hear the little girl no more! It roared! The women and men were all crying. And the children! You'd have sworn we were all dying out there. The cattails around us were burned to the waterline. Even the water began steaming! I'm not kidding!

"When we came out, the train was gone! Just the wheels and iron carriage was all that was left. But old Root, he had pulled nearly four hundred lost souls out of that doomed town and everyone of them crawled out of Skunk Lake alive.

When he was done, Tyler spoke first. "What happened to her?"

"The girl? I never got her name. She couldn't remember. I think the fire wiped out her memory on that. We gave her to the Benedictine sisters at the hospital in Duluth. She needed a lot of care; had a lot of bad burns. She was an orphan as far as we knew. Her parents never came forward. She stayed with the sisters, and today she's a Benedictine sister, herself. She runs a hospital in Hibbing up on the Iron Range. A saintly lady bound for heaven. God knows, she's already been through hell."

At 9:20 the milk run reached Duluth. When it slowed to go through the residential section on the west end of town, they jumped off and walked down towards the waterfront, to the Jungle.

Duluth was a muscular city. On the east end of town large mansions lined the London Road and enjoyed a grand view of Lake Superior. There lived the timber barons, shipping magnates and iron kings. Their proud houses stood as grand testimony to the riches that were being taken from the wilderness of northern Minnesota.

The city spread out from the protected St. Louis River estuary, reaching up the sides of a high bluff that towered eight hundred feet above the lake and afforded a spectacular view of Superior and well beyond into the Wisconsin woods.

On the western edge of town, lay the blue-collar neighborhoods, each one distinguished from the others by the church spires of its particular denomination and ethnicity.

Down by the harbor, the housing transitioned to warehouses, staging yards and loading docks. From the docks flowed the timber and iron ore that formed the backbone of the Duluth economy. Heavy trestle works reached out over the water and supported the groaning ore cars from the Mesabi, Vermillion and Cuyuna Ranges. They crept out over the docks and disgorged their 'red gold' into the hoppers that fed the cavernous maws of the ore boats.

Gantry cranes and derricks loaded timbers and sawn lumber onto the decks of schooners. The ships made the dangerous passage over the stormy waters of Superior to the steel mills of Gary, Detroit, Erie and Pittsburgh. The lumber built the sprawling cities of Chicago, Minneapolis, Omaha and St. Louis.

Older buildings, no longer suited to the fast growing commerce, were abandoned in favor of new structures on the abundant land. The poor and transient reclaimed these neglected derelicts. Shacks built from prosperity's trash piles dotted the empty back lots along the St. Louis River. It was an area that still bustled with heavy industry by day, but sighed with quiet despair by night. To the people who lived there, it was called The Jungle.

About the same time they neared it, another man, Patrick Donlin, was leaving, striding out with the proud walk of a man with a job to do and the confidence to get it done.

Donlin was a jack-of-all-trades, but like the old adage, a master of none. His situation did not result from a dislike of work. He loved physical tasks. He was a big strong Irishman and enjoyed heavy work. It was just that Donlin was a free spirit. He had left Ireland when he was fifteen. His father was a tenant farmer on the estate of a wealthy nobleman. The caretaker of the estate, Harold Waldron, had a beautiful young daughter. Paddy was a beautiful young man and, in the course of one spring, their infatuation blossomed into love and her belly eventually blossomed too. The enraged father, intent on redeeming his daughter's honor swore to kill Patrick. Paddy narrowly missed having his hair parted with a shotgun and fled to the coast where he made a steamer for America.

Ten years later, he was still searching for something to satisfy the romance and adventure he had been denied. Because he never stayed in one place long enough to develop a trade, Donlin was, instead, given ample opportunity to develop his muscles. He loved a ribald joke, could carry a tune, dance a jig and possessed a rich laughter that emanated from his soul and made him a hail-fellow with the men and a 'catch' with the ladies. He was on his way uptown to butcher hogs for a man named Beltrand.

Butchering was well suited for Paddy. One at a time, the fattened porkers were driven out of the pen. As they went past a gap in the chute, Paddy drove a killing knife into their neck and, with a sharp downward thrust opened the jugular vein. He dragged out the kicking animal; collected the gushing blood in a bucket, hung up the animal and gutted it. Next, he slid it into a scalding tub of water and shaved off the bristles with a hog scraper, split the carcass into halves and hung them up in the cooler. With twenty pigs on the wagon and two hundred pounds apiece, it promised to be a full day's work.

About the time Donlin had stuck his first pig, the ragtag troop entered a ramshackle old tenement building at one-ten Front Street. They dropped off their turkeys and, ignoring the come and go of the morning traffic, went to sleep on the wooden floor. They woke at noon and cleaned up to go job hunting.

"Come on, boys," Socrates ordered. "Let's get out and find Hungry Mike before he buys up all the Swedes!"

There were several ways to hire out to the woods during a big cut year. One was to walk right into a camp and sign on. Some camps had such a poor regard for their help that they had three crews going all the time: one working, one leaving and one coming. They were constantly hiring men just to maintain a steady flow of manpower.

Others, like Hungry Mike Sullivan, kept the same crew all winter long. He expected no less work than the other camps, but kept his men well fed, the camps clean and the equipment in good condition. It was a cause for bragging if a man could say he had wintered in a Sullivan camp.

Another way to get a job was to leave a name at the employment office. Good men were kept on file from year to year and could generally command a job just for the asking.

The third route was to go by way of the man-catchers; agents that cruised the lumberjack hangouts trying to sign men on for resale to logging camps. Good camps didn't need man-catchers;bad camps couldn't get by without them. Gathering ten or twenty unemployed jacks around a jug of cheap whiskey, they'd get them drunk and get the poor man's "x" on the signup with fists and billy clubs. It wasn't Socrates' intention to accept a free drink and wake up lost in the woods for six months.

They walked over to Superior Avenue and into the district office of the Itascan Lumber Company. Socrates went up to the clerk and addressed him by name.

"Morning, Jack, how is everything?"

"Well, Socrates! Everything's fine. How have you been keeping?"

"Good, Jack, good. Say, Jack, I came up with a whole passel of guys looking for work. Logging this winter?"

"Plenty of that, Soc. We can always use a cook. Who else is with you?"

"Well, there's me and Snoose here. Then there's Schnapsie; Old Toad, you know him; Siefert, he knows the woods; and this big kid here, Tyler."

"You're a big enough man," Jack said looking Tyler up and down. "Where have you worked before?"

Socrates spoke up for him. "In the woods? He hasn't. He's from Chicago. He's a young, tough kid with a lot of grit."

Jack eyed them for a moment. "Well, like I said, Socrates," Jack said lowering his voice, "I need cooks anytime, but everyone else is either getting long in the tooth, or showing green behind the ears. I'm not sure."

" Jack, we came a long way for work."

"I know. I know. Listen, we have a small project up in the Arrowhead; cutting pulpwood by the piece. I think you boys could handle that. And I need a good cook there, too."

"We're looking for timber work, Jack."

"I can't say I have any for you. Where can we reach you? I can put you on the list and if something comes up I'll give a holler.

"Where's Sullivan?"

"Hungry Mike? Isn't here. He's building a new camp on the Pine Island. I'd guess he's in for the winter by now."

"We'll wait for him."

"I don't think he'll be coming. You better take this job at Isabella."

"No, Jack, thanks just the same, but we're together. We'll wait for Mike. He'll be coming."

"Suit yourself. Maybe he will come. I don't know. He's running his own camp this year. He can hire who ever he wants. Try the man-catchers if it's timber you want.

Socrates snorted in disgust and gesturing to the others, walked out. Jack watched the curious collection of misfits leave the office and turned to his superior in the back room.

"I don't know, Barry, but if Sullivan hires those men, he isn't the foreman I heard he was."

Barry looked up from his desk. He was older than Jack, had seen hundreds of men come and go and knew Mike Sullivan personally.

"If you believe that, Jack, you don't know Mike Sullivan." And, he thought, you probably don't know lumberjacks, either.

Out on the sidewalk, Tyler was confused. That clerk hadn't even given them a good looking over. Looking at the others, Tyler wasn't much impressed either. Snoose and Schnapsie appeared to be more suited for rocking on a front porch than lumberjacking. They were a couple of eccentrics, all right. The quiet Seifert hadn't said a word since they left Minneapolis. Maybe he didn't speak English. And Toad! If half the things he had already heard about this man were true, he should be locked away.

Then there was this Sullivan. Why the big whoop-dee-doo Socrates made over him? Would he really come and take them out of the Jungle? If so, when?

Socrates had no trouble appraising the situation, "That Jack always was a jerk. If he's too blind to know a good catch when he sees one, that's his loss. Could be Itascan is getting too big for its britches. Good food and clean bunks and all, they still got no right to be that choosy. And as for them unholy man-catchers, why, they'll put you in a louse-ridden, gray-meat camp and then charge you a month's wages for the privilege of being there! He spat in the gutter.

"But," he continued, "Sullivan, there's the man to work for. He'll let every man decide how he's to be treated. If you act like a first class gent, and work like one, you get respect. If you act like a jackass, you get to walk. He's tough on the camp, but he's fair 'cause he never shows himself no mercy neither. If I had my druthers, I'd go to my grave working for Sullivan. When I can't work anymore, I'll be ready for the grave, anyway. And when I am, it's Sullivan I want shoveling in the dirt."

"The way you talk, that's where we're liable to end up." Socrate's speech had done nothing to reassure the youth.

"Have some patience, boy," his mentor scolded. "All things come to them who wait. We'll wait."

"Well, that seems to be what we're best at," Tyler said in a sniping tone.

They spent the rest of the afternoon in a saloon blowing the last of Tyler's money and about an hour before dark, started back to the Jungle.

About that time, Paddy Donlin was hanging up his last pig. He washed the skim of blood and fat from his face and hands and went in to be paid off. Beltrand, was locking up for the day.

"Say, now, Mr. Beltrand," Paddy began. "I'm finished out back and I'll be asking for me wages now."

"What?" The man with the high-pitched nasal voice turned abruptly from the door. He seemed to have forgotten about Donlin. "You startled me. Your wages. Yes, of course, but I'm closed up now. I've locked the safe. Besides, I have to inspect your work and I've no time for that now. I'll not pay for bad work."

"Surely, Mr. Beltrand, you'll have no bad work coming from this Irishman. Come and take a look. They be all snug in the cooler and cleaner than a hound's tooth, they be."

"They had better be but I have no time now. Come back in the morning. I'll have the register open then."

"Tomorrow? Mr. Beltrand. I toiled all day without a bite, and I would sorely like to eat tonight. I haven't a penny but what you owe me."

Beltrand seized on this. "And it's my fault you haven't a penny in your pocket? Come here. I'll let you out and we'll square up in the morning. There's no other way."

Paddy sighed audibly, knowing this Englishman was trying to take advantage of him. "Very well, then, if it must be tomorrow, it must be. But I'll leave by the back way, if you please. I left my sweater on the stoop."

"Fine, then. Goodnight." The butcher was pleased to see it go his way. He planned to spend the next two days with friends in Two Harbors and, with luck, this bum would be moved on by the time he returned. With a wave of his hand, he dismissed him and bent to the locks on the door.

What Paddy did next would go with him to his grave. He walked into the cooler in the back of the store, lifted a side of pork off its hook and, balancing it easily on his shoulder, walked away from the butcher shop. Approaching a cop at the corner, he tipped his cap and proclaimed with an accent drenched smile, "Good evening, Constable. Top 'o' the evening to you."

The officer tipped his cap in reply and responded, also in a beautiful Irish brogue, "Now, that it is, laddie. Now, that it is. And that's a fine pig you have there."

"Isn't it though? Yes. I'll be now delivering it to the good sisters down to the convent."

"Would that be at Saint Monica's?"

"Aye, St. Monica's."

"Well, give Sister Bridget a fine hello from Officer O'toole, now won't you? She's my mother's sister, you know."

"Sister Bridget. What a saint! I'll shower your blessings on her, you can be sure."

"Good evening then." The officer tipped his cap again and turned away to hide the grin on his face knowing there was neither a St. Monica's nor a Sister Bridget anywhere in Duluth.

Six blocks later, Paddy and his pig met Socrates and his misfits. Inside two minutes, it was agreed to throw the pig, their two jugs of whiskey and a sack of potatoes that Snoose had 'found' into a common pot.

The lot next to the Front Street tenement was empty. They built a roaring fire to lay a bed of coals. Old iron bars and wire were fashioned into a spit and an assortment of broken furniture was dragged out of the building to sit on. They sat up late into the night roasting the pig, and lay around still later into the early morning eating it and washing it down with the harsh whiskey they dressed up with a crock of spring water. As the whiskey went down, the quality of the stories went up.

"I remember, as a young man," Schnapsie began in the traditional manner of reminiscing, "I used to spend a considerable amount of my valuable time in the pool halls. My best friend was a Finlander. Toivol. He still is Toival for all I know. But he's dead now, too. So there you have it. Fell out a bedroom window one night. Not his. I helped the mourners carry him home. We shot a lot of pool together. Straight pool, 8 ball, Snooker, you name it we shot it. He had a great stroke, my best friend Toivol, a great stroke. Then he got married. I forget which time, exactly, but when he did, there wasn't a rumor of him for three months. They say that Tina, that's the girl I'm referring too, they say she didn't do a stitch of laundry for that whole time. Didn't have to. Didn't wear nothin' Hah!

"Then, all of a notion there my best friend is back at the pool hall. And, Lordy, she's there with him. In a pool hall! Boy, she was a looker! We all figured the passion had done burned off like the alcohol on a shot of good whiskey, don't you know. But she sure lit afire in the rest of us. But best friend Toivol and me, we started shooting some straight pool, just like he had never left. We're shooting away and I notice pretty soon that every time I come around the table to where Tina is sitting, she rubs her foot up and down my leg. Toivol can't see this, of course. But I'm pretty sharp about that stuff. I think she's just trying to bother me to help him win my bet. Then, later, when he's out back to the john, she comes up to me and starts whispering sweet nothings in my ear. Silly things like women say when they feel lovey.

"Well, I'm tryin' my best to ignore all this. I'm getting warmed up and it's ruining my game and 'cuz after all, he's my best friend. Did I mention that? But, by thunder, later still, he's up to the bar gettin' the jars filled and I'm looking at her and she slithers up to me again. She asks do I like what I'm looking at? And, you know, she's got this dress on with two buttons missing on the front like some terrorist tore them off, and she fills it out pretty well anyway. Well a man's a man, and I can't take much more of this, and I figure if Toivol can't keep his heifer in her stall than who's fault is that? I say, sure, I like it. So she says, would I like to spend sometime with her? I nearly spit! But by then, I'm leaning to that possibility, myself. I say, sure, even if it was the beer talking a little. But, I says, what about Toivol, my former best friend? She says, don't worry. Come Saturday, he'll be up in Northome all day on business he tells her. This being Thursday, we were shooting pool. But, she says, bring twenty dollars. Twenty dollars, I say? What for? You know, says she, a proper gentleman always brings a girl a present. I agreed with that.

"So Saturday comes and the weather is cold, so to get warmed up a bit I decide to go over to see Tina. We have a lot of fun together and I give her twenty dollars for a present, like she says."

"That's a good story," Snoose allowed.

"Hush up, Snoose, that's not the story, that's just leading up to it. Let me finish."

"Sorry," Snoose muttered, studying the buttons on his mackinaw.

"So, anyway, come Sunday, Toivol gets home and the first thing, the very first thing, mind you, he says, Tina, did my friend Schnapsie come over on Saturday and give you twenty dollars?

"Well, Tina is so scared to death she said the truth. Yes he did Tivoli, but how did you find out?

"That's good, says Toivol, I borrowed my friend Schnapsie twenty dollars on Friday and he promised to stop by Saturday to pay it back. Now, wasn't that clever of me?"

"By God, that was grand, true or false," laughed Paddy. "You are a clever man, indeed."

"1 used to be," allowed Schnapsie, "Back then. You know, young man's hunger can make him turn his back on friendship and do the craziest things. Now? Now, I'm so old, I can't for the life of me remember what the feeling was even like."

"Gripes sake, Schnaps, I'm gonna cry." Socrates used this as an intro to a story of his own and so it went around the fire until by dawn only the quiet Seifert was still feeding the coals. The bashful man had finally worked up the courage to tell a story but with no one left awake, he quietly told it to the flickering flames.

Eleven

Sunup came and passed. The boys snored on until eight-thirty when the front door burst open and in stomped the butcher followed by a Duluth police officer.

"There he is! There's the filthy beggar that stole my pig!" The man was shrieking and pointing in the general direction of Paddy.

"Which one of them are you indicating, sir?" The constable whispered. The floor was littered with men.

"That one right there!" The butcher wailed. "Are you blind, man? The big Irishman with the red hair! He's the thief!"

"Right. I see him now. But let's keep this civil if we can." The officer stepped carefully over several bodies until he was alongside Paddy. "Beg your pardon, sir," he asked, pulling out a notepad, "but would you mind answering a few questions for me?" Paddy didn't stir.

"Oh, hell, man! Wake him up before you arrest him, you fool!"

The constable gave Beltrand a baleful look and, bending over, gently shook Paddy by the shoulder. "Wake up now, man. We have to speak with you." A quiet murmur was all that came back.

"No, you oaf, let me! You got to rock him!" Shoving aside the policeman, the butcher applied his boot generously to Paddy's rear end. Paddy came to his feet like an enraged beast. He grabbed the butcher by the neck and began to shake his head off.

The officer jumped on Paddy's back and tried to pull him off the bug-eyed butcher. Paddy finally woke up and recognized Beltrand!

"Boss!" Paddy exclaimed, "Why, I thought you were a demon from my murky past come to fetch me off to Hades. But it's only you then, isn't it. You've come to pay me, then?"

It took a moment for the butcher to get his voice and color back, but when he did, he screamed even louder than before.

"You, you, murdering bugger! Yes, I'm a demon all right, by God, and I'm here to have you arrested, convicted, imprisoned and entombed, you dumb Irish piece of crap. I'll have your hide hanging in my shop, and your carcass in my cooler, you filth.!"

Paddy was nonplused. "Now whatever is troubling your soul to cause such concern?"

Beltrand shouted in a lather of spit, "And to the charge of theft, I want to add attempted murder!"

"Well, I don't know, governor," the constable replied, "you kicked the man quite hard. He only ..."

"Man? Man? You call this barbarian a man? I tell you he's a thief and murderer, and everyone here is part of his gang for all we know." With a sweep of his arms he implicated the others who were up and shaking off their sleep.

"I demand justice, and by God, you had better deliver! He stole my pig and away he ran!" He finished that sentence with both his nose and index finger thrust towards the sagging ceiling.

"I stole nothing." Paddy stated matter-of-factly.

"What's that?" The constable welcomed the rebuttal. "Can you explain yourself, then."

"What!" The butcher shrieked, "You'll take his word over mine?"

"Now you behave yourself, sir," the constable cautioned him.

"Thank you, your honor," Paddy said.

"Proceed with your statement," the constable replied, confidant that he had asserted control over the matter. Licking his pencil stub, he addressed his attention to his notepad.

"Well, your Lordship," Paddy began with a great show of respect. "Yesterday I slaughtered pigs for this man for wages we had agreed on. When I had finished my go, this crafty fox declined to pay me."

"That's not true! That's a clever lie. We agreed that you would be paid today."

"No, you agreed after the fact," Paddy asserted. "I had no say in the matter."

"So you stole my pig and away you ran, huh? Isn't that right? Like in the nursery rhyme?" Beltrand thought that very clever of himself.

Socrates came to Paddy's aid. "Beg your pardon but you already made that silly joke. However, to the case at hand, I see no pig here. There is no pig here. Does anyone here have a pig in their sack?"

"So you ate it, then." The butcher was quick to guess.

"I couldn't say," Socrates replied. "Maybe a pig, but not necessarily yours, was eaten here, maybe it was not. However, I don't think, Mr. Butcher, you have enough evidence without a corpus."

The butcher, the constable and Paddy stared in amazement at the shabby, old man. Socrates permitted himself a smug smile.

Beltrand sensed that things were not going well and seized a different tack. "Officer! You would take the word of these bums over that of a taxpaying citizen."

"Let's not be unkind," the constable cautioned. "Every citizen is entitled to due process of law." It was working in Paddy's favor that the officer was the son of immigrants and knew better than to judge an Irishman on appearances.

"We are not bums," Socrates replied with a quick parry. "We are lumberjacks."

"Do they look like lumberjacks," laughed the butcher, eyeing the ragged bunch. "No, they're bums and vagrants. Duluth has a vagrant law! I demand you arrest them as vagrants or I'll speak with my alderman. I'll have your job, officer!"

"Surely, sir, you don't intend to . . ."

A gust of cold air blew in through the door, carrying the words of the man who had opened it and silence fell upon the room.

"These men work for me."

The exasperated constable turned and addressed him, "And who might you be, now?"

The man standing in the shadows of the door he filled answered. "Sullivan. Michael Sullivan."

Socrates detached himself from the crowd. "Mike, I knew you'd come, by golly."

Hungry Mike Sullivan walked over to Socrates, his physical presence dominating the room.

"Well, Soc, what have you gotten yourself into now?"

"I swear, Mike, I had almost nothin' to do with it. This man," he said pointing to the butcher, "says we're a bunch of tramps."

"Did you say these men work for you, sir?" the constable asked.

Sullivan calmly looked at the officer. "That they do. Everyone of them is hired out to the Itascan Lumber Company.

"That is a lie!" The butcher screamed in the constable's ear.

If any man could shoot fire from his eyes, it would have been Sullivan right there.

"I say again, every last man here is one of mine." Mike reiterated, moving a step closer to the butcher.

The butcher backed off, his fire extinguished. "Well, I still say this one here owes me a pig. He took my pig."

Mike gave him another riveting look; the look of a man who had stood toe to toe with dozens of men in his life and never came off second best; never gave an inch. "Why don't you come and visit us up north some day. I will see that you get all the pork you want."

"Wonderful! Then it's settled," completed the constable starting for the door. "You collect whatever your due is from this Mr. Sullivan. I have other duties to return to."

The butcher had a mind to stay for more, but as the constable gained distance from the group, he thought the better of it and hurried after him, still chewing on his ear as they left.

Socrates grabbed Mike's hand. "How have you been keeping yourself, Mike?"

"Fair, Socrates. Aging a bit. The work gets no easier with the years. You look the same as always."

"No better, no worse, more's the pity. I knew you'd come. I told the boys."

"I have." Sullivan took in the others with a practiced eye. "I know some of the men here. Seifert there. Schnapsie and Snoose. Toad, how did you escape your sisters? The big man and the boy I don't know."

Socrates did the introductions. "This youngster here is Tyler. Tyler Caldwell out of Chicago."

"Tyler, eh? That's a good name and Chicago is a big town. I was there once. How old are you, son?"

"Nineteen."

"Plenty old enough. Have you ever worked in the woods?"

"No sir, I haven't" Tyler felt the need to say more. "But I am sure I'll be up for it. I played football."

"You played football?" Mike considered the merits of this qualification. "That's good. If we need a football team, you can be the captain. Okay?" Tyler flushed at the laughter. Mike looked at his cook. "Socrates, you know this boy. Will you vouch for him?"

Socrates stared at Mike blankly. Vouching for someone who took on problems by running from them? Vouch for someone who was stubbling along with no goals, no control of his immediate fate? Vouch for someone like himself? Not likely. Then, without really knowing why, answered, "I will," and became inextricably bound to Tyler and his destiny.

Sullivan turned to Donlin. He liked the cut of this man. He had the look of one who could take wear without being worn out. "Who would you be, then?"

My name is Patrick Donlin from Dublin, Ireland. I'm honored to meet you, sir."

Sullivan took the hand of a countryman and in the handshake they took the measure of each other.

"And you like pork, I understand, Mr. Donlin?"

"I do, sir. I eat what I can when I can get it."

"But there was no theft?" Mike wanted no thieves in his camp however strong they might be.

"No sir. I earned every snort and squeal on that hog. I swear on St. Patrick's crosier that I am not a thief; unless you consider a stolen kiss here and there."

"There be no better witness than that of the good saint," Mike agreed. "I trust you'll not try to steal kisses in my camp? And what do they know you by, Patrick?"

"Paddy to me friends, sir."

Then from out of the back row Snoose gave him the name that he was to carry forever. "Paddy the Pig! Our own Paddy the Pig, now, eh?"

They gathered their belongings and climbed into the last of three trucks that were parked outside. The other trucks were already full of men hired out directly by the Itascan office. They were husky men, for the most part; bearded faces with a look of calm resignation about them. They sat quiet and passive. Tyler saw no excitement, no prospect of high adventure in the eyes that watched them through the slat sides of the trucks.

There was a wooden bench lining each side of the truck bed. Tyler pulled himself up, moved up to the front and sat down in an empty place. Across from him sat a slightly built man reading a book. He wore a long, heavy coat and his face was almost completely hidden under a muffler. He wore a gray, wool cap. At his feet was a small cardboard suitcase. What attracted Tyler's curiosity most was the book, a copy of Marcel Proust's Swan's Way. Just as he was about to comment on it, the truck jolted into motion.

The small convoy corkscrewed it's way slowly out of the deep valley of the St. Louis River, through the small town of Carlton, past the monstrous mill in Cloquet, and onto the flat, hard-rock country above Duluth. So far it was everything Socrates had promised him. The previous night's stories, the way they handled the mean butcher, the heroics at the Hinkley fire. A lusty adventure was shaping up. He was in man's country.

Twelve

Two hours out of Duluth, the trucks rumbled into Floodwood. Though the road was the major highway across northern Minnesota it was narrow, rutted and slippery with fresh snow. The constant jolting had left everyone stiff, and nauseous. If that hadn't been enough, the frigid air pouring through the stake sides of the truck made sleeping impossible.

They piled out, grateful for the stop, and walked to the edge of the brush to pee. Those who still had money in their pockets ran into the Floodwood Tavern to throw down a glass of beer or pocket a bottle of Old Crow.

After five minutes, Sullivan ordered the men to load up. Two laggards came out of the tavern as the trucks pulled out. They ran after the trucks shouting for them to stop. The men in the trucks yelled back and waved them on. One was young and long-legged. He came up to the truck and held out his arms. They grabbed him and dragged him a ways before they got him aboard. The other man was too old. He lost ground and fell farther and farther behind, finally falling in the road. He lifted his hand and made an obscene gesture at the trucks, then lay quietly in the road. The trucks kept going. They could see him lying there until he was nothing but a small speck and then they went over a hill and he was gone. One man muttered, "Sullivan's suitability test. He flunked."

Tyler had settled onto the hard plank bench before it occurred to him. The man across from him had remained in the truck during the brief stop. He cleared his throat and shouted above the growl of the engine, "Too bad about that guy. We should have stopped." There was no answer.

Tyler tried again. "Hey! You sure can hold your water!"

Several heads turned in his direction. One guy poked another in the side and grinned. The person across from Tyler carefully placed a bookmark in the page and closed the novel. He then unwound his muffler and, pulling off his hat, shook out a cascade of brunette hair.

"Oh, my God!" Tyler tripped over his tongue, "You're ... you're a girl!" She threw back her head and joined the rest of the truck in the laughter. Her face was well shaped, the cheek bones high, her eyebrows full and long. Her laugh was bright and cheerful, providing a perfect introduction to a flashing smile. She had a pretty mouth, marred only by a small childhood scar at the left corner.

"Why, yes," she replied with a flutter of eyelashes, "I've been a girl for almost eighteen years now. I enjoy it enough, I believe I'll stay one."

Tyler blushed deeply, and not wanting to appear any less a man than he already demonstrated, continued nonchalantly, "Oh, I'm sorry, I didn't know the camp would have women in it."

"Whoa, boy," cautioned the man next to him. "You're jumping your traces."

The smile dissolved from her face. "Really? And just what kind of 'woman' do you think I am?"

"Well, I ... but are you ... Oh, God. I'm going to shut up now."

"No need to shut up. What I'm doing in this truck, you erroneous young man, is traveling to Grand Rapids. I believe that is all you have to know, isn't it?" She was angry at being made a part of the men's rough humor, however innocent, and even angrier at being mistaken for a prostitute. Her eyes smoked with indignation daring him to speak again. He didn't.

The girl returned to her Proust. Tyler was subdued, reluctant to take his eyes off the truck floor. They rode in this manner for another hour until, on the south shore of Trout Lake, the lead truck overheated. Again the small convoy pulled over and, while the driver went for water, the men once more climbed out to stretch. This time the girl also got off and, while the men lined the north of the road, she discretely disappeared into the brush to the south.

When she returned, Tyler watched her climb back onto the truck. She looked younger than the age she had given, moved with a sturdy walk well suited to the country. Her eyes and complexion had a softness that seemed out of place on the iron range. She was dressed as the others; woolen trousers, a heavy plaid shirt under her coat. She obviously did not favor form over the practicality dictated by the weather.

Still embarrassed by his mistake, he reluctantly returned to his seat waiting until most of the others had climbed on and the engine started up. She had moved and was now sitting next to his open space on the bench. The book was closed on her lap.

Tyler sat next to her, prepared for another scathing attack. When they got back onto the road, the sudden jolt threw him against her.

"I'm sorry," he said, quietly enough so the others wouldn't hear.

"I am too," she whispered. "That was very abrupt of me."

"I mean about my earlier remarks. They were rude. I apologize."

"Accepted," she answered. She looked up at him and a soft smile crossed her face. "I had no reason to bite at you like that. You couldn't have known. It isn't good to bear grudges against anyone. Forgive and forget is my father's philosophy and I agree."

"Your father sounds like a wise man. It's something I aspire to but it seems I have a long way to go." Tyler shifted his weight so as to face her. She had a pretty face. Not beautiful with the glamour of his girlfriend Ellie, but just pretty.

"I think so, too," she agreed. "I mean about him being wise."

"I'm Tyler Caldwell," he volunteered, encouraged by her openness. "I'm from Chicago and I have a gift for doing stupid things. Just ask anyone who's ever talked to me."

"Jennifer," she replied. "And you're right, but then, all greenhorns are like that for awhile." But this was followed by another smile so he continued.

"Jennifer is a beautiful name." This caused her to blush lightly and she hurried to change the subject.

"Chicago? I've never been there. I only know it's a lot bigger than Grand Rapids. What do you do there?"

"I was a student, at Northwestern. First Year."

"Really? I was a student in Duluth. I graduated last June."

"Graduated?" This confused him.

"From high school," she laughed, brushing a lock of hair out of her face.

"High school? Oh!"

"I took a teachers certificate this summer. That's what I'm doing now, going back home to teach grammar school."

"To teach grammar School?" He was suddenly aware that he was repeating everything she said. "But you won't be using Proust as a reader for grammar school?"

She looked at 'Swan's Way' on her lap and laughed. "Oh, heavens, no! I don't even like Proust. His writing moves so slowly. You know. It creeps at a snail's pace and goes nowhere. I personally think it would make a good doorstop."

"Then why do you read it?"

"The sisters at the convent where I boarded thought it would be a nice addition to our library. The dears. I shouldn't be surprised if it gathers more dust than readers in The Rapids. Adventure, romance and timber contracts are all they read back home; those who read at all."

He tried to flatter her now. "I should think that a person of your abilities will change all that, Jennifer."

Again she blushed and nibbled at her lower lip while thinking of a way to again move the subject away from her.

"Tyler Caldwell," she began, "Tell me, Tyler, what are you doing here? You aren't a lumberjack. You aren't at all like the others. I can tell by the way you talk; your vocabulary. Also, you haven't sworn once hardly since we left Duluth."

Now it was his turn to be embarrassed. He was tempted to concoct a boast but didn't. "No, I'm not. I have never been north of Evanston, Illinois. But I'm not a greenhorn," he lied.

"Then what are you doing here? Research for a journal? You implied you were going to a camp? It isn't part of your school work, is it?"

"God, no!" he laughed. "I am, though. Going to camp. Sullivan's camp. I'm with a man named Socrates. He's a lumberjack."

"He's a cook, now."

"You know him?"

"I know most of these men. I've seen them come and go since my childhood, through my father's work."

"Does your father work in the woods?"

"Yes, he does. But tell me, why? Why does someone intelligent enough to attend university leave school and come up here to work for a dollar a day? Are you in trouble?"

He was annoyed at her directness. "Let's just say I left home under difficult circumstances and it's best I don't return for awhile. But my family knows of my plans," he added hastily.

There was a brief silence before she said, "It must be hard for you." Her concern surprised him as much as her intuition.

"It is a sore spot and I'd rather not discuss it," he answer closing the subject.

"Then we shan't." She smiled reassuringly. "You may change the subject if you wish." She spoke as a teacher would. "And you may call me Jenny if you wish."

"Jenny is also a pretty name." He fell silent for a time. "I don't really understand these men or their work." He began again. "I find them accepting at times but also quick to take advantage of someone's newness. They can be cruel. Like Sullivan. They way he left that man on the road rather than stop. Do you understand them?"

"I think I understand them as well as anyone can. All of them are different as people are apt to be. Yes, they are intolerant at times. The work is harsh and so is the discipline. If you can't adapt, you have to go. It takes a special type of person to agree with the work. Actually, my father says there are three types of lumberjacks."

"Broke, dirty and uneducated?"

She shook her head. "No. Listen carefully now and see where you might fit in. First, there are the local farmers. They farm in the summer and go to the woods in the winter so they can keep their little farms. In the process they risk losing their families to a better provider. Does that sound pessimistic?"

"I would hate to be one of those farmers coming to you for a job."

"But they are the best of the lot. By far. Next is the local man. That's someone who was born here, or if he lost his way, chanced to move here. Either way, he doesn't have the sense to leave. He homesteads forty acres of what they call cut-over. That's land that's nothing more than brush and stumps. The big logging companies have already taken the trees. You'll see them on your way north. One cow, two pigs, three dogs, four cats, five chickens and six children." She ticked off the numbers on her fingers. "The lucky ones work for the county or state, building roads during the summer, but in the winter they leave their little plots and follow the trails into the logging camps. The real lucky ones lose everything and move out.

"Good times if they stay on. They chew tobacco, slap bugs and tell dirty stories. If they wander astray, there's a good chance they'll catch some social disease and end up in the Pest House. That's where the men are sent to die when they catch Syphilis, Tuberculosis or any number of pretty diseases."

"Sounds like another happy ending to an otherwise dreary existence," he said.

"Oh, but that still leaves room for the rest. Guess who?"

He was listening intently, hesitant to answer.

"That's right. Look around. It's all of you, Tyler Caldwell, or Lucky, or Lefty or whatever they will eventually call you. It's people you never really get to know nor care to. Why? Because you won't want to admit you've become like one of them. You never know where they come from, or where they will go. You are a secretive group. Most of you are running from something; running from families, like yourself, or maybe crimes you have committed. Maybe you just couldn't take the pressure of city living. Only you will know the answer because, like the rest of them, you will eventually forget how to speak." She was leaning close to Tyler entreating him. "You will become, I fear, a silent stranger even to yourself."

"Please," Tyler said, holding up his hand. "Do you have to get so worked up about this? I mean don't make it sound so god-awful. It's a living, anyway and what about the legends, the heroes of the woods."

"Oh, like Mr. Toad back there? Living in a box all his life? Sure they call him a legend. But what good is a legend when it's all finished? No, most of you will just climb onto train cars and disappear over the horizons. You'll consume all your money in liquor and your teeth in fist fights and, for romance, you'll consort with those foul women you confused me with. Is this you? You're better than that aren't you?"

"I am not a drunk, Jenny."

"Not yet, but that's my point."

"Well, sure, but what suddenly made you so angry?"

"Tyler, I don't mean to be." She reached over and briefly touched his arm.

"I'm sorry, I've spent my whole life around lumberjacks, and they depress me. I look in Grand Rapids for nice companions my age and there are none. They neglect their educations and rush off to their bitter futures."

"But, come on, not everyone has such a bitter future? I don't intend for mine to end like that."

She put her hand on his sleeve, begging his attention. "Nor do I, but how can I make you understand? Listen. When I was a little girl and we lived on a small farm by Black Duck. There was a man who lived at the end of our road. His name was Hagen, I don't even know if he had a first name. Maybe that was it. He was a lumberjack, or rather he had been. Now he was just old and very crippled and bent. He had retired to a little shack in the woods. In the summer, he probably went outside to get away from the mosquitoes."

"Almost every day we would see him walk to town with his little sack, the things they call 'turkeys'."

"I know what they're called," he said. She had a way of making everything about lumberjacks sound shallow.

"Poor old Hagen," she continued. "After an hour and a half, he would come home again. My mother said once, 'I don't think he even has anything in that packsack.' How right she was. He was so poor, so alone out there. We used to bake bread to take to him.

"One day, my father stopped by his cabin to visit and found him dead. Hagen had died during the night. Sitting at his little table over dinner. It wasn't much of a dinner, either, a cup of coffee and a slice of our bread. I've since wondered what it would be like to die with no one to hold your hand or listen to your last words. To give you a final kiss.

"I went back with my father and the coroner to collect his things. There was nothing. A chair, the table, a mattress on the dirt floor. It was an old mattress we had thrown out years before. We were looking for something of his past. There wasn't much. He had carved little holes in the wall, Tyler, and in one of the holes, I found a small wooden jewelry box. Inside was a small lace hanky and a piece of pink ribbon. That's all, for a lifetime of effort. Just a bit of lace from his past." She drew a sharp breath. "I want more out of life."

"I'm sure you deserve it. We all do. I feel bad for this Hagen, but you can't believe that all lumberjacks are like that."

"Tyler," she said, "If I could I would make a wish, a wish to replace each and every camp with farms and hamlets, schools and churches. That would be my wish."

"And what would you wish for these men?"

Her eyes were full of concern. He was interesting, as out of place in this society even as she imagined herself to be. She was really wishing for an opportunity to get to know this handsome young man better. He was different than the bumpkins she had grown up with. But that was not what she said.

"I'd wish for all young men to stay out of the woods except to picnic. I wish for them to go home to their families."

Tyler smiled at her passion.

She cast him a stern, parental look. "What do you think is going to happen up there? Really."

"Well," he shrugged, "we're going to cut down trees."

"That's the least of it!" She whispered so harshly it shocked him. She looked quickly at the other men and lowered her voice. It was almost a whisper, fearful and prophetic. "Tyler, you are going to lose your soul."

He was stunned by her words.

"Go home," she begged. "Go on home." She took his arm again, gripping it tightly.

He spoke with a simple honesty to match her own, "And if I have no home?"

"Then," she said with finality, "At least you shall not have destroyed someone else's." She sank back and stared at him. Tyler returned it for a moment, than turned to the front of the truck.

It was two-thirty when the trucks lumbered into Grand Rapids. The lead vehicles turned off to the train depot. Tyler's continued on for two blocks and turned right. When the road threatened to run onto a small frozen lake, it turned right again, rolled past several small cottages and stopped in front of a trim, white frame house with green shutters. There was a tidy white picket fence around the front yard. A small grotto with a statue of St. Francis was set in a corner of the front yard. Chickadees and juncos were flitting around the gentle saint.

"This is my home," Jennifer said possessively. She stood up to leave. Tyler took the handle of her suitcase.

"Let me carry this for you. Please?"

She resisted at first, then gave in. On the walk up to the house he began, "I don't know if we ever get into town."

"You don't."

"But if we did ..."

"You just won't." They were on the porch and she was reaching for the doorknob.

"Please, just let me finish, won't you?"

"All right, but quickly. I must go in." She kept her eyes down and listened.

"When I come back from there, may I talk to you again?"

"I don't think it would be best."

He was surprised, never having been so rejected by any girl. "Why not?"

"Because you are young, handsome if you don't already know that, and, I think, intelligent. In spite of that, if you return you will have become like all the rest and it would just depress me. What future would there be for me in that?"

"But I'm not like that. I won't become like that. If you knew me better, you could see that."

She shook her head emphatically. "They never really come back once they've gone in there."

"I'm different than them. I swear. I'm only doing this because I .... I've got to find out something about myself and I don't even know what that is."

"Tyler, after a winter in those woods, there will be no distinction between you and anybody else. I said I expect more out of life than that. I meant that."

She took his hand to say goodbye and held it for a moment. He started to say more but she put her fingers over his lips. She smiled at him and then turned and opened the door.

"It's me father, I'm home," she called.

Tyler made a last attempt. "Jennifer. ... I ..."

Socrates shouted from the truck, "Hurry, kid, we got a train to catch."

"Go, Tyler, you have to find out for yourself. Your friends are calling. Thank you for carrying my suitcase." She went into the house and was gone.

"All right, then! I'm sorry I tried."

He ran to the truck and climbed in. It started up, turned the corner and was gone.

Jennifer's father greeted his daughter with a kiss. "Who was that at door, dear?"

She answered distantly. "Oh, just a boy I met on the truck. He wants to be a lumberjack but I don't think he has any idea of what he really wants. Or needs."

Thirteen

Over two hundred men were waiting at the depot. They were standing and lying everywhere; crowded the station platform and overflowed onto the tracks. Socrates led his group into the waiting room in search of Sullivan. There, another throng was gathered under a blue haze of tobacco smoke. Many of them were drunk or quickly becoming so. Four women sat on a wooden bench, the only one in the building. Socrates saw Hungry Mike by the freight manager's office. Mike spotted him at the same instant and waved him over.

"Socrates," he said, "The train is five minutes out. Our flatcar is 10176. In the warehouse is a stack of boxes for us, all marked Itascan # 2. When it pulls in get 'em loaded and the men also. Okay?"

"Sure, Mike, do the other fellows know?"

"Yes. They're out there now, but don't know the number."

"10176."

"You fix it up. I am going to see to something else and then I'll join you."

"You heard Mike," Socrates sang over the noise to his group. "Let's go." They tramped back to the door.

In the center of the room stood a large potbellied stove with a tall stack that stretched up and out through the vaulted wooden ceiling. Beside it, two men had squared off against each other over an argument that only they would understand. Backing off to gain some swinging room, one, a tall blonde accidentally stepped on Socrates' foot. He turned to apologize, "Sorry, Brother," he said.

"Don't mention it," said Socrates, "Happens all the time."

Seizing the opportunity, the blonde's opponent, smaller, more of a bantam-weight, rushed in and slugged the Swede on the jaw. The

Swede staggered, but instead of falling, he reached out and grabbed the runt by the arms.

"Say, that vas not fair, vas it? Not fair at all." That was all he said before he picked the man up and threw him into the potbelly. The stove shuddered and rolled over, smoke belching from the flue covered by a cascade of falling stove pipes. Others rushed to take a hand in the fighting and a general brawl broke out. Socrates shepherded his group upstream against the press of rowdy pugilists. They got out on the platform and walked over to the warehouse just as a whistle and a plume of black smoke signaled the arrival of the freight.

Tyler grabbed Socrates arm. "They're tearing the place apart!"

"Naw. Like I said, it happens all the time."

They piled the groceries and equipment onto the train and settled into the car for the next leg of the journey. The train was pulling ten cars. There was one standard passenger car; the other nine were flatcars with sides four feet high for hauling pulpwood. Each car was loaded with a group of men shepherded by some type of boss. They were all bound for one of the many logging camps between The Rapids and Craig, or beyond.

The whistle blew and the trainload of humanity pulled out leaving the station empty except for four dazed women who had been driven outside by the smoke. They stood watching the departing train with a mixture of wonderment and revulsion.

Tyler settled back against the wall of the car and stared out, wondering where he was headed next. If he had the ambition to consider the situation pragmatically, he would very likely have jumped the train and returned to Chicago, a chastened but wiser young man. But already he was feeling a sense of responsibility to the group. He had hired out to Mike Sullivan in Duluth. Socrates had vouched for him and to cut out now would leave him no better than when he had left home. Leaving may have been easier than staying, but to do either required its own brand of courage. It was simply easier for Tyler to acquiesce to the situation and do nothing.

Without realizing it, he was already becoming what Jennifer had cautioned against; a man without purpose, a man without direction, a man without a home; a stranger to others and, ultimately, to himself. A man who would ultimately be defined not by who he was but by what others made him.

They were riding on Great Northern tracks that extended north-west out of The Rapids, through Bemidji and out to the endless prairie expanses of North Dakota and Montana. The roadbed was well maintained, the ride smooth. This small comfort changed abruptly when, forty minutes out of The Rapids, they came to Deer River and were switched onto a track that ran north to Craig and the endless forests of Pine Island. They were now on the notorious Gut and Liver Line.

The Gut and Liver got its name because a ride on it could homogenize a man's insides beyond reconstitution. The tracks stretched across miles of tamarack bogs and glacial ridges. Along the entire stretch, the rock ballast was minimal and, for miles at a time, totally nonexistent. The track, often as not, was laid directly over rough log ties piled on heavier timber floating on top of the peat bogs.

The rails stretched in an uneven, undulating ribbon of crooked steel. Derailments were so common the trains carried their own equipment to recapture the track. A trip up the Gut and Liver was one of excitement and frustration.

Half an hour out of Deer River, they stopped while the crew shunted a flatcar onto a siding. Four-foot cordwood was piled for hundreds of feet along the track.

The boss jumped down and divided his men into two groups. One he sent forward into another car for transit farther down the line, the other was ordered stay there, load the shunted car with pulpwood and then catch the return trip to Deer River to pick up another empty. Everyone set to the task without question except for one man. When the boss had split the group, he had drawn the line between this man and his buddy. The man was adamant that he would not leave his friend but, being unable to speak even passable English, he had trouble explaining himself.

"No go," he insisted. "Me stay. Here! Friend!"

"Come on, get your ass on down from there!" The boss ordered. "You ain't staying here and I ain't your fuckin' friend!"

"Me, stay!"

"I said, get down!" The boss man had neither time nor inclination to tolerate this type of behavior. He wasn't used to having his orders questioned.

"Me no get! Me stay. Friend." The man picked up a tool from a pile of equipment and brandished it at the beefy boss. "Me stay!"

"Oh yeah? You'll stay when I'm dead, dumb son-of-a-bitch." He glowered, climbed up the ladder and swung into the car. The immigrant backed off a step.

"You get your butt up to that other car, you crazy Pollock!" He ordered. "Me stay!" The tattered man in bib overalls was defying him, but in a pleading way. He may have been a little drunk.

"You son of a . . . !" Shouted the straw boss as he rushed in.

The man swung high, and the boss displayed the quick footwork borne of a lifetime of brawling and ramroding. He slipped under the arch of the wrench and hit the man across the face backhanded. With his other hand, he ripped loose the wench, threw it away, and, grabbing the man by his britches, heaved him over the car walls and into the drainage ditch alongside the track. The Pole foundered in the water and finally stood up.

"Now git, you!" The red-faced boss was pointing to the next car. The man stumbled out of the ditch and meekly went up the track.

The incident was witnessed from Sullivan's car.

"Socrates," Tyler said, "that man, why didn't he let the poor guy stay with his friend?"

"He couldn't, Tyler. Every outfit can have only one boss. There's no democracy north of Grand Rapids. Now, if you want to be the boss you have to do it by besting the other one. Then you're the new boss. But there still is only one boss. See? That Pollack just applied for the job but came up short."

"But it wasn't much to ask, was it? He could have picked someone else."

"It would be a big thing if everyone got to pick the work they wanted." Besides, he only wanted to stay with his friend because he had a bottle hidden on him."

"You think so?"

"Oh sure, I know so. There's two things you won't see much of up here, sentiment and free booze. That poor devil is gonna go a long time now without either."

"Do they really fight to see who's going to be in charge?"

"Heck, yes! Years ago I was a section boss on a track repair crew. Gandy-dancers. There was another guy, a real gorilla. As big as he was, I should have just said, sure, you can be the Great Cahuna. But I was a young buck, too, and there was a little extra money in it. So we squared off.

"They made a ring, cleared off the ground and all the guys stood around to keep us in a circle. He came out to face me, and, I swear, his hands were touching his shoelaces! I did pretty good for awhile, bobbing and ducking. I'd crawl between his legs and whack him in the groin. Finally, I thought I'd take a shot at his face. I reached up, and he just grabbed me by the arm and held me. He hit me just once. On the kisser. Well, those guys weren't much of a ring because I just flew right over the top of them. Landed in Tofte, about ten miles away in the middle of a chicken dinner at the church social. By the time I had eaten up and got back, he was boss.

"We got to be pretty good friends after that. It was just a matter of respecting each other's wants. He wanted to be boss and I wanted to keep my face."

"I still don't think it's right to order people around like that," Tyler insisted.

"Oh, no?"

"I'd never put up with it," the kid boasted.

"Okay," laughed Socrates. "Hope you enjoy your short happy stay." But it bothered him. With an attitude like that, the kid was bound to get in trouble eventually. And Socrates had vouched for him. That meant something. The last thing Socrates wanted was to have Mike Sullivan on his case. He had his own problems to worry about. His and Gertie's.

Fourteen

*I*t was dark when they pulled into Craig. It wasn't Craig, actually, because the tracks ended on the south banks of the Bigfork River, where Craig used to be. The Bigfork River was the boundary line between Koochiching and Itasca Counties. The rivers all flowed north in this country, so a railroad was necessary to move the timber south to the mills of Bemidji and Grand Rapids, the county seat of Itasca. The big lumber company owners up north avoided the expensive railroad construction costs because the Bigfork and Littlefork Rivers, being good water, flowed north to the Rainey River which flowed through International Falls, the county seat for Koochiching county.

Craig got started as a railhead and end of line for the Gut and Liver. It didn't cross the Bigfork because they never built the bridge because the people up north refused to pay up to extend a line down south to meet it. The town grew into twenty-six "blind pigs" that served cheap whiskey and a number of lice-ridden "hotels" provided cheap sex. Eventually, because of its notoriety and public prostitution, the constables from Grand Rapids started to go up on the train, raid the houses and destroy the illegal booze.

What Craig did, one starry night, was move the town, buildings and all, across the frozen Bigfork and into Koochiching. It wasn't because the Koochiching commissioners had a more liberal attitude towards this type of behavior but to raid the newly located Craig was an expensive proposition and time-consuming task. It meant traveling pitted gravel roads and rail down to Northome, on to Bemidji, down to Deer River and back up the Gut and Liver to Craig. The law would have to arrest whoever they could catch, and cart them all the way back to the Falls for trial. A three hundred mile round trip meant very infrequent trips.

In its new digs Craig prospered. Although it never grew beyond a single street, the street got to be quite long. A dozen brawls could take place simultaneously without any of them inconveniencing another.

Craig satisfied the simple needs of lumberjacks for fifty miles around. It was one of many "first stops, first drops" for men coming out of the woods with money in pockets and cotton in their mouths. The jacks would come into town, walk in a bar and yell "Timberr!" That meant a round of drinks on the house for everyone still standing. It was tradition and also insurance. When that jack had drunk up his stake, he'd wait for the next man to come in the door, yell "Timberr!" and he could keep on drinking.

"When these guys all come into town," Socrates explained, "they'll have bills left from last year. So they pay off the tab first. They will, too. If anything, a lumberjack is honest. If a man doesn't come back to pay his bill from last year, you know he got himself killed somewhere. Pride, you know. They'll drink up their own money and then drink off the cuff for a time. Then it's back to the woods and the whole thing starts over again.

"You get into one of these places, Tyler, watch yourself. They always got a bartender that's a pretty tough guy. He keeps everything in order and will break your arm with a club if you try to bust up the place. Most guys just come to town, drink, raise a little hell and fall asleep on the floor. In a few days they'll be broke or gone, but until they are, there are plenty of folks there that would take it away from you if they could."

"It doesn't sound like my family's country club." He was thinking of champagne flutes and ice sculptures surrounded by huge arrays of food [prepared by chefs schooled in France. The dropping of a napkin was enough ado to cause two or three waiters to rush to pick it up.

"Yeah," Socrates chuckled. "A country club! The only clubs up here are made of dried oak. Here, let me tell you a story. This happened right here in Craig and Schnapsie will back me up on it. This old lumberjack came in and gave the bartender fifty dollars and drank awhile. Didn't collect all his change. Let the barkeep hold it for him. But he took ten dollars of it and went to some of the other joints in town. Nickel a glass for whiskey. It was the same for a beer.

"I'm getting off track. Catch me. Anyway, this guy was gone most of the day working joints up and down the street and when he came back in the evening, he wanted some more money, the rest of his fifty."

"The bartender said, 'No! You're broke'. He told him to go back to the woods; if he wanted any more money, he'd have to work for it. Well, that bartender, he's gone now, dead, I imagine. He was stealing all of the poor jacks' pokes.

"He was all riled up, standing in this tar paper shack and banging his fist on the counter. He says, 'I vant my money and I vant it all right now. I gave you so much money and I took ten dollars this morning and I spent it in other places. Now pay me the rest or I'll sort you out. That lumberjack knew his arithmetic and the bartender didn't figure for this. He didn't figure that old jack would stay sober long enough to add things up.

"So he says, 'Settle down, you old woodchopper. I value my teeth. I'm going to look it up in the back room. Maybe you have a case after all.' He didn't want a big ruckus in the bar 'cause if one jack fought, then all the others would want to fight too, and they'd bust up everything and stop drinking, too. But he had something cooking in his head.

"So he set up a big drink at one end of the bar and said, 'Why don't you come down here and drink this up while I go look up your record. This one's on the house.' He made the drink big enough that the other guy would need some time to drink it up.

"The bartender went out the back door. And wouldn't you know it, he had set that man up at a certain place so he could count the strips of tar paper to where he was standing. There was a rifle shot and the lumberjack dropped dead right where he stood with that 'free' drink in his hand.

"Then the bartender came back in and looked around the bar. He said, 'What the hell is going on here? You men been scrapping? Say, that man is dead!'

"He was lying in a big pool of blood by this time. It had soaked the sawdust all red. Awful sight. He said, 'One of you fellas shot this man.' Well, they all looked blank and said they hadn't. But, they didn't know who did it, either. They suspected.

"Then the bartender says, 'Well, I got to get this guy out of here! I don't want anybody to see a dead man in here! We'll get rid of the evidence right now!'

"In Craig, in the winter, they draw their water out of the river. That would be the Bigfork. So they keep a hole in the ice. They drag this guy outside and throw him through the hole and he's gone. He's chucked down the hole and is gone. Like he never was. A lot of good men have gone through that hole in the ice. Some bad ones, too."

Tyler didn't know if he was having his leg pulled or not but he was learning not to challenge a story unless he had a better one. "What about the police? Didn't they investigate?"

"Police?" Socrates scratched his beard. "No, there never was ... Oh yes! There was a cop up here once. Swen Lundstrom. He got shot and killed on the street. They carried him in and laid him on the bar and there he died. Some guy was pulling something in one of the saloons and started waving a gun around. They called the law and when Swen started chasing him he shot Swen. Haven't had legal law since."

Schnapsie had followed the story with interest. "It's true, all right, I heard it the same way. But about the river, I know one story personal that I was at. I was up in Craig, middle of winter. Snoose cut in on him, "Schnaps, we all heard this yarn a million times. Your moment of glory it was!"

"Oh, shush your face," Schnapsie snapped, "Tyler ain't heard it and he wants too. Tyler, don't you want to hear it?"

"I do." Tyler was enjoying their B.S.

"Okay then, shut your yap, Snoose. Where was I? Oh, yeah. There was a fight up on the street and some man was killed in the forehead with a pole ax. This was right in front of a bar up there. But the fighting went on, not me, others, and nobody was paying any attention to this guy that got laid out.

"Well, pretty soon, the bartender came up to me. I was doing my fighting from behind a barrel. He asked if I'd take the body over to the Smith's wanagon on the river and put it through. That's a barge on the river. A wanagon. I said no, I wouldn't touch a dead man. Dead men give me the willies. He said I'd get a bottle of moonshine for it. I said, hell yes, a dead man can't hurt nobody. So I wrapped him in a blanket and the bartender put him on my shoulder and off I goes to the river.

"I get down there and I'm thirsty. So I put down this dead man and I've got my face in the hole drinking and all of a sudden, by God, he comes to! He comes to! Holy saints in heaven, he says when he comes out of the blanket, what's going on! I'm getting out of here!

"No, I says, I'm getting a jug of shine to dunk you. If you go back now, they won't pay me. Your tough luck says he. So I'm wondering if I should hit him again or what. But I'm thinking real fast and I says, wait here until I get my gallon, and I'll split it with you. Okay, he says, that sounds fair. That's just what we did."

Tyler groaned, "You nearly drowned that man."

"Maybe," Schnapsie shrugged. "But if I had, he'd have been dead, anyway."

Tyler looked at the nodding heads in disbelief.

They transferred the camp stores onto logging sleighs. Since the camp lay north and west of the Bigfork, there was no need to cross into Craig. Tyler had to satisfy his curiosity from afar. The shacks and shanties, separated by a broad street of frozen mud, began at the riverbank and stretched back into the trees beyond. There were lumberjacks everywhere; most of them working, sober. The season had just begun and they had no money to spend.

Sullivan's men climbed onto the sleighs and followed the narrow trail west along the river. The powerful horses soon left Craig behind. The quiet ride over a new carpet of snow was a total departure from the smoke bone-jarring rattle of the railroad.

Tyler stared in awe at the woods. He had imagined a pure and endless stand of conifer trees stretching to the Arctic Circle. Instead, he saw sweeping groves of paper birch and poplar, pioneers that followed the cutting and fires in area. Here and there stood great white and Norway pine, too crooked to cut, lonely sentinels waiting for the return of their brothers. Tall black spruce, their conical shapes forming perfect shadows in the gathering dusk, indicated the locations of low land and competed with the cedars for the wetter parts of the topography.

Oak, ash, cherry, alder and willow, now leafless, claimed their spot of ground. Hazel brush and raspberry brambles marked the sites of former logging. Tamarack, cousins to the cypress of the south, also stood bare and dormant, up to their knees in the swampy waters.

The sun was down, leaving a great red slash across the western sky and, except for the occasional comments of the men and the breathing and farting of the horses, it was quiet to the point of eeriness.

One of the jacks, a stranger to Tyler, began singing in a deep and beautiful baritone:

"On the Big Rock Candy Mountain
The jail is made of gin.
You could get out again
As soon as you got in.
There ain't no short-handled shovels,
Nor axe, nor mauls, nor picks.
There ain't no snow,
The wind don't blow.
You paddled downstream in a big canoe
On the Big Rock Candy Mountain."

By the end of the third verse, Tyler had gathered his mackinaw around himself and fell asleep. He dreamed not of his troubled past, nor his flight from home, but of the Gut and Liver Line. He dreamed of holes in the ice, and dead men in the streets. His mind was filled with tyrannical bosses, stinking bodies and filthy living conditions. Several times he jerked involuntarily. He would wake up confused and frightened, staring into the dark, the grip of the arctic air pressing about him.

Finally, in his exhaustion, he slept without dreams; and in his dreamless he failed to notice the scrub and low brush of the cut over land quietly give way to a new and taller landscape. Then, as if the transition had taken place in a heartbeat, they were moving through the massed battalions of the lordly pines. They had entered Pine Island, the forest primeval.

TIMBER!!

In the Woods

Book 2

One

"Come on, boys, warm beds inside," prodded Sullivan, rousting the men from their sleep." They were in camp. It was three in the morning. He pointed out the bunkhouse, then walked Socrates up to the cook shack. Silently, groaning with stiffness, the weary men rolled off the sleigh, entered the building and quietly scattered among the bunks.

Warmth! That was the Tyler's first sensation. Cherry-red coals showed through the draft in the big barrel stove that dominated the center of the room. Four kerosene lanterns, their wicks turned down low, gave a muted yellow glow to the interior of the dark, cavernous building.

Along each wall stood a row of two-tiered 'muzzleloaders'–bunk beds built foot to the wall, extending straight out, the side of one abutting the next. At the foot of each was a deacon bench, hewn out of a split log with four peeled sticks for legs. A small table for the card players stood behind the stove. Along one side of the stove was a shelf that held the enameled wash-basins. Rope and wire for drying clothes was strung up in every direction. Beyond that, the bunkhouse was unfurnished.

The room was a menagerie of odors. Each bunk had a padding of hay that gave off the smell of new-mown meadow. In contrast, rows of sweat-soaked, unwashed woolen socks were hung on the wires. The pine logs of the building oozed with fragrant pitch still being cooked out of the wood. There was the smell of aromatic birch coaling in the stove, and here and there a whiff of tobacco, new leather, and kerosene mingled with the musky aroma of unwashed men.

Tyler stood in the middle of the dimly lit room and listened to the snoring. So this would be his bedroom, his home for the next six months, if he made it that long. In time his own odors and manners would be indistinguishable from the others and Jennifer's words flashed through his head.

Paddy came up and touched him on the shoulder. "Tyler, lad, it looks like we're the new troop here. Why don't you and me take that empty spot there in the corner?"

Tyler agreed, looking over to the end of the line. The bunk had been left because it was the farthest from the stove, but like Patty had indicated, they had no claim to anything better.

They pulled off their clothes and climbed in, Patty on the bottom. Each bed had two blankets; a heavy wool one covered the hay, and a heavier woolen one covered the man. Their turkeys, stuffed with clothing, became their pillows. As soon as everyone was in bed, the bullcook threw two chunks of green birch in the stove. Its wetness would keep a fire going until dawn. He blew out three of the lanterns and turned the fourth down to a barely discernible glow and went back to his own bunk by the door.

Tyler lay back and stared at the roof slats. Spiders had already spun a fine webbing between the wide gaps in the boards. They stood out in shiny relief from the thin layer of tarpaper and boards separating him from the cold night outside. A wave of homesickness swept over him. He missed his pillow. He missed his deep comforting mattress and heavy, familiar quilt. In this crowded room he felt abandoned by everyone and everything that he had grown to feel secure with. He had yet to realize that, in a great irony, he would eventually come to abandon himself. He was so scared, he was about to cry when a childhood verse came back to him, "Now I lay me down to sleep, I pray the Lord my soul to . . ." He was asleep before he finished.

Two

The door burst open followed by the brusque call: "Dat's all boys! Up and at em! Daylight in the swamps! Biscuits and gravy in five minutes." Sullivan's voice boomed through the darkened bunkhouse. The bullcook was already out of bed lighting the lanterns and throwing fresh wood in the stove. Flames sprang into life and soon the barrel was glowing red.

Tyler's eyes popped open in terror. For a moment he couldn't remember where he was. "Oh, Lord," he moaned. "What time is it?"

"Five a.m. damn near time for lunch if you lay around any longer," growled the bull cook. "Haul it out! Chow's getting cold."

From every corner and crevice, long-john clad men slid out of their bunks and the large room suddenly became a chaotic mass of white and red scarecrows, scratching, stretching and bumping into each other as they crawled into their clothes.

"You would think that we'd get a late sleep-in after all that travel," complained Tyler.

"Doesn't appear so," said Paddy from down below. He was already out on the floor and hauling on his trousers. "Better hurry if you want a clean towel, lad."

Two large tubs by the stove were filled with lukewarm water. The men pushed in close to them, splashed their faces and wiped off with the towels that were being passed from one to another. By the time Tyler got to one, the dirty cloth put more water on his face than it took off.

The floor was cold and drafty even through their heavy socks, a boding of the weather outside. They dressed quickly and poured out of the bunkhouse. In five minutes, it was empty. The snow between their door and that of the cook shack packed hard by the boots of the hungry men.

It had started snowing hard during the night. By now there was nearly six inches of fresh white on the ground and large flakes were still falling. The sky was an inky black; the moon already fallen, the sun not yet up. A light breeze of super-cooled air hit their necks and slid down their backs.

"Good God, Paddy," Tyler said through chattering teeth. "I've never been up this early in my life."

"Oh? Am I to believe that we have a member of the aristocracy in our presence?"

"No, I just tend to be a late sleeper."

"Tyler, my lad, I have a feeling in my bones that late sleeping shall not be your problem in the future."

Tyler and Paddy, again in deference to the veterans, entered last and took their places at the end of the farthest table. Right off, Paddy started to ask a question, but Tyler grabbed his wrist and mouthed the words, "We don't talk here."

"What?"

"I said we don't talk here," Tyler whispered with the tone of one who knew about such things.

"I cannot hear you."

"Sssh!"

"Why?" Paddy asked in a voice loud enough to attract attention from the men around him.

Tyler drew a finger across his own throat and grimaced. Paddy shrugged as if to say, no matter, and transferred his attention to the food spread before them.

Platters of fried fatback and bacon, hotcakes with syrup, steaming oatmeal, donuts, fresh bread and large bowl of stewed prunes were spread over the table. The thick, black coffee, served in tin mugs, warmed the hands as well as the stomach.

For every two tables of men, an assistant cook stood by to refill the cups and platters. No sooner would the last hotcake disappear than another platter of fresh ones would drop in from behind them. It was impossible to eat up the last scrap of food at a logging camp table, especially Mike Sullivan's camp.

Back in the kitchen Socrates, Old Mike, and Spooner, were turning out more cakes on the large cast iron griddle.

The men sat in order of their status. At the head table, was Sullivan; Schnapsie, his clerk; and Rube, Mike's straw-boss and second in command. A new daughter had just broken Rube's string of boys. Next to him sat the stable boss, Old Hoss Anderson, then Johnny Quick and the chief smithy everyone just called Smithy. In descending ranks were the teamsters, fellers, jammer crews, saw filers, swampers, road monkeys, bull cooks, various assistants and several as yet unassigned new hires. At the end, sitting among the undistinguished were Tyler, Paddy and five other newcomers, mostly straw-headed farm boys from central Minnesota who had come up with their fathers to help support the families.

They ate silently and fast. In ten minutes Mike stood up and left the room followed by his staff. The other men weren't far behind. A last donut, another slug of coffee and the cook shack was empty but for the men in the long white aprons.

"It went well," Spooner judged, "but we should have some music for dinner." "Fine," Socrates agreed, "how about the sound of a ladle slapping up alongside your head, boy?"

"Hee, hee," Old Mike tittered. He had a way of laughing that came across as effeminate but had the arms and build of a wrestler. He and Spooner, Socrates and the Cookies made up most of the kitchen staff. Mike never said much, at least not to other people. He spent the better part of each day stirring his huge cauldrons of soups and stews and blowing ashes from his ever-present pipe. The food he did talk to. He'd coax it into digestibility, discuss the weather with it, complain about the cold and luxuriate in the fragrant steam. He'd even apologize to the potatoes for having to stew among carrots that were a little less than firm and socially on the outs.

The cook shack in a logging camp had all the capabilities of a good-sized restaurant, serving three hundred meals a day in three fast sittings. The idea was to get the men in and out as quickly as possible.

As chief cook, Socrates, besides preparing menus and overall direction, was in charge of pastries, bread and desserts. To him went the job of baking eighty loaves of bread or the equivalent in biscuits each day as well as keeping the sideboard well stocked with donuts, pies and other desserts for the sweet-toothed.

Old Mike was second cook; the meat cook. From Craig by way of the Hay Run came sides of beef, pork and lamb as well as poultry. Jacks didn't care for sheep so it was normally mixed in with beef stew. The meat was stored in a small room built off the back of the cook shack. The temperature could be regulated from cool to freezing by adjusting the size of the small openings in the outside and inside walls.

The cooks never cooked fish in camp because they believed that fish had no staying power for a man in the woods. But there was always a crock of pickled fish, mostly northern pike taken in the spear house on the lake out back, to satisfy the Scandinavian palate.

Spooner was the third cook and at twenty years old, the youngest. Old Mike was in his mid-fifties but his habit of fussing about and talking to his food gave him the mannerisms of a much older person. Spooner was young but he had three year's experience in a Bemidji restaurant and was given the job by Whittier as a favor to his father, James Spooner, a long time fishing companion. Socrates took to the well-mannered young man immediately. Spooner, in turn, loved the old cook's stories and the banter they exchanged constantly and never complained about the work.

Spooner cooked the vegetables, oatmeal, coffee and other sundries that the veterans avoided or simply deferred to him. The 'cookies' were mostly young boys hired to serve, clear, wash dishes, dice, stir, chop, sweep, knead and carry.

The food that made its way to the table was rich and fat laden to help fill the eight-thousand calorie a day need of the lumberjack. Even the grease was saved and poured back over the bacon to be mopped up with sourdough biscuits.

Each nationality had its own dietary preferences although none was catered to over another. The Finlanders liked their food greasy; the Swedes preferred it clean as in boiled potatoes. Germans yearned for a touch of vinegar and sauerkraut; the Irish cried for corned beef and cabbage. Socrates tried to satisfy all the tastes, particularly on Sunday when the men could lay in and rest up.

It was still dark outside but graying up. Tyler watched as the crews dispersed; teamsters to the barn, the woodcutters to the blacksmiths to collect their saws and axes. Schnapsie had a few words with Sullivan and then went to his office in Mike's quarters. Seifert joined the sawyers. Snoose, the permanent bullcook, went to take over the job of maintaining the bunkhouse, outhouse and sauna.

Rube rounded up the new men. The farm kids were sent off with a man owning a bulbous nose and the handle, Stumpy, to continue extending the Northern roads with axes and brush hooks.

"And you would be Paddy the Pig," Rube said, gesturing to the big Irishman. "Maybe you can catch up with Seifert and see if he can't make a cutter out of you. Mike says you got the muscle for it."

"A wise decision, your honor," Paddy agreed, running off. "Top o' the morning, boss," he greeted Sullivan as he loped by him.

"Top o' the morning, countryman," Mike nodded.

"And you, Chicago lad," Rube addressed Caldwell. Mike had related to Rube what he had heard from Socrates about this boy. A kid with problems bigger than his body. He would be given work to quickly test his mettle. "Down by the barn is a man named Johnson. We have eleven Johnsons here. He's the Johnson with no cap on his head. He'll be putting horses on the water tank. Give him a hand."

"Yes sir," Tyler said, starting for the barn.

"Better get your mittens, first," Rube hollered at him.

"Tyler looked at his bare hands and swore to himself.

Mike watched him hurry back to the bunkhouse. We'll set him to it, he thought, and see if we can find the stuff Socrates sees in him. With that he went up to the office to help Schnapsie sort out the X's in the time books.

Tyler came out of the bunkhouse and ran to the stables. A barn hand directed him to the water tank, a rectangular wooden box sixteen feet long, mounted on sleigh runners. Once filled with water, eight horses hauled it over the roads. Petcocks at the back of the tank were opened and water poured out to flood and freeze the roadbed. When it had built up to a certain thickness, a heavy iron drag with two cutting teeth chiseled the six-inch wide grooves that the loaded log sleighs would track in. Without these ruts it would be impossible to keep the loaded sleighs on the twisting roads.

Tyler grabbed the ladder mounted on the side of the tank and started up it.

"Whoa, boy, who be you?" A man came out of the barn with a big load of harness.

Tyler recognized him as the singer from the night before. "I'm looking for Mr. Johnson."

Johnson spat a stream of brown tobacco juice. "You found him. Now who vould you be?" Johnson pronounced most of his 'w's as 'v's.

Tyler dropped to the ground. "Tyler Caldwell. Mike said to come find you."

The menacing voice dissolved into a crinkle of a smile. "Good, good. That's very good."

Johnson set to work. He was a blur of motion throwing leather over the horses, buckling, hooking and snapping. In five minutes he was fastening the final rings. "Did you watch how I did that, Tyler?"

"Yes sir."

"Understand it?"

"No sir"

"Good, good. Tomorrow I vatch you hitch up the team. Today, I think we're ready."

Tyler started moving back up the ladder but again Johnson stopped him. "Whoa, boy. Now vhy are you so all fired anxious to git up on that box?"

Again Tyler dropped to the ground, frustrated. "I said I'm supposed to help you. So you tell me what the hell I'm supposed to do."

"Sure. I ride up there. You don't. You got to git up there on the back of that lead horse."

"Ride the horse? Why would I do that?"

Johnson pointed to the right front horse, a large bay gelding and spat again.

"'Cause I said so. Now git up on his back and, if he falls asleep tickle his ears."

Caldwell had never ridden a horse in his life but he knew falling asleep wasn't a good reason. "Really, what do I do up there?" he said suspiciously.

"Do? Why, you got to watch for them damned snow snakes, of course. Vhy else do you think Mike sent you? And then too, a horses rump is a lot warmer than a vooden bench."

At the mention of Mike's name Tyler went up to the lead team. Rube and the other men still in the barn area watched with amusement.

"Hurry up, son. We'll pass ourselves coming back for lunch before we leave camp if we don't git outta here. So haul your britches. What did ya say your name vas?"

"Tyler ... Caldwell."

"Well, my name is Johnson." He pronounced it 'Yahnson'. "You can call me Johnson if you vant. Now you jump up there quick before our runners freeze to the ground and I'll tell you about 'dose dangerous snow snakes."

Reluctantly, Tyler found a handhold on the harness and boosted himself onto the animal's back. He came to rest facing Johnson.

"No, no, Mr. Tyler," Johnson was spinning his finger in a circle. "You've got to turn around so you can see the snakes coming through the woods. Look vhere we go not vhere we been."

Tyler finally got himself turned around and Johnson flicked the reins on the backs of the big draft animals. They stepped out easily under the weight of the empty sleigh. As the water tank pulled out of the yard, Johnson was giving Tyler a loud and dramatic dissertation on snow snakes.

"Now, your common snow snake is, on average, maybe five, six feet long. The girls get bigger with pups in the spring. They like to eat mice and chipmunks but when they get feisty, they will hide in the road ruts and try to take down a horse. 'Course they can't do that but it still scares the pee out of old Clarabelle here. Why, boy, I seen a team take off one time. It didn't stop until Nebraska. You see one up there, just holler, 'Snow snake, Mr. Yohnson!' loud as a bull moose and spit some tobacco in it's eye. You chew, don'tcha?"

"No sir, I don't."

"Vell, now's a good time to learn. Here." He pulled out a pouch of tobacco and threw it to Tyler. Tyler took a quantity of the foul smelling tobacco leaf, stared at it and gingerly put it in his mouth as he had seen the others do. He gagged on the taste but managed to keep it in. Soon the brown, tobacco choked saliva had filled his mouth and was oozing out the corners. The big Swede seemed to be enjoying the entertainment. Finally he could stand it no longer.

"Spit, you damn fool, spit!" Johnson ordered. "If you swallow that stuff you'll have the shits 'til next June!"

Tyler spat out the dark brown fluid. It came out not in a thin, liquid stream, but a broad, flat gush laced with stringy discharges. It hung on his stubble beard, ran in rivulets down his coat and froze hard on the horse's mane. He took a deep breath and some of the juice ran back down his throat causing him to retch violently. He managed to expel the last of the tobacco while still retaining his breakfast.

"Good, good." Johnson declared. "You spit like that, them snakes will run off helter skelter." His student was coming along fine. "Now remember, it's the ones with the red eyes you got to take most care with." He kept up his chatter until well out of earshot of the camp.

The men broke up quickly. Two groups went up the two roads leading out of the camp.

A third crew walked out of camp to the edge of the clearing. Because the camp was new, there was an abundance of good timber right out the front door. The swampers set to with axes and brush hooks grubbing out the undergrowth so the cutters could get at the trees and the one-horse skidders could work in their rigs to hook on and drag out the logs. When not busy with this work, mature timber often having little understory, the swampers also helped notch the big pines.

The deep notch was cut across the face of the tree on the side they wanted it to fall. Then the fellers took up the two-man crosscut saws and began the back cut opposite the notch. They carried a pint whiskey bottle full of kerosene to pour on the blade periodically to cut through the sap that built up during the cutting. The cut was low, a foot off the ground. This meant dragging the saw back and forth while bent over at the waist. All the power came from the arms and shoulders while the back and legs contributed little but a solid base. A career spent felling trees produced either a broken man or an extremely powerful one.

Within fifteen minutes after the first axe bit into the dark gray bark of the big white pine, the cries of the jacks began echoing across the clearing. From all directions came the traditional cry of warning and triumph, the bellow of the victor: Timberr!

The jacks called the fall and then quickly stepped away and watched the tree, one hundred and twenty feet tall, swing in a wide arc, slowly at first, almost feeling its way to the ground. Then it gathered speed and slammed its tons of bulk into the frozen ground in an eruption of broken limbs and flying snow powder. Wagers were common between the confident jacks to see who could fell a tree most exactly. A stake would be placed in the snow and a bet would be entered upon as to how close to the stake the tree would fall. As often as not, the stake would be shattered by the falling tree.

Stopping only long enough to put a fresh chew in their mouths, the fellers and swampers set upon the carcass of the fallen giant. The remaining limbs, some of them as large as a man's thigh, were severed and the trunk 'bucked' into seventeen-foot lengths; sixteen plus one for trimming.

One or two-horse teams came to take the logs, one at a time, and drag them to the nearest landing, nearly always within a half mile of the cutting. There, the logs were decked; laid side by side across two rows of poles. Laying the logs on the poles made them easier to roll in the crusty snow.

The decked logs were then loaded onto the wide-bunked sleighs for transport to the rollways along the rivers and streams. Logs were piled on the sleighs in tiers. Up to thirty or forty thousand board feet of timber was worked into a stack measuring sixteen feet wide by seventeen feet long by sixteen feet high. More typically, they were loaded three logs high to save the horses and men.

They used a jammer to pile up the bigger loads. It was a simple invention that made the hauling of large loads long distances practical but was also a logging camp's idea of modem mechanization. A wooden crane set up in the woods, used to lift logs off the ground and onto the sleigh, it was fashioned of two long poles erected so that they were six feet apart at the base and touching at the apex from which hung a pulley. Two cable backstays kept them erect and leaning over the sleigh.

A cable ran up from the log to the apex and back down to another pulley where it came out and was hitched to a single horse. At the log end, the cable was split about twelve feet before the end so that two lines, each with a metal hook on the end led to the log deck.

The deckhands jammed a hook into each end of the log and the horse would walk off and life the log into the air. The jammer poles slanted enough so its peak was hanging out halfway over the center of the sleigh bunk. The horse was backed up and the log dropped into place with the help of the toploaders. A good crew could load a sleigh in half an hour; less if there was another crew competing for bragging rights.

It took Johnson and Tyler twenty minutes to get to Skunk Creek. A hole had been dynamited along the shore to let the water tank to get alongside deep water. Within a week, the mossy shore of the camp lake would freeze hard enough to let them haul water out of there. For now, they had the longer haul from the creek.

The water wagon had a set of rails that ran from the ground to the top. Johnson crawled back and untied a wooden barrel, then lowered it against the rails with a rope and pulley rigged from the top of the tank. He threw the other end of the rope down on the opposite side of the tank. Then he lifted a wooden cover from an opening on the top of the wagon and climbed down.

"Here's how the work lays out, son. There is a hole under that cover," he said pointing to another board cover lying on the creek ice. "You take this barrel and wrestle it into that hole. I will unhitch a lead pony and use it to pull up the water. We fill the tank like so. Then we build a little fire in the stove to keep it from freezing." The water tank had a small stove, with a stovepipe that ran up through the water tank.

"Do you understand, Mr. Tyler?" Johnson was considered to be especially patient with new hands. In fact, he enjoyed their company more than that of the older, crabbier jacks.

"Yes I do," Tyler affirmed, rubbing the stiffness out of his butt. He wrapped his arms about his already chilled body.

"You do this job as good as you watched for snow snakes, you will be all right." He tossed off the remark with a big grin on his face. He was missing three of his front teeth, and more further back. "And we work hard to keep warm. Yah?"

"Yah, sure," Tyler said, buying himself back a bit of bruised dignity as he bent to remove the water cover.

"Good. Good!" responded Johnson, unflustered by Tyler's sarcasm, "I learn you to talk like a Svede, pretty soon you come to think like one too!"

"I sure as hell hope not," the boy muttered.

The hole measured two by four feet in ice that was already two and a half inches thick. Tyler broke the cover off the hole and stepped up to the barrel. He picked it up and, holding it to his chest, moved over to the hole and dropped it in. It took some wrestling to get the open end under the water. Finally he watched it settle into the creek and when it had filled, signaled to Johnson with a shout of "It's full!"

Johnson walked off with the horse and the barrel rose up alongside the skids. When it reached the top of the wagon, it tripped on a wooden cleat and dumped its load into the tank. He backed off the horse and the barrel slid back down to Tyler. Thirty more times they cycled the barrel up and down the tank. The work was repetitious but once he got into the rhythm of it, Tyler forgot its monotony. In fact, the repetitious aspect of the work gave him the freedom to ponder his situation. He was quick to place blame enough to cover a lifetime of misfortunes but he never came close to working out a plan to move on. True to his immaturity, he was finding solace in self-pity.

By the time he dropped the barrel into the hole for the thirty-second time, Tyler was confident enough to lose his concentration. His boot soles had built up an icy crust. Water sloshing out of the hole had flowed onto the ice and frozen, forming a slippery surface over the cover board he was balancing on. His mittens were stiff from more ice buildup and he was caught totally off guard.

He had dropped the barrel wrong end up so the water didn't flow into it. He leaned forward to tip the barrel down but it slid off to the side of the hole. Tyler tried to push off from the barrel to regain his balance, but it slid forward and rolled. His shoes lost traction and, with a cry of panic, he fell into the creek. When the icy water reached his shoulders, his feet felt bottom and he instinctively pushed off and up and threw his elbows onto the ice. He clawed frantically trying to pull himself onto the ice, but the weight of his saturated woolens were dragging him back into the water. He screamed at Johnson, "Help! Help me! I fell in!"

Johnson came running around the sled. "Holy smokes!" he cried. "That is sure a hellava place to be taking a bath, Tyler."

"Get me the hell out of here before I freeze to death!"

"Yah, yah, gotta get you out right away. Give me your hands." Johnson stripped off Tyler's mittens and grabbed his wrists.

With his spiked boots, he got a grip on the pond ice and dragged Tyler gracelessly onto the frozen creek. He flopped about like a huge fish, finally regained his footing and staggered up the bank where he fell again, sliding back down on the ice. Johnson got under his arms and hauled him onto the ice road. Tyler lay there for a moment watching the water pour out of his clothing. Even as he stared, it began freezing on his pants and sleeves.

"Oh fuck," he croaked, "I am going to freeze to death in this hole!"

Johnson wasn't about to assume such a responsibility. "No you won't, young fellow. On your feet," he ordered, "and get moving about! We'll get you home right away."

He pulled Tyler to his feet. The wool clothing, even totally saturated, still had an amazing capacity for retaining heat and Johnson knew that only if he stopped moving would the boy's life be in jeopardy.

"Johnson, let's get going, now!" Tyler started to climb onto the wagon.

"No!" Johnson stopped him. "If you ride up there, you will freeze like a dead fish. You must keep moving. Walk back to camp. Run if you can! I will harness the horse and follow quickly With the sleigh. And keep flapping your arms. Try to fly, my boy!"

The sharp command in the man's voice got Tyler moving. He started down the road. The water was no longer running off his cuffs.

"If you freeze up and fall, I will come and collect you," Johnson shouted after him.

"Great," groaned Tyler as he stumbled off down the road. "My first job and I turn myself into an icicle. What a target for a snow snake." He began laughing through his clinched chattering teeth in spite of himself.

"Move!" Johnson shouted and Tyler began to run. Moving faster, he had to fight the heavy weight of the clothes and the chattering of his teeth. His feet began burning from the water-filled boots and, as he thought of coming back to the men at the camp, any last thoughts of laughter died away. Tyler had never known an ounce of humility in his life. Even when his brother bested him at something or his father bestowed his limited capacity for affection on Graham, Tyler would feel only envy and anger, never humble. Like his mother, both of them 'kept' people in a sense, a mantle of pride was its own security.

Johnson tied the barrel to the tank, replaced the hatch and pond cover, lit the fire in the stove and put the barrel horse back in harness. He unhitched the lead team and, hitching them to the sleigh runners at a forty-five degree angle, gave them a switch of the reins. The team jerked forward, breaking free the frozen runners. He harnessed the team, climbed onto the seat, lit his pipe and started off down the ice road.

As soon as the sleigh was tracking right, he jumped down, ran to the back of the tank and knocked out the plugs. The water cascaded onto the road. Johnson scrambled back onto the tank, and with an occasional cluck to the team, settled in for the trip.

He didn't want to catch up with Tyler but not because he was callous. He had admired the determination with which Tyler had tackled the job at the creek. But Johnson was a man with a focused mind. Wet or dry, their job had been to build up an ice road. Tyler's predicament did not alter that. Rather than dump the load of water back at the creek, or risk a freeze up and tank rupture, Johnson took the most natural course of action; carry on in spite of the incident.

Even then, there was more to it. He recalled, as a young man, his own experience. He remembered, as a young man, having chopped a notch in the ice and laying two sticks of dynamite in the crack. He had run, not up the bank but farther out on the ice. When the charge blew it had opened a fissure beneath his feet and the water had swallowed him up. He remembered the heavy, wet clothing, the pull of the cold sucking at his innards, the fear of drowning, then freezing. He knew the need to keep moving, the urge to stop. An old-timer had saved his life that day and Johnson would do no less for this boy.

He knew that on a day like this, maybe fifteen degrees above zero, Tyler would probably not risk hypothermia. He hadn't. But it was important that he not catch Tyler. The kid had to keep on his feet; had to keep moving or he might freeze up. If he tried to climb up on the sleigh, he'd turn into a chunk of ice. So he kept the team at a steady pace and watered as he went.

Tyler got back to camp at a bad time; fifteen seconds ahead of Johnson. His clothing was so frozen that he could no longer move his arms, and his knees only with some effort. It would have been merciful if he could have made it to the bunkhouse without being seen. Johnson spoiled that. Trying to be considerate of Tyler and realizing the threat to the boy's health, Johnson stood up on the water tank and set up a shout.

"Hello, the camp! Frozen man here! Give a hand!"

Men that had been setting up the jammer behind the camp office saw the bizarre parade and came running. Another bunch from the edge of the cutting heard the call and hurried in. They gathered around Tyler and at first made as if to carry him straight off into the bunkhouse. But he was still moving under his own power and there was a 'don't you dare touch me' look in his eyes. So they formed a corridor for him as he waddled across the clearing. They were silent at first, then encouraging with talk like "Atta, boy!", "Push on, Lad", and "Almost there now". In time, inevitably, the snickering began and then the jokes.

"Couldn't get your fly open, son?"

"Wouldn't have believed a man could sweat so much."

"You'd look right good floating in a glass of whiskey."

Tyler looked neither left nor right nor changed his expression, but kept a course straight for the kitchen.

Socrates opened the door of the cook shack and watched in stupefaction as Tyler waddled up to him.

"What'll it be," Socrates asked, feigning nonchalance, "hot coffee or an ice pick?"

"If you have any pity in you at all," Tyler spoke through chattering teeth, "you'll get me out of sight now."

"Come on in then" he said. "We'll get you undressed. I think I have an ice pick somewhere in here."

He shuffled in and Socrates shut the door.

The boy stood over the stoked up barrel. Soon steam began wafting off his body.

Socrates brought out a bottle of Old Crow.

"Here," he said gently, "take a good pull."

Tyler stared at the bottle. "You said you didn't allow whiskey in your camp?"

"We don't. This isn't here. It's strictly for whatever Hungry Mike sees fit. Right about now you seem like a good fit."

Tyler took the bottle, smelled it and swallowed a big slug of the sour mash. He gagged, and took another.

"God! It burns good."

"You put it right down for such a young pup."

His clothes softening, Tyler sat down and began unlacing his boots. "I wouldn't do this again for French Cognac." He took off his shoes and socks and wrung them out on the floor. Finally, he leaned back and sighed, "Guess I messed it all up, huh?"

"Guess you did but why would you say 'all'?"

"Yes, I know I did. I do that. It's a gift from my parents who never taught me a damned practical thing in my whole life." He recalled using similar words with Jennifer. "Crap," he said, chasing off the memory.

"Alright, have it your way. Maybe you did. I gotta admit, when I saw you coming in like a runaway scarecrow, I kind of wondered how you manage to do these things to yourself. But, Tyler, it ain't by a long shot the worst that could have happened to you. It probably ain't the worst that will happen."

"Like what? Name something worse that won't kill me."

"Like drowning. 'Course, that would kill you. I bet I've helped drag a dozen or more men out of lakes and creeks over the years. Good men. Experienced. Accidents creep up on us sometimes, we can't avoid them. And, well, tomorrow's another day. Just try to learn from this and then forget it happened."

"Tomorrow? It better not be another one like this. I get sent to work with a dumb Swede who I can barely understand and told to do something I'd never knew existed before today and somehow, for awhile, dammit, Socrates, I was doing so good! I really was! Ask Johnson."

Socrates handed him a cup of coffee. Tyler cupped it in his hands and sipped on the scalding liquid.

"I'll tell you what, boy," Socrates said, pouring a cup for himself. "If you're gonna ever grow up, now's the time to start. Growing up means living with who you are."

"Go to hell," Tyler said, ignoring Socrates' advice. Then he had a thought. "Tell me something."

"Yeah?"

"What's a snow snake?"

" A what snake?"

"Snow snake. They spook horses, right? And don't tell me there isn't any such animal."

"Oh, they got'cha on that one, huh? Boy, there ain't no such animal. Not unless you figure sticks and roots sticking out of the snow. They'll spook horses all right."

"Shit! I knew it. Have I been a jackass today or what? It isn't even noon and I've got myself fired."

"You ain't fired! Who said you were fired?"

"If I'm not, I should be. No, I should quit."

"Well, quit if you want! You begged to be here. You don't need to beg to leave."

Socrates saw the pained look on Tyler's face and softened. "Boy, there's a world of difference between messing up and just having an accident. This was an accident, a laugher, sure, but no one's going to think the less of you for it. But quit if you want, no skin off my nose. That would be a mess up. It's not what you did to yourself but what you make of it. I always thought maybe I can't control what happens but I can control how I handle it."

"How could they think any less of me than they do now?"

"Humph. Give 'em time," Socrates chuckled. Then he put his hand on the boy's shoulder. "If you can walk, why don't you get into the bunkhouse and get undressed? Grab an extra blanket and get to bed."

"What?"

"You can still get a good sick. Retire for the day before you risk pneumonia."

Tyler stood up. "Hell if I will! I'm not going to let them come in and see me lying in bed. "He slipped on his boots, shuddering at the cold wetness, and walked to the door, then stopped. "And another thing."

"What's that?"

"I don't like working with anyone who shows me up like that. I got enough of that at home. I have a good mind to nail him one."

"Johnson?"

"Yes, Yahnson!"

"Have you noticed how many teeth he's missing?"

"What of it?"

"He's not much of a fighter. A good joker and tease, maybe, but not mean. If folks hit him, he won't hit back. He goes down and lies there and just looks back at you. It'll make you feel pretty low if you hit him.

"Oh hell!" Tyler kicked a chair across the floor and stormed out of the cook shack with a parting shot to Socrates, "And don't call me boy!"

"Then don't act like one. But you're right on one thing," Socrates spoke to the departing figure, "A man shouldn't have to stand for being shown up like that. Man or boy."

Tyler didn't quit. He changed his clothing, put on a pair of dry boots, and ran out the door. Johnson had gone to the blacksmith shop to make an adjustment on his harness and was ready to pullout when Tyler caught up with him.

Johnson looked down at the kid. He hadn't expected to see him again, ever. "You think you're ready for more, son?"

"1 am." There was defiance in his manner.

"You will not have to ride on the lead horse again."

"No, I will not."

"Then climb up on top with me and we'll go to work."

Tyler grunted and moved up beside Johnson. Johnson pulled out his tobacco and offered it to Tyler who grabbed a healthy wad and stuck it in his mouth. Johnson watched him settle back then shot him a big toothless smile.

"You are a good sport, Mr. Tyler. I like you. Maybe you like me, too, some day." He slapped the leather to the horses and the sleigh jolted ahead.

"Yeah, well, don't bet on it happening anytime soon," Tyler growled.

As they slid past the office Sullivan watched them. Then, across the yard by the door of the cook shack he saw Socrates. Their eyes met for a moment. He watched the smile creep over Socrates, then, with a shrug, Mike walked back to his books.

The icing continued without further mishap. At noon, they brought in the team to the strident call of the Gabriel Horn and wolfed down a meal of pork stew and bread. The mess hall wasn't as full as at breakfast. The crews were scattered at midday and came in groups and bunches. As the work reached out farther into the forest, the cooks helpers and bull cooks would eventually go out in small sleighs to serve dinner in the woods. Some smaller groups that were too far out and too small to be catered to packed their own lunches.

Eventually all the noon meals would be sent out and for the next three months the men would not see camp in daylight again, outside of Sunday.

Tyler and Johnson hauled five more loads in the afternoon. They were beginning to operate efficiently. At the creek, Tyler had learned how to unhitch the barrel horse and rig the set for the water lift. Johnson, being a fair man, traded off with Tyler on the barrel. It gave Tyler a chance to become familiar with the horses.

At five o'clock they pulled up to the stables. The sky was already black. Tyler helped unharness the team, inspect and put away the leather, and brush and grain the horses before turning them over to Old Hoss. It wasn't until Tyler swept the last of the hay off his coat and started for the mess hall that Johnson dropped the bombshell.

"We really should put on the fresh team now, so it's ready for us after dinner."

"A fresh team of horses?" asked Tyler. "Who would be dumb enough to go out at this hour?" Johnson smiled at him.

"Is someone going out?"

Johnson held his smile. "Unhuh. Yep."

"Are we going out?" Joohnson added a nod.

"No! You're pulling my leg. We've been busting our butts out there all day. No! They don't cut trees down at night, do they?"

"We gotta go," Johnson said. "I'll tell you why as we hitch up." It was Johnson's willingness to make allowances for greenhorns that made him so valuable. Breaking in the dumb and the innocently incompetent in camp was a difficult job. "We have to water all night, you see. By the moonlight. Then we can sleep tomorrow. In the morning someone else will water some more and then we can cut the ruts so they can start to haul the logs to the rollway. It is important that we finish quick so the logs don't choke our little landings."

"And after that, then are we done with this miserable job?"

"Are you in such a hurry to find another miserable job? In time you may think that this one was not so bad."

"Even so," Tyler persisted, "what is next for us?"

"All right, we go through it. Tomorrow night, we will start icing the other roads. In a month, I would say, we'll have her all done."

Tyler groaned at the thought of riding the icy tank for thirty nights of freezing work. "Oh, lord."

Johnson slapped him on the shoulder. "Come on, my young helper, we will get us a hot meal. Then we feel better."

They ate another big meal and washed down with more black coffee. In spite of four cups of the stuff, Tyler began nodding off at the table. He woke with a start when Johnson came by and tapped him on the shoulder, and only began to shake off the numbing fatigue after they got out into the night air.

They ran the road ten more times before dawn, driven on by numbing cold. Tyler began to doze off on the tank. Only his partner's quick hand and firm grip kept him from getting thrown off any number of times. In time, the drowsiness left him and he worked on. His fingertips grew stiff and his face was so cold he found it a labor to talk. Johnson, too, became quiet and somber. The horses for all their size were relatively silent. Their breathing and the clinking of their shod hoofs on the ice provided a steady rhythm.

The sound of the forest coming to them in the night offered the only conversation. The snap of a snow-ladden branch and the hooting of night-hunting snowy owls, pushed south by the harsh emptiness of the Canadian winter. Timber wolves howled back and forth across the forest, while the higher pitched cry of the coyote offered a soprano harmony. Small creatures, ermine and mink, not yet into hibernation moved stealthily in shadows beneath the low-lying brush. Deer, seeking to escape the hindering depths of the snow, stood silhouetted in the moonlight at every bend in the road. In such company, the time passed quickly and helped to dispel the monotony of their task.

Four times they stopped by the deserted cook shack for hot coffee and donuts left on a sideboard by the cooks. At 3:30 a.m., Socrates greeted them with fresh bacon and eggs.

"Here, boys, might as well have your breakfast now," he said. "There aren't eggs enough for the rest of the camp, anyway, and I know Tyler does like his eggs." He fixed them some hot chocolate made with a can of condensed milk.

Sullivan came in as they were finishing up and called Johnson aside. "How's the boy doing," he asked, gesturing toward the exhausted Tyler.

"He's doing all right, if you ask me," the Swede answered. "I've worked with a lot of men who done worst.

"Good. So he's holding his own? Not too green?"

"Oh, he's green, all right. I tell you, he's a good kid, Mike. He's older than either of us were."

"The times were different then."

"Not much."

"The people were different," Mike insisted. "We were."

"Maybe a little," Johnson agreed grudgingly.

"Yeah, well," Mike said, mollified by Johnson's comments, "if he isn't up to it, tell me. If he isn't tough enough."

"I'll tell you, sure," Johnson promised.

Tyler saw them talking. He couldn't make out the words, but he knew it was about him. He was angered by Sullivan's failure to include him in their conversation.

The other new men got easier jobs and now were sleeping in warm beds. He knew he had been singled out to see how he could stand up to this punishment and he resented them for this. Sullivan. Especially Sullivan. He reminded Tyler of his father. Domineering and Intractable. The other men were about to wake up and greet the new dawn, refreshed and prepared for another day's work. But Sullivan was killing him just to test him. Let someone else do the dirty work. He didn't have to be here. He only came to humor the old man. Yes! He could walk out of camp anytime he wanted to. And should! Yes! Just to put these power hungry assholes in their place."

"Come we go now!" Tyler bolted awake from Johnson's hand on his shoulder. "It's okay, boy, you were dreaming."

"Huh! Yeah. Okay. I'm ready."

They ran back down to the creek, filled up and spread their last load of water. Back at camp at six-fifteen, they unhitched the team, and walked up to the bunkhouse. Tyler barely heard the greetings from the few men in the camp, but "Iceman " and "Frosty" were among the nicknames tried out on him. One old hand even offered "Snakey", but if Tyler's response was essential to a name sticking with him, then none stuck, because Tyler had no response left in him.

In the bunkhouse, he undid his shoes, and pulled off his sweat-heavy stockings. He shook out the water from his mackinaw and, rather than go up to his own bed, climbed into the lower bunk. It was still warm from Paddy.

There was a pair of boots on the blanket, well worn but still serviceable. The soles were spiked up under the hollow where the sole meets the heel and across the face of the toes. Attached to them was a note: 'Tyler, your first bonus check. Wear them with the same pride that the last man did. Socrates' He crawled out and tried them on. Satisfied, he placed them on the deacon bench, crawled back in, lay down and was instantly asleep. Snoose, who had taken an unlikely liking to the young man, tiptoed in, hung his clothes over the stove and pulled his blanket up tight.

Three

Johnson and Tyler finished working the roads in less than a month. The days stayed cold enough for twenty-four hour watering. Two crews began drawing water from a small clearing they had opened at the camp lake and in two weeks Tyler and Johnson were ordered off nights. For the rest of the season, the job of keeping up the roads would fall to some of the older hands.

The change to days brought Tyler into the mainstream of the daily camp life. Up to this point, he had known most of the others only as shadows passing by on his way to or from the bunkhouse. Through his willingness to stick to the hard work of the night flooding, he had begun to gain the respect of the other men. Men, who as yet unknown to Tyler, seemed to know everything about him. Quiet as camp social life appeared, there was always enough gossip to ferret out a man's personal life.

Admiration would have been too big a word. Lumberjacks were not given to admiration and even if they were, there were only a handful of men in camp that would have been deemed worthy. Still, Tyler was winning his spurs. He was still often abrasive, often immature, but there was a willingness about him, a defiance that was slowly turning into persistence, that went beyond his youth and the chip he still carried on his shoulder.

Recovered from the overwhelming fatigue that had driven him to sleep so quickly after every shift, he began to stay up with the others and participate in the camp life. The two or three hours between dinner and "Lights out" or, as Sullivan called it," 'Dat's all, boys," contained the lion's share of the camp atmosphere.

There were boots to be greased, clothing to be mended and wounds to be tended. The camp store was open for an hour after dinner so basic needs such as clothing, tobacco, soap and such could be purchased from Schnapsie.

In the bunkhouse, the jacks broke into small groups, in part because of diverse interests, but also out of necessity. There were five languages spoken in Sullivan's camp: English, Swedish, Finnish, Norwegian and French. Some claimed Irish as a sixth. There was also a scattering of Slavic dialects; some German, and occasionally an Italian added spice to the melting pot. Everyone learned enough basic English to get the work done, but for extended conversations, most reverted to their native tongues and hung out with their own nationalities.

Every country had its own bunkhouse songs, its own brand of tales and every curse had a particular ethnic sting to it. If this worked to create a polarization among the men, it also provided each of them with a touchstone of security.

There were card games at night. Poker was a favorite, and Tyler was a regular. He had played it regularly at the Evanston Country Club and loved the game. It was one of the few practical skills his father had taught him.

Others favored cribbage, euchre, schmear or pinochle. Buffalo Bill Brody, an old hand on the jammers, loved cribbage above all. He had been a cowboy down in Nebraska but traded the lonely life on the range for the lonely life in the forest. He loved the cold and the lumber camp grub, but he loved cribbage above life itself.

"I was born to play cribbage," he told Tyler. "There isn't a day goes by that I don't play a bunch of cribbage. I don't need a board 'cause I just don't. I remember all the points in my head. If someone starts talking I might get a little confused. Then I just start over."

"Doesn't that make the other guy suspicious?"

"Naw. He don't mind much unless I'm way behind. I ain't hardly ever, though. I usually play by myself, anyway. But, I'll tell you, if you can play cribbage, you'll never need a compass in the woods. You'll never be lost. See, if you're ever lost out there, all you do is pull out your cards and start playing cribbage. In no time at all, someone's looking over your shoulder telling you how to play your hand.

There were the regulars on the deacon's benches. Every evening the talkative jacks would pull up in a quiet place and tell stories. The master of them all, Schnapsie and Socrates possibly excepted, was a man named Liver-Lips Hoover. He got his name not only because he had thick lips, but also because of the way he kept them flapping.

"Lips like a horse lapping grain," someone once said. Hoover would start off with a story, nearly always something from that day as a starting point and always a new story. He could stretch them out forever if he wasn't rushed. Finally, he'd wind it up and then the next guy on the bench would light his pipe and take over.

That was usually Pete Apple, a lumberjack with a constant craving for apples and things made from apples. He could put down a full pie at a sitting. Only Hungry Mike could out eat him at pies but then, Mike could eat three.

Apple was an amiable guy, not crabby or short-faced like a lot of men and he loved to tell "supposing" stories. "Supposing the Spanish had come north and the Swedes had gone to Mexico? Then what?"

Around it went until only the quiet Seifert was left sitting alone. He'd bend forward a bit to keep his words from spreading too far and out would come the story no one would be there to hear.

Paddy the Pig became a favorite of the deacon benchers, often regaling the men with stories of great loves, great sea voyages and great fights. Tyler sometimes left his cards when Paddy began a tale. Though ten years Paddy's junior, he felt a bond between them. Paddy felt it too and took to keeping an eye on Tyler, like a big brother yet not so. Other than Paddy, there was only the Oregon kid, a young but experienced woodsman that Tyler really felt comfortable with.

When mail came, it usually included an old newspaper. Socrates would come over from the cook shack and go through it cover to cover for the men. He'd read a few headline stories about the war and the weather and then he'd turn to an inside page and begin an article about a great scandal or ax murder. He'd go on at great length until he'd come to an especially critical part, then stop, fold up the paper and say, "Boys, I've got a cake in the oven. Got to get back." Half a dozen men would grab for the paper but they'd never find the story.

Sometimes Socrates would hit on a true story that was so good he'd keep it running from one paper to the next. Margorie Reynolds was one such story.

"Well, lookee here," he beamed one night, "Here's one for all you married gents and all you guys who were never so fortunate.

*"Marjorie Reynolds socialite wife of Victor Reynolds of
Reynolds Cooperage, Oshkosh, Wisconsin, was arrested
last Wednesday for assaulting her husband. She is charged*

with sewing him up in the sheets while he slept and then
repeatedly sriking him with an iron poker. Mr. Reynolds
was taken to St. Ignatius Hospital where he was reported
in serious condition with multiple fractures and bruises. In
a statement to police, Mrs. Reynolds was quoted as saying,
'I just couldn't take the abuse of his drinking any longer'."

"That's it. That's all it says."

"Whowee! Can you beat that," Hoover chortled. "It just goes to show that the bridal bed isn't all flowers and bowers after all, don't it, boys."

"If you ask me," Schnaps went on, "it says you can't trust any woman, period, in or out of bed."

"Least wise none that know how to sew," Snoose agreed.

"Oh, shut up, Snoose. The closest you ever came to a wedding was when the judge did a double ceremony and married that couple the same time he was sending you up for exposing yourself on the street."

"Oh, hush, not everyone knows about that."

"Well, they should. Can't tell where you might be taking your clothes off next."

"Won't neither, Schnaps. Besides, one look at me and that filly wanted to throw off her groom on the spot."

"Sure, she thought you were his old man standing there and didn't want to bear no children that looked like gophers."

"Oh, go on, you liar!"

"If I went on too long, these other guys would have to take you out and hang you."

"Horse turds! You been smoking sawdust again."

Every time Socrates picked up a paper that winter someone would ask him about Marjorie Reynolds, and every time he would oblige them.

Tyler approached Socrates one evening when the old man was mending a pair of socks.

"A question?"

"Speak up, I'll listen."

"It's personal."

Socrates nodded and finished a final stitch and bit off the thread. "Let's go for a walk," he suggested, reaching for his coat.

It was a typical Minnesota winter night. The air was quite still and thick with cold, as if it had been frozen too hard to move and was captured in a great, clear, icy blanket. Socrates pulled up his collar and lit his pipe. Tyler put in a chew. He had become accustomed to its taste and chewed as constantly as the other men.

"Beautiful night," Socrates declared. "Look there, the North Star, bright as a ball of fire and cold as a diamond. Kind of like some women I've known. Yep, kind of like a woman's breast when she's taken to another man."

Tyler looked into the brilliant stars, seeded across the black, cloudless sky. He traced the line of the Great and Little Bear and, turning, located The Hunter, Cassiopeia and the Scorpion. The belt of the Milky Way ran like a gauze veil through a field of pearls.

"Socrates?"

"Umhmm?"

"How am I doing?"

"Well, how do you think you're doing? That's what counts." Socrates countered smartly.

"Good, I think. I think I'm doing good." Tyler nodded at his own summation.

"Than what I think don't matter, Tyler. But, just for the record, you're holding your own. Doing all right. That's the word on the street. Why are you asking?"

"Well, it's Sullivan."

"Mike? What about him?"

"I can't figure him."

"Oh?"

"I mean, I just don't see what you see in him. That he's the greatest jack of them all and the finest man you've ever worked with."

"Well, some folks might not see what I see in you either, son. That's 'cause they aren't looking with my eyes though. Maybe that's your problem too."

Tyler turned to Socrates, "Well, I don't think I like him much."

"Tyler, you're not paid to like him, just work for him. Sometimes that's the nature of the boss. If he gets too chummy people take advantage of him. If he's too distant, people don't want to work for him. You got to sit somewhere in the middle."

"Yeah, I know that. But he's cold. Reminds me of someone."

Socrates was squinting into the bowl of his pipe. "You know, you get to a certain age, nearly everyone reminds you of someone."

"No. It's mostly Sullivan. I don't like Sullivan."

"Is that so?"

Tyler nodded.

"Hate his guts, huh? Curse his parentage? Spit on his name?"

"I didn't say that."

"Oh? I hear you saying something. What is it?" Tyler let out a deep breath. He had to rethink the matter.

Socrates let him ponder for a while and finally stopped when they reached the camp. A squat silhouette of the spear house stood out on the ice fifty feet off shore.

"So, Tyler, tell me what's really eatin' you about old Hungry Mike?"

Tyler spat, wiped his mouth and spat again. "I don't know. He makes me angry just by talking to me, which isn't very often. I know he thinks I'm a greenhorn and he still rides me like I've been here for years. I don't like taking orders from him and he never gives me a word of praise."

"Yes, we all want praise for doing what we're supposed to be doing anyway, don't we?" Socrates agreed, "I get mad at things I can't control or run from, too. It's a thing with me. But, maybe that's not what it's about, hey?"

"What do you mean?" asked Tyler, "I don't follow you."

"Oh, I was just thinkin' of Gertie there." Socrates said. Then he got back to the matter at hand. "Maybe you've already met a Mike before. Before you came here. Or someone a lot like him."

"I know what you're suggesting. My father. That's rich, isn't it? My father follows me all the way up here just to harass my butt. It's crazy, isn't it? I can't get away from it, dammit."

"Maybe," Socrates had to raise his voice. "But from what I know, what you said about your pa, he was tough, gave orders, never backed down and made no bones about who ran the show. Is that right?"

Tyler stopped. "No." He spoke very quietly.

Socrates waited.

"He's a first class son of a bitch is what he is. Sullivan isn't my father but I marvel at the similarities."

Socrates smiled and shook his head.

Tyler stopped, turned, and began talking again. "You think I can't take orders from anyone, don't you? You think I ... Well, why don't you just say it?"

"Son, most of the time I talk without thinking. That's a sorry fact. But here now. Ask yourself. Have you ever taken orders from anyone other than your old man? Did you? Did you ever have too?"

Tyler didn't have to think on it very long. "And you think I'm a spoiled rich kid, don't you? That's what I expected you to tell me. That's what you think, isn't it?"

"Sure. Okay. Like I say, don't matter what I think, anyway."

Tyler stopped again. "That's right. It doesn't."

Socrates caught up with him and they walked in silence most of the way back.

When they reached the bunkhouse door, Socrates caught him.

"Listen, son. Just think about this. That's all you got to do. It's gonna take time but we got a lot of that up here. Maybe your old man is the devil incarnate you make him out to be. Maybe not. I don't know him. I do know this about Sullivan. There ain't no man dead or alive I ever knew quite like him. He is what he is and if you come to like him, like I do, you'll never have to ask yourself why. You won't look for praise because just knowing you're his friend is enough. You will never have another friend like him."

Tyler wasn't buying it, so Socrates pushed harder. "Look inside you, boy! You got problems with someone, all right. Look in here." Socrates poked his finger in Tyler's chest.

"Don't call me, boy." Tyler brushed the finger away brusquely.

"Then," said Socrates emphatically, "maybe you never had much of a daddy, but don't use that as an excuse for not becoming much of a man."

Four men in particular always stuck together. They had come up from Bemidji, sent by Itascan Lumber when Mike was in Duluth and represented themselves as seasoned jacks. Rube had sent them out cutting their own tract. In the woods they turned out to be an undistinguished bunch. Their work was below par, their stamina was found wanting and their ambition left much to be desired. The timber that flowed from their efforts was so marginal that if the logging demand hadn't already taken all the good jacks, Mike would have gone looking for replacements.

"I don't know," said Rube one night in Mike's office. "They sure aren't a friend to work. I'd like to see them sent away if we get a chance."

"Are they as poor as all that, Rube?"

"Yes, they're a bobtailed crew if I ever saw one, Mike. They must have built up their credentials to get the work but they only put out enough to keep from being fired. I'll say this. In the bunkhouse they're real campaigners."

Their leader was a man named Stankovich. He liked to soapbox and claimed to have ancestry from Latvia where he said only royalty was entitled to a proper full name and he always swore when he talked about someone who held any title or power over another. He resented authority in others yet always seemed to be preoccupied with exerting his own whenever the opportunity presented itself. He railed on in a secretive manner about the camp management and living conditions pontificating about how he would do it differently and better. He loved to agitate unrest over every little inconvenience even if it was one of his own making.

Stankovich curried favor with the jacks, especially the foreigners, newcomers and those with lowly jobs. He sought out the green, vulnerable and confused, so it took no time before he found Tyler and Tyler found something strangely appealing about this dark complexioned man. It was the third night after Johnson and Caldwell had come off the night shift.

"Hey, lad." He stopped Tyler in the space between the cookshack and bunkhouse and waited until a group of teamsters had walked by. "Stankovich," he said extending his hand. "What is yours?"

Tyler glad for a friendly word shook the man's hand. "Tyler Caldwell."

"I've heard you called Frosty and I've heard you called other names. Tyler is a proper name. I'm proud to know Tyler Caldwell. I hear you have been doing the work of two men and drawing the pay of a chambermaid."

"I do my share," Tyler agreed, expanding his chest a bit.

Stankovich was older than many of the others. There were streaks of gray in his straight, greasy hair. He had penetrating eyes that bulged out of his face.

"You seem to be in need of a friend. I offer my friendship to you." He did not smile. The man had only one face: long, dark and sullen and he acted like someone who had all the warmth beaten out of him as a child. In its place was left a quiet rage; a resentment for all the world and those who controlled it. He rarely looked anyone in the eye when he spoke, but he spoke with a directness that commanded the attention of the listener. His pattern of speech was rhythmic and mesmerizing, like that of a messianic herald. He spoke in declarative pronouncements, avoiding any casual conversation, rarely sought another's opinion and never expected or solicited a reply or reaction. He was an outsider intent on forming his own discipleship. He didn't wait for Tyler's reply now.

"Johnson did a cruel thing to this boy, putting him on that horse like a circus rider."

"I didn't like it much," Tyler shrugged.

The fact that Stankovich brought it up again told him that others had not forgotten and this rankled him more than the actual incident.

Stankovich went on. "A man has no right to treat another like that."

"I told him I wouldn't let him do it again. We're okay now."

"He made a fool of Tyler Caldwell for the whole camp and a man like that should be whipped I say. What he does belittles all of us workers. To tolerate it is a worse crime than the persecution itself."

"I said I think the matter is finished."

"There are some of us that haven't forgotten. We remember on your behalf. If Sullivan were any kind of boss, Johnson would be gone. If I were boss, Sullivan would be gone. He is domineering to a tyrant's degree and a man consumed with his own power. Power is an evil thing and it makes men evil and then the evilness must be driven from the man or his soul will suffer in eternal damnation."

Tyler was drawn to Stankovich's attack on Sullivan because his opinions were amazingly consistent with his own. But the man's ferocity scared him. His habit of reducing people to third person subjects disturbed him.

"Johnson's all right. He helped me when I went swimming and he didn't mean any harm. We have an understanding."

"You should have beaten him. The man needs a beating." This was only the second time since they met that Stankovich had acknowledged his presence with a pronoun.

"No," Tyler shook his head. "Johnson doesn't fight. My friends thought I fought too much. Anyway, I said it's over."

"I say it isn't." Stankovich stuck a fist in Tyler's face. "There is much more to be done before it's over." Tyler didn't know he was talking of a larger cause. "Men like Johnson and that slave driver

Sullivan are vipers. They only live to destroy the dignity of other men. Without dignity a man has no reason to live. When a man steals another's dignity, he forfeits his claim to life."

It had an impact on Tyler. He remembered Socrates using the same words towards Gertie. It sounded harsher and melodramatic coming from Stankovich yet it appealed to a young man adrift in his emotions and lost on his journey to manhood.

"A friend who takes advantage of another's greenness is no friend," Stankovich railed. "Remember that. I offer a friendship that asks for no compromise, not like some here who claim to like you when you do their bidding but spit on you when you turn your back."

"Sullivan doesn't do that." He was so confusing with his talk that Tyler suddenly found himself defending Hungry Mike. "He's tough but Socrates says he's fair."

"So, Socrates says this and Socrates says that. Is Socrates your mama? I hear talk, Tyler. And laughter. I only say this, chose your friends carefully."

That was a decision Tyler had already made. "I will."

Tyler was surprised to see someone break ranks so quickly and completely with the camp culture. This was by and large a closed society. Everyone thought alike and acted in a lockstep manner. It disturbed him but also aroused his curiosity. He was drawn as a moth to a flame. The flame. Socrates had spoken of the flame. He wondered, was it the same one? He was an eccentric, no question; but no more so than others he'd met, Socrates not the least of them. And he could hypnotize affectable young men, so much so that, even as the boy grew more distant from Socrates, he unconsciously drew closer to Stankovich totally, naiively unaware of the use Stankovich planned for him.

There were men in camp with special bunkhouse skills. The Oregon Kid could walk across the bunkhouse floor on his hands, do backward somersaults, reach back and grabbing his foot with his hand, do a standing forward flip. To Tyler, it was reminiscent of the Gayety. The Oregon Kid was a top loader, the best in camp. As fast as the logs were swung up by on the jammer, he'd steer them in place, leap up on the newly set log, and be calling for another. Tyler enjoyed his company as much as any of the others, partly because they were only five years apart in age and partly because the Kid had graduated high school, had a quick wit, and had even played football. The Kid was so confident in his own abilities; he never begrudged seeing another lumberjack distinguish himself, either. He would take the time to talk with Tyler about the work and give him tips to help it go easier. Even Paddy, to whom physical work came easy, was too engaged in his own fun to do that.

The majority of the jacks were observers. They sat on the benches or the end of the bunks, smoking or spitting the endless streams of tobacco juice while the more socially precocious went about their games and chatter. Like Jennifer had predicted, they were generally a quiet, taciturn bunch. To accidentally knock someone's sock off a drying wire was liable to create as much complaining as if the culprit had cut the man's toes off with an axe. But then, the next moment the same crabby lumberjack would be at the sock-knocker's side bumming tobacco.

Every night at nine Hungry Mike would walk in, call "Dat's all, boys," and, in minutes, the room would be dark and still. The snoring would commence and the camp would sleep with a blanket of calm descending over the smoldering unrest that Stankovich was creating.

Four

Tyler's promotion off the water tank came not so much from his own good work as the mistakes of another. Those who knew such things saw it as more of a replacement than a promotion. It involved a teamster named Okie and a raw kid called Perfessor. The kid, a farmer's son from Hubbard County, Minnesota, got his name not because he was book learned, but rather, because he was so totally lacking in common sense that he became confused by everything that was told to him no matter how trivial or explicit. Everything he was ordered to do came back to the boss in a reworded rendition. He did it to the extent that eventually one jack said, "He should be a school perfessor, 'cause he ain't got the common sense to know how to wipe his butt."

He had a habit of sleeping with a soundness that bordered on hibernation. Most mornings it took a rude kick to turn him out. His father, a teamster, and a good one performed the honors out of long practice. There came a time, however, when Perfessor's father, Nathan Blum, was given a week of hay runs into Craig and Perfessor's bunkmate was put on the night water crew. The harmless coincidence of these assignments meant the end for both Perfessor and Okie.

The Perfessor was a road monkey, a job reserved for the too young, the too old, or the too weak. Perfessor qualified on the last count if not also the first.

The road monkey's job was to walk the ice roads each morning and evening; cleaning horse manure, ice chips, and blown limbs and other debris from the ruts with a narrow wooden shovel. Manure, especially, worked as a brake on the sleigh runners and put extra strain on the teams. There were certain places, however, where such braking was necessary; the hay hills, so named because the lumberjacks piled hay alongside the road. When the loaded sleighs approached these downhill grades, the teamster would call to the road monkey for hay. The monkey then threw enough hay in the ruts to keep the sleigh from picking up too much speed and running over the horses. There was no worse fear for a teamster than a runaway sleigh. Stories of such occurrences abounded in the camps and everyone swore to have witnessed disaster that resulted in the death of either the team or the driver.

Putting on just the right amount of hay was more art than science. Too little hay and the sleigh might run off out of control. Too much hay could cause the sleigh to come to a halt and the monkey would have to crawl under the load and dig it out by hand while the teamster scorched his rear end with foul language. More than one road monkey had lost a joint or two off his fingers from a stuck sleigh suddenly breaking free. While the Perfessor still had all his fingers, his rump had been singed regularly his first week on the job.

There was only one good hay hill coming in from the outer cuttings. It was on the Spruce Swamp Trail a quarter mile out of camp and about that long. It didn't really end until it crossed the small bridge Mike had built over the creek that drained Pickerel Lake behind the cookshack. It was assigned to the Perfessor and, because of his particular nature, he was fairly competent at it, unless he wasn't there.

On this particular day, Blum was laid over in Craig from the previous day's trip so he couldn't put the boot to his son. Okie had gotten an early start. He had left his sleigh at the jammer that evening because there weren't enough logs to make up a full load.

Stankovich's crew was cutting out there and claimed it was because of the outrageous brush they had to contend with. In fact, one of his men had been whipped in the face by a green Hazel branch that morning. As cold as it was, his skin split open in a long, burning cut. The man was so enraged that he had taken an ax and cut down every small piece of tree or brush he could find while his team sat and laughed.

Because of this delay, Okie had to go out extra early to pick up his sleigh and bring it in. It took him ten minutes to break the runners free, but once on the ice road, he made decent time.

He had just two horses, his own team from home. One was a robust gelding with a proud chest, and the other a little gray mare with great ambition. He was as fond of them as any animal he had ever owned.

They moved along at a brisk walk, their shoes grinding at the icy surface. Okie was whistling an old ballad, and turning the snow brown with the juice from his Redman tobacco. He was riding on the rollway, a single six-inch log that rested across the front runners and put the driver a whisker's length from the swishing tails. Okie stood there, whistling and warming his face in the rising sun. He was a religious man and knew that the good Lord had sent this morning for his personal pleasure. When he saw the slope of the hill dropping away in the foreground he instinctively pulled back on the reins and called for hay.

"Yo, road monkey! Put 'er on, son. Okie's coming heavy loaded and there's no holding this devil back. Give me the green grass."

There was no answer and as he reached the crest of the hill he got worried. The sleigh leaned forward and started gathering momentum. In seconds it was unstoppable and impossible to steer.

"Monkey! Wake up and get me some hay!" Okie screamed.

A second later he broke over the hill. There was no monkey and no hay! The road was clean, still snowed over from the night before.

"Holy Jesus! Sweet holy Jesus!" Okie prayed and began climbing up the face of the load. He held the reins in his teeth, his hands searching frantically for the binding chains to pull himself up with. He could have jumped clear at this point and been rid of the sleigh, but he knew that the only chance his horses had was if he stayed with them and tried to ride it out. The team needed him on the sleigh if they were to make it down and even then the odds were terribly stacked against them.

Okie made it to the top of the load and starting putting the leather to his animals, whipping up the team to try and keep them in front of the runaway sleigh.

"Oh, my God! Oh, my sweet Jesus," he prayed.

The hill rushed up at him. The trees flew by in a blur. He had no choice but to trust to the horses and keep them moving. If they fell they would be crushed, man and beasts together. There were no turnoffs, no brakes, nothing to slow the sleigh except the forest itself and to run into that would be disastrous.

"Run you beauties," he bellowed. "That's my boy. There's my girl. Run!"

The runners were banging and jumping, skipping from hump to bump, threatening to break free from the ruts. The logs began to shift, settling into new positions, working beneath the chains, flexing them and leaving slack. The load bulged and strained, expanded with every jar and shrank with every recoil. The binding chains worked loose and were on the verge of giving out entirely.

"Oh, Jesus. Oh, Jesus! Where are you? Hi yah! Up Beauty! Up Dusty!"

The push of the logs threatened to overtake the horses and grind them up beneath the runners. The spring pole reared up between the team and began ripping apart the harness, lifting the horses and throwing them back and forth. Suddenly the tug strap on the mare snapped. With the sudden release of tension, the little mare began to slow down and the sleigh caught her. It hit her in the hind legs. She went down for an instant, screamed and caught herself. With help from her partner she pulled herself out and got back on her feet. Okie whipped her with the line and she took off and the sleigh never caught her again.

The gelding was holding out all right. He was still in his harness and running at a flat out gallop, pulling the mare along with him. But with all the tension of the harness on him, he was pulling off to the side. They were nearing the bottom, but the sleigh had jumped clear of the ruts and was sliding back and forth across the road, bouncing off the big trees and crushing the smaller ones. Okie had lost all control. He was blinded from the burning wind and the water in his eyes. Still he stayed with the sleigh, praying for mercy and laying on with the reins.

The bridge was coming up and Okie tried to make for the center as best he could. It had railings of short posts connected with poles, to help the horses distinguish the sides. Just before he came onto it, the mare, fearing again that the sleigh might hit her, jumped against the spring pole crossing it with her legs and swinging the sleigh over enough so it ran far to the right, enough to miss the bridge.

"Please, Mother of Christ, save my ponies!" Okie sobbed. "Just a little longer, I beg you!" The sleigh was still moving at a tremendous pace, but coming up to the level. He thought they had a chance. He screamed at the horses, "Haw! Haw! Haw, you team!" to bring them left and nearly tore the bit out of the little mare's mouth. She threw her head around and screamed at him. But she responded and pulled away from the gelding and drew left.

They flew over the little bridge and the sixteen-foot wide bunks, barely holding the edge, and mowed off the railing like grass.

Snoose and a cookie were below on the creek. They were pulling out water for the camp and looked up in time to see the sleigh and the wild, foaming horses. They dove under the bridge as the pieces of railing began to rain down on them. The cookie made it but Snoose slipped and went down into the ice hole. He came up spouting water and icy blue curses.

Okie was still whipping up the horses and made for the loading yard in the meadow behind the stables. All the time he had been screarning, "Runaway! Runaway!"

Out on the jammer, the Oregon Kid had just set the fifth tier on another sleigh. As yet, it had no top chains on it. Men from the log deck and jammer team scattered in every direction as Okie's sleigh roared into the meadow. As it flew past the jammer, it caught the corner of the Kid's sleigh and tore loose the lower binding chains. A runner cut off one of the jammer stays.

His logs started rolling free and the Kid, still on top, began dancing for his life, clawing his way up; trying to stay on top of the shifting, rolling logs. At one point he was waist deep in them, flailing for higher footing and then all of a sudden, he was above it and the last log, still hanging from the jammer, was hovering in his face. He leaped for it and climbed onto the log just as it swung behind the unsupported jammer. The jammer started to topple, logs, cables and frame. Whipped around like a trapeze artist, the Kid looked desperately for a chance to let go. He flew off just before the whole outfit crashed down and landed in a brush pile twenty feet away.

Okie was leaving a trail of logs across the meadow and doing his best to stay with it. He was pulling hard now to stop the hysterical horses and would have made it unscathed, but the last of his logs rolled off and he fell between the bunks and got caught up beneath a runner. Still he held onto the reins and got dragged until the weight of his body finally brought the horses to a stop against a blow-down tree.

Another cookie had heard Okie's screams. He ran to the front door and grabbed the Gabriel horn. To blow it at any hour but mealtime signaled trouble and would bring everyone within earshot back to camp.

Socrates ran out and added his own voice to the uproar. "All men and the cook! All men and the cook!" The traditional cry in a crisis. Realizing the significance of his words, he said, "Cook? Lordy, that's me!" and ran for the clearing.

The Oregon Kid was the first one to Okie. He found a bloody hand sticking out of the snow. Crawling beneath the sleigh, he began digging into the drift. The arm and Okie were still attached to each other. The Kid dug out his head and brushed the snow out of his face.

"Okie! Okie!" There was no response. He slapped him hard. Okie's eyelids fluttered, his face screwed up with pain, and then they opened wide.

Okie looked into Oregon's blurry face. "So, you are an angel, then?"

"Sorry, partner," the Kid answered "You drew a short straw. Start shoveling coal."

"Oohh!" Okie tried to laugh. "God, something hurts!" he moaned. "No, everything hurts."

"Take it easy and I'll get you out of here."

"You better not, because once free, I'm gonna kill a road monkey." Then he remembered. "My ponies. How are my ponies?"

"The horses are okay," the Kid answered. He glanced over and saw that both animals were still standing, cut up some but in better shape than Okie. The kid grabbed Okie under the shoulders and tried to drag him out but the man screamed and fainted. The Kid stopped pulling and cleared the rest of the snow off him. A leg was still pinned beneath the runner.

Other men had come running to help gather up the pieces. They unhitched the team and lifted the heavy sleigh and dug Okie out.

His pant leg was gone and the leg was badly torn. The shattered bone bulging against the skin. They bundled him into Mike's office where Socrates forced a pint of whiskey down him before resetting the bone as best he could. Socrates and Rube stitched the worst cuts while Okie drifted in and out of consciousness; the pain first waking him and then making him pass out again.

Snoose was toying with the idea of catching pneumonia and begged for the forbidden whiskey bottle without success, while the Oregon Kid didn't know whether to be scared, angry or prayerful. In the end, he just figured he had seen and been through worse.

The little mare that had fought so valiantly was laid up for a week. When her foot had gone under the runner, it bent the shoe together so the open ends were nearly touching. Her hoof was compressed so badly, she couldn't carry weight on it for some time. In spite of the pain she had run with a magnificent heart.

Mike had been out when the Gabe blew. He threw down the hunk of ham he was lifting out of a man's lunch pail and raced back to camp. After seeing the damage and listening to Okie's story, he set out to find the Perfessor. Still sleepy-eyed, the farmer's kid was standing in the door of the bunkhouse rubbing his eyes.

Mike had his piece with him right there. "Son, do you know what happened just now?"

"No, sir. Should I?"

"You should. You caused it."

"I did? Was it good or bad?"

"A damned good man was hurt bad and may yet lose a leg. Others were saved by God's providence. All because you let down your end of the bargain."

"Oh, God, was it as bad as that, Mr. Sullivan?"

Mike grabbed Perfessor's collar and shook him. "You almost killed him! You damn near killed one of my men. Do you hear me?"

The Perfessor was caught in his slothfulness and fearing that Sullivan was about to kill him, began to cry. "Is there nothing I can do to keep this from my father, Mr. Sullivan?"

"My business is not with your father but with you. "Are you a good walker?"

"Yes! Yes, I am, sir!" Here was perhaps, a chance to make amends.

"Fine, then. Pack your belongings. You're going for a walk."

"Where shall I go?"

"Wherever your feet lead you, boy. Home, I should think. Schnapsie will give you your time. You're done here."

"Are you firin' me?"

"You did that yourself. Now walk out of my camp." That was all Mike had time for. It was all he trusted himself to say. He went off to clean up the mess of the morning, leaving the Perfessor crying in the street. Eventually the young man got up the ambition to pack and pick up his pay.

Socrates had watched Sullivan with the young farm boy. It was rare to see his boss lose his control over anything. "Too hard, Mike, too hard," he wanted to say. "He's just a fool kid, not a murderer." Socrates could see that Mike was scared, scared bad over something the old cook didn't understand. "What awful secrets are you hiding, old friend? Tell me, then, where is your runaway taking you?"

The boy caught a log sleigh down to the rollway and began the twenty-mile hike into town. At noon he met the hay run coming back on the trail. His father listened to his story of the runaway. The young man made no attempt to whitewash his part in it. After giving it some thought, the elder Turnham said, "Give my best to your mother," touched the reins to the team and drove on.

Okie was put in traction and sent on to the Deer River hospital by way of Craig the next morning. It wasn't until the following year that he saw a camp again. The doctors saved his leg. They credited the cold air with preventing mortification during the wretched journey over the Gut and Liver.

Mike kept him on the camp books at half pay for the use of his team and Itascan Lumber paid his doctor bills. "All in all, a nice little holiday," said Schnapsie searching for the silver lining in the dark cloud.

Ironically, the Perfessor's father was given Okie's job sledding logs. A man who had been driving a one-horse skidder was promoted to the hay run and a young cutter off Stankovich's group was put on as the new skidder.

Five

Tyler was taken off the ice road and put in the woods to fill out Stankovich's team. They started him swamping right off. Twelve hours a day he cut down brush and limbed trees. His axe was constantly in motion and for the next two weeks, he again fell into bed as soon as dinner was over. His large frame kept adding strength and weight as newly developing muscles began to swell his body and ego his head.

In Tyler, Stankovich found an easy disciple for his rhetoric. He would lean on his saw at every opportunity, spit in the snow and lecture Tyler on the mistreatment and abuse that was rampant. Perfessor had been railroaded out of camp, not because he had made a mistake but because Mike couldn't accept the responsibilities that should have been his. Okie had no right to run a loaded sleigh on that road in the dark. No, it was obvious that Sullivan just wanted to throw his weight around and the kid was an easy, helpless target.

"Why lose two men for one man's mistake? It's no different than with Tyler. These men here lie in wait for someone to spit on; grind down with their awful righteousness and indignation. Oh yes, they treat us like animals and pay us like slaves and when they have no more use for us, you see, they'll show us the road, too."

Stankovich made some sense. His diatribes began to erode the last of Tyler's romantic notions of the lumberjack. The self-made man, the woodsman by choice were fast becoming mythology. He talked about how they were kept in perpetual subjugation by the logging companies with low wages and cheap booze until they were worn out and worthless. He used the same words, same descriptions as Jennifer but found a different reason for the tragedy: The human factor, man's eternal inhumanity to man.

"To perpetuate the myth of supermen," Stankovich said, "they encourage the lumberjacks to compete for top dog honors. Whores of the woods. Who is the best feller? How big are your loads?" Stankovich loved to call them that. Whores, fighting among themselves to curry favor with the boss. The more the young man heard, the more he found agreement. But there were other times that made him wonder. One day Tyler was out working the perimeter of their cut. Their crew had fallen into a heavy stand of white spruce and because it straddled a camelback between two swamps, it had to be cleared before they could move forward. He was alone in the thick of it, limbing the thick, sappy branches because the others in the crew disdained such work as beneath them.

He stopped to mop his face and in the stillness heard angry voices coming from the clearing. He dropped his axe and ran out of the spruce grove. By the time he reached the clearing, the shouting had stopped. Stankovich and his friends were standing in a circle in the center of which knelt a man, his head bowed. His hat lay beside him. As he drew near, Tyler saw flecks of blood in the snow.

Tyler pushed his way in. "What happened? Who got hurt?"

The man on the ground turned his face to Tyler. It was Johnson. His face was bloody and swollen.

"Hey, what is this?" Tyler asked as he stooped to help him up.

"No!" Stankovich ordered. "Do not touch him!"

The words carried such a bite that, together with the attitudes of the other men, Tyler obeyed.

"Why?" he asked, "I told you Johnson was alright; that he wouldn't fight. You didn't have to do this."

Stankovich shouldered his way over to Tyler. "Don't believe for a minute that we beat him for you, boy. The man has a big mouth. He came here and he challenged our work. He said we were lazy and shiftless. We showed him that out here he is a hen among roosters."

"But he doesn't fight."

"Because he is weak!" Stankovich shouted. "If a man is weak he will be consumed. This man is of Sullivan's chosen. Now he knows his place with us."

Johnson got up and wiped his bloody mouth. He picked up his cap and looked at Tyler. Their eyes met and Tyler saw only sadness. When Johnson had left the landing, Tyler returned to his work, confused, and didn't talk or listen to them for the rest of the day.

To Stankovich, the bunkhouse game of Hot Ass was another example of men trying to gain some prominence at another's misfortune. It was played regularly in the evening among the jacks and, to Stankovich, it was just another way to degrade and humiliate.

There was one lumberjack everyone called the Sheepherder. He had served his youth as a Montana shepherd. Somewhere along the line he had also learned to play the fiddle fairly well. He was shaped like a pear, narrow at the shoulders and very round in the middle. His rear was three feet wide by popular estimates and he weighed in at well over two hundred and fifty pounds. His body was the frequent butt of jokes. The games and the humor were often coarse and insensitive.

One night some of the boys were playing the game. In Hot Ass, the man that was "it" put a sack over his head and bent over. People took turns walloping him on the butt and he had to guess who it was. If he named the hitter correctly, that man got the sack and went in the middle of the circle. Everyone wanted a shot at the Sheepherder's butt, but he never played the game. He was a quiet, gentle soul and pretty much kept to himself.

One night the others set him up. A straw boss that had been pushing hard on the Sheepherder's crew that day was in the middle wearing the sack. Some of the other boys went over to Sheepherder and whispered, "Fats, now's your chance to get back at him. He'll never guess it was you because you've never played the game before."

That convinced him. The Sheepherder snuck up behind the straw boss and hit the man so hard that he nearly drove him across the room. The straw boss rubbed his backside and whistled in amazement. "By God, that was hard. I've not had my stormy side hit so hard since I last told my stepfather to stop fighting with mom. It can't be none of you other guys. There is only one man here could put such weight behind the blow as that. It must be the Sheepherder. Was it you, Sheepherder?"

So Sheepherder got his head covered with the sack, but, instead of using the flat of his hand, the straw boss took a slat out of a bed and, spitting in his hands for a good grip, laid it full alongside Fat's billboard rear end. The board shattered. Sheepherder plunged forward and slammed into a bunk so hard, it brought the whole thing down. The men split their sides with laughter. When the Sheepherder crawled out of the collapsed bed he didn't talk to anyone the rest of the night nor play his violin again. It took a couple days before he was back to normal but he never played Hot Ass again.

Stankovich took hold of the incident and wouldn't let go of it, using it as yet another argument against the inhumanity of the system that it could drive those men to such cruelty towards one another. When he told the Sheepherder that he had a legitimate grievance over it, the big man told him to let it go. He said it was just a camp joke and it was done with.

"You see," Stankovich preached to Tyler, "Sheepherder is too cowardly to speak up for fear he will be fired for criticizing the straw boss. He will then appear weak and cowardly. That is what he is after all, weak and cowardly. It is not fair," Stankovich hammered. "There should be others willing to stand up for him."

"Well, who would that be?" Tyler asked skeptically, "You?"

"Yes!" Stankovich exclaimed jubilantly, his eyes gleaming with the fire of an evangelist, "I, and a thousand men like me. Even now, we are waiting with barely restrained impatience, ready to change the world for the worker. There is an unstoppable movement rolling across the land." He neglected to tell Tyler that when he had approached Sheepherder, the big man told him to go get a church if he wanted to preach.

"And run it for him, too?" Tyler asked doubtfully.

"No, Tyler, no! Agents of the workers will run it, a committee elected by popular vote will. Their qualifications are to be based on the ability to lead and get results. You see? We will be democracy in its highest state."

Hungry Mike came into their cutting during his tirade and saw them sawing words instead of wood.

"You men," he chided, "if you plan to talk these trees down, you'll need more bite in your words. I have seen better men than you fail."

"We were taking a well earned break, Sullivan," Stankovich said sourly.

Sullivan grunted in disapproval and then noticed a lunch pail left out in the open.

He studied the area, gauging the meager amount of work performed since morning and, picking up the lunch pail, proceeded to eat its contents.

"Hey!" One of the crew, one of Stankovich's cronies, yelled, "that's my meal you have there. You're eating my lunch."

Sullivan nodded. "Good, I didn't want it to belong to anyone who deserved it. I think, looking at the chips and sawdust here, that none of you have worked up the appetite to eat it, anyway." He polished off the contents of the pail, stood up, and walked over to Stankovich. "I don't like what you are doing out here. I expect better of my men or I don't keep them on. You advertised yourselves as cutters but you cackle like old women. Maybe you should work harder or work somewhere else."

He turned from the crew and retraced his steps back down the road, knowing that to wait for any protestations would be a waste of time.

Stankovich watched him go and made sure he was out of earshot before he raised his voice in defiance before the men. "That man is a lowlife bastard! In my plan he shall be the first to go and I promise you he shall go violently. There will be no easy walk down the road for him. The movement will deal with him and his lot. And the time is coming soon!"

"Movement?" Tyler wondered, "What movement are you talking about?"

"I'm talking about the greatest movement of working men in the world today," he shouted, shaking his fist at the departed Sullivan. "The Industrial Workers of the World is its name! Others have called it something else, but today we wear that label as a badge of honor on our chests. We are the Wobblies, by jesus, the Wobblies!"

Six

*E*very time Mike criticized Stankovich's work, it fueled the man's hatred and increased his zealousness, for Stankovich could always find the words to turn the situation to his advantage. He used every opportunity to promote his version of the Wobbie philosophy. In the camp he found many willing listeners; men who for one reason or another, had been given a bum deal in life and now were open to the argument that life owed them a turn or two. Through the Wobblies, a promise was given and a dream rekindled. To the homeless, came suggestions of free land and livestock, to the lazy came a cornucopia of promised blessings: free food, free lodgings, free booze and freedom to vegetate in pastoral repose. Compared to lice-ridden beds and greasy beans, even the thought of an enclosed outhouse would open a man's mind enough to let a Stankovich fill it with dreams, however impossible or impractical.

Now that Stankovich had dared to make public the name of his organization, his mission was open to the scrutiny of all except Sullivan and the other bosses. He began to promote more actively, though still in quiet groups and under the curtain of night. A movement in the hands of one man is just an idea, but when it is accepted and embraced by a larger following, it becomes a real and dangerous threat to the status quo. Tyler discovered this when he mentioned the Wobblies to Socrates one day.

"I heard some guys mention it," Tyler lied.

"What guys?"

"I don't remember. What are they?"

Socrates knew it was a lie and wanted to challenge it but didn't. He tried to be reasonable. "It's a fearsome lot more than a word, lad.

It's the touch of death itself to some. It's the torch of anger, and the club of brutality.

"Socrates, you're exaggerating. I heard it was a worker's organization. We even studied it in school."

The old man smiled. "I suppose it's hard to argue against book learning no matter how wrong it might be. Well, it's what they call a labor movement, all right, Tyler. But just what is the Wobblie brand of talk? That's when the labor is suddenly told that they don't have it as good as they thought, nor even as good as it is, and definitely not as good as it can be. These Wobblies come around and get everybody worked up with talk of gettin' up the wages and making the owners treat their workers better. They promise things like linen napkins and featherbeds knowing full well that ain't possible. Oh sure, they might have a case here and there, but in general, their methods are right out of a jungle. They're apes with clubs, is all!"

"Why do you say that?" Tyler wanted to draw out Socrates without betraying Stankovich. Stankovich, for all his vehemence, hadn't mentioned violence, at least no more so than he had already witnessed among the men in daily life.

"Let me tell you about the Dakotas. They went out there saying they wanted to work. Well I was there, so I know what I'm saying is the gospel. They looked over the work, looked over the pay and said, let's have at it. Well, they just couldn't take the heat, the work, but they didn't have the good sense to pack it up and go home and leave the jobs for men who wanted them. No. Instead they started preaching about abuse and slavery and then tried to wreck every thing they touched. They threw rocks in the threshers, burned the fields, even poisoned some of the water. Things like that. These weren't big business folk they were hurting, but farmers! In the end they just cost a lot of good men their jobs."

"They promote violence?"

"They attract a lot of violent men. Men who can't do that sort of thing in a bar without going to the pokey, they do in a labor movement and it seems acceptable. Don't get me wrong. Both sides know how to make use of violence. I do believe this, if a man's got a job that ain't to his liking, and it's the same job he once laid claim to, then if that man's got a lick of sense, he'll pack his turkey and go find something else. Most often it's the job, itself, decides how good or miserable a man's work will be, so there ain't always much room for improvement. Hell, I've packed up many a time because I couldn't stand something or the other. It's no big deal. That's how it should work. If no one accepts the work then the boss has to make the situation better. Vote with your feet, I say."

Socrates paused to ponder what he had just said. Then he made his final appraisal. "But in Dakota, I heard of a fight last year where three men took another and threw him into a running threshing machine because he spoke out against the Wobblies. It chewed him right up. When he came out there weren't any pieces bigger than a pork chop, and that's just what they looked like. Now to my way of thinking, that's murder, ain't it!"

Tyler was listening.

"Tyler?"

"What?"

"Don't make light of this. You keep your nose clean, not bent. One way or another, if the Wobblies come in here, and I'm not sure they aren't already, stay clear. You promise me that."

When Tyler finally answered, he lied again. "I promise."

"'Cause if you don't, you're on your own. I can't help you. Do you understand?"

As angry as he became over Socrates' dictating his behavior, Tyler managed to hold his tongue.

If Stankovich's dark aura held a strange attraction for Tyler, it also projected a disquieting side. He was the flame that could warm and burn at the same time. Unlike the flame Socrates had spoken of in the quiet of the church, this flame was of flesh and blood. Tyler was undecided about the beating of Johnson. Maybe the man had it coming and it was just part of the pattern of a camp pecking order. t was the way of camp life, but it still struck him as cruel and unnecessary. There were things about Stankovich, too, that seemed to contradict his own preaching.

One evening there was a card game between Tyler, Stankovich, two of Stan's followers, and an immigrant Swede named Ole. They were playing seven card stud for pennies. It started out in a friendly enough manner but as it wore on, Stankovich got into the Swede for quite a bit of money. It reached a point that he questioned the luckless Ole's credit.

"I be square," Ole responded in his broken English, "Okay, Stan, I lose, I pay."

"Well, just make sure you remember that, you dumb yokel." Stan said it too fast for the immigrant to comprehend. The Swede just nodded amicably.

There was one particularly large pot. Stankovich was dealing. He gave Ole a pair of five's, down and dirty. Ole opened the betting with a nickel. Without looking at his cards, Stan saw the bet and raised the limit. Ole matched his raise. The others dropped out at the show of power.

"Here's some royalty for you," called Stan, as he laid the king of hearts face up on top of Ole's two down cards. He dealt himself a four of clubs, another king to Ole and a three to himself. Ole laid on the bets, hitting the limit each time. Stankovich, still ignoring his hole cards, saw him every time and parried with a limit raise of his own. Stankovich pulled a four for a weak pair, and dropped a five on Ole's pile with a look of contempt. "Well, he said, "I guess I should have a look at my mother lode here." Stankovich picked up his bottom cards. He was sitting with a three and a pair of fours showing and nobody knew what he was hiding. Ole couldn't contain his delight. He had a pair of kings, a pair of fives and a pair of sixes. There was only one card to go and he guessed Stankovich was holding trash.

The sixth card came down. Ole was blessed with the King of Spades! A full house, kings over sixes, a winning hand. A lone ace for Stan. Well, no matter, it would take a miracle to improve on those cards and the die had already been cast. Stan had been bluffing him all along and Ole knew it. The man had not even looked at his hole cards. Ole was not the kind of man to be treated like such a novice. That Stankovich would get a lesson in poker tonight.

Ole bet again, and again Stankovich raised the limit. Ole smiled through his beard, "No matches? More?"

Stan leaped at the opportunity. "Sure, Swede, no matches." He swept the coins to the floor. Reaching into his pants pocket, he pulled out a gold railroad watch and held it in the air. The shiny metal hung from a shoelace and twirled in the lantern light with a soft golden luster. "Match this, you crazy Swede," he challenged.

Ole stared hungrily at the watch, but shook his head no. "No have," he said. "No watch."

"Then bet that." Stankovich pointed at Ole's wedding ring, a large, unadorned gold band.

"No!" the Swede cried, shaking his head violently. "No!" The ring was a family heirloom, the only contact he still had with his wife and child back in the old country. They were waiting for him to save enough money to send for them. His dream of a homestead.

"Then fold, mama's boy," the zealot challenged him. Stankovich had risen off his stool and, bracing his hands on the table, leaned over to Ole. Their faces were inches apart. The challenge was about more than a card hand. Both men knew the real stakes in this game.

Ole looked at his ring and studied the watch on the table. Solid gold casing and easily worth one hundred and fifty dollars. Five months pay. Reluctantly, he licked his finger and drew off the precious band. Gently he placed it on the table and with great deliberateness turned over his cards to reveal the three kings and two sixes. Sighs of relief emanated from the men gathered about them. A formidable hand in any game much less a golden jackpot.

Stankovich met Ole's look and hardened on it until Ole's grin began to dissolve in uncertainty. Stan snorted and reached for his cards. He rolled them. A four, another four, the lonesome ace, and then he reached for his two hole cards. With the tip of a fingernail he flipped them over: Ace of hearts, ace of diamonds. Fullhouse, aces high. With a whoop of glee, he reached out and pulled the booty from under the eyes of the stricken Ole. He held the ring to the light, bit it with an assayer's skill, and slipped it on his finger. "Does this mean I get your woman, too?" he said with a smirk.

Ole threw the table aside and swung at Stankovich. Two men jumped forward and held him back. Ole wrestled with his captors for a minute and then grew limp. He struggled to find the words to express his anger. "You, you, a, a, you cheat!"

"Hey, wait a minute there, you dumb Swede. You're just sore. You'll have to prove that!" Stankovich broke into ridiculing laughter and flashed the ring about the room.

Ole shook himself free and went to his bunk, heartbroken.

The game broke up quickly, no one caring to stay around such a disheartening affair. Tyler was the last to leave, but he had not spoken, not even to say how he had seen Stankovich deal the first two cards from the bottom of the deck and steal the man's wedding ring.

Later, Stankovich went over to him as he sat on a deacon's bench, taking off his boots. When he was satisfied that they were alone, Tyler said, "It doesn't seem right to take a man's wedding ring like that, over a card game."

"The man was a fool, a sucker," Stankovich glared at him. "He's a sheep and I'm the shearer. This," he said flourishing the ring, "will add its value to my purposes. Do you understand, that?"

"1 guess," Tyler muttered, but he didn't.

"Young man, the game I play is not for the weak. Nor the timid. Nor for the ignorant fools who are washing ashore every day. I promise to give back America to the men who built it; to wrest it away from the leeching immigrants who now suck its blood. To hold it back from the men like that dumb Swede who fled their homes rather than stand in revolt against their own tyrannies. Do you understand now? Do I sound like a bigot? You ask me, so I tell you. There is not room in my empire for the unclean brethren. There is no room for those who suck at the breast of other men's toil. Do you hear this? Do you now understand my dream?"

Tyler turned his back on him.

"Do you believe in my dream?"

Tyler had finished undressing and crawled into his bunk, leaving the question unanswered. Stankovich stood up and whispered into his ear.

"You will, my son, you will."

Moments later Sullivan came in the door, called "'Dat's all, boys!" and blew out the lights.

Seven

*T*he days wore into December. The crews were in heavy cutting now, up on the ridges where the white pine grew tall and majestic. The woods were alive with axes and saws, the cries of "Timberr!" and the crashing of trees; the grunting of men, the snorting of horses, the tinkle of chains and the grinding of sleighs on the ice roads. The roads had been extended as far as the contract allowed and there was a steady flow of logs pouring through the camp and down to the rollway at Skunk Creek.

There had been little turnover of men after the first two weeks and Tyler was still with the Stankovich group. Socrates thought that because Mike didn't trust Stankovich, he was counting on Tyler as Socrates' protege, to report any talk back though the old cook; talk that might allow Mike to send the foursome down the road. That wasn't Mike's motive at all. Nor would it have done any good. As it turned out, Tyler was keeping his own council. As a young and liberal thinking kid, he had trouble disputing the philosophy Stankovich was spreading even if his language was vulgar and egotistical. He held Stankovich in no great esteem. Indeed; there were many in the camp that he admired more simply because of their work and quiet dignity. But he found many of the dark man's words comforting when held up against the harsh reality of the camp life. Tyler's own upbringing had been soft and luxurious. He could find no justification for the depravity in which he now found himself, no comfort in its base crudeness. Even Socrates' daily quotations, so pointed in their subtle attacks on Stankovich's methods, didn't carry enough weight to refute the other man's sermonizing. One emanated from the reality of life, the other from old Hebrew mythology. Stankovich spoke the words necessary to sooth his ego and inflate his pride.

"That Stankovich," Socrates warned one day, "talks a good spiel about the working man, Tyler. Dignity and all. Myself, I see his kind already written off in the Good Book."

"How so?"

"'If anyone will not work, neither let him eat. For we hear that some among you are leading an undisciplined life, doing no work at all, but acting like busybodies.'

What do you think, son?"

"Why? You think he's a busybody?"

"I asked you."

"I haven't thought about him much. He talks a lot. Besides, who says that was written for Stankovich?"

"Who says it wasn't? I think that's about all he does is talk. And eat. He sure ain't much of a lumberjack. He reminds me of a guy that got hired into my camp out by Remer once."

"A story?"

"A lesson in life. This guy went out in the woods and began attacking a tree with his axe. He chopped all the way around so it looked like a beaver had gone at it. So the boss sees this and goes over and asks him which way he thought it was going to fall.

'How the hell do I know?' said the chopper. I'm a woodcutter, not a prophet."

"I suppose he got fired, too?" Tyler was thinking of Perfessor.

"Suppose right. That's not the lesson. You ask me, if Stankovich is a better prophet than a woodcutter. Follow the wagging tongue, men." Socrates demonstrated by sticking out his tongue and rolling his head. "He was hired on as a woodcutter, he should cut wood."

"All right, I understand. So how do you think a man should lead?"

"A man, Tyler? Why, all the real men I know lead by what they do more than what they say. They lead by showing here's how we do it; watch me and do likewise. That's how Jesus led his men. Your Stankovich seems to stand back and say do this, do that, you sweat and I'll watch from the comfort of the water bucket. Know what I mean?"

"You're saying that the biggest and the toughest should be in charge, then?"

"Hell no, I'm not. But then again, maybe that's right, if they use that toughness properly. Here, you got to be that way just to hold up. You don't find any soap boxes in the woods, and a man who uses a stump to speak from is only talking off of yesterdays work. You think about that. You think Mike Sullivan only cares about the work. Would it surprise you to know that he gives half his pay every year to those in need?"

"It would, and why do you call him 'your Stankovich'"?

"Yes, why would I? Maybe you can answer that."

"But what he says is true, a lot of it, anyway. I look around here and see things exactly as Jennifer said they'd be. Rootless men with no future. Working until they die. Is that right?"

"A man's existence decides its own value, I think. I think what each man does is the measure of his value. Does, not says, Tyler. And, I think you're starting to talk a bit like a Wobblie."

"So now it concerns you how I talk?"

"Not just concern, son, it frightens the crap out of me, to be honest. You got to think what you believe, but don't miss the big picture either."

"And what the hell is the big picture?" Tyler challenged him. He was tired of being preached to.

"Ask anyone of these men, Tyler. They're here because they got no place else to go. If it weren't for the camps, most of them would be bums. At least here, they have a bed, good enough food, and work to give them dignity. If you got the stomach for one more of those Hebrew myths, I'll tell you how Ecclesiastes fits my idea of life."

"Go ahead, if you want to talk, I'll listen. I'm getting good at that."

"Now, don't be sour, boy, cool off a little and you could learn something valuable.

Then Socrates reached into his marvelous memory and drew out the fabric of his being: *"'Here's what I have seen to be good and fitting: To eat, to drink and enjoy oneself in all one's labor in which he toils under the sun during the few years of his life which God has given him; for this is his reward.'"*

The simple words silenced the reticent youth for a while. When he finally responded, he simply said, "Then that's all there is? That's the great reward?"

"For me son, that's all there has to be. For the others, that's probably enough."

They had been taking a Sunday walk. They had just crossed the little bridge that the horses had crashed though and were reentering the camp.

Down in front of the bunkhouse were groups of lumberjacks engaged in the Sunday relaxation. They weren't doing much of anything. Johnson, Oregon Kid and Rube were throwing axes at a log. They had chopped a notch and placed a sliver of wood in it, then paced off fifty feet and were trying to see who could split it. It was a skill many lumberjacks perfected out of boredom and constant use of the tool. Rube threw and imbedded his axe four inches off the mark. Tyler and Socrates watched for awhile. Finally Tyler spoke again.

"Look at that. These men are just sitting around waiting for tomorrow. Then they can go back out and break their backs again. That's no future. Just a lot of sorry past."

Johnson took hold of a double-bit axe, licked his finger and drew it over the shining edge. He hefted the handle to find the balance point. At that moment Stankovich came out of the bunkhouse and began to walk across the yard, oblivious to what was going on. Johnson lifted the axe, drew it alongside his head, and threw just as Stankovich moved alongside the mark on the log. The axe tore through the air, passed within a foot of Stankovich's head and split the wood chip. Stankovich jumped back so quickly he lost his footing and fell. Then he screamed at Johnson as he picked himself up and ran off.

Socrates thought that was pretty funny. "Of course, life does have its moments," he said. If Johnson had wanted too, he could have split that ape's skull and no one would have sworn it wasn't an accident. The man does know how to send a message. Funny how things even up after awhile, isn't it?"

"Well, it's not enough for me." Tyler left him and walked back to the bunkhouse.

"I don't need it, anymore," he threw over his shoulder.

"No," Socrates agreed disgustedly, "and I guess you don't need me anymore either. Aw, good riddance, boy." He spat and went over to join the axe men.

Eight

For days on end, they slogged their way through a snow filled bog, trying to get through the huge stand of white spruce that seemed to go forever. The butt logs, often twenty-four inches in diameter, buried themselves in the snow and peat moss when they fell. Double and even triple teams of horses could barely drag them clear. Many trees fell in such awkward circumstances that they had to be abandoned.

Hazel brush whipped at their faces and hidden deadfalls made the footing impossible. The trees were heavily limbed and demanded all of Tyler's energy to clean the trunks off and clear the path for the skidder. Even so, he stayed far enough ahead of his fellers that he also did more than his share of bucking and notching for the cutters. The other men in the crew let him do as he pleased. The more work he accepted, the more they were willing to forgo.

Tyler was aware of the inequity of the labor and often said so to the other men of the crew. He was becoming as caustic and irritable as they.

One day Tyler had four trees notched and ready to fell and was working on a fifth. The fellers behind him had moved up and dropped their next tree but in their carelessness failed to shout a warning. At the last second Tyler saw the shadow of the falling tree cross him and looked up. He dove alongside a stump as the falling spruce crashed down, burying him in a tangle of branches and needles.

Stankovich came running and worked his way into the tree. He was met by a furious Tyler.

"Are you all right, boy?"

"Out of my way, I ain't your boy!" Tyler's anger tore through the afternoon air. He pushed past Stankovich and went over to the two fellers.

The one had a bemused look on his face. Tyler was covered with snow and needles. "Well, well. He looks a little green, don't he," the man joked.

That was all he had time for and the other didn't get to say anything. Tyler knocked one down with a right to the jaw and, grabbing the other by the neck, he drove him to the ground and started beating him mercilessly.

"You almost killed me," he screamed! "I going to break your fucking neck!"

Stankovic stopped him in time to save the man's life.

"Easy, there, easy! It was an accident."

"Accident, hell! These men have been goofing off ever since I've been here and I'm not going to take it anymore! Do you hear me! I won't put up with it!" He went at the man again, but Stankovich held him back. But he also saw the wisdom in siding with Tyler. The boy was just mad enough to report the incident to Sullivan and, even if Stankovich had Tyler thrown out of camp for fighting, Sullivan would be quick to send them along with him.

"You're right, you're right! That was damn inconsiderate and you're lucky to be alive. If it happens again, I'll be the first to put an axe handle up against the man's skull."

Tyler was eventually mollified, but rather than correcting the situation in the group, the incident only made things worse. Tyler took to doing his own swamping, felling and bucking and let the rest of the crew do theirs. Thus the drop in the production became even more apparent.

Stankovich had difficulty reading Tyler's loyalty. All of his followers were generally loners with surly reputations. They often questioned Stankovich's speechmaking, asking when talk would turn to action and change their lives for the better. To an outsider, Tyler would seem to fit right in. Stankovich saw something more and it caused him concern. The boy was smarter than the others. Most lumberjacks would consider an argument and if they accepted it, that was that. Tyler on the other hand, was smart enough to read both sides of the coin, then question and evaluate. He could discern the subtle shifting of positions and emphasis.

That made Tyler less than dependable in his scheme. And yet, he knew Tyler was keeping his confidence. If not, Sullivan would have chased him out of camp long ago based on Tyler's say alone.

Stankovich decided the question of his loyalty would probably not be settled until the last moment, and that made him feel better. Young men, he knew from experience, acted impetuously and in doing so, always seized the most emotional and impossible causes to fight and even die for. It was as Napoleon had once stated that it was amazing what men would do to win a piece of ribbon. Well, the cause of the Wobblies was all of that and come the moment of truth, Tyler would have to acquit himself. If not, it would be as Stankovich instructed his inner circle:

"We will winnow the chaff from the grain and the chaff shall be thrown into the fire. There shall be no brothers, there shall be no sisters, only those who believe in me and keep the faith with me shall be given shelter."

In the depths of his heart, Stankovich feared that Tyler might eventually supplant him in leadership, a thought that had not escaped the boy either.

Stankovich and his men were becoming intolerable for Sullivan. He hated the thought of losing any crews, even a marginal one, but rumors of goldbricking and dissatisfaction kept circulating and he knew that, if Stankovich was the organizer he thought he was, then he would soon force his hand in the matter. Thus he waited impatiently for an opportunity to reassert his control over the camp.

It came in the second week of December. Heavy snow had fallen for four days, shutting down the roads and much of the logging. Most of the crew was turned out to shovel and plow.

The hay road to Craig was covered with drifts of five feet in places blocking all attempts to bring in fresh supplies. The camp was isolated and, as time went on, Socrates had to resort to using more and more canned meat.

In a ranking of disgusting food, canned meat was second only to a straight diet of sheep or venison. It came out of the can gray or even blue, smelled and tasted of tin. It consisted of the poorest cuts of beef, if it happened to be beef at all, which was why the men simply called it gray meat. As the quality of the food went down, the restlessness of the men rose and gave Stankovich the opportunity to make his play for control of the camp.

The men had just come in from a back-breaking day of attempting to open the roads. Sixty men had shoveled nearly four miles of hay road, only to find on their way in that the wind had driven in enough new snow to obliterate much of their work. Sullivan and a smaller crew were still out, fighting their way through the fresh drifts. They were exhausted, famished and at the point of mutiny. Supper was sparse and made around their emergency rations: canned horse meat, green boiled potatoes, and bread from wormy flour. The coffee was made from old grounds and 'a dirty sock'.

The men ate quietly as usual, but there was an undercurrent of resentment. Forks stabbed at the cruddy food. Coffee cups rattled on the table out of synch to their normal rhythm. Here and there came an occasional murmur, a quick and nasty epithet. Back in the kitchen, Socrates could feel the tension. He understood the mood and even shared their irritation to a point, but the situation was quickly going past that.

Old Mike wasn't much help. "How in the hell am I supposed to make mulligan stew like you says when there ain't no carrots. Huh? How you figure that? Okay?"

"Mike, I know there ain't any carrots in camp. Just keep your mouth shut and do the best you can, will ya?"

"We got cabbage, Mike," Spooner suggested.

"You got a recipe for rock and cabbage soup you'll want for tomorrow I suppose too?" Mike retorted.

"You don't put a lid on it we'll be having head cheese made out of that bump on your shoulders, you old fool."

"Don't you be taking your crap out on me," Mike said. "I didn't do nothing. Okay?"

"Than keep doing nothing quietly, understand?" Socrates hissed. He was hoping to get through one more meal and then hear from Sullivan that the road was open again. "Who's side are you on, anyway?"

"I'm on the side of my belly, smarty pants, and my hide if you wanna know the truth. I hear things. They ain't good. Okay?"

"What have you heard, Mike?"

"I never been in one but I heard that when a crew goes mad and wrecks a camp, they always kill the cooks. Okay?"

"That's crazy talk, so you just keep it to yourself. You hear me?"

"I'm just sayin' what I'm thinking. And I'm thinking there's not much stretch left in the suspenders. Somethings gonna drop."

"So you said it," Socrates snapped. "Now button it and cook. There ain't gonna be any trouble. Understand?"

"Sure, sure. Just what in damnation am I supposed to cook? Shoe leather?"

Halfway through the eating, Stankovich seized his opportunity. He threw down his spoon and stood up. "This slop is not fit for pigs!" he shouted. "I will not eat it!" The words shot through the room like a thunderbolt.

The chewing stopped and heads went up. The silence held the weight of an anvil. The men were stupefied at Stankovich's insolence. The tension hung in the air like a storm cloud about to break into a raging fury. The crew looked to Stankovich and then to Socrates. Socrates knew he had to act quickly. He came around his stove and stepped into the dining area, a cleaver in his hand. There was a duel of stares, but before another word was spoken, Stankovich spat on his plate and stomped out of the mess hall. Three others got up and followed him out. One man took his grub and heaved it against the wall. Then another dozen did likewise. They were outside and halfway across the street, standing in a tight, defiant circle by the time Socrates and Rube got to the cook shack door. The rest of the men were filtering out behind them, the uncertainty of their loyalty made the two extremely uneasy.

"You men," Rube called into the moonlight. "What do you think you're about out there?"

Stankovich was ready. His audience was in place. "We're about to see some changes in this camp, we are! We are tired of your slavery! We've had enough of this work and enough of this slop you call food. Men have been poisoned with better food than this."

Socrates was spitting tacks, but Rube cut him off.

"So, what do you mean to do about it?" Rube demanded. His feet spread and solidly planted beneath his broad shoulders. His hands were on his hips and his jaw was set and thrust at Stankovich. From a lifetime of experience, Rube knew the importance of a bold front, but for the life of him he sorely wished Mike came back soon.

"We mean to propose a new order for this camp and all other camps like it. We want representation for the men. We want relief and, by God, we mean to have it." Stankovich was waving his arms and stomping around in a circle.

Socrates was incensed by the desecration of his kitchen and the insults to his cooking. He called him out in a voice that echoed with the righteousness of Moses himself, "The Lord God says, 'In the *sweat of thy face shalt thou eat thy bread, until thou return to the earth out of which thou wast taken.'* My food is more than the likes of you will ever earn, you worthless Wobblie or tramp or whatever name you be truly worthy of. If it's dust you're hankering to become, I'll be happy to oblige you." Socrates stepped off the wooden board-walk of the cook shack, but Stankovich brought him up short. He pointed at Socrates, the fingers rigid and spread like as if he were casting a spell.

"You hypocrite, you degenerate old man! You talk of prophets and accuse me of being a weak one, but I quote with the authority of the prophets, for I am a prophesy fulfilled! For we," he swept his arms about him, indicating the men at his side, "we are the living presence of that which was written. We are the Four Horsemen of the Apocalypse! We are the issue of the first seal of the retribution of God and of the second, third and fourth seals. We are the white horse of Conquest, and the red horse of the Great Sword and the black horse of Famine. And I myself," he stopped to draw deeply of the cold night air, his face contorted, red and dripping with sweat even in the cold night air. His eyes shined malevolently in the glow of the cook shack door. "1 am the fourth horseman of the Apocalypse. I am the pale-green horseman! I am death! I have been given power over the four parts of the earth, to kill with sword, with famine, and with every form of disease and every beast of the earth! I am sent to do the will of God for all mankind!"

His voice rose to a crescendo, and then he simply stared at the men confronting them. Even his believers were dumfounded.

Spooner whispered, "What the hell is he talking about?"

Rube spoke first, under his breath. "Bullshit, bullshit, bullshit," he muttered and then in a loud voice so all could hear, "That's bull-shit!" He started to go after him but this time Socrates caught his arm and held him back.

"No, Rube," he cautioned, "That man is crazy. We do something now and there's gonna be a lot of bloodshed, mostly ours. We have to wait for Mike."

Socrates guessed that Stankovich may have reached more men than were standing beside him. As it was, there were very few that could be counted on; himself, Rube, the three straw bosses and a few others. At best, most of the other men would just stand by and watch. They would obey whoever gave the orders and laid the best table. And the table that Socrates had been setting lately was nothing to brag about.

Stankovich had twenty men gathered tightly about him; most of them illiterate and unable to speak more than pidgin English. In a fight, though, an axe handle spoke many languages and every man in camp had fighting experience of some kind. There was no telling how many more were sitting on the fence waiting to see which way the wind was blowing.

It was a standoff, the two sides continuing to stare at each other for some time. Stankovich had hoped that his speech would enflame the others enough that they would rush the cook shack and save him the trouble of being the first to taste Rube's fist. But they were uncertain, undecided.

An assault from the camp leaders would work in Stankovich's favor because the momentum was his. But Rube and his men refused to come down from the cook shack porch. They sensed the strength of that poor, little piece of high ground and dared Stankovich to come take it. The stalemate went on for several minutes with each side hurling threats at the other.

Finally, one of the bull cooks disappeared into the cook shack and emerged with a rifle, kept to protect the larder from bears, wolves and thieves. He handed it to Rube who chambered around and pointed it at Stankovich's heart. He stared at the weapon, reassessing the situation.

"Do you intend to shoot me, then?"

"1 intend," Rube answered, "to shoot whoever thinks he's going to have the first turn at me. I just hope it is you."

"You are a coward."

"So be it. My woman would say I was being practical. Where will you have it? In the chest or the head?"

Stankovich was in check. He knew Rube would absolutely shoot him if necessary and there was no law that would punish him for doing it. In a camp, the boss had almost absolute authority in matters like this. His dream was one of conquest, not martyrdom. He had to save face and perform a tactical retreat before his support faded. He decided to husband his strength and try to incite his men enough to do the job for him. Soon the camp would sleep and then he would strike.

"That will change nothing," he challenged Rube. "Come for us if you will. If you are a man, then come like a man, not a faceless bully hiding behind that gun." With that he turned from the line of fire and led his men in the direction of the barns. Rube lowered the rifle and wiped his hand over his eyes.

"You should have shot the bastard," Schnaps said from inside the cook shack. "Yes. But I couldn't shoot a man who just stood there. He didn't come at me. If he had, I would have shot him for sure and felt no sorrow over it, but it would still be a hard thing to live with."

"No," Socrates agreed, "He's crazy but he's still too smart for that. But put the rifle in his hands, and your mother would be saying prayers over her favorite son's grave."

Rube nodded and handed the gun to Schnapsie. "Hide it well, but keep it close. There may be work for her yet. Are there any other guns in camp?" Guns were a common item in a logging camp. Men who had rifles brought them in and used them for hunting or target practice.

"There's two over in the bunkhouse," Snoose said. "Old Hoss and Red's. They're okay."

"Just the same, go get them so someone who's not okay doesn't get any ideas." Snoose and Spooner ran down to the bunkhouse and returned in two minutes with the carbines. Rube took his men back into the cookshack and waited.

An hour later, Sullivan and Johnson returned to camp. Mike jumped off at the cook shack while Johnson drove the team on down to the stable. By the time he came running back, his eyes wide with alarm. Socrates and Rube had briefed Mike on the dinner revolt. It brought a relief of sorts for Mike. He wasn't used to having unsettled accounts gather around him. All accounts would be settled tonight.

"How many?" Mike asked Johnson.

"Well, I t'ink I saw about fifteen or twenty. It was pretty dark and there might be more in the corners. They have a lantern, but it was dim, by golly. That dark man Stankovich was talking to them like a Baptist preacher, really stirring them up. I saw a crazy man once and he talked like that. I'm for thinking if they can't take over the camp, they'll try to take the horses and light out."

"He's crazy all right," Socrates said. "Sick is what he is. Wobblie talk but there's not any sense to it. He's got everything all twisted. Four Horseman and everything. Blasphemy!" He spat out the words.

"How many were there at dinner, Socrates?" Mike asked.

"There were upwards of a couple dozen. They might quit by morning. Maybe they'll get froze out."

"Wobblies like to play with matches. I don't trust them not to burn the hay," Mike said.

"We could lock the bunkhouse door, if nothing else than to keep the others inside," Rube suggested.

"That might set them off. A door won't hold back angry men."

Mike looked around at his people. There were about fifteen men in the cook shack, a few outside the door. Some were hankering for a fight but there was no way to tell which way they'd go, if any, when it started. Some guys just liked to fight anyone. And then, many were the farmers who logged in the winter. Not the kind of men to fight dirty if at all. The last thing he wanted to do was set the camp upon itself. It was only the head of the serpent he had to cut off.

He looked at Rube. "I would be grateful if you and Red came down with me."

Red was a beefy teamster and trustworthy. Both men agreed without hesitation.

"I'll be at your side, if you'll have me?" Paddy the Pig sat nursing a cup of coffee. "Your choice," Mike nodded. "I'd most welcome it."

He turned to Socrates. "Where's your boy?"

"Tyler? He ain't mine no more, Mike. He's got his own mind now."

"Is he theirs? Is he with them?"

"Yes and no," Johnson said. "He's hanging around outside with three or four others in the shadows."

"Where will he stand, Socrates?"

"I honestly don't know, Mike. I honestly don't know." He resented being so closely associated with Caldwell. "Hell, he wasn't even here at dinner. He was out with you. They've been talking, that's all I know. I'm hoping he didn't realize how insane that bastard is."

From Stankovich's prophet remark Socrates knew Tyler had betrayed his confidence, but this he kept from Mike.

"Tyler Caldwell from Chicago. He still has a good name." Mike nodded to Paddy.

"You watch him, all right? If he gets out of hand, we have to do for him like the others."

Paddy accepted the order reluctantly. He liked Tyler in spite of his propensity for dumping his own failings on other people. But he liked and respected Mike more. "I will."

Sullivan stood and walked to the door.

The Oregon Kid was waiting there. "I'm here if you need me," he said.

"Come along," Mike answered, "You take the little ones we throw out to you."

The Kid fell in behind the group.

Schnapsie took the rifle and held it out to him. Sullivan waved it away. "Take that piece and unload it. We're hunting men, not animals."

They went down to the stable; Sullivan, Red, Rube and Paddy shoulder to shoulder. Behind them came Socrates and his cooks, Schnapsie, Snooze and the Oregon Kid. It wasn't much of an army. Tyler was at the barn, quiet and confused; hanging on the edge of the group, refusing to make eye contact with them. Like Judas, thought Socrates, trying to make his decision.

When they reached the barn Mike took the lead, stopping just inside the doorway. The light was dim but enough to make out the men. Stankovich and his soldiers were sitting on horse blankets, gathered about the lantern as if it were a campfire. Stan was in a frenzy, working them up to a fighting mood with his preaching. His shouting was loud enough to be heard clear over at the other end of camp. The horses were spooked; stamping and shying nervously at the ruckus.

One of Stankovich's men was wrapping a rag around a stick of wood. A can of kerosene was close by.

When Sullivan stepped into the barn Stankovich's harangue came to an abrupt halt. Mike looked into the eyes of his men and saw the smouldering anger, but also the confusion and hesitancy. Stankovich' s eyes were fixed and distant. They bored through Mike rather than focusing on him.

"So," he said, jabbing his fingers at Mike. "It is the Satan, himself."

If the lunacy in Stankovich's words bothered Sullivan, he didn't show it. "If there be any devils in my camp," retorted Mike, "then we best get them out of here. Is that also your intent, Mr. Stankovich?"

"By the righteous power borne of slavery's unholy oppression, we will drive out the unlawful master."

"Fine," Mike nodded. "It comes to an end tonight."

Stankovich's three disciples were ready to fight. There were twelve with Stankovich. Fewer than he expected. Mike hoped, they might still be won back with the right words. But he would not negotiate with a man past the edge of sanity. Stankovich had crossed an invisible but clearly defined line. The camp could tolerate but one boss and that boss was Mike until someone more powerful took it away from him. If Stankovich had that power, than Mike would force him to show it. The law was unwritten but clear; if Sullivan went down and stayed down, the leadership would change hands. Whether or not one of his lieutenants would pick up the mantle did not concern him.

He considered the odds. Aside from himself, he had four that could be counted on. Socrates and the cooks would do little more than add confusion and probably need some help themselves. He wanted to cut them down a bit.

"You there!" Mike spoke to the men standing in the back of the circle. They began to fidget uneasily. "You there!" he commanded again. "Listen to me now!"

Stankovich cut him off. "Those men are mine! Speak not to them unless it be through me."

"No!" Mike roared, the rage in his voice rising to match that of his challenger.

"Their X is on my time book! Now what say you men? Do you stand with this flaming idiot or with Hungry Mike?"

It was silent. Even if they did understand the torrent of words being thrown at them, they were still undecided as to what to do. Mike took another step forward. "You men get out and we forget this happened. Git!" He waved his arm towards the door. There was an interminable five seconds of hesitation. Then they moved. So did Stankovich.

"No!" he screamed and jumped forward to bar their path. A match flared in the hand of the man with the torch. In an instant, he had touched it to the kerosene soaked rag and was brandishing the flaming club above his head.

"Come, Wobblies. We'll burn the camp to the ground and Sullivan with it!"

Stankovich screamed.

They rushed at Sullivan. The torch man swore mightily and swung at Mike's head. From the edge of the shadows, a man flew forward, grabbed the arsonist around the waist and drove him beneath one of the horses.

"You Judas! You betrayer, spawn of hell!" Stankovich screamed at Tyler.

Mike grabbed Stankovich, hit him hard and tossed him back to Red and Rube as the other two Horsemen rushed him. The Red Horse struck first, driving a fist into Sullivan's face. Mike took the blow and hit back, breaking the man's nose, the rush of blood justifying the name Red Horse. The other horseman tried to hit him but failed to connect. Mike stuck up a huge paw, caught the other man's fist, and crushed it in his own. Driven to his knees, the Pale Horseman could only watch in horror as Mike buried his free hand in his face.

The others methodically set about their work. Paddy connected for good measure on the Red Horseman and then grabbed for one of the immigrants who threw up his hands in a gesture of surrender. The other's, having little stomach for the brawl quit and went running from the barn. The Kid and the cooks tongue-lashed them back to the bunkhouse.

Paddy grabbed the Black Horseman and Tyler by their boots and pulled them out from under the horse. The Horseman continued to struggle until Paddy brought him down with a kick in the groin. He screamed and began to vomit, then quietly curled up in a fetal position. Paddy pulled Tyler to his feet and brushed him off before giving him a playful chuck on the cheek.

"What was that for?" Tyler asked.

"Nothing. Mike asked that I look after you knowing your affection for a scrap. I'm just grateful to the good Lord that you are all right."

"I'm alright but you just kicked that man's balls into his throat."

"Aye. Well you know all is fair in love and war."

In thirty seconds it was over, the mutiny broken like a dry twig. Stankovich and his three cronies, in the end, had stood alone against the camp command and so had they fallen.

They dragged the men outside and let them lie in the snow while the bull cooks gathered their property from the bunkhouse. They threw the bags at their feet and Mike passed out the sentence.

"That's all for you boys here. You can take a walk now." Twenty-one miles in the cold and dark and, God willing, they might make it to Craig alive.

"That's murder!" Stankovich cried in a voice considerably less strident than earlier. His face, was puffed and bloodied. Another man, thanks to Mike, was nearly toothless. The one Paddy had hit was spitting blood and holding his hand from the impact with

Hungry Mike's lantern jaw. Tyler's opponent was limping badly from Paddy's ungentlemanly boot. Still he managed to beg for clemency.

"For the love of God, man, not at night! We'll die for sure!"

"If you truly are the four Horsemen as you claim to be," Mike snorted, "than mount yourselves and ride into town."

"You can't mean it!"

"You have two minutes to clear this camp or these boys," he pointed to his own crew, "will go at you again. If you come back, I promise you will never leave again."

Stankovich painfully picked up his bag and wiped his face on it then, with a final command to his poor army, started off. The other three staggered after him. Four they had come and four they left. There were no others to walk with them. The rest of Stankovich's followers had slunk off in the dark and were cowering in their bunks, fearing for their jobs.

"Rube," Mike said. "Have the bullcooks take the Gabriel and watch the road tonight. Tell them to blow if that bunch comes back for more mischief. We do not need any horses in the bunkhouse again."

"I'll do that."

"And where is that Tyler lad?"

Tyler had been following Mike with Paddy and Socrates. He came up to Sullivan. Mike took a hard look at him but this time Tyler met his eyes, refusing to be cowed.

"Well," Tyler demanded, remembering the first night of icing the road, "was I tough enough to suit you?"

Mike liked what the kid had done, in spite of his belligerence. "Tough hasn't much to do with fighting, son. You made the right choice. It would have gone hard for you if you hadn't."

"Maybe," Tyler said with an attempt to gather his dignity.

"I saw a game of football in Duluth once," Mike said, his tone suddenly soft and conciliatory "What you did there is called a tackle, is it not?"

"Yes," came the hesitant response.

"It was a good tackle, I think. It kept him from burning my whiskers and earned my appreciation. Tell me, what made you do it?"

Tyler started to answer, but his words were inadequate. "I don't know, he tried to hit you first."

"Yes," Mike said, thinking that one day Tyler might understand his part in the affair. "You go off to bed now. There's work tomorrow."

"Yessir!" This time Tyler's reply had some pep to it. He broke from the group and walked towards the bunkhouse door.

"Lad?"

Tyler stopped and turned.

"Thank you. You did make the right decision. I'm proud you are part of my crew."

Tyler had everything riding on what had just transpired at the stable and, in the end, and not knowing exactly why, he had sided not only with the stronger but also the more righteous. He was just now coming to that realization. Sullivan's compliment struck him like a blow on the chest but he caught himself before answering and so tempered the response, "Yessir. I did at that."

Nine

With the departure of the horsemen, Mike had to realign his crews. He sent Paddy, the quiet Seifert, and Tyler up the Spruce Swamp Road. Tyler was put on a crosscut with Paddy, felling trees. Seifert and a raw farm kid teamed up while an old hand, Lumpy, became their swamper.

Lumpy had earned his name as a bunkmate in the old camps. He had a habit of rolling around so much in his sleep that his partner in the old muzzleloader bunk always ended up lying on him. He claimed that, as a mattress, he was just that: Lumpy. He had a good attitude and worked hard but like many lumberjacks was a crab.

Like Toad, Lumpy worked in the camps all winter. If he didn't get signed on as a summer caretaker, which he normally did, he'd find an abandoned homesteader shack somewhere and spend the off season picking blueberries and fishing. He neither smoked nor chewed nor drank, odd for a lumberjack, yet he was always broke. He sent all his money to care for an older sister living in a Duluth nursing home.

They made up a good crew. The men worked their way quickly through the big spruce of the low country, the trees that had frustrated Stankovich so much. From there, they traversed a small stretch of white cedar the boughs of which were a favorite browse of the white tail deer. Each morning as they came to the cutting, they would surprise a herd of the delicate animals feeding on the limbs of the previous day's cut. One morning, Lumpy took the carbine from the cook shack and killed a big buck.

"You shot a doe, Lumpy!" Tyler protested when the animal fell.

"Whatta ya mean, I shot a doe? Use your eyes, you little twerp!" Lumpy replied.

When they got up to the deer, Lumpy rolled it over. "Look there. You young city slickers don't know anything about deer."

"But it didn't have any horns?"

"Antlers, Tyler," Lumpy sniffed. "They drop their antlers after the rut you know. Shoot, you don't need antlers to tell a buck. Just wait till he takes a pee and watch where it comes out from."

They dressed it out and sent it back with the skidders. By the time they came in that night, Socrates had made a stew of it. They killed several more deer after that, which helped make up the shortage of food in camp.

They moved out of the low table and up into the pine-laden ridges. There they found the fabled trees of Pine Island, white and red pine trees so large of girth that two men would wield axe and saw for an hour to bring one down and leave a stump five feet in diameter upon which to eat their lunch. Unlike before, no one chose to use it as a soap box.

Pine Island had no high hills. The ridge they were cutting was only forty feet from crest to bottom. It was an ester from a long ago glacier, narrow but long, snaking off for miles into the northeast. Still, the view from the crest was spectacular; mile after mile of rich green conifer forest spreading out well into Canada. To the south, they could see the smoke from camp and hear the Gabe when it blew the noon hour.

Seifert pointed out the wood smoke of three other camps as well as Craigville; tiny camps and an obscure shanty-town squatting in the midst of God's immense magnificence.

"It's unbelievable," Tyler whispered. "It goes on forever, more than we'll ever log in our lifetimes."

"Look again," the moody Lumpy snorted, "but don't blink, it might be gone." "No," Tyler disagreed, embracing the vista. "We'll never cut all this. We couldn't."

"Yeah?" Lumpy retorted, "You don't know nothing, boy. I've seen a dozen forests like this in my time and they're all gone now." Lumpy sneered at Tyler's greenness. "A whole state."

Tyler looked to Seifert for support but got none. "He's right, son," Seifert whispered. "She's going away for good. This is the last of it for Minnesota, for us anyway. She won't be so green again in our lifetime."

There was sadness in the quiet Seifert's words that day, a melancholy borne of experience. Tyler looked over Pine Island and where he saw the future, the old lumberjacks saw only the finish.

Mike visited them several times a week, pleased at their progress. The loss of the Horsemen, rather than hurting the cutting, only generated more production from everyone and Lumpy knew Mike well enough to carry out chow to feed his crew two times over; once for them and once for Mike. The fires were another benefit of Lumpy's experience. Every day at noon he would build up a small fire and boil up a gallon of coffee. Tea, Mike called it, but he drank it up like blended whiskey.

Building a fire in the woods was a risky business, not because of the danger; forest fires were almost unknown in the winter, but because of what it implied.

Seifert, in one of his rare story telling moments related the story of a man he knew in another camp, in another time.

"The weather was terrible cold," he recalled bashfully, shivering at the recollection. "I bet it was maybe forty below. Who knows? The mercury had gone to Florida for the winter. It was a true blue snow winter. One of us, a swamper, was given to easy work and poor habits. He was starting to stiffen up bad from the cold so he went off under a balsam tree and built himself a big fire. Pretty soon three or four other guys, not me, thank God, joined him. Well, wouldn't you guessed it, just then along comes the straw boss, no cap, no mittens, mackinaw flapping wide open.

"He walks up to the men and says, well then, what's going on here?

"Well, they replies, we're cold. We were cold so we built a fire to warm up a bit. "Got the chills, huh? Well, if that's the case, you'd better go home, he said, we can't use you. If you can't work hard enough to keep warm, then I can't keep you. You're fired. And he did! He fired the whole bunch on the spot."

But Mike liked his "tea" and he liked his food and, if the logs kept coming in from the Spruce Swamp Road, the fire never caused a fuss.

December held no further incidents of unrest. The road was finally reopened after a herculean effort and supplies flowed in. Word came back that the Horsemen had made it to Craig alive and healthy except for their wounds and the loss of a couple frostbit fingers.

Tyler continued to think about the dark man long after his expulsion. He was slow in recovering from the trauma of the fight at the stables and more than a little surprised at his intervention on Sullivan's behalf. He had often thought that Sullivan was as much bully as leader.

If both Stankovich and Sullivan represented what he hated most about his father, then the removal of Stankovich should have transferred all of the boy's hostility to Sullivan. But it was more complex than that. Mike's great abilities in governing the camp commanded such respect, even Tyler's, that he found it difficult to assimilate both attitudes into his emotions. With his father it was so easy because Patrick Caldwell had called him out and disowned him in public. The lines of conflict were definite and irrevocable. Tyler was still unable to understand the differences and similarities in the two men.

He found even more contradictions in the people he had confided in. Jennifer had declared the lumberjacks to be homeless men, existing barely above the level of tramps. Socrates espoused the dignity and honesty of these drifting souls and declared the logging camps a safe haven for their vulnerable spirits. Tyler began to see the truth in each philosophy, but if he accepted their ideas, then he was also forced to accept much of what Stankovich said. Didn't we deserve a greater share in the wealth than thirty dollars a month so quickly consumed in whiskey and tobacco?

Tyler heard more stories of Wobblie violence; of equipment destroyed and men maimed and killed. He had discounted them at first as exaggerated and biased but he couldn't deny the attempt to burn the stables. The thought that he had nearly become an unwitting party to this act made him feel stupid.

He hated Stankovich for his insanity and how he had bought into it and he resented Sullivan for exposing the man's insanity. He resented Socrates for his damnable common sense, and he hated just about everyone else for their sheep-like submissiveness. In a great contradiction, he even hated Jennifer for her refusal to be submissive to the life that now held him in such turmoil.

The key, rationalized Tyler, was to retreat inside himself and never make himself vulnerable to such temptations and manipulation, again. He began to keep his own counsel, held away from public scrutiny. He became more and more of a loner, a man without friends. He was taking, without being aware of it, one more step towards the completion of Jennifer's prophesy. She was becoming his Cassandra, the truest prophet of them all.

Socrates had given him up, not out of anger, but of resignation. He had never sought the boy's company to begin with. Socrates was off the hook. Tyler could go one way and Socrates, as always, would choose another. He had other matters to keep busy with.

This was not to say that Tyler was a social leper. He was admired for his action in the stable and respected for his work in the woods. Nor was he always sullen and resentful. He used moods to suit his purposes, and like the moodiness of a child, it would often slip away and reveal the true Tyler Caldwell, the man-child deep inside him. He didn't realize it but the flame that had eluded him thus far was still flickering dimly deep inside him.

Ten

A week before Christmas, the camp began to take on a different appearance. There had been no indication that the surly lumberjacks would care to celebrate Christmas and Tyler had been content to bury himself in the exhausting work. In his own love-less house Christmas had always been more of a country club event than a family one anyway.

Suddenly, all about him, men who had whistled and sung bawdy songs heretofore might now be heard crooning a refrain from Silent Night. The suet feeders for the birds outside the cook shack received an extra portion and an air of civility and peace settled about the troops.

Then Tyler started strangely disappearing after dinner. He was spending his evenings down in the stables. Smithy gave him material and tools to use but, even so, had no idea what the lad was making. It had all the potential to be anything from a hat to a ditty bag.

"What're you making, boy," Smithy would ask.

"None of your business."

"I give you my leather and it's none of my business?

"You said the leather was worthless to you."

"Maybe so, but don't you think I got a right to know?"

"Smithy, if I told you, you still wouldn't know what it was, and if I explained it you'd tell everyone in camp."

"You ain't shy about it? It ain't a truss? You got a hernia?"

"No," Tyler laughed. "It isn't a truss. It's just a surprise and I don't want anyone to know."

"Well, why didn't you say so. I can keep a secret. It's the people I tell it too that can't keep secrets. I don't have to know a word." And as much as he still persisted, Tyler refused to tell him.

Three days before Christmas, the men cut a fragrant balsam and set it up in the bunkhouse. Socrates made popcorn and big men with fat fingers sat on their deacon's benches stringing it onto thread. Cherry red rose hips were added for color. Homemade ornaments fashioned from tin cans, wood, paper and fabric adorned the richly aromatic limbs. Through the decorating Sheepherder would play Christmas songs on his fiddle. When Sheepherder wasn't playing, Snoose would pull out an old harmonica and blow out a poor rendition of Away in a Manager. It was always Away in a Manager.

"For Chris' sake, Snoose," Schnapsie wailed, "that's terrible! Don't you know any other songs?"

"Shoot, I don't know this one either," Snoose said. "That's why I haf'ta keep practicing it."

Even the work-load gave way to the spirit of Christmas. Hungry Mike let the men sleep-in an extra half-hour during Christmas week.

On Christmas day, the men breakfasted in slippers, long johns and other manner of casual dress. Socrates laid out a magnificent breakfast of canned fruits, fried donuts, country sausage patties of his own creation and buttermilk pancakes. With only minor objection, he pulled out his bible and read the nativity story during the meal. The men ate quickly, out of habit, and then left the mess hall.

Some of them, the younger ones, went back to bed. Others, again from force of habit, went about their usual chores. They sharpened tools, mended leather and repaired equipment. For them a day of rest was simply a day of waiting for the routine of work to begin again.

Those veterans on the far side of youth pulled the deacon benches outside and sat in the glow of the warming sun. Like old cats, they leaned against the log walls of the bunkhouse, stretched their legs and arched their backs. They picked at their nails and scratched their beards and putzed with small talk. Conversations were slow, interrupted by long lapses, even snoring.

The temperature hit a balmy twenty-eight degrees. A bright cloudless sky spread a blue umbrella over them. "God's pause for the weary," Socrates called it. It was that, and so the morning passed. Lunch came and again the meal was uncommonly good. Somehow the cooks had come up with ten large turkeys and ten hams for the feast. Mashed potatoes, cranberry sauce, brown gravy and real buttermilk biscuits.

Finally, at 2:30 in the afternoon, when the crusted main street was softening and the day was at its warmest, Tyler came up from the stables with a bundle under his arm. He had a bashful smile on his face. Nearing the bunkhouse, he saw the Oregon Kid dozing in the open doorway of the bunkhouse.

"Hey, Kid," yelled Tyle unwrapping the bundle. "Get up, you lazy devil!"

The kid cracked his eyelids and pulled himself to a sitting position. A second later he was hit in the belly.

The Kid watched the strange object bounce and roll drunkenly away. He stared at it as if he expected it to get up and start walking. It didn't. Then he recognized it.

"My, god, that's a football!" He reached down and picked up the misshapen leather object. "No it ain't. Yes, it is!"

"Absolutely! It isn't Ivy League but it is a football," agreed Tyler. "Merry Christmas, kid!"

The Kid turned it over in his hands. "For me?"

"Hell, yes!" Tyler said. "Who else knows what it is? Besides," he added sheepishly, "you've been a good friend to me."

"Well, gee," the Kid blushed in embarrassment, "that's nice."

It was fat, heavy and ugly. Still, when the Kid threw the first wobbly pass to Tyler, it carved the air with a presentable spiral, nestling snugly into the young man's hands.

"Well, come on, Tyler, throw it back!" yelled Oregon.

The Kid came off the porch and began playing catch with Tyler. The other men perked up at their frolicking. Drowsiness soon gave way to curiosity, which in turn melted into interest. In short order, there were sixteen young men, Sullivan's finest, out on the slushy street receiving a crash course in football rules and techniques. Tyler and the Kid broke them into two groups. The distinctions between blocking and mugging; tackling and maiming were explained. A field was laid out using buildings as sidelines and tree lines as end zones. Plays were roughly interpreted as ending when no one was left standing and the ball, by natural conclusion, was to be advanced every way but at gunpoint. Teamsters and jammer crews were pitted against sawyers and swampers. Brawn against quickness. Boldness faced off against gile. The underlying natural competitiveness of the different work gangs rose to the surface as sure as steam on a lake in November.

Socrates volunteered to referee. He had never played, or even seen a football game, but insisted that, having read about them, he had a fair knowledge of how they should be conducted.

On the opening kickoff, a young Frenchman, lithe and nimble of foot, took the ball and slithered up field along the bunkhouse sideline. He reversed his course, then swept right towards Mike's office. The over-eager tree fellers, trying to converge on him, had left the rest of the field unguarded. Finally, only Tyler had a chance to bring him down. He made a diving attempt at the goal line, but the swift Pierre showed his corked heels and scampered to a score.

Fistfights broke out on the play and even Socrates got in a lick or two. In short order, he, the referee, was ejected for jumping on Old Sheepherder's back and knocking him down on top of two much smaller men, crunching them beneath his expansive girth.

"Listen, you knuckleheads," Tyler yelled, "you aren't in some town getting drunk now. This is football, not wrestling! Football. Get it?" Everyone nodded and went back to their brawling. Another quick session included a crash course on gentlemanly behavior and the game recommenced.

They reformed in the slop and Tyler's team took the ensuing kickoff. The ball skittered frantically along the ground until picked up by a man in the back row. The heavier lumberjacks drove a wedge up the middle of the field and may have scored themselves if the Oregon Kid hadn't vaulted over the top and dragged down the ball carrier in the shadow of the end zone.

Eventually, the game settled down into its basic elements. There were handoffs into piles of husky men, swift dashes for the flanks, an occasional attempted pass, a minimum of fakery and cleverness. Paddy the Pig led the blocking for Tyler. Tyler led for Paddy. Blocking and tackling merged into one. Shoulders, forearms and fists all served equally well for fending off would be tacklers. A well aimed kick was found to down a ball carrier as efficiently as an arm tackle.

Steam poured from the laboring men. They shed coats, then shirts and, in some instances, pants. The game went on without letup or pause throughout the afternoon. Halftime was ignored. Men who had to visit the john did so between plays. Old timers on the benches were the wildest of all, goaded on by the robust cheerleading of Snoose and Schnapsie. The players bestowed themselves with fanciful fictitious names dredged from their memories and imaginations.

Tank, Killer, Legs and Shifty tore into the defence. Tree, Rock and the Blocks of Granite held them off. Even Hungry Mike drew up a chair on the steps of his office and watched with curious amusement.

As the sun closed on its course, a fog began to creep into the clearing. Contained within the misty twilight, the game began to take on a surreal appearance. Their movements, slowed by exhaustion and poor footing, hung transfixed as in a Currier and Ives engraving. The grunts and groans reached out into the forest and echoed back at them. Even the trees watched in muffled curiosity at these big stoical men turned loose at childish play.

Tyler's team had fought back to tie the score and then scored again. Meanwhile, the Kid, using the greater speed of his men, led them on quick and unexpected scoring thrusts only to have the crunching blockers of Tyler's crew drive them time and again across their own goal line in retribution. The score became confused and meaningless. It was the physical dominance over each other that they sought; the feel of triumph, the ability to be macho in a ribald, exuberant way never permitted in their work.

The day had grown old. The sun stabbed the tops of the spruce and the slush was reforming in crusty hardness as quickly as the heavy boots could crush it down.

In the end it was Tyler's possession, fourth down and deep at his end of the field. Neither team had punted all day nor would one. Socrates stepped out on the porch of the mess hall, Gabriel horn in hand and blew a blast. Tyler guessed there was time for one more play, the most daring one of the afternoon.

He had one young swamper who possessed better than average speed and an endless silly grin. At the ends of very long arms hung a pair of enormous hands, fingers like the tines on a potato fork. He had spent the entire game with his arms in the air rushing the opposing passer and hadn't been used on offense at all.

"Farley," Tyler told him. "You go deep. Run around a little and then, go as quick as you can downfield. I'll fake run to the left behind Paddy. Everyone else go with me, but you, Farley, you go deep."

"Why should I do that, Caldwell? You're going to need some help."

"Because, you cushion head, I'm going to throw the ball to you."

"Oh. Oh! I like that," Farley exclaimed in sudden illumination.

They lined up over the ball. Socrates stepped up and put the horn to his lips and blew again. The signals were called, the ball rotated back to Tyler. He fled towards the sideline behind the flow of his protection. The teamsters surged forward to meet him. Farley ran over a small top loader and hid for an instant behind the bunkhouse woodpile. Then he took off. A deckhand saw him make the break and gave pursuit, but he was a step too slow, a shade to late.

Tyler stopped, slid on the ice and planted his skittering feet. He rotated his arm back and then forward high over his head at the same instant he was buried by tacklers. But the ball was in flight! It shot downfield in a great, arching, crippled spiral, casting no shadow in the gloom. It was a black dot in the twilight but twisted off to Farley's blind side. It might have been a game ender, a game winner. It might have meant bragging rights for weeks! But it was going to be too long!

Then came the bark of the rifle shot. The ball jumped sideways in the air and dropped softly into Farley's net-like paws. Touchdown! It had been blown out of the air by Mike Sullivan from the door of his office. Hungry Mike met the startled looks of the players, especially the glower of Tyler, and calmly ejected the empty cartridge from the carbine. He set it in the doorway of his office, shut the door, said, "That's all boys," and with more than a whisper of a grin on his bearded face, walked off to supper.

Socrates didn't bother blowing the horn a third time. Christmas was over and it was time to return to work.

Eleven

The weather stayed warm for another week, fueled by great blasts of Chinook winds that burst out of the northwest. It was the January thaw.

The ice road became too soft to haul over. In places it just disappeared as if it had gone from ice to vapor without melting to water first.

Mike sent out most of the teamsters with brushhooks. There was more than enough standing timber to keep everybody busy cutting, but a man marking time doing what he didn't like doing is an ornery man. The sawyers didn't like "those French hens comin' in and trashin' up our woods. Better they keep to the ruts so they don't lose their way " So they let the teamsters cut brush and limb the trees and make firewood for camp and do the hundred small jobs that go undone during the timber flow.

Evenings were mellower in camp in spite of the poor weather, because that "nasty brood had been swept out good" as Snoose liked to boast. The card games were more convivial and the stories more relaxed. Sheepherder played his fiddle every night and Ole rejoined the poker circle. The men had pretty much settled into their winter isolation. They had already passed through a good piece of it and could feel the downhill run to the spring breakup.

One evening, the talk turned to horses and teamsters.

"If you ask me, I say we got as fine a crew of horse drivers right here in camp as there is anywhere," said a man called Buck getting it started. He had come to camp with a matched team of black Morgans.

"Horsepoop," Liver Lips snorted, "there ain't a man here can hold the reins for some what I seen."

"So I'm asking you, then," Buck rose to the bait. "Tell us about your great teamster friends you says are so much better than us."

"Since you're gonna keep badgering me 'til I do, I guess I will. How about 'Gallopin' Bill Gavin? There was a sleigh runner for ya. He once hauled a load with forty-thousand feet on it out of the Akeley camp north of Bemidji. He had just two horses and a little bit of a tail wind. He worked them up from a heave to a walk and then a slow trot. Finally, when he come out on this big lake, he broke 'em into a gallop. I can still see them come blowing across that lake. Their shoes were chewing up that ice so fierce, they were striking sparks. I'm not just pulling your whistle, either! There were sparks coming off that ice!"

Schnapsie was laughing as hard as the next man, but he prompted Hoover to finish up old Gavin. "So tell them how he bought the farm."

"Oh, yeah! His speed killed him come by and by. He was bringing out another big load one time. Old Bill lost his grip on the ruts goin' down a small grade and when the sled plowed into a curb log, his chains busted apart. He could of jumped for sure but stayed on so he could keep whipping up the horses, just like Okie did here. Saved the team but when the logs broke loose, they rolled him out like a gingerbread man. They buried him between two slices of bread. Embalmed him with butter."

"That's good," Schnapsie agreed, "but that Gavin was more joke than jewel.

Anyways, he weren't no match for old 'Talkie'."

"Who's Talkie," Buck asked. He wasn't from Minnesota so all the names were new to him.

"Talkie. Einar Taakala. He's the only Finlander God ever made who could make a horse understand him. How he did it was he never said nothin.'"

"Well, how in the hell could you understand a man who never talked?"

"He figured folks who talk too much get misunderstood more than otherwise, so he'd just smile and nod, chirp and cluck, same to horses as to people."

"Where is he now?" Paddy wanted to know.

"Talkie? Oh, he's been gone now twenty, twenty-five years. He was walking in outta somewhere up around Squaw Lake. A little snow started falling and before he could shelter up, it blew up a blizzard. A trapper found him snugged up under a fir tree but it wasn't enough. He was blue as sky and hard as ice. Eyes were shut tight, but you know what?"

"What?"

"He froze with his mouth wide open. The trapper swore there was a pile of frozen words layin' all around him. Cuss words, prayer words, even 'How's the weather?' words. Seems he had a lot stored up in him and spilled it all out the last day."

Socrates dared to be the first to cut in on Schnapsie's tease. "Sure he was a character, boys, but that don't make him the world's best teamster."

"Who's your pick?" Buck asked.

"Well, I'll tell you," Socrates answered, filling his pipe. "Now, I don't have to think hard to come up with a name, 'cause to my reasoning, there's only one top driver ever lived in this country. Jack-the-Horse."

A murmer of assent went around the group. Other than Buck, only Paddy had never heard the man's name before, so he asked, "Who was this man, then, someone bigger'n a horse?"

Socrates settled back. The others were quiet. Jack-the-Horse was Socrates' nomination, so it was his story to tell. He struck a match and got the tobacco burning, then took three thoughtful draws off it.

"Oh, no, not at all. He weren't much bigger'n you, Patrick, not to say that isn't big, but he had a heart so big his chest could hardly hold it. And he was strong as a horse.

"Jack was a Frenchie, just like a lot of teamsters. But he looked more like a lumberjack: barrel chesty, big arms, hands. He could'a been Tyler here if he were twenty years younger. He could crack walnuts just like this." Socrates put an imaginary walnut between his thumb and forefinger and squeezed. "He had the darkest hair you'll ever see; head, beard, moustache. It was all black and curly. He always wore those big cruiser boots that come up to his knees and he wore a gold ring in his right ear. If anyone said anything about it, he'd just say, 'It's yours if you're man enough to tear it off.' A lot of fellas got their manhood sorted out, a few women, too, but he never lost his earring. "Anyway, he was sledding logs for some ugly boss many years ago. They were working an area around Marcel. The Gut and Liver had been laid that far then, but just as far as North Star Lake. They loaded the logs with cross-hauls and sledded them straight out to the railroad. See, there were so many streams and lakes in that area, it was like a whole spider web of roads. They'd just haul to the west and wherever they cut the G and L, they'd drop that load.

"So, Jack was doin' his hauling on these lakes and creeks, but, see, wherever you got water, you're gonna have otters and beavers and fish working that ice thin in spots."

"For god's sake, just tell the story, don't give us a lecture on the birds and bees.

"Oh yes? Snoose, what would you know about such things, anyway. You're too dang nervous. Go outside and pee if you gotta."

"Oh, shush! I can hold my water a lot better than you can hold the B.S."

"Then try holdin' your tongue, too, you old woman. Paddy here doesn't know this stuff." Socrates re-lit his pipe and resettled on the bench. Schnaps threw a couple more birch bolts in the stove. A chill was beginning to creep down the walls and across the floor.

"Like I said, Jack was hauling his logs. He had come through the woods and dropped onto this no-name lake and started across it. There was a snow cover; the weather was cold enough. Nothing should have happened. But, of course, it did. Maybe the ice started cracking, maybe not. I wasn't there. Surprised, Tyler?

"But, all of a sudden, the front of the right horse, Angel, dropped through the ice. The horse's head went under the ice and the sled crept up behind her just enough so she couldn't pull herself back out. The other horse, Satan, was scared as a sinner meeting St. Peter. He was busy holding his own, trying not to get pulled down with Angel. But being harnessed together, something had to give. And it did, all right. The poor Angel drowned and hung like a dead weight in the traces.

"Jack had jumped off right away and ran up to help her, but her whole body had gone down by that time and even a giant wasn't going to drag a thousand dead pounds out of a ice hole, but she were heavy enough to pull her partner down with her.

"When she went, he pulled out his knife and began cutting leather to save Satan. He was right down in the water, freezin' cold, slashing away, and when he finally cut the last trace Satan reared away from the rig. Jack held on to the lines and got dragged out. By now he must of weighed a thousand pounds, too. It froze on him quick; icicles were hanging off his ears and nose. They were a foot long on his beard. But he didn't worry about that. Jack just tied himself into that harness, looked his horse in the eye and said, 'Come, Satan, we'll pull her off now!'

"And they did! They dragged that big loaded sleigh off the lake and all the way out to the Gut and Liver. By the time they got there, he had boiled off all that ice water and his clothes were rock dry. The story got around so they named that lake after him. Jack-the-Horse. You can go look at it. Over there by Little Dick, south of Bigfork. You can go look at his tombstone too, if you want, down in Deer River." Socrates stopped and went to work on his pipe again. Finally Snoose couldn't hold back.

"Well, for cripessake, then, spit it out!"

Socrates gave them a little smile and went on. "See, Jack finally retired from the woods and took a job bartending down in Deer River. I think he owned a piece of the joint, too. It wasn't much, but it kept him around the men and the stories. He was a legend by then and his name was good for business.

"One night an Indian come down from Cass Lake and got drunk in Jack's place. Jack wasn't working that shift. Another man was. That guy finally got tired of this buck's shenanigans and kicked him out. Soon after that, Jack came on duty. Well, this indian fella was so mad, he goes on the warpath. He put some paint on his cheeks, gets a rifle and went back to the bar. He walked in the door and points the gun at whoever's standing behind the counter, which was old Jack by now. He shot him right in the forehead and killed him. The Indian hanged for murder but Jack was dead too. He had meant to kill the other guy. That's all."

"That was a good story," Buck agreed.

Mike blew in through the door and stomped his feet." 'Dat's all boys. Save the best lies for tomorrow. Weather's coming down fast." He blew out the lanterns and left.

That night, Tyler dreamt as he often did after getting a hard day's work and a head full of stories. He was pulling the sleigh across the lake. Suddenly, the snow-covered ice grew black and ugly. Huge rotten teeth appeared along the edge of a yawning icy mouth and swallowed him whole.

He was in the water! Under it! Fighting for air! A knife flashed through the black curtain of cold water. Leather ripped and parted. The harness fell free. But, instead of being pulled clear of the lake, Tyler felt himself sliding down, further into the blackness. He was deep underwater, suffocating. The pressure was collapsing his chest, crushing his eardrums. He was drowning! He had drowned!

He woke and sat up. His blanket was soaked with sweat. Tyler ran his hands over his face. He stared into the bunkhouse blackness, fighting to recognize his surroundings. He was back in camp, in his bed.

Slowly he lay back down and pulled the covers over his trembling body. He remembered the dream, the water, the panic and terror. Then the truth hit him! He wasn't Jack in the dream. He was the doomed Angel!

Twelve

*T*he next morning frost covered the ceiling of the bunkhouse and stood out in the chinking between the logs. The mercury had plummeted to twenty-five below zero. Rousted from bed, the men danced across the cold floor and paused at the washtubs only long enough to splash the sleepy crust from their eyes. They hurried to the cook shack and dallied over breakfast so long that in the end Rube finally stood up and called an end to the meal.

Sullivan set his men to work with a vengeance. Crews went down to the lakes with dynamite, blasted holes and drew water to re-ice the roads. Sleighs hauled sixteen hours a day bringing in the logs that had piled up at the landings. Supplies came in from Craig with coffee, chocolate, pork and beef and beans in hundred pound sacks. The camp was soon running on a full belly and Mike was happy.

But the reverie was short-lived. Out on the northwest trail, on the edge of a cedar swamp where the snow had drifted in deep, the warm weather had done no more damage than put a heavy crust on the surface of it. There was a grove of big white pine growing in a small tight depression. Nourished by a pocket of rich, moist humus, they had grown extraordinarily tall and heavy. It was hard to reach. A poor chance, old timers might say after such a snowbound grove was logged, "When the snow melts off, the stumps will make good bar stools." It would take four-horse teams to skid the logs. But Mike needed them taken out because the company had ordered it. The straw bosses knew the dangers of working in tight places with deep snow to flounder in. Trees could do funny things when they fell. They would spin like tops, bounce off each other like billiard balls, or loose a shower of dead, rotted branches on the people below.

The men knew the dangers, too, but when the bosses sent them in, they went. They went because Mike wanted the trees down and Mike was the boss. Now Mike was back in camp, waiting for one of his men to die and doubting the wisdom of his decision.

"Is he dead yet?" The man spoke the words as one might inquire about the chance of rain.

Sullivan had been staring at the ground. He was loath to respond but finally looked over at the man who had spoken to him. The swarthy lumberjack was waiting for the answer as though the question weren't really that important. Mike had no desire to talk now but he answered, thinking that was all that need be said.

"No, he ain't. Not yet." He spoke slowly, the words coming out grudgingly as though not saying them might change what was to be.

The man looked out into the forest. "It weren't me what killed him, you know."

Mike didn't lift his eyes from the ground. "No. It wasn't you." He already felt bad enough over his own part in the accident.

"There's some might say it was, Mike," the man said.

Mike didn't answer but looked out to the woods himself. He watched a whiskey jay work on a piece of fat hung in a tree out behind the cook shack, then turned his attention back to the ground. Anything but face the other man. With the toe of his boot, he began to worry a small chunk of ice into tiny crystals.

"They know it wasn't your doing. It just happened."

"If they do, I'll answer for myself."

"It won't, but if it comes to that," Mike said, "I'll not interfere." He was tired and in no mood for this conversation, but the man addressing him warranted his attention.

Sullivan watched the burly jack disappear into the stables. Hec was Irish, like Hungry Mike, big as a barn and dark like his ancient Spanish forebears. Timber Beast, years ago had chosen to sleep with the horses rather than in the warmer, more social atmosphere of the bunkhouse. He, even more than most other lumberjacks, rarely spoke. He lived totally within the isolation the forest provided. He was a woolly hermit. The words he had just exchanged with Mike would be the longest conversation the foreman would ever be able to recollect having with him.

Timber Beast rarely took sides in an argument, never siding with any opinion but his own and rarely bothering to campaign for that either. In the fight at the stable he had watched from the back of the hay pile, silent, uninvolved. If the barn had burned he might have helped to save the horses. Almost certainly he would have let the men fend for themselves. He lived in a prison of his own design.

But, like Sullivan, the Timber Beast was as hard on himself as he was on anyone else. Be it crosscut or double bit axe, he was without peer. He could cut two or three times that of any other man.

His latest partner, a husky young lad from Maine, had come to camp advertising himself as Tamarack Jack. In the bunkhouse he'd sung his song. "Call me Jack, Tamarack Jack," he said. "I'm a rip snorting son of a double bit axe. Timber is my middle name. Hard work is my fame. Where I come from, the tip of Maine, none ever cut more than me. Tamarack Jack, a crackerjack I be." But he was too young to be taken seriously and then a cat had five kittens on his bunk one morning and old Hoover had said, "Let's call him Maude, 'cause now he's a mommy." Tamarack Maude stuck. The young man protested at first, but a name well struck was a name that stuck and he accepted it in time.

The door of the office opened and Socrates stepped down into the yard and walked over to Mike.

"Is he dead yet?" Sullivan quietly asked, regretting at once his use of the Timber Beast's blunt words.

"Not yet," the old cook answered. "He's conscious and talking like a crazy man. Most boys you can't get them to recite their age. But I seen it before. You put a man on his deathbed and it's like cutting their head open. Their whole life pours out. Like he's afraid to die until that stuff gets out."

"What's he saying?"

"Oh, hell, he's been talking about his mother and how she'll never see his grave.

Then he started talking about a sweetheart in Michigan. I said, do you want me to write her for you? But he says, no, she'd not be likely to remember his name, anyway. I think, maybe, she's just a calendar sweetheart."

"I'll go back and sit with him," Mike said.

"1was thinking I should get back to the kitchen," Socrates said, but he didn't move. "It's hard, ain't it, Mike?"

Mike looked at Socrates. For a moment it appeared he would say more but all he could say was, "Yes, it's hard."

"Can I help?"

But Mike shook his head and looked away.

"I'd lighten it if I could," Socrates offered. He left for the cook shack while Mike walked back to the office.

They had put the young man in Mike's office when he was brought in from the woods. The other men in his crew had made a stretcher of poles and jackets and carried him in. His legs were paralyzed then and they rightly guessed a broken back.

Tamarack was conscious the whole time. They tried to be as gentle as possible, his burly companions, but, even so, he screamed so much, they had to put a glove in his mouth. But they held his hands so he'd have someone to share his agony with.

Now, he was lying on Mike's cot. Blood he had coughed up was splattered on the wall and over the blanket. The boy was talking to himself, fast but still intelligible. When he got closer, Mike realized Tamarack was saying the Lord's Prayer. Mike sat down on a stool and quietly prayed along with him.

"... and lead us not into temptation but deliver us from evil. For Thine is the kingdom ... and the power ... and ... the glory ... forever. Amen."

When Tamarack finished, he looked over at Sullivan and struggled for recognition. Finally he smiled weakly, relaxing his stare. No words passed for some time. Then, tears began to form in the boy's eyes and his jaw began to tremble. "I'm awful scared, Boss," he whimpered. "1 don't know how to do it," meaning how to die.

Mike reached over, his huge paw closing over the boy's own pale hand. Every year the big timber cost him one or more of his crew. Every year it became harder to deal with. At one time, they were all of the same age, he and his jacks. As he had gotten older, the men seemed to get younger. Mere boys, like sons now. In the end, their youth and strength was so puny against the power of the forest.

"I believe in God," said Tamarack. "1 swear. I believe in all three of them." He was talking about the Trinity. "I'm an altar boy." He said it as if it were still so. "Mike?"

"Yes, son?"

"Mike, do you believe?"

"Yes, son, I believe."

"Do you believe in the resurrection, too?"

"I do."

"Who taught you?"

"The priests, son. I, too, was an altar boy."

"I am, Mike. I am an altar boy."

"That's right, son. Try to rest easy." Mike could see the boy was having a hard time with the pain. But Tamarack wanted to talk.

"Promise me, Mike. Make an altar boy's promise. Promise … to bury me.

"I promise, son."

"Say it, Mike." Maude knew the practice of wrapping a corpse and putting it in a lake to save the work of thawing out the frozen ground for a grave. "Please."

Mike had trouble getting the words out. "I promise, son. We'll bury you like a Christian. We'll read the prayers. But don't carry those thoughts in your head now. You'll be all right."

"It's all right, I just wanted to … make sure. I know it don't make any difference really, I mean after you're … dead and all. Will you stay with me, Mike? Until after?"

Tears were running down his cheeks. "I don't want to be alone then it comes."

"You're not alone, son."

"Stay with me," he asked again.

"I'll not leave you."

Tamarack Maude had nearly broken the Beast's record. For twenty-seven days the two had worked together and the kid was holding on. By the end of each day he was sleeping in his boots, but he was holding on. He was a tough kid and getting stronger with each passing day. Some men wore down and others got stronger. Tamarack was one of the latter. He was quiet about it. It wasn't a matter of boasting that he was as good as the Beast. He knew he wasn't. If it weren't for the constant pressure of the Beast, he would of sat down long ago. But Tamarack Maude made an honest effort and it almost stood up.

"It … weren't the Beast that killed me, Mike." He was saying the words between coughing fits now. The blood from his lungs was over everything. "I was … tired, but that ain't why it happened."

Sullivan knew better, but he was proud of the lad for defending his partner. If he lay there cursing the Beast, he'd not be blamed for doing so. Teams, like horses, were only effective if they were evenly matched and well rested. Lumberjacks paced themselves to the length of the day. If a man became too tired, he was dangerous to himself and the others around him. Out in the brush and snow, to be slow to react could mean injury or death. To the Kid, it was death. There was a fine line between pushing a man and beating him. He wouldn't say the Beast had crossed the line. Maude could have quit at any time, as others had.

"Mike, are you there?" The boy's eyes were glazing over. "I can't see you."

"It's night, son. The room is dark," Mike lied.

"Tell them, tell ..." his body was wracked by violent coughing. But for the spilled blood, there was no color at all in the boy's face. "Tell them I was a good man."

"The equal of them all, Tamarack. As fine as the Timber Beast, himself." Mike took a towel and wiped the blood from the kid's face.

"Yeah ... as fine as the Beast." The boy repeated the glorious words. "That's going some ain't it?"

"Yes, son, that's really going some."

Tamarack relaxed and closed his eyes. His breathing became more regular again.

Perhaps he would sleep now and pass away quietly.

God knows, thought Mike, how long that old white pine had been standing there, waiting for its own end. Then the men had come to finish it off. The snow was well over their knees and hard to move in. At five and a half-foot diameter, the tree had been a true monster. It was the kind of tree the Beast, or any proud lumberjack would seek out, fell, and brag about. But there was no way to tell how sick it had been; how fractured its heart.

They couldn't have known that, after the saw had sliced nearly to the point of the axe cut, the old monarch would fail to fall clean. Instead, it had turned on its stump, ripping and tearing its few remaining inches of wood. In the twisting, it split. It started at the cut and shot up the trunk until fully half of the huge tree split off and jackknifed back along its other half. It threw itself directly at Tamarack Maude.

Even if he knew it was coming, he may not have been able to avoid it. As it was, he was standing in deep snow, his head down.

The Beast had yelled a warning. Witnesses attested to that. But the kid was too slow. He looked up, saw the tree come at him and, throwing up his hands in a futile effort to fend it off, had tried to turn away from it. He had taken just one, slow, tortuous step when it slapped him in the back. Right then he began his dying. His back was broken, his ribs were driven into his lungs and his right arm and shoulder were crushed. It was only because of his refusal to die at once that they carried him the mile back to camp and put him in Sullivan's bunk. A lot of men had met their maker in Sullivan's bunk. The unlucky one's that didn't die outright in the woods.

Tamarack opened his eyes and looked for Mike. He was blind now. Another rush of pain surged through him. His grip on Mike's hand tightened desperately as his body stiffened. His eyes closed again. He arched his back, incredible in his condition, breathed a last anguished sigh and fell back. There were no last words, no heroics.

After a moment Mike pried Tamarack's frozen fingers from his own, made the sign of the cross over the dead man and again for himself. Sullivan rocked back in his chair and covered his face with his hands. He could never bring them back.

"Tankja," he moaned, "I've sent you another child."

He pulled the blanket over the Kid's head, closed his eyes and went outside. At the door of the office he stopped. The other men in Maude's crew were standing there, watching him. Mike slowly shook his head and walked over to the cook shack. Entering it, he approached Socrates.

"Coffee?" the cook asked.

"The other."

Socrates didn't have to ask. He went into the larder and came out with the bottle of whiskey.

"I'll sit for you if you want," he offered.

"No, Soc, thanks just the same," Mike answered. "I have to keep a promise. One altar boy to another."

Mike took the bottle and walked back to his office. He stopped outside, removed the cap from the bottle and with a thumb and forefinger again wiped the moisture from his eyes. Then, as was his practice, he went inside to begin his vigil with Tamarack Jack.

Thirteen

*I*t was Tyler and Timber Beast. The young man they had started calling Bull because of the way he ran with a football was sent to stand across from the man they called Beast because he approached work like a huge, dumb animal. They were told to finish up the cutting in the grove that had killed Tamarack. From sunup to sundown they stood, joined by the steel band of the cross cut saw. There was no escape from the relentless monotony of the singing, seven foot blade. Again and again it flashed before Tyler's eyes as he strained to pull it from the iron grip of the Beast, but as soon as Tyler would rip it through the kerf, it would disappear again from the insistence of the Beast's tireless grasp. When the blade grew dull and useless in the frozen wood, the Beast would take another, for he always carried three into the woods.

The others had grown to respect the strength and determination of Tyler, the Bull, but their feeling toward the Beast transcended respect. No one, not even the most callused and hardened of men, wished to be served up to this raging woodcutter, this feller without peer, this destroyer of men. They knew of men who walked out rather than work with him and spoke of them in whispers of respect in the bunkhouse.

Tyler was not privy to the stories. They were afraid to tell him for fear it might break his spirit. This insulated him for a time from the truth of his hardship.

But money was quietly wagered on the match-up. A piece of chalk registered each passing day on the bunkhouse wall. The marks accumulated slowly, laboriously, as though they were being scratched out in blood rather than chalk. None of the men believed that Tyler could survive to thirty. No one ever had.

Tyler refused to talk about the work or acknowledge the marks but he noted them every day in passing. They became a testimony to his doggedness and determination. Every new mark was one more than most men had been able to record, one more than they expected of this hotheaded runaway. Each new mark made him hungry for another one.

He began to sit apart from the others in the evening. He had a cancer, inflicted on him by Mike Sullivan. To even associate with the lad may lead to a contagion for the next man. Tyler had the monkey on his back and every lumberjack knew that a monkey traveled fast.

The consensus was that Mike harbored a grudge against Tyler for his association with Stankovich and was determined to send him walking. Tyler knew otherwise, but wasn't sure and rather than face Mike over the matter, he let it fester in his gut and it stiffened his own resolve. Every day finished he considered another day of vindication for the young Bull, another day of embarrassment for Hungry Mike Sullivan.

Mike never thought of abusing Tyler or anyone else so. If he had reflected beyond the simple need to find a saw mate for the Beast, he might then have justified his action by the boy's need for further seasoning. In the final analysis, the kid was big enough and strong enough. He would be okay if he was tough enough; if not, then Mike would find another. Failing in this, Mike would be satisfied to let Beast cut alone.

The days wore on and Tyler again felt as though he had just arrived in camp. His body had to fight every night to recover from the punishment of that day and, even though his back and arms burned in agony, he didn't let on. He'd lay on his bunk and stare at the ceiling, listening to the stories, yet not hearing them. At night he would dream of the lake. The dream would wake him, trembling in the cold, dark bunkhouse, sometimes with a cry of fear, sometimes with a whimper.

Beneath him, Paddy would feel the movement and hear the cries. He knew what Tyler was going through but he said nothing. None of the men, including Socrates, who watched throughout as the father watched for his prodigal son, said anything. They could only watch and wait while Tyler fought his private battles.

Tyler was finishing up his second week with Timber Beast when the Reverend Amos Houghton arrived. He was still holding his own.

Even the Beast began to recognize the young man's spunky determination. Though he rarely talked other than to grunt and point, there were times when he would pause just before laying into the saw and look at Tyler with his coal black eyes. One time Tyler could have sworn that he saw the suggestion of a smile. When he smiled back he saw only a dark brooding stare that projected nothing.

But there was no camaraderie at night. Arriving back in camp, they would go to dinner and sit apart. Later, the Beast would leave alone, going down to the barn. The boy didn't understand the dark man's behavior. Mike would have taken a hundred like him, but it seemed God had created only one and then left off doing others because he couldn't accept a world so lacking in humor and good will. If the Beast had feelings, they would remain a mystery to all but his creator.

That Sunday, the Creator became the center of attention in camp.

Fourteen

The Reverend Houghton was a Lutheran preacher who chose to minister to lumberjacks. He wasn't the only man who followed such a career, but there were many jacks who claimed he was the only honest one so he was accepted as one of them. He lived in Grand Rapids but had a warm bed waiting in a thousand shacks, homes and logging camps throughout Itasca, Koochiching and Beltrarni Counties. He traveled about the country in a small sled pulled by a big Newfoundland dog named Luke after St. Paul's companion in the Acts of the Apostles. His methods were simple: be a friend, lend an ear, and bring Jesus to the lonely hearted. He carried no food, no bedroll and very little extra clothing. Every cubic inch of tightly packed space was devoted to the men in the camps. There were bibles but also newspapers, stationary, hard candy, medications and even a small surgical kit.

In the course of time Houghton had dug out bullets, sewed up knife wounds and was even prevailed upon to attempt an emergency appendectomy in a logging camp one winter. Unfortunately, the man died just the same, but even if he couldn't cure them, Amos Houghton still applied the same enthusiasm to burying them.

He brought paper and pencil and wrote letters for the unlettered. Many an immigrant maintained contact with his family through Amos. Likewise, many farmer lumberjacks did their banking through him, passing on time checks for him to deposit on accounts throughout the state. To these same farmers he was also a messenger, bringing news of births, deaths, baptisms, funerals, weddings and divorces.

It was Saturday evening when Amos approached the camp; his dog barking an eager greeting to the familiar kitchen smells. In the most blinding snowstorms, Luke had never failed to find a camp's cook shack.

"Are we nearly there, Luke?" asked Houghton through his muffler. "Can you smell the biscuits?"

The big dog whined in response and surged forward. Another quarter mile and Luke broke into the clearing, raced past the yarding crew and stopped at the doorway of the kitchen.

Alerted by Luke's barking, the men came out to welcome the Reverend. Old familiar faces brought smiles and greetings from Amos as he warmly shook hands with his friends. Amos was good with names, especially the nicknames because he had grown up with these men and their livelihood. Now, as a minister to their spiritual needs, he knew most of them by name.

"Well, Socrates, my philosopher friend, "Amos said greeting the old cook. Their relationship went back twenty-five years. "And here is Rube, Johnson, Schnapsie and Snoose," the litany went on. "God has, indeed, led me to a place in need of His word," he teased.

"Oh, shoot, Reverend," Snoose retorted. "What your elephant dog did was lead you to the Garden of Eden, and all of us are his little angels."

"Maybe," Amos replied good-naturedly. "After the fall I would surmise."

Sullivan came over from his office. Though not of the same religious persuasion, the two men had a quiet, common bond. Mike had known Amos nearly as long as Socrates and, as an example to his men if nothing else, he presented a clean and brushed face at every service Amos ever gave in his camp. Some thirsted for God, others drank of the entertainment Amos offered. Anyway you looked at it, Amos was good for camp morale.

"Welcome to Itascan #2, Minister," Mike said, shaking his hand. I'll have the boys take your bag up to my office."

"Thank you, Mike, but I can't take your bed away."

"I'm already set up in the kitchen. We'll hear no more of it."

"Well, in that case, thank you for your hospitality."

It was a gentlemanly formality that had been played out without variation many times in the past. As they walked to Mike's office they chatted.

"How are things, Mike? I saw a mountain of logs on the creek bank. And a lot of snow."

"There is a lot of both this winter. I can't complain. We've had better and we've had worse. I would call this fair."

"Did you lose much time with the thaw?"

"We live with whatever your boss gives us."

"Absolutely," Amos agreed.

Mike grew silent and Amos could tell that something else was on his mind. "What is it, Mike?"

Mike cleared his throat. "Amos, we have a funeral for you.

"No, Mike! Is it anyone I know?"

"I don't think so. A good young lad from out east. We called him Tamarack Jack. This was his first camp. Tree fell on him."

"How sad. Did he suffer?"

"Yes, he did … but as bravely as I've ever seen."

"And you?"

Mike considered the simple question and answered. "You know how it is. I promised him a Christian burial. We've waited for you."

"Then we will bury the dead and comfort the living. In the meantime, you wouldn't have a little liniment for a sore back would you?"

"Rubbing kind?" Mike asked.

"The other if you please," sighed the Reverend.

"It's already on your pillow," Mike said, pointing the way.

At dinner Houghton blessed the meal and ate, at his own request, with the swampers at the foot of the table. He was as quiet as the next man with every bit as large an appetite. Later, in the bunkhouse, he gave the newspapers to Socrates and a group of men gathered around the stove to pick up word from the outside world.

"Read us a story," someone requested, so Socrates began to read. There was sporting news about a young Goliath from St. Cloud who was making his mark as a University of Minnesota wrestler. He read several amusing stories from the Gossip and Popular Items column. He read, very slowly, a front-page expose of a prostitution ring in Minneapolis that ended with the arrest of twenty-one people including four police officers and six businessmen. Eleven women were taken into custody, only four of them notorious enough to be identified by name. Gertie wasn't mentioned.

I hope she's out of it for good, he thought.

Finally Snoose couldn't contain himself any longer. "See if there's anything about that Margorie, Soc. What's she up too?"

"Well I don't know now," mused Socrates turning the pages. Suddenly he stopped. "Yes, by God, here it is." He began reading to himself. "Well, I'll be skun," he suddenly exclaimed aloud.

"You got it? Read it so we can hear," Snoose ordered.

"What?" Socrates said, shaken from his concentration.

"Read it, you old fart."

"Sure! Sure. But you aren't going to believe this.

> *Marjorie Reynolds, convicted husband beater escaped from the state penitentiary for women in Madison last Thursday. Authorities have failed to apprehend her at this time. A note was found in her cell. 'I'm leaving. I can't stand living without having a man around to lay my poker on. I hear the Minnesota woods are full of them and, what's more, they like getting beat on as much as I like giving it out.' Reynolds was reported last seen in Aitkin, Minnesota, driving a dog team pulled by four fuzzy whiskered old lumberjacks.*

"Snoose, it looks like she's headed straight for your bunk."

"Oh, hell! She ain't either! You made that up!"

"Better sleep on top of your blanket, Snoose," Apple Pete laughed.

"It doesn't say that! Let me see that!" Snoose tried to grab the newspaper, but Socrates held him off.

"Why are you grabbing at this for? You couldn't read it if I gave it to you."

"Well maybe I gotta use the john and the catalog is froze stiff, that's why. And why are you always trying to fool me like that?"

"Oh, settle down," Socrates cooed, "You asked what she was up to, didn't you? I just told you."

"But I wanted the truth!"

"And who says it isn't? Any of you other guys?"

"I believe," Paddy volunteered with a solemn face.

"Every word," Hoover agreed. There wasn't a dissenting voice in the bunch.

"Well, then, I think Pete gave you some sound advice, Snoose."

"Oh hush. Go on, read something else." Snoose had been in a sulky mood ever since he had dropped his best pipe into the outhouse pit and couldn't talk anyone into going in after it for him.

"How's the Kaiser doing?" someone wanted to know. Socrates dutifully flipped through the small stack of papers looking for an appropriate headline.

"Here's one," he volunteered. "A Navel Action, it says." Socrates read the headline"

"Wolfpack Attacks convoy: Submarine Sunk. The largest Allied convoy to steam to France this year was struck on the morning of fifteen December. British Corvettes successfully drove off a fierce attack by an undetermined number of German submarines. At least one submarine sinking was confirmed during the battle which took place within three hundred miles of the convoy's destination of Brest, France.

"Several merchantmen in the convoy of over seventy-five vessels were struck by torpedoes and surface gunfire during the coordinated attack in the choppy, windswept waters. Only one ship was known to have gone down."

Socrates finished the article and then glanced ahead to the next column. "Wait!"

Here's another story about the sinking.

"Troop Transport, Mary Celeste, Reported Sunk. Four Hundred Lives Saved By Convoy Escorts. War Hero Lost At Sea.

"An eye witness from the converted passenger liner, Mary Celeste, described in detail the loss of the ship: 'From the lookout station forward, I saw the tracks of two torpedoes. Due to the rough water, they were not visible until nearly upon us. We were struck just aft the starboard beam although only one, I think, actually detonated. The explosion caused the entire vessel to heave up and then heel over after it slammed back into the seas. Two Corvettes came to our rescue immediately. They laid down smoke and began taking off soldiers, mostly American volunteers and French convalescents coming home. Due to her stout construction, she did not sink at

*once, but settled slowly in the water, bow first. This gave
us time to put out life boats. Nearly all hands were saved,
I think.*

*   'Among those lost were a number of seamen still in
the forward crew 's quarters which quickly flooded. An
American pilot drowned while assisting other wounded
seamen into a lifeboat. A tender from HMS Vanguard
was unable to retrieve the body. He was identified by
witnesses as . . ."*

Socrates abruptly stopped his narration.

"Oh come on, Soc, don't play that game of yours now. Finish
the story."

Socrates read the rest of the article to himself then looked
towards Tyler's bunk.

"Tyler, were you listening?"

Tyler was staring at the frosty ceiling. "I heard. Why?"

"Maybe you should read this first."

"No. You finish it."

"It's Graham."

Tyler sat up in bed. "What happened," he asked quietly.

Socrates slowly finished the article.

*   "He was identified as Lt. Graham Caldwell, an
American war hero fighting in the French Espandrille.
Lt. Graham was returning to France following recovery
from wounds incurred in combat while flying over hostile
territory.*

That was all. Silence hung over the bunkhouse. Lumberjacks,
although living with the possibility of it every day, were embarrassed
by another's tragedy. Finally, Tyler pulled himself out of his bunk,
put on his coat and left the room.

Amos watched him depart then asked Socrates who he was.

"That's Timber Bull," Paddy said.

"Did he know this Graham?"

"They were brothers."

Amos' distress was reflected in his face. "Oh, what a terrible
thing to hear of it in the papers," he whispered. "The shocking loss

of a loved one is so difficult to accept even when prepared for it. He must have loved him dearly. Oh, the pain!"

Maybe, thought Socrates, it hurts more because he hadn't loved him enough.

Tyler walked out onto the camp lake and sat down in the dark spearing house. In front of him was the two by three foot hole in the ice. Tyler sat and stared into the green, iridescent water. Watching.

Amos pulled back the canvas door flap and looked in. "May I come in?" he asked. Tyler didn't answer so the minister quietly admitted himself. He squeezed into the small hut and took a seat alongside Tyler. After some time, Houghton broke the embarrassing silence.

"I know most of the other men here but we haven't been introduced. My name is Amos Houghton."

Tyler continued to stare at the carved wooden decoy hanging from a string in the hole.

"Your friends say they call you Timber Bull."

Tyler spoke without looking at him, "Yes, my friends call me Timber Bull." "What is your Christian name?"

"My friends call me Timber Bull. If they like it, then God can like it too."

"I suspect He does at that." Amos shifted uncomfortably on his stool and slipped onto the icy floor. He grabbed Tyler's arm for support. Tyler stiffened but the Reverend's reaction brought them into eye contact. Amos held the boy's arm for a minute longer as he shared his condolences, "I am saddened at your brothers death. Socrates told me something about him. He died a heroic death." Amos held out his hand.

Tyler ignored it and, looking away from Amos, spoke. "Everything Graham did was considered heroic by someone. He was even a hero at birth; first child born in the new hospital. Heroic birth, heroic death. Very consistent. So what was his prize this time? A nice marble headstone? A nice heroic tombstone? He won't even get buried. The sea just. . . ." Tyler's voice broke off. He began again, "Oh, what the hell! It doesn't matter a damn anyway, does it? Aren't we just born to die anyway?"

Amos had not planned to debate a man called Bull, especially on the occasion of his brother's death, but Tyler had chosen the ground and Amos believed in sowing seed wherever fertile ground presented itself.

"A man's actions are often their own reward, or punishment, son. His motives are not ours to question or understand. His plans are obscure. We merely ..."

"We merely accept our fate? Is that what you believe?" Tyler turned around and squared up with the Reverend. Is that what you were going to say? That we don't have the right to bitch or scream or get angry over the dirt we get covered with?"

"Your interpretation has put me at a disadvantage, but, yes, I admit I was about to say that. I also believe it to be true. It is the basis of everything I believe." Houghton said this with conviction.

"Well, the hell with beliefs! I have no intention of putting my fate in the hands of someone else again. It doesn't work. I place my faith in no one but myself." Tyler went back to watching the hole.

"Not even the countenance of God? To trust in God, young man, is the foundation of faith."

"Especially the countenance of God, no less than that of man. I trust very few people I know and have no faith at all in strangers."

"And God is a stranger to you?"

"It was His decision, not mine. I'll get by without Him."

"Man cannot live alone. He is conditioned to seek others. Nor can I accept your position that God has not revealed himself to you. We know He is made known to all men in time. But we must prepare ourselves for the moment of His revelation. Do you understand this?"

Tyler was barely listening. "If you followed me here to preach, you might as well leave now."

"I'm sorry it came out that way," Houghton apologized, "I get caught up in my own enthusiasm. Try to understand me young man. I only came to express my deepest sympathy for your loss."

Tyler was not to be mollified, however, nor did he care to be drawn back to the subject of Graham. "They call me Bull because I can bend the moment to my will. I have tried the other way. I have relied on the goodness of other people and found only personal greed, trickery and self-interest. My reward has been abuse and disappointment."

Tyler's voice rose and began to quiver. He caught himself before it broke. "That was yesterday," he finished.

"And tomorrow?" Amos insisted.

"Tomorrow?" Tyler repeated. "Tomorrow and every day thereafter shall be my day to use as I want."

"Judging from the newspaper account, your brother seemed to be cut from a different cloth."

Tyler's took the spear that was leaning against the wall. His hand closed tightly on the cold metal shaft, his knuckles growing white as their breath.

"Let me tell you about my brother. My brother's cloth was velvet, mine was sack cloth. He was royalty in our house. I was treated like a stepson. My father never had a kind word for me. Graham bathed in them. My mother ignored both of us. All she cared about was her society friends. We were raised by nannies. I can't begin to recount all their names there were so many because they never measured up to her standards of ignorance. Now I can think of no kind words for any of them. I regret that Graham is dead but he brought it on himself."

"But he was still your brother." Houghton was incredulous at Tyler's lack of feeling. "We were never close. Five years separated us. I learned from the experience. I can't say that of him. I don't care now."

"Why do you say that . . . that he didn't learn?"

Tyler stared at the hole, gathering his thoughts. "Graham was a moth, drawn to the flame of public adoration. He gave himself over to the hands of others and became a victim."

"And you are not?"

Tyler fixed Houghton with a freezing look. "I was but I've learned to live with pain. No, I have come to welcome it. It is part of my life now. Look here, Reverend."

A Northern Pike had appeared in the hole and was nosing the wooden decoy. "See that fish? That's my brother as he was, Reverend, drawn to the prospects of a meal just as Graham was drawn to the prospect of glory. Even as my father is drawn to his money and my girl was obviously drawn to other men. Greedy people all of them. But, like them, this fish hasn't considered the risks, only the rewards. He can only see the satisfaction of this moment and that will be his undoing."

Tyler's arm flew down, the spear slid soundlessly through the water and impaled the Pike just behind the dorsal fin. It hung paralyzed for an instant and then began to thresh wildly, beating the water, struggling uselessly against the steel.

Tyler raised the fish from the hole.

"Behold the victim," he said, "drawn too close to the light." He hit it over the head with a hatchet blade. It quivered and was still.

He pulled it from the spear, examined it with mild curiosity and, pulling back the canvas flap, threw it outside.

"And then it's gone," Tyler pronounced with finality. "The glory, the money the beauty, nothing can save the greedy fish. That was Graham."

Amos was appalled at Tyler's analogy. "Didn't you love your brother?" he asked incredulously.

"Hah!" Tyler laughed, "Did I love my brother? You can still ask me that?"

"Yes," Houghton said softly, hopefully.

"Didn't that old gossip, Socrates, tell you?"

"No. He said nothing."

"Graham and I hated each other. The night I left home, we had a fight. Over my girl, my girl mind you. At a society ball, given in his honor, naturally."

Houghton was shocked. "And because of that, a mere fight between siblings, you forsake your family, your heritage?"

"No!" Tyler roared in his face. He jumped to his feet, shaking the fragile walls of the shack. His voice carried over the frozen lake. "I left home because my father beat me! He beat me in front of three hundred people because I hit his favored son."

Houghton was stunned. "Oh, Lord no! I don't know what to say. A father taking sides between his sons. Son, I am so sorry." Tyler, his rage spent, sat down again.

"And that is my little secret. You ask, did I love my brother?" Tyler repeated the question." I thought I knew what love meant once, but that was so long ago. Now I love a pair of dry stockings. I love fresh coffee and a sharp saw. I love what I can control. I love being left alone. Do you understand me?"

"And for yourself? Do you not even care for the welfare of yourself?"

"Not even he," responded Tyler returning to the hole. In his final remark he had written even himself out of his life.

For the Sunday service, the men walked to a small rise back against the little creek that flowed out of camp. There, they had built a fire, keeping vigil over it night and day for three days until the ground thawed enough to scrape out a shallow grave. Next to the mound of raw earth, before a small rustic cross, Amos read the Service for the dead over the body of Tamarack "Maude" Jack. Then they committed him to God's care. If Tyler was mourning, it went unnoticed and unobserved, for he did not attend the service. He was absent from camp until dinner.

Snoose also had very nearly missed the service. Someone had sewed him into his blanket during the night.

Two weeks after Houghton's departure, it was quitting time far out on the Skunk Creek Road. Quiet Seifert turned to his men, still hard at work. "Wind it up, boys!" he called, "Let's catch the sleigh into supper."

The Timber Beast and the Timber Bull, halfway through a white pine log, never looked up. Their saw was still chewing away, spitting out sawdust as the blade swept back and forth, twenty cycles, forty strokes a minute; the pace they had kept all day, all week, all month.

In another minute they were through and the log rolled clear. Tyler straightened up and looked at his hands. They glowed a moist, cherry red in the frigid air. He was working without coat or shirt, his suspenders hung from heavily muscled shoulders covered only by the top of his red flannel long-johns. His long sandy hair and full beard gave him the appearance of a mountain man. Standing with Timber Beast they were a pair to be reckoned with.

"Bull."

Tyler looked at the man with the soft, deep voice who had just spoken his name for the first time. Taking a step forward, the Beast reached his swollen red paw over the fallen log. Tyler looked at it, took it, gripped it firmly in his own and felt the comradely pressure given in return. Beast's single, unadorned word rang approvingly in his ears.

"Partner."

Tyler turned from the Beast to hide the tears that, in spite of the promise to himself, were welling up in his eyes.

Fifteen

There was still thirty-six inches of snow in the woods on March third. Sixteen loads a day were running over the ice road between the main camp and the rollways. And yet, the mild weather and the rising angle of the sun heralded the approaching spring.

The camp birds were livelier than ever. Whiskey jays and chickadees flitted back and forth from the roofs of the buildings, and whistled for handouts from the lumberjacks. Red squirrels were out darting across the raw ground that was starting to show around the buildings; fighting for long ago discarded pieces of fat and bread. Ermine were seen standing boldly at the cook shack door where Spooner doled out their daily scraps of meat trimmings. Frequent late storms rushed through, dumping up to a foot of snow with each pass.

Between the storms the sun burned ever higher in the sky, melted down the drifts, and honeycombed it with tiny rivulets of water. The water, in turn, flowed over the frozen ground, softening it, absorbing the frost and filling the cedar swamps and ash swales. It worked its way through alder and willow-girded streams and rivulets, through the cattail swamps and into the black-bottomed lakes. It flowed out onto the ice and mixed with the packed snow cover. The snow on the lakes grew heavy with water. Beneath it, the ice turned black, rotted until it was so honeycombed it could no longer carry a load. In less than a month, the embracing shackles of winter would be broken. Spring breakup would be on.

"Socrates," Mike said, "I'll be grateful to have a sober crew coming tonight." He spoke without much conviction.

"Oh, Mike, don't worry about the boys. They'll behave."

"It is not the 'boys' I am thinking of," Mike grunted. "Just promise me you'll stay where we can watch you."

"I will. I will," Socrates huffed, put out by Mike's admonishment.

"And keep away from the river."

"I will, Mike! Dammit, you'd think I'd never crossed a street before, the way you carry on."

"Well, I just don't care to lose my cook," Mike shrugged, "at least not until he learns how to cook." He met Socrates' frown with a grin.

They were going in to Craig. Mike wanted to inspect the two wanigans that had been left tied at the riverbank. Last fall, when the river had dropped to its lowest level leaving the hulls exposed, a crew had been sent up to re-caulk and tar the bottoms. Mike knew they should be in good shape but with vagrants, vandals, squatters and what not, checking them out now might save a lot of trouble later.

The wanigans were twelve by thirty feet, flat-bottomed skiffs built of heavy planks, covered with oakum and tar. Large cabins squatted on their decks. They were built light so they could be worked over shallow rapids, yet strong enough to hold together on a trip that would take several weeks. They were large, clumsy and difficult to steer, not unlike a house set upon a flood. They were Noah's Ark without the manure, but they were home to the crew. In them, they could find a dry change of clothes, eat a hot meal and sleep with a minimum of mosquitoes and gnats.

Mike had thought it might be a good time for some of his men to shake out the sawdust from the winter. He brought along those few who had not left camp all winter: Snoose, Socrates, Schnapsie, Paddy the Pig and teamster Johnson. The Timber Twins, Beast and Bull were along, too. Mike figured that if anyone had earned a day off, it was them. Unlike the others, only Beast had to be persuaded to take the ride. Finally, Mike had ordered him onto the sleigh. He was restless and anxious the whole trip and acted fearful about coming out of the woods.

Tyler sensed Beast's uneasiness and confided it to Socrates who just nodded in agreement.

"Why is he like that? You'd think a day off work would ..."

Socrates cut him off, "It's his past. It's none of our business."

"No one knows anything about his past."

"That isn't necessarily so," Socrates said impatiently. "You stick around a man long enough and you pick things up. I don't know all of it but what I know I might tell you sometime."

"Why not now."

"It's his past, not mine. I don't gossip."

"You don't gossip?" Tyler asked incredulously.

Socrates tried to look serious. "Do I look like a man who would betray another man's confidence?"

Tyler was excited at the prospect of discovering something about the Beast. "I'm his partner. If anyone should be trusted to know, it would be his partner."

"Maybe, but if anyone should be trusted not to ask, it would also be his partner."

It was left at that.

The early morning woods were already awake. They encountered deer on the trail; fawn-heavy does a month or less from delivery. Ruffed grouse were actively working the manure on the ice roads for oats. Several times they caught the sounds of drumming. Like an old two cylinder engine stubbornly coming to life the male grouse advertised for mates. Red squirrels, chickadees and whiskey jays scolded them at every turn. The bears and otters were still sleeping, but before long, they too, would shake the cotton from their heads and came out in search of food.

Paddy was the most talkative of the group. He fired an endless stream of questions at Snoose and Schnaps, laughing at the conflicting answers. If one man claimed there were twenty bars in town, the other swore there were forty. On only one thing they agreed; mind your manners and your purse and mostly the latter.

"If any man says he's extending his hand in friendship," advised Schnaps, "bite it off 'cause all he's after is your poke."

Mike had advanced them five dollars each from petty cash, although Socrates had slipped out with a bit more. That would be more than enough to clean the moss off thir tongues.

By 11:00 Mike was treating his men to a big lunch at the only legitimate restaurant in town, Sad-eyed Sam's. Sam was in his early forties but he had suffered a stroke out in the woods when he was only twenty-four. It left the right side of his face paralyzed. That gave him a serious speech impediment. When he talked, it sounded like he was chewing on his words and clipping the edges off them. The only way you could tell if Sam was telling a joke or a tale of woe was to assume that everything he said was laughable, which it invariably was.

He set up his restaurant like a cook shack with long rows of tables and a central serving line. A meal featured one main course that he wrote on a little blackboard by the front door. At thirty-five cents a head and all you could eat, all Hungry Mike could eat was four helpings, primarily because Sam's helpings were so large to begin with.

Eventually Mike wiped his face with the big, checkered napkin and stood up. "You boys now," he said clearing his throat, "you be careful you don't get your pants ironed while you're in them today." The general attitude was that they'd all be careful. "We'll meet then at the sleigh when the train comes in if that's all right?" Everyone was very polite and cooperative.

After Mike left, Paddy allowed again, he was forever commenting back in camp, that he had never seen anyone eat as much as Mike. "Oh, that's nothin'," chirped Schnaps.

"Socrates, you were up there in Bemidji that one Thanksgiving, weren't ya?"

"Sure I was."

"Tell 'em about that time."

It was one of Socrate's favorite Hungry Mike stories and he wanted to tell it to show Tyler a little insight into Mike's personality.

"Mike and I were back in town for some mucky-muck's funeral. We stopped in at the Regis Hotel and had turkey dinner together." He stopped then and went for his pipe, a sure sign that the story would be a long winded one. He packed it and swiped a match over his pant leg. Several savored puffs later, he continued.

"There was maybe ten or twelve other people in there. Well, we sat down and had a couple of drinks and then the waitress brings us the menu. Right away, and you didn't have to be a wizard to know it, we saw the daily special was turkey dinner. Yeah, turkey, mashed 'taters, dressing, biscuits, gravy, cranberries and punkin pie. The works for forty-five cents. Maybe fifty, I don't remember exactly but things were a lot cheaper then. I remember it was a pretty high-class meal, though.

"Naturally I take the turkey dinner, it being the occasion and all. Then she looks at Mike and he says, how much for a turkey and she says, like I mentioned, forty-five or fifty cents. I forget which. Well, Mike says, no, I mean how much for a whole turkey? She looks at him and says you're joking me, but Mike don't crack a smile so she excuses herself and goes in the back room.

"Boom, she's out again with the manager. He asks Mike if he's serious and Mike assures him he is so the manager looks him over pretty close and he notices the other diners are looking on, you know, being entertained by all this. So he tells Mike, listen, a whole turkey with the fixings will cost you six dollars, but if you clean up the plate, I'll not charge you a cent. I don't think you can do it.

"1 think he expected Mike to back off at this 'cause he's got a big smile under his dinky moustache. Well, Mike wiped the smile away quick. He just said, bring on the turkey.

"Everybody turned their chairs around so they had a good look; the cooks all had their heads in the door and Mike dug into that fifteen pound bird. He started eating at exactly five-thirty that night. An hour and a half later, he had about half a slice of minced meat pie on his plate along with a small dash of dressing. He held up his hand, weak like, and waved over the waitress. Mike's kind of bashful around strangers, you know.

"Now she looked down at his plate and she got a little smile on her mug, too. All the same she acts real professional and says, yes sir, is there anything else I can bring you, sir? And Mike takes a little sip of his tea and says, yes, there is. You wouldn't have another slice of this delicious pie back there would you? I swear she dropped her teeth when she heard that! Everyone in the place stood up and started clapping, you'da swore Mike was a politician or something!"

Paddy shook his head in admiration. "And he ate the whole turkey?"

"Every blessed piece, white and dark. Even chewed the knuckles off the bones."

"Well I'll be go to hell!"

"Well, I'll be go to the other end of town," Schnapsie said, standing up.

"That's a good idea," Snoose agreed. "Socrates, you want'a come with us and see we don't misbehave too bad?"

"Soon as I shake hands with a friend," he said standing up.

Tyler, Beast and Paddy left soon after. They worked their way across Craig, stopping to look in on some of the dives along the main drag. The Beast would go in and hurry to the darkest corner he could find while Paddy and Tyler went up to the bar for the drinks.

There were about three hundred men in town most of them farmers passing through with their teams, leaving the camps that were closing out early. There was a sprinkling of salesmen and hustlers. They were the few wearing suits and overcoats. Here and there was a company man.

Mike found Tyler, Beast and Paddy coming out of a joint and asked them to wait with him for the Gut and Liver. He had picked up a bottle of Old Crow that he offered to share. It looked better than the rot-gut they had been drinking so they went down to depot with him. The four men sat on benches on the rickety platform, not talking much, content to lean back and take in the sun.

Every so often someone would come up the track or over from town, hoping to catch a ride back to The Rapids. They were mostly jacks with empty pockets, heading for no place special. They were just trying to get a head start getting someplace they hadn't been before.

A tall, emaciated logger crossed from town and shuffled up to them. With a heavy sigh, he slumped down on the edge of the platform and began rubbing his palms on his pants, then scrutinizing them, looking for something that wasn't apparent to the others ten feet away. A look of concern and he'd rub them again and again. Finally, Paddy's curiosity got the better of him.

"Say, bud, you got something the matter with your hands, don't you?"

The lumberjack looked around at the sound of his voice.

"Over here," Paddy directed him.

"Oh, sure, there you are," the man squinted at Paddy.

"I said your hands. You don't seem to like them much?"

"Oh?" The man looked at his hands again. His eyes were red and rheumy and as he spoke, it sounded like the crackle of dried leaves. "No," he said. "No, I can't get rid of the awful stuff."

"What are you trying to get rid of?"

"The blood. I went and got blood on my hands. Some fellow's blood and now they're growing hair all over them." He stretched out his hands. "See?"

"What are you talking about, blood?" Paddy asked, sitting up. The man spied the bottle and licked his lips. "Mighty dry," he said, changing the subject. "I'm mighty dry. I sure could use one."

Timber Beast stuck the cork in the neck and rolled it over to him. Fuzzy Hands took the cork between his yellowed molars and pulled it out. He pulled off three big swallows, stoppered it and politely rolled it back. The whiskey seemed to buck him up.

"They killed a feller over there two nights ago. There was a big fight and he got shot. So they paid me to dump him through the ice but he bled all over me when I tried to carry him down there. I had to drag him by his boots. No! His feet. Someone took his boots right off. I had to drag him face down because they had blown off the back of his head and it was leaving a big streak in the snow and the bar owner said roll him over, I don't want that blood in front of my store." He held up his hands. "I got it under my skin. Now they're furry."

"You're brain is furry, man," Paddy said. "Ah, man, they just feel that way now because you've rubbed them raw. Go take a bath and rub them with some lard instead."

"That takes money and I ain't got none," the old reprobate moaned. Sullivan caught the man's attention. "Say, you ain't Hungry Mike are you?"

"Michael Sullivan, yes I am," Mike answered. "But I don't know you, do I?"

"Used to. I was thirty pounds heavier then and mean as black tar spit. They still called me Beanpole. Anyway, now you remember?"

"Sure. Beanpole. You worked in the Cass Lake camp."

"You remembered. That's nice. You were good to work for, but I didn't like that cook much. What was his name?"

"Socrates," Mike grunted.

"Yeah, Socrates. Never put enough grease in the soup for me. Who you got cookin' for you now?"

"Same man," Mike answered.

"Oh," Beanpole nodded. "Well, like I say, you were good to work for."

Mike nodded at the compliment. The man began working over his hands again, then suddenly stopped. "Mike, didn't you run a dark faced man with a high and mighty manner out of your camp a month or two ago?"

"Stankovich," Mike acknowledged, his eyebrows rising.

"Yeah, yeah, Stankovich, that's the one."

Tyler stood up. "Is he still here?"

"In town? Hell, he's the one that shot the no-name. Only no one would own up to saying it was so. He's got a place now, last one at the other end of Craig. Calls it the Four Horsemen something. It's a bad place. Lot's of free booze 'til you're blasted. Then they clean you out."

Mike stepped off the platform and started walking back to Craig. At the sound of other boots moving on the platform, he stopped and turned. "You boys wait for the train.

I'm just going to collect the others."

"I'll come with you," Paddy offered, standing up.

Mike shook his head. "We're not here to pick a fight with gunfighters." He held up his hand. "I'll bring them back. You finish the bottle."

He went down the riverbank and crossed over the ice. In a minute he was through the brush and out of sight. It took him five minutes to walk the length of Craig's main street. It gave him time to think, and remember. If Stankovich was there, Mike knew he'd be eager to see him. If he had killed the one man, or more, killing Sullivan would be easy. And he'd have muscle with him, enough to commit murder without getting lynched, anyway. It didn't matter. Mike still had to collect his men. If Stankovich got between him and his men again, Mike would go to the wall for them. Too many times he was forced to watch helplessly as good men died following out his orders. He wasn't helpless now.

Long before he reached the end of the street, he saw something, a figure, maybe, lying on the street outside one of the bars. As he approached it he realized it was a lumberjack curled up on the ground.

He studied him for a moment, then rolled him over with his boot. The man groaned. His eyes opened slowly. He had been sleeping.

"Well, I thought that was you," Mike said, his heart pounding, "but I couldn't tell if you were dead or alive." Socrates was drunk but not so he couldn't talk.

"Well, what the hell else could I be, Mike." Then, "Oh God, I sure do wish I were kind of dead right now."

"I told you to behave yourself."

"I know. I know. And I promised myself to listen this time. Don't you know the first advice I ignore is always my own. God! Do I have a headache? Yes, I guess I do." He rubbed a large welt on his noggin.

Mike leaned over Socrates and gently parting the thin scalp, examined the bump;

He clucked in quiet admonition. "Well, I can't do much for your head but get you out of here. You don't need stitches. Where are the other boys?"

Socrates rolled over and sat back on his haunches. He put his hands behind his neck and rubbed. "Oh, Lord, that was some bad stuff," he moaned. He pointed across the street. "They were right in there when I left 'em. Or they left me. I don't remember." Mike saw the garishly painted sign on the front of the wood-framed, tar-paper building. It read, "The Four Horsemen Saloon."

"Good holy St. Patrick, Socrates! Didn't you know any better than to go into his joint in the first place?'

"Mike, when I'm sober, I don't go into any joints. This was the fifth one we hit."

"How'd they treat you?"

"Like kings for awhile, at least until that s.o.b. threw me out."

"And tell me why a saloon keeper would ever turn out a gentle soul like you."

"Get me off this frozen crud and I'll tell ya." Mike gathered a handful of Socrate's coat and pulled him to his feet. The old man brushed the frozen horse manure from his pants. "I'll be honest, Mike, I had a twenty dollar bill with me. Schnaps advanced it out of my poke. Yeah, don't give me that look! I know I done wrong."

"Finish your excuse," Mike said, impatiently.

"Soon after we got in there, we spent the last of the other stuff, so I brought out the twenty. I didn't think they'd … well, I guess I didn't think at all. But there was only three or four guys layin' around. It was real tame. We knew them all anyway, nearly, so Schnaps spoke up for me and yelled 'Timberr!' and we all drank up together. When we come to move on down the street, the bartender says that'll be eight bucks. I say all right and brought out the big bill."

"And he couldn't change it?" Mike interjected.

"That's right! That's right! The guy looks at that bill and whistled out loud. Then he said, fella's, I ain't got change right now but here's five on account and I'll hold the rest 'til you go. Have another."

Mike looked at him skeptically.

"I know! You'd think I was born yesterday, wouldn't ya. Well, right off I said we weren't coming back, we were heading for camp. So he said to have one more and he gave us part of the bottle and we sat down to finish it and that's just what we did. Now don't look at me like that, Mike, everybody does it! But you know what he said when I went back up to the bar again?"

"Yes. He said, 'There ain't none left, old timer, you drank it all up. 'Dat's about what he said now, wasn't it?"

"Yeah, 'Dat's about what he said," said Socrates mimicking Mike's accent. "'Dat's about exactly what he said. How'd you know he'd say it?"

"If you were sober, you'd remember your own stories."

"Socrates, it's bad enough to buy your booze from a crook, but to buy from a crook that insults your cooking? That place is owned by an old friend of ours."

"Well, if he's a friend, why don't he treat us civil"

"That friend is the renegade Stankovich. Did you read the sign over the door before you went in?"

"No, signs are just a lying promise, anyway." He squinted at the sign over the saloon, read the words out loud, fumbled for his lower lip and bit it. "I guess I could of been hurt, huh? Well, It wouldn't be the first time."

"It could have been the last time with those boys," Mike said.

"I'm due, I guess."

"Well," Mike said with a final sigh of resignation, "I think I better go in there and find the rest of this miserable crew." He hitched up his trousers and walked up to the Four Horsemen.

Socrates stumbled after him muttering, "Verily, they shall see the might of the Lord smite them down."

The saloon reeked of stale beer and stale bodies.

"Whatta ya want, Sullivan?" the bartender demanded. He already had a pretty good idea. "You ain't looking for a free meal, are you?"

Mike studied the man carefully. He wasn't one of the men who had worked his crew. "No. I've come for my boys."

"They can stay as long as they want. They're old enough," the bartender said with a malicious grin. But there was a nervous edge on his voice.

"And I'll have that money you stole from Socrates," Mike added in the same quiet manner.

The grin melted away and the bartender turned and disappeared through a doorway on his right. Several men stood up from around the barrel stove. Then, Stankovich, trailed by two more men, came in from the back room. That made seven.

A smile broke across Stankovich's face. "So the fly has come to the spider." Delighted at the improvement in the odds since their last meeting, he spread his arms to take in patrons and goons alike. "You see, Mr. Sullivan, the Four Horsemen are now seven. And there's not a colt among them."

"At this rate," Mike said, "you might run out of colors to name them."

The smirk left Stankovich's face. "Your men are here until they go, Sullivan," he said, "The money is mine. When you called my man a thief, you called me a thief. The price of slander in my establishment is high."

"I'll accept honest money from a thief as soon as from an honest man," Mike answered.

This time Stankovich's face hardened. "You won't leave here without a fight, money or not. And not on your feet, either, after we do our work."

Sullivan took another step into the room. The men at the stove stepped back and spread out in a semicircle to his left. The men with Stankovich moved off to his right.

"If that's how you'll have it," Mike said watching them position themselves, "I'll fight you fairly." He began taking off his Mackinaw.

Stankovich laughed, "Oh no, Sullivan, not just me. You will have to fight us all, together."

Mike shrugged and dropped his coat to the floor. The goons had begun pressing in on him when another voice carried in from the doorway. "Mike, we finished the bottle and got lonely. And look here now. You wouldn't be going to a party without your friends, would you?" Behind him stood Paddy the Pig flanked by Tyler and Timber Beast. Timber Beast swept a table off the floor and ripped off a leg for a club, his eyes were dark and malevolent.

If Stankovich was shaken by the arrival of reinforcements, he didn't show it. His eyes bored into Tyler, "So, it is that runny-nosed traitor from the logging camp. It was good of you to come by so we can settle all accounts at one time."

Beast and Paddy moved up to stand alongside Sullivan.

"You've grown," Stankovich observed. "Not the empty-headed cub you used to be. That is good. My men don't take to beating up on children but you look ready enough to learn some manners, if you are tough enough."

Tyler didn't take his eyes off Stankovich. He couldn't. The dark man had not changed at all. He was just as condemning as always, but he had added another quality to his persona. He had found his Eden in Craig. If his ultimate goal had been to make money out of robbing and murdering old lumberjacks, then he had arrived. If it was to acquire a small army of thugs and villains, then, yes, he had nothing more to work for. If it was to circumvent the common law and live by his own, he had found a place that would accommodate him.

"There need be no trouble," Mike offered. "I'll take my men and the money they have coming. That'll be the end of it."

Stankovich threw up his arms and let out a loud whoop. "Yes! Yes, the great Hungry Mike Sullivan thinks he will walk out of here as easy as he came in! He thinks that he can still dictate the rules and order us about at his whim. No! You know what he really thinks! He thinks he is so scared, he might crap in his pants. He is horrified that he will be beaten unconscious. He thinks that we might kill him and throw him in the river with all the other mangy men that have preceded him." He reached behind the bar and brought out a three-foot length of dried ash. "See my friend? See my scepter? We have lots of friends like this, do we not?" All around him similar clubs appeared in his men's hands.

Suddenly, Socrates detached himself from Mike and staggered up to Stankovich. "Whoa there, fellas. That isn't necessary. You're liable to hurt someone with them fly swatters."

"What are you mumbling at, old man?" Stankovich demanded. Socrates grabbed hold of Stankovich's shirt for support.

"I just said," Socrates shouted, suddenly very lucid, "'*The fool immediately shows his anger, but the shrewd man passes over an insult.*' That's Proverbs 12:6, you know. Or don't ya? No, I guess you wouldn't. You're pretty much a Revelations man."

The words had a poor effect on Stankovich. "I have something to pass over you, old man," he said, striking him with his club. Socrates slid to the floor with a groan. Stankovich raised it to strike again.

"You fucking bastard!" Tyler screamed and threw himself at Stankovich. He buried his shoulder in the horseman's chest and drove him into the bar, collapsing it beneath them. Then all hell broke loose as the two factions rushed at each other.

Paddy, Sullivan and Beast waded in, ducking, deflecting blows, punching, gouging and kicking at any target that left an opening. Paddy held up a chair to absorb the initial rain of club blows, then drove them back by whipping that piece of disintegrating furniture in their faces.

Mike caught one cautious blow with his forearm. It went numb but still he reached in and drove his powerful fists time and again into the ugly face in front of him.

Timber Beast struck pay dirt immediately. Swinging the chair leg like an axe, he caught one bearded man on the arm. The bone snapped like a twig, the crack sounding incredibly loud even in the din of the brawl. The hairy thug went down and lay writhing in pain. Timber Beast dropped the table leg like a child caught in mischief. "Sorry," he muttered and turned to meet the next attacker with his fists.

Tyler had his hands around Stankovich's neck and was mercilessly pounding his head against the floor, his scalp splashing blood into the sawdust. Stankovich, out of his head with rage and oblivious to his own pain was beating Tyler's head with his club and spitting his venom in his face. Realizing its futility, Stankovich finally dropped the club, and tried to loosen the strangle hold of the maddened Timber Bull. Two men came to his rescue just before he lost consciousness.

They dragged Tyler off and began pummeling him but Socrates had gotten back up and picking up Stan's fallen weapon, he slammed it against one man's face. He went down, his eyes rolling up into his head, his nose smashed into a mask of blood.

Sullivan pulled off the other man and threw him across the room, bringing down the barrel stove in a shower of smoke and soot.

Free again, Tyler set himself once more at Stankovich and renewed his attack on the man's battered head.

The Beast and Paddy had three men backed against a wall, systematically beating on them, each hitting first their outside captive and then collectively cracking the jaw of the one in the middle.

Then, like all truly vicious fights, it ended quickly. Sullivan wrapped his arms around Tyler, and pulled him off the helpless Stankovich. "Come, lad, don't kill the man. Let's leave that for the wolves."

Beast and Paddy backed off and the three toughies slid soundlessly to the floor. They looked at each other and solemnly shook hands.

Around the smoke-filled room, clusters of drunken jacks were still wrestling on the ground. Schnapsie and Snoose were at the bottom of a pile of grunting humanity. Mike went over and sorted out the knot. Then he picked up the spilled cash box, calmly counted out the exact amount Socrates had claimed and dropped the rest. Turning to the crowd, he shouted, "Dat's all, boys! Everybody out. I'm burning this pest hole down."

People began running or crawling for the door. Tyler, Paddy and Beast began dragging out unconscious and near conscious bodies as Mike picked up a can of kerosene and splashed it around the room.

Striking a match, Mike dropped it on a pile of saturated sawdust and stepped into the street. People gathered in small groups on the frozen street tending wounds and being tended to. The smoke began to billow out of the eaves.

Sullivam's men were clustered off to the side. Tyler's hair was matted with blood. Socrates was bleeding from behind his ear. They would both need painful stitches but they were grinning now, exalting in the victory. The Beast had already returned to his old withdrawn self. Snoose and Schnapsie were shadow boxing with each other, feeling feisty, having just worked themselves into the game. Paddy was playing with a tear in his coat.

"Will you look at that?" he complained, "You go to town for a wee libation and quiet conversation and the next thing you go and catch your coat on a nail someplace. Now, how did this happen, do you suppose?"

Mike went over to Stankovich who was lying in a heap with his buddies. "How are you and your horsemen?" he asked matter-of-factly.

"You're burning me out, you bastard."

Mike leaned over and pointed his finger in Stankovish's face. "You meant to harm my people. I would burn you with your hell-hole if I could. Do not ever do this mischief again!"

In spite of Mike's anger, Stankovich was not cowed. "I'll find you and I will kill you for this, you bragging devil spawn," he mumbled, but he was having difficulty getting the words out.

Mike put on his coat and buttoned it. "You know where I live. You come, you don't come, it's all the same to me," he said and started down the street.

Socrates threw in the last line, "*A simple reprimand does more for a man of intelligence than a hundred lashes for a fool.'* Proverbs 17:10. But I guess you didn't know that one, either, did you?"

Stankovich tried to spit at him, but all he could muster was a bloody drool that hung from his broken jaw.

The loggers went back down the street, out over the Bigfork and up the bank to the station. The whole town watched them go, outlined as they were by the blazing fire from The Four Horsemen. Only Tyler spoke at all, muttering one time under his breath that he'd cut the man's heart out if they ever met again.

The train had come in. They loaded over the supplies and climbed on for the trip home. At length, Johnson began to sing an old lumberjack ballad in his mellow baritone:

> *"You ask for me to sing a song*
> *As through this world I jog along*
> *I jog along through thick and thin*
> *And I can sing most anything!"*

A dozen verses and a dozen choruses he sang, the miles sliding by, wrapped in the muffled sounds of the runners on the snow. Eventually Johnson's song worked down to its final lines:

> *"Little did my mother think*
> *When she sang sweet lullaby*
> *Of the lands that I would find*
> *Nor the deaths that I would die."*

"Yes," the sobered Socrates said. "We sure enough come close today, didn't we?"

Sullivan looked at him as only a true friend could. "I wonder what made you step forward like that."

"The whiskey, Mike. Whiskey makes you frisky. It'll put courage in a one-legged midget."

"No, not the drink. I've seen the demon rum make you hide more often than fight. You think it was something else?"

"It weren't nothing."

"No? You stood up for old Hungry Mike. I felt good about that."

"Don't mention it," Socrates said, trying to laugh it off, "I won't be so careless next time."

Out on a far ridge, off beyond a great black spruce bog, a pack of wolves took up the chorus for Johnson.

If Socrates had hoped to find a meeting of the wills with Tyler, in the end, the trip to Craig might have only fed Tyler's ego even more. He and Timber Beast had reached a high level of mutual respect, and with the other men of the crew, he began to garner much admiration.

It wasn't that he was overtly abusive, but he let it be known in his mannerisms that he was no longer a green kid in the woods. He moved up in the cook shack too, bumping older, more experienced men from their places just because he knew that he overmatched them physically.

He redefined toughness to suit himself. His attitude clearly said, 'If you want your place back, take it. If you can.'

Socrates was especially concerned because this new change had a worrisome look of permanence.

"That thing back in Craig wasn't toughness, boy, it was just a brawl that's all. In the end, it won't prove nothing."

But Tyler refused to listen and Socrates understood why. In his own youth he had lived through a similar phase. He had once been a feisty, scrappy young feller, tougher than any tree he ever put to the ax. But, even then, Socrates felt he had always kept a decent respect for others. True, he didn't have the size of Tyler, but still, he had been tough enough and still kept his friends and his respect. But Tyler, he just didn't seem to care about others. And tough or not, a man needed some friends.

Yet, hadn't he thrown himself at Stankovich for striking the old man? That was something. But that was all the farther it went. A gulf still remained between them.

Tyler's attitude toward Sullivan changed. He began to admire the boss in much the same way as he did the Beast. He associated their quiet strength and bull-like stubbornness with aggressiveness, belligerence and anger, although neither of them was like that at all.

For all his concern, there was little Socrates could do to change the boy. His efforts to get inside Tyler were rebuffed as just more Bible spouting. "Don't go sucker punching me with one of your Proverb quotes like you did Stankovich." Tyler judged that, "In real life, it's a man's guts not his heart that get him ahead."

"Maybe so," Socrates would retort, "but guts are gonna get old and then another man with more of them and younger is gonna come along and then you end up with a different rooster ruling the roost. Look at Stankovich, Tyler. That man was just living for the day someone beat him down. So you did it. Fine. I'm proud of you for it. Just don't become the next one to take his place."

And every time, at the mention of that man, Tyler would fly into another rage over the man who had used his emotions so callously. Once he picked up an axe and brandishing in a two handed grip, threatened to bury it in Stankovich's head after which he drove it so deep into the end of a log the next man broke the handle off trying to pull it out.

"Damn kid!" Socrates cried. "He don't listen to his elders no more. Aw, he ain't a kid no more. And I guess I'm not what I used to be either. Do I have to die to get through to him?"

Sixteen

They finished the logging just ahead of the thaw. Mike began paring down his payroll, paying off most of the teamsters so they could head home for spring planting.

For the men who remained, there was still work to be done before the log drive. Earlier that fall, a driving dam had been put up below the rollway at the confluence of Spud and Skunk creeks. It was built of wooden weirs filled with rocks and mud and anchored with timbers and strong enough to hold back an eight-foot head of water over a fifty-foot wide span. In the early spring the water would stay high enough so logs could be passed day and night, but if the logging company took too long in getting them down, they might have to stop and build water for six hours for every hour of driving. Mike intended to get all of his logs off early.

To make sure he would have enough water he built four smaller dams farther up the creeks. The squirt dams were holding a good amount of water in back sloughs and marshes. There were also three sizable beaver dams that would be blown when needed.

The rest of the lumberjacks, they who were not employed in construction, were still in the woods, clearing brush, blazing new side trails for the next year, or repairing and storing equipment in camp.

He chose thirty-five men for this drive. On a faster river with more rapids, he would need more. The Bigfork had its share of rapids and one major waterfall, by the town of the same name: Big falls. But it was a predictable river and well known by its drivers. A crew of thirty-one would be enough.

He and Red would boss, Mike at the Head and Red at the trail. Socrates and another to cook with three bullcooks; two on the cook wanigan and one to run the sleeper would do. He picked ten men to work at the head of the drive. They would cover the front third of the drive and anticipate those areas where jambs might occur. Another ten men would take the middle of the drive working the bends and breaks in the river to keep the logs moving. The other four, one of whom was Tyler, would bring up the rear, picking up logs that had gone ashore or in any other way worked themselves aground.

Paddy, Oregon Kid, Old Toad, two cutters from Bemidji, Tall Jim and Curly Bob, Snoose, Johnson and Schnaps and twenty-five others were hired on straight from the camp.

To the great surprise of Tyler, the Timber Beast was leaving camp at breakup. He had taken a contract to cut summer pulp at an Itascan camp farther south.

Tyler asked him to join the drive but Beast refused. "You don't swim?"

"No."

"I'll teach you. Socrates doesn't swim either and he does it." The Beast gently shook his head. No, swimming wasn't the reason he wouldn't drive. He shook the boy's hand and that was it.

"Next year," he whispered and went to the barn to gather his belongings. He left camp early one morning a week before they blew the dams. He had already said farewell to Tyler, Paddy and Mike. The others didn't matter to him.

"Why did he do that," the crestfallen Tyler asked Socrates. He felt abandoned, his own reputation diminished by the loss of his cutting partner.

"If I tell you, don't call it gossip. The man is gone and I suppose his partner has a right to know if anyone does."

"It isn't gossip."

"Tyler, Beast took to the woods to keep from being hanged. That's why he was so nervous all the time in Craig. He won't go near towns if he thinks the law is about."

"Hanged? For what?"

"He killed a man in International Falls a while back. Broke his neck with his hands. He ran and got to the woods ahead of the law and he hasn't been out since.

Better than ten years now."

"And they're still hunting him?"

"Nope. Never were. Eyewitnesses said it was self-defense. They even told him."

"I don't understand. Why does he stay hidden?"

"Any number of reasons. Some would say he's trying to kill himself with work.

Others say he's afraid to face his family and friends. Like you."

"What does that have to do with anything?"

"He isn't like us, Tyler. He isn't like anyone, anymore. He's gone over the edge, only he did it young while he was still fresh, not old and worn out. Now, he's just waiting for it to catch up with him. It's like I've been telling you, if a man can't trust others; if he can't be part of the world then he must live his own punishment. Beast chose it and it'll one day kill him."

"But this man he killed ...?"

"It was his brother, Tyler. He killed his brother and now he's living a self-imposed life of imprisonment."

That story affected Tyler as much as any He had ever heard from Scorates. He tried to understand how a man so incredibly strong could be living a life so empty because of an act of passion, a momentary loss of self-control. Suddenly Timber Beast was no longer a demigod but, rather, just a man with human frailty.

Mike figured his crew was already pretty well set the evening three men walked into camp wanting to sign on. They had come west to see the rivers, hoping, eventually, to see the Columbia out in Washington. Instead, they were piece cutting pulp wood about two miles out of Craig and not enjoying it much. But they were broke and willing to do whatever necessary to get on.

"Where are you boys from?" asked Mike. He wasn't thinking he'd need them but there was something about the way they carried themselves that aroused his curiosity.

"My name is Willie," said the spokesman of the group. "They call me White Water Willie. I'm from Maine, same as these men." He put his hands on the shoulders of his companions.

"You wouldn't be from Bangor now, would you?"

"Hell if we ain't. We're all from Bangor. We're Bangor Tigers if you've ever heard of us. We let ourselves get drawn out on the world, following the stories of great rivers and big logs. Here we are now, cast afoot and cutting matchsticks for a living. We need a river to run on Mr. Sullivan. We sure do."

That was all Mike had to hear. Men of their reputation who would do anything to work were worth having. And Tigers at that!

Even in Minnesota the Bangor Tigers were legendary. They had started out as a company of river rats in New England in the 1800's. Formed by John Ross, they became the proudest, most organized, most sought after river men in the country. In time, anyone who worked that stretch of the country, or worked under a former Tiger was entitled to claim the title, Bangor Tiger. And they were special!

You could tell by the way they dressed and walked. They had already shed the heavy cap of the lumberjack and were wearing the black felt hat of the river man. Their lightweight wool pants were pegged higher than any man's in camp. Their boots were heavily corked, guaranteed to hold on any log and chew up any wooden floor.

By reputation they were agile as a panther, surefooted as a mountain goat, strong as a horse and hard as nails. They could fight like two grizzly bears when aroused, but they preferred to establish their manhood on the water rather than in the bars.

They had a swagger in their walk, part boast and part affected from the nature of their work; like a sailor that walks that way because of a life spent on a rolling ship. They were loose jointed, with a swing in their shoulders and arms, a happy-go-lucky edge on their personality. Their faces were braced with a reckless, good-humored gleam in their eyes. One of the men had a number of small scars alongside his temple that Mike recognized as "logger's smallpox", the result of a spiked boot in a barroom brawl.

"What are your partner's names?"

Willie grabbed the man on his right. "This is Boots. We've been together for four years now and he saves my life at least once a year. There's no better man than Boots. This other one," he gestured to the one with the smallpox, "I can't vouch for his past. We've only traveled together for the past year. I'll say this, he's a good cutter, and from what I've seen, he's a good river man. And we're Tigers, all, for sure. His name is Moustache," he said of the whiskerless young man. "Just call him 'Stache."

"We can use good men, anytime," Mike said. "Men from Bangor I've heard of. We pay forty dollars a month for drivers, be it lead or trail, all the same. Cooks, too. You have any problem with that?"

"Sounds fine to us," Willie said. The other two men nodded agreement. "How is the grub?"

"I'll apologize for that up front." He knew Socrates was standing behind him eavesdropping. "I expect to start driving anytime. You boys go find an empty bunk. Gabe should blow in about twenty minutes. We'll see if your appetites match the stories, too.

Early next morning, Socrates and his trail crew left for Craig to run the wanigans down to the mouth of Skunk Creek.

Sullivan made the rounds of his dams every day now, checking the water. The Tigers had been sent up to a good-sized holding dam near the head of Skunk Creek. It was a good distance to walk on the rotting road. One night Mike showed up there.

"Put on the kettle and let's boil up some tea," he exhorted Willie.

Willie hung the kettle over the fire and soon had a gallon of hot coffee brewing. "You wouldn't have a bite to eat here, would you?" Mike asked. He knew the men had left camp with two day's rations.

"Sure, boss, we got some bread and a good sized ham," Willie answered.

"Well, let's break it out and have a little bite while we chat."

Three hours, and a bag of stories later, Mike went back to camp, leaving the dam tenders holding a bare ham bone and a book full of experience.

Mike was so contrite he returned the next morning with another sack of food. But while at the dam, he got into more conversation and polished of most of that one off too, so he wisely sent a cook's helper out that same afternoon with another load. When the cook got there, he found the Tigers, cooking a red squirrel on a stick.

There was a lull for two days while they waited for the last of the ice to clear on the Bigfork. The roads turned into a sea of mud and the woods had taken on a cast of pale green as buds began to swell. The work came to a standstill. Axes were greased and packed away. Black bears dug in the garbage pit every night.

One night, Mike walked in on his little bunkhouse crew and called, "'Dats all boys, tomorrow we blow 'em."

TIMBER!!

On the River

Book 3

One

*F*eeling his way by the shadowy light of the quarter moon, Rube
led the men down the rotten ice road to the rollways. The air
was cold, wet and heavy; the kind that could drive away a week of
sleeplessness yet not so cold that they wore their heavy clothing.
During the night a quarter inch of ice had reformed on the pond
behind the driving dam. Five thousand logs were already sitting in
the ice while on the banks rested twenty thousand more.

Sullivan handed the dam tenders a tin of bread and sausage,
and coffee.

They had been on the job for twenty-four hours straight and
were exhausted. Still, knowing the importance of their work, they
hadn't gotten much sleep. If they lost the driving dam, the logs
would be stranded in a dry streambed until the next spring flood.

The tenders were good men, proven at other jobs and worthy
of their keep.

"How is the water, Arvid?" Sullivan asked.

"Still comin' down, Mike. There's a good head to work with
right now."

"Leaking?"

"Not much. Some squirts. Say, Mike, I'm out of snoose."

Sullivan handed over his pouch and walked out on the working
decks that floated against the back of the dam.

From the crib of logs he looked down to the dam base. Leakage was
producing a good flowage alright, but nothing beyond the expected.

Mike squinted through the dark mist and turned back to the
rollways. The jacks had already dropped their baggage and were
stationing themselves among the logs, ready to break loose the check
blocks. Others had come out on the dam and were standing by with

long pike poles ready to guide the logs into the sluice gates and shoot them downstream.

"Finish your chow and help load the turkeys on the sleigh, Arvid. Run 'em down to Socrates on the wanigans. Take some sleep down there if you've any time. You're done here."

The two tenders scampered off the dam, not so eager for the sleep as to get started before the sun turned the roads back to mud.

"Okay, boys!" Mike shouted loud enough to wake the men in Craig, "Break 'em free! Take 'em by the ears boys, and get 'em out! Get 'em wet, boys!" For the next thirty minutes he was a bawling, cussing, woods boss. Up and down the bank he walked, exhorting his men as they flew at the logs, prying at the wedges and breaking out the frozen logs.

"Give it some head, boys," he shouted to the men at the dams. Four men hung on the big gin pole that raised the gate, and a flume of water shot ten feet out beyond the base of the dam. It filled the narrow creek bed and rushed downstream.

A rollway broke loose and a dozen logs, bumping and grinding, echoing like giant drumheads, rolled into the creek. The ice heaved up as the water billowed beneath it, then broke into thousands of silvery shards. The logs and the dozens of others that followed drifted toward the gate, drawn by the current of flowing water.

Pike men took the logs at the gate. With their long, iron-spiked poles, they guided the timber into the opening of the sluice. One at a time, they slid into the water filled chasm. Left to their own random wanderings, the logs would have quickly choked the flue opening, requiring hours of labor to clear them out. It was a tough job, and dangerous. Many good river rats had fallen off the icy decking to be swept into the gate and drown in the turbulence or get crushed by the timber that rained down on them.

Once drawn into the maw of the opening, the logs shot clear of the dam, and landed with a spectacular explosion downstream of the dam. There, the bend and rapids crews got hold of them. From the dam to the Bigfork, men were strategically positioned to fend logs off the banks and keep them floating. Overhanging brush and trees at the narrow points had been cleared to prevent jams. They called them widow makers for the unwary jacks they swept off their logs and killed in the underwater web of branches. In two and a half-hours, a driven log would be at the mouth of the Spud.

Down on the Bigfork, Socrates and his small crew had finished rigging the catch boom over the big river. They had come down in the wanigans the day before and tied up on the bank.

The previous November, a crew had cut four forty-foot cedar logs, dragged them down to the end of Spud and rolled them off the bank. When Socrates found them, they were still lying eight feet above the creek bed. They were blocked off from it by an impenetrable tangle of alder brush.

"Well, I'll be dead and gone to St. Louie!" he swore. "Look at this guldarned mess! We got us a jungle here and all because some jackass hay puller was too lazy to look over the bank before he dumped! Well, what are you clowns looking at?" he growled, "Maggie's Drawers? Get some brushwackers out and let's get out of here before some lion comes along and eats us!"

They grabbed axes and peavies and worked well past the turn of the night digging out the boom logs, sweating them down into the river and joining them end to end with iron hooks.

To string the boom, the crew took a small skiff over to the far bank. They trailed a long line fastened at one end to the cedar logs. Gunnar took two wraps around a strong ash tree and they warped the string of logs across the swollen Bigfork, three feet at a time. The men had just cleared the halfway point of the river when a floating snag came down river and hooked itself over the rope. The extra weight was more than they could overcome even with the back eddy from Spud Creek working in their favor.

"Gunnar, row out there and free it up," Socrates ordered

"On it, boss," he answered with the snap of a West Point cadet

Gunnar jumped in the skiff and rowed along the upstream side of the cable. When he got to the half-submerged snag, he groped around in the dark water until he found the offending branch, and chopped it free with the axe. The boom came free with a sharp recoil that nearly threw Gunnar out of the boat.

"Holy saints and sinners!"he said, crossing himself. "I nearly took a bath a month early." Regaining his balance, he signaled Socrates. "She's free. Can you feel it?" "Pulling easy!" Socrates hollered.

"I will come back to you, then."

"Don't bother," the cook called back in the dark. "Me and these young studs have got it. You go on and watch the other end so she doesn't kink up. And put the coffee on! We'll come back on the boom."

Carl nodded at the voice in the dark and rowed back to the wanigans.

After tying off the north end of the boom, Socrates stood up and gestured at the floating string of logs that led back to their beds. "Any of you young bucks care for a race?"

The logs were stout enough and, being cedar, rode high in the water. There was just enough moon showing to display their black silhouettes in the twinkling glimmer of the river. Tyler looked at Socrates. "You are not serious."

"Sure I am."

"Crap, Socrates, I'll fall in the river."

"Unless you know how to fall out of a river. We'll all go swimming before the drive's over, boy. Might as well learn now before you have an audience."

"Go get the boat, will you?"

"You want the boat, you go get it."

Tyler could sense the grin on Socrate's face as the old man edged away from him.

"Listen, I'm not going to put up with this. You hear?"

"It's called 'wet ass', Tyler, and everyone gets it some time or another." Tyler lunged at him but Socrates was already well out of his reach, out on the first log. Spooner and Carl were in front of him and moving right along, their backs straight and their heads up. Tyler stood alone on the bank, two hundred feet from a place where he hoped to put his hand around the old fool's neck. He saw the others make their way across the boom. They moved quickly, with a surefooted scamper constantly correcting their pace against the bounce of the logs. It looked easy. Maybe, thought Tyler, it wasn't so difficult after all. It just looked hard.

He stepped out on the first log. It wasn't nearly as solid as it appeared when the others were on it. Why had he thought it would be? "Oh, hell, I'm going under!" The end he stepped on sank until it bottomed out along the shore, the other end rearing up. "They don't float at all! I can't do this. No one can do this. They didn't even do this. What in the hell did they do, anyway?"

He stepped back onto the bank.

A bemused Socrates watched him from the other end. "Move quick, Tyler," he urged. "Don't look down, keep moving and walk heel to toe. Keep your eyes out in front about ten good feet."

"Sure! You had a hollowed out log for a crib! You think this is like going down a sidewalk. What am I saying? None of you ever been in a city before. I'd like to get you guys in Chicago for just one week." He began coaching himself." All right, just like dancing, heel to toe, heel to toe. One. Two. Three. I'm going to do it. Here I go. Now! Now! Okay. Now!"

After four false starts, he was off, moving with the fluidity of a ballet dancer, albeit a stiff one. His boots were biting bark and holding firm.

Halfway across the river, reality hit him on the jaw and almost knocked him off.

Tyler slowed, hesitated and stopped.

"Don't stop! You'll freeze up!" Carl yelled. He remembered his first trip on a log.

When you get that fear and your body goes rigid, then the log takes over.

Tyler began settling in the water. Slowly he worked his way to the middle of the log. He stood there, his knees bent, his waist forward, his arms out as if he were about to dive into a pile of leaves. He wasn't moving at all except for the trembling. He was only thinking of not falling off; always a sure way to fall off. He was perfectly willing to stand there until the river went dry. The encouragement turned to anger.

"Move your butt, dammit!" Socrates screamed. Tyler was off like a shot, finished that log, did another and was just twenty feet from home when his toe caught a small stub of branch that should have been trimmed but wasn't.

He flew out over the water and hung suspended for a moment, struggling to fly, and made a perfect entry.He went under and came up gasping for breath; the cold water already constricting his chest. It was the dream all over again! He couldn't breath! He flailed at the water, panic stricken, searching for an escape but with no idea where to go. And suddenly it was there. Carl had run back out on the boom with a pike pole and began poking at Tyler. His thrashing hands found the pole and stuck. He nearly pulled Carl in, but Carl was ready for it and towed the boy the rest of the way off the boom where he was hauled aboard the wanigan and dried out by the barrel stove.

"I ought to kill you for that," Tyler snarled at Socrates. "You'd better sleep with one eye on your throat is all I got to say."

"I know you're just funning me and besides, then who'd be around to show you the good times, boy?"

"Don't call me, boy!"

"Son, I did you a favor."

"How do you figure that? A favor?"

"Oh? So tell me what you planned on doing for the next three weeks, walk on water?"

Maybe I will, dammit!" Tyler shouted. "I just didn't want to get wet. I've been there and I didn't like it." He still remembered his dunking in the creek but even more acutely, his drowning dream remained in his consciousness as an omen of his future.

"Tyler, there's two hundred miles of water and river bends between here and there and the only way to get down is on a log. I did you a favor all right. You got the first taste without thirty guys looking on. Don't matter who you are, they'd all laugh to see a man get baptized off a log."

"I'll walk the shore."

"Can't. There ain't no shore, especially on the hungry side. Some places, sure, but most others it's just muck and branches and slippery banks a man can't stand up on. See?" Socrates swept the river with his hand, "This river is a road, Tyler and that log is your buggy. You have to learn to drive it on the road is all. It takes practice but come a week from now, you'll be a river rat like the rest of us."

"Then I won't have to kill you?" Tyler said, his anger abating.

"Guaranteed. Have another cup of muck." Socrates turned them in early knowing that in a few hours the logs would be coming.

"Shorty!" Mike shouted to the little man. "Touch 'er off!" Shorty was holding a long pole with a stick of dynamite tied to one end. He ran out to a clearing a hundred feet away and lit the fuse. He stood the pole up against a dead snag and retreated. Seconds later it blew, sending a thunderclap into the woods. Scarcely a minute later another rumble, far off but loud, came back as a tending crew blew one of the beaver dams in response to the signal. The detonation tore a twenty-foot breach in the mud and sticks and loosed a five-foot wall of water into the Spud. Three minutes later, it hit the driving dam, carrying with it another thousand logs from the rollways.

They had been sluicing for six hours. Over three thousand logs had shot through the gates. Over on Skunk, a smaller crew was wrestling with the three thousand pieces that had been landed there. Thirty-three thousand logs by tally count. The demand for water was great, the pace of the work exhausting.

That was the second beaver dam Mike had blown. There was also a squirt dam across Skunk Lake still holding a good head. With luck, Skunk would be clear in another twenty-four hours. Spud would take considerably longer. To get them off before the water gave out meant working around the clock.

That night an icy rain began to fall. It started as a drizzle and turned into a steady downpour, saturating their clothing and soaking through to the skin. The rain turned the creek bank into a quagmire and put nearly as many men as logs into the water. But it also ate away the last of the frost from under the rollways and added thousands of gallons to the reservoirs.

At two in the morning they blew the third beaver dam. Mike was satisfied in spite of the weather, maybe even because of the weather. He knew everyone would step up the pace to keep warm. But, as always, he was among his troops, down in the water, running the length of the rollways, and lending a powerful arm when the logs out-manned his men.

"Put your backs in it, boys," he exhorted them. "You got all summer to sleep. Turn 'em! Turn 'em! Roll 'em out and wash 'em down! Put your heads back and drink from the clouds. We'll wash it down with whiskey at the end of the drive!"

Too wet to sleep, too tired to bitch, they swarmed like termites over the logs, knocking free the blocks, throwing themselves clear of the careening timber and rolling the balky laggards into the dark water. By now there wasn't a man among them who hadn't fallen in any number of times. What the rain didn't soak, the creek did. But they knew and respected that, among them, Mike was the wettest of all.

The second morning he finished off a big pail of stew and, stomping down the bank, stood in water up to his thighs. Splashing the muddy stream in his face, he shook his dripping head and roared, "Roll 'em out, boys! By the ears! It's daylight in the swamps and she's warm enough to wash your long johns. Let's finish her up!" And later, "Here comes the sun! She's a new day and God is smiling on his river rats! Let's do 'er! Get in the water, boys! In another month you'll be paying someone to put this in your whiskey!" Grabbing a peavy, he worked his way back up the bank, throwing logs into the creek behind him.

In two days and two hours Spud and Skunk creeks were empty of logs save for those that were still enroute to the Bigfork. The stew kettle was lashed to a log and run down the creek while the men were marched down to the wanigans for a dry change of laundry. The Bangor Tigers and the Oregon Kid were still fresh enough to ride the backs of the last three sticks.

"Climb aboard," Willie called to the Kid. Last one to the Rainey buys the first round!" And the Oregon Kid amazed them all by jumping on the last log and riding it clean through the sluice gate. He disappeared in the spray when he went in. Reappearing down-stream, he screamed a bloodcurdling cry of elation and, passing them all, went hell-bent around the bend and out of sight.

Two

"*D*at's all boys, roll 'em out!" It was pre-dawn on the river. There was another freeze during the night. The clouds had cleared and under the full starlight the cold came down and a last breath of winter stole into their blankets. Ice had formed along the shore and extended ten feet out in a fragile glaze forming a shining latticework around the waiting logs. Over thirty thousand of them distended the boom like a huge engorged belly.

The men crawled off the wanigan deck and rubbed the sleep from their eyes, stretching out the soreness of the last three days. Tyler walked out on the deck. Mike was out on the boom with Rube, looking down river, surveying the lay of the work. The drivers were clustered in small groups, out on the logs, along the bank and at both ends of the wanigan.

A short, naked, wiry man with a tattoo of an equally naked lady lounging on his chest stepped alongside Tyler looked him over with quiet amusement. "Hey, ain't you the Timber Bull, so called?"

Tyler kept his eyes and hands on his own business. The other man came only to his shoulders, but he wasn't deterred by the cold rebuff.

"Yeah, you're him. You fit. Big as a mountain and cute as a button. They were telling me about you up on the creek. Said you ate a small jack pine for breakfast and cut timber with the flat of your hand. Not pine, mind you, just spruce."

The callous runt reeled off a short burst of brag. "But I ain't no kid, either! I ain't new to nothing! I'm Willie, the Bangor Tiger. We heard you got the wet ass stringing the boom so Mike signed me on just to pull you out of the drink once a day so you don't get too wrinkled." He pulled up his pants and skipped away before

Tyler could get his hands around him, but his eyes burned through Willie's back as the skinny little man jostled his way back into the wanigan.

Mike wanted daylight for starting the drive. Rube would have to march a good share of the boys across the boom and down the tote path where he'd drop them off at the places where trouble was liable to occur, and it didn't make sense to walk through brush country in the dark. Even so, Rube fed his men and started them out as soon as they could distinguish the ground from their boots. Most of the drivers stayed back at the boom to ride out with the logs, get a feel of the flow and take notice of the best places a log might curl up on a bank and stick. Then they would drop off and work that spot until the bulk of the drive had passed by before moving ahead again.

The Bigfork flowed like a snake. The longest stretch without a bend or rapids was never more than half a mile. Big trees that favored the water's edge, basswood and ash, overhung the river from the high banks, placing much of it in shade for the greater part of a day. It had a peaceful and tranquil appearance, broken only by the rapids that intruded periodically. Once wet, a man stayed wet all day. Water seeped in the stitching of the boots and turned the feet soft so tubs of lard were kept on hand to coat both the leather and the feet.

If the drive was hard on the body, it was doubly so on the lower extremities. A river man with foot rot couldn't work, and men that couldn't work might as well be on the dole. Mike had no use for them and worse yet, they had no use for themselves. If a river driver was anything, he was proud and would just as soon work crippled than not be able to work at all. It was a system that perpetuated itself, based on pride and supported by pride. As Socrates had said months ago, "The boys are sorted out quick enough."

Fifteen minutes after Rube moved out, Mike took a maul out on the boom. With one swing he split the binding link. Willie let out a whoop and jumped the first log out, and the drive was on. For three weeks the river rats would ride, wrestle and roll the waterborne logs down the Bigfork. Until they hit the Rainey and handed off the timber to a tugboat, it would be work, work, and then more work.

"See you women at Big Falls," Willie hollered back to the wanigan as he floated off with the others. Bull, don't get your diapers wet."

"Why are you riding Bull?" the Oregon Kid asked. "He's all right."

"1 know that," Willie retorted. "That's how I make friends."

"But he's big enough to stick you in a snuff can and carry you around in his back pocket."

He grinned. "I know that, too. A man don't make a name for himself by picking on children, does he, Kid?" Willie couldn't say 'Ouch' without smiling.

"Just be careful your name doesn't get worked into an epithet. He can be touchy."

Back at the wanigan Socrates had heard the cat-calling and saw the look in Tyler's eyes. "Bothers you some, doesn't it?"

"Aw, he's a nuisance, like a fly buzzing around a fellow all the time."

"You plan to swat him?"

"If I can catch him." Tyler looked over at Socrates.

"He likes you," the cook offered. "That's his way. Like a young kid. Too proud to show outright friendship so they tease. Maybe he thinks he's tough, too, eh?"

"And what would you do?"

"Give back same as you get. He'll think you like him, too."

"Well, I certainly would, if I could catch the little shit."

Sullivan came back onto the wanigan. "Socrates," he said, "I wondered. Have you got another stack of them griddle cakes for the boss?"

The Bigfork wasn't a wild river by New England standards. But it was crooked and had its share of dangerous rapids and flowed two hundred and more miles long from the source at Lake Dora to its mouth on the Rainey River. A crow could cut off a hundred pig-tailed miles flying in a straight line. It flowed better than four miles an hour when it was swollen and deep, as in spring. By August it would be gutted, its rapids fully exposed, swift, turbulent and shallow, impossible for passage of logs. In March, there were only three rapids of any consequence: Powell's Rapids, Muldoon's and the drop at Big Falls.

Other than Big Fork and Craig upstream, the only towns were Big Falls and Linford farther downstream.

The logs moved with a lazy fluidity with and yet apart from the water that bore them. Starting as a compact mass in the beginning, they stretched out with a fluid elasticity as the days wore on. Logging drives ran night and day, especially in the swift rivers of the east where logs were dumped in at the rollways and, barring a jam, never stopped moving until they hit the sorting bins at the sawmills.

Minnesota used a system uniquely adapted to the terrain. Because the water ran slower, and the Bigfork was a longer river than most, the drives lasted longer and the logs strung out farther. Not all logs would float at the same pace nor did all water flow at one speed either. The center of the river held the greater current. Eddies and backwaters trapped logs while sandbars, and rocks created shoots and runs that boosted the speed of other logs considerably. To run night and day without a chance to regroup periodically would have made feeding the men a logistical nightmare. There had to be opportunities to gather up and tend to housekeeping.

Sullivan liked to run four or five days without letup and then throw a catch boom over a narrow part of the river to hold back the vanguard. When the rear tenders got to within three or four hours of the front, he'd let them go again. Holding logs in the river for too long was bad business. They would soak up water and when sodden sink in the muddy bottoms or snag on the rocky bottom of the river bed.

Sixteen hours a day was every man's lot, rain or shine, hot or cold. Lunch was likely as not a cold pork sandwich that may have been dropped once or twice in the water and a man's company all day was just as likely to be a muskrat, kingfisher or a bald eagle as another man. To a river rat that was part of the lure: to be alone with his thoughts, no boss to bully and harass him, no woman or colicky kids to distress him. He was his own boss, the timber was his client, and the river was his sales territory, his responsibility, his best friend and his worst enemy.

In good times, the river made a man's life easy; in bad times it stole his life, but without it there would be no drive and no logging so the lumberjack never pondered the philosophical implications. He went about his work as an integral part of the landscape and yet was of fleeting consequence only. A river rat left no footprints, turned no sod and planted no seed. He floated through the land as quiet as the log on which he rode, rounded the next bend, and was gone.

Sullivan's outfit moved out in fine style. By noon the boom was empty and the wanigans were running with the logs. Socrates let it ride free among the timbers because moving at the same gentle pace as the logs was jostle free. The wanigan, left to its own nature, however, would also get trapped in an eddy or wrap itself tight against a deadfall. One cook had to be at the sweeps almost constantly. Their destination was twenty miles on, where they would pull into shore, tie off to a tree and set dinner for everyone. Although he always kept a pot of something good simmering on the stove, Socrates never fixed lunch on a big scale. The men carried their own midday meal, either in a cut down gunny sack or in a container fashioned from an empty tobacco or food tin. They hung them from their backs when out on the river, or buried them in the cool riverbanks if working a bend or rapids. Only the greenest kid would be foolish enough to hang his lunch pail from a tree branch with Hungry Mike on the prowl. All the same, Socrates kept a lookout for men working the shore.

"There's three at that creek entrance, Spooner, grab the pot."

"Yessir, boss!" and Spooner would take the coffee pot and a satchel full of donuts and go running off across the logs, to the cheering and encouragement of the hungry men.

Tyler was working the hungry side of the stream. Wanigans always tied up on the same bank if possible, normally the right one, so jacks heading in wouldn't have to worry about which side to cross too. People on the left packed their food and hoped it held out until they could clear the last of their logs and then ride one over to the other side and find the barge. Hence the name, 'hungry side'.

For similar reasons, Sullivan never spent much time over there. He kept mostly to the tote path on the right bank. The tote path was a trail carved out as close to the river bank as possible. Both animals and people had a hand in its creation. Beaver dragging branches to the water, deer and other animals looking for a place to cross or hunt provided the first definition. Indians and trappers clarified it and cleared the major obstructions. Finally the loggers and their horses put on their stamp of permanency. It followed the path of least resistance, often disappearing inland to bypass a backwater or creek mouth. Sometimes it petered out entirely because of a meadow or swamp. But a patient man who knew the river, knew the tote path and never completely lost it. Tyler rarely had the luxury of walking the tote path.

He was partnered with Carl, a good man, quiet and modest about his skills, easy to work with. He was no challenge to the better whitewater men so he never showed off, but Carl knew all the techniques of working a log drive and wasn't too proud to pass them off to Tyler. He reminded Tyler of Johnson who had gone home with his horses. They were both Swedes, both taciturn yet also friendly and loyal with a humorous side. They had known each other in camp. Carl had been a cutter at the other end of the forest. They knew of each other's reputation and Carl respected Tyler's ability, both to work and to fight.

Carl taught Tyler to ride the logs. "Always save a good one," he advised. "To go home on." So Tyler learned to ride the logs between snags. He learned to steer them into shore, wrestle out the snags and then mount his log and move on to the next work.

Their working tool was the peavey, a six foot pole with a spiked metal end and a hook for rolling, pushing and dragging the logs around. Carl showed Tyler how to climb on a log and steer it into the whirlpool by shifting his weight and dragging his peavy in the water. He showed him how to work a log sideways by spinning it, running on it with the corked shoes and so, cross the full width of the Bigfork in under ten minutes. He showed Tyler all the good things he knew about the river and, in time, Tyler became better than Carl at most of them.

He fell in often at first and later, infrequently and finally, never. Carl only fell in once, but it made a lasting impression on Tyler.

Carl had finished a small job upstream and was riding past him, fifty feet out from shore. He was watching Tyler, gauging whether or not the youngster needed help. Comfortable that he did not, Carl, in a playful gesture, doffed his hat to Tyler as he drifted by. He was bent over in a silly bow, when he hit a submerged log.

Carl fell in and disappeared under the surface. Tyler broke out in a fit of laughter over the dunking. Twenty seconds went by, thirty and Carl still hadn't come up. Frightened, Tyler pushed off to where his partner had disappeared. He drifted over the spot and looked down. Carl's hat was floating high on the water. There was nothing else. Tyler could make out the sunken log in the river but there was no sign of Carl! No bubbles, no thrashing arms, no body. His mind raced trying to figure out what had happened! My God, he's drowned, Tyler thought. He's hit his head and went under. Where? By now he could have been swept two hundred feet downstream. Or lodged in some underwater . . .

"Bull! Pick up my hat when you're out there please!" Carl was standing by the shore, waist deep in the river, his peavy on his shoulder. He was dripping wet but unruffled.

Tyler was dumfounded. "What in the hell? How'd you get over there?"

"My hat! I said pick it up!"

"Your hat? But, how'd you? What happened, Carl?"

"What do you mean, what happened?'

"How did you get over there?" Tyler had snagged the hat and was working his way in.

"Well, I walked, of course."

"Walked? On water?"

"Of course not. On the bottom, the ground. I went to the bottom and walked in."

Tyler couldn't believe what he had heard. "Why in God's name? You mean you walked in along the bottom?"

"Well, what did I say, Tyler?"

"You did that just to scare the crap out of me."

"No, no. Of course not."

"Then why, for God's sake did you just disappear out in the middle of the river and then come up like that just when I thought you were drowned?"

"Because, you donkey-brained student, not yet a river rat, I can't swim very well and with a peavy in my hand not at all."

"My Lord, he walks on the bottom of rivers," Tyler muttered, at a loss for understanding. "I'm living with a river full of freaks."

It wasn't until dinner several days later that Tyler sat down next to Carl over a meal of beans and ham.

"Carl, I was wondering?"

"About what, sonny."

"What is it like under the water?"

"You really want to know, Bull?"

"Yes. Yes I do."

"It is wet, just wet. No, more than that it is dark and lonely, too. It is a place where just you can say what is going to happen to you. And you dasn't try to breath down there. But if you become to much afraid, you will die for sure because you get frozen and can't move."

Three

*I*f a river's beauty is defined by the grandeur of the land surrounding it, the Bigfork was not a pretty river. Aside from the hardwoods along its banks, it was bordered by desolation. As far back as visibility permitted, the loggers had done their work stripping out all the good timber and dumping it in the Bigfork. The early crews always took the easy chance.

It was a boggy area with islands of up-land intended by God to grow great trees. But once logged, it grew back in brush, a thick low, growth of alder and hazel brush punctuated frequently by the stabbing fingers of tall stumps and snags. It grew mosquitoes and drew homesteaders who read the invitations of free land from the government and lived too far away to inspect the tract before packing up and coming. What they found was low and boggy, or high and full of rocks, a perfect habitat for wildlife and fish, less so for humans. Beneath the ground the network of roots grew strong enough to stop any plow man had yet devised, and if the roots weren't deterrence enough, the ground, itself, was. Carl talked about the dirt as "Just enough mud to hold the rocks together." The glaciers had done their work well. During the last ice age, they had scoured Canada, collecting millions of tons of gravel and boulders, and dumped them in Minnesota. In time, a pitiful thin topsoil had developed, rarely more than an inch thick. It was a land meant to grow trees and blueberries, nurture wildlife and run water. That was the extent of it.

When the pines were taken, the ground was opened to sunlight and other species established themselves. Oak, ash and basswood were plentiful. Beneath them, the brush: hazel, juneberry, serviceberry and chokecherries. The sugar maples, able to grow in near darkness encroached on the richer pockets of loam. And scattered among them the pine, spruce and balsam seedlings slowly began their return. Birch and poplar and other pioneer trees claimed entire tracts. Only God knew where they had come from.

One night after supper, Tyler was pitching in with the cleanup and he mentioned this to Socrates.

"It's so desolate, Socrates. "I think this is what a war zone must look like."

"It is, isn't it? I can't deny that," Socrates answered. "And I can't deny I had something to do with it. We've done a lot of wrong to this country all in the name of getting out the logs. The only ones who ever got anything out of it is ... hell, I guess nobody really. What the timber barons did, they did because it was a chance to cash in. Uncle Sam said, 'Come children, the party's on me.' I can't say they were bad, probably greedy. But maybe all of us were wrong to cut the trees. At one time, no one could have guessed that we'd run out of trees. They went forever. It doesn't seem possible that we're getting to the last of it."

"You were one of them, weren't you? Not an owner but a logger?"

"I was. As you are now. And there were thousands before me. Strong backs with tallow between the ears. They're nothing but unkempt mounds of dirt now. Back when I was your age, I couldn't have cared less. Maybe you do. Maybe things will change. If we left it alone for a hundred years it might be the same as God first made it. But people like to change things, make their mark like a wolf pissing on a rock. Oh, I'm running on about nothin'."

But Tyler wouldn't let it lie. "What was it like?"

"Tyler, you should have seen it in its glory." Socrates nodded, running again with the subject. "God spent his summers up here. Adam and Eve had a cabin right south of us. Trees so tall, you'd of thought you were paddling down a tunnel. The sun never hit the forest floor. The river was clean, too, not all filled up with snags and deadheads and sandbars. You could count the fish. You could see 'em so plain except there were too many to count anyway. You could walk across this river on the backs of pike when they were in their spawning runs! Yep, it sure was beautiful. I remember that time, or the end of it, anyway."

"I still see a lot of game."

"Game? Oh, if anything, it's better, at least for the deer and partridge. You see them all along here, That's because they like the cover of brush better than the open woods. Fishing might be better, too, what with all the cover from these sunk trees and what not, though I doubt it. Now, it ain't, of course. The water's too high. But later this summer come down here and you can give your soul to the Lord if you like fishing. You do like fishin', don't you, Ty?"

"I never fished. Except for the spear house."

Socrates grabbed at his heart. "You poor, neglected child. Tell you what. Tomorrow we'll go fishing about noon. You come in for lunch and we'll get us some nice fish."

"You said it wasn't any good now."

"I know the tricks. Here, as long as you're helpin', scrub the mold off these spuds, so I can boil them."

Tyler sat down in front of a sack of potatoes and began scrubbing them down with a stiff wire brush. Socrates went out the door with a bucket of slop and threw the garbage overboard. He rinsed out the pail twice, then filled it. Across the water a pair of yearling whitetail deer were standing at the foot of the embankment, drinking. They lifted their heads and watched him until he disappeared into the wanigan, then lowered their noses back into the water.

"Just throw them in here," Socrates said, putting the pail along-side Tyler.

The wanigan was warm and comfortable. They were alone. Socrates sat beside Tyler, picked up another brush and joined him with the potatoes.

"You've been acting pretty calm lately, Tyler. You feelin' it?"

"Feelin' it? Am I feelin' it?" Tyler played with the words. He sensed what Socrates was about. It raised his hackles and it showed in the tone of his voice. "Feeling what?"

"Don't think I'm prying, son. I just couldn't help but notice so I thought I'd say it." He took Tyler's lack of a rejoinder as an acceptance of the matter so he went on.

"You've grown a lot in the last while, Tyler. I'm thinking that you might be ready to leave some things behind for good."

"Like what?"

"Like the demons in your heart, son."

"Demons?" Again Tyler got defensive. "What are you talking about?"

"People. People who got inside you and turned you around for awhile."

"You mean Stankovich?"

"Him, yes, and maybe your pa. Mike and other things, too. People who gave you wrong notions about being a man. Back in my time, and I know I can't expect you to respect the memories of an old fogy like me, but back in my day, Tyler, it was an alright thing to come up here and make a name for yourself. We all did it. It was a new world and a man could come in and stomp around, good and bad, and set himself up for life. Still can. But it's no good if you're just out to make the name."

"It worked for others."

"Not anymore. See, kid, it's dying out, the old breed and the old ways. Ten, fifteen years and it'll be all over. There won't be any more timber; there won't be any more camps. The old bums like me will be all dead and forgotten. If we don't fall under a tree in the woods, or if the river don't shut the hole on us, then we'll sure drown in the booze. Good riddance, I say. You young guys, well, maybe you're too smart too soon. Maybe you think you know it all. Huh?"

"And tough. Don't forget how tough we are."

"Yeah, tough. You laugh. Maybe that's good, too. But don't joke about your future, Tyler. Sure you're tough, some ways at least. I brought you in here to toughen you, didn't I? And I gotta tell you, honest now, you've learned well. But up here everyone's tough. They all put kerosene on their hotcakes. That don't prove nothin'. That ain't the right kind of tough."

"Well, you're either mean or you get beaten down like a dog. It's a dog eat dog world. Am I mean, Socrates? Am I any different than the rest of you?"

"Not really but you mix up toughness and meanness sometimes."

"Am I meaner than any of the others?"

"Yes, I think at times you are. It still shows on you. You take advantage of your size and muscle. Not so bad that the others want to sew you in your blankets, but, yes, there's a roughness there yet. It's a little sad, is what it is."

"If I'm nasty, it's because I've had good teachers. Damn near everyone up here has given me a lesson at one time or another."

Socrates held up his hand to settle Tyler down before going on. "You're feeding on a lot of pain yet. Hurt! Maybe I don't know the half of it. I don't know your family. I always thought families were something to go home to. Maybe not. What do I know? I never knew my folks. Funny thing, everyone who ever tried to be my family, I run out on. I guess I ain't so tough either. Hell, give me another spud."

Tyler examined his potato thoughtfully. "It isn't your fault. Shit, I don't know my family either and I lived with them all my life. Once Graham got going good, ma and pa figured he'd raise me, I guess. Maybe Graham didn't do such a proud job of it."

"Listen, I do know this. There's a man named Tyler Caldwell inside the one called Timber Bull. I ain't sure yet which one will go back to The Rapids with me, but it's getting time to find out. Coming from a bad beginning is no excuse to go to a bad end. A man gets old enough to make that decision for himself and in the end, there's no room for blaming others because nobody cares but you. You get my drift?"

"I get it. Maybe I won't go back. I can make out okay where I am. I'm doing fine here and I'll do the same in the next place."

"Listen Tyler, if whatever's out there pulling at you is good, I'll not argue it. I don't wonder if you can't know what you want. Just so long as you're thinking on it. Just think on it."

Tyler threw down his brush and stood up. He was frustrated by Socrates' quiet persistence, his gentle needle. "Well, what the hell difference does it make? Everyone here is either a tramp or about to become one. You! Underneath all the words, you're just an old drunk!"

The words hurt. If said in jest they would not have stung so much, nor if anyone else had said them. Tyler knew he had gone too far. He stood there dumb, his hands trying to speak for him. Socrates stuck another potato in one of them.

"You're lagging," he said. Tyler sat staring at the potato. "Son," Socrates began again, "all of us up here are pretty well down to our last hurrah. We're pretty near the end of the trail. And it's a drunken trail at that. But, except for a few exceptions, the men have kept the most important thing, their souls. Now, there's pride, and salvation in that. So drunk or not, and we've all been drunk as often as sober, a man can still have some good in him. So don't fret about what you said. The truth hurts, but words can't kill. Not like silence anyway."

Tyler stopped scrubbing again and took Socrates's wrist. "I'm sorry I said that. Honest, if it wasn't for you, I . . . well, you helped me a lot. You know that. But here you're talking about your final reward and I'm still trying to find my first one. You have to give me that. What difference does it make? The world is full of soul-less men. They still get through it. The best ones get by pretty damn well. That's all I'm asking; just a chance at being someone. A shot at the brass ring. When I get to your age, I'll dig out my soul and polish it up. Front pew, I promise. Okay?"

Socrates patted the boy's hand and began playing with his pipe. "I hope to God you get that chance, son. I really do." He cleared his throat and changed the subject. "You say this stretch of the river is pretty ugly. Tomorrow it will change a bit for the better. There's a place up ahead called the Klondike Rocks. It's real rugged with hills and boulders. Lots of boulders, like the Alaskan gold fields where I spent a little time. Yeah, I been there too. That's how it gets its name. It was damn near impossible to log so it's got a lot of old growth in spots. It's the kind of place a man could get lost in and just hole up until his Maker calls. The Indians have a story about it."

"I suppose I'm going to hear it." Tyler said with a sigh.

"You darn right you're gonna. You think I just talk to exercise my whiskers?"

"What kind of Indians?"

"Now? Chippewa. Ojibway is what they were to the French and something else before that, but you know the white man, always trying to improve on perfection. There used to be Sioux but the Ojibway drove them out. Now there's tough for you. Anyway, they say there's a hole up there in those rocks and ledges that nobody has ever seen and come back to report on. Guess that makes it a legend. I know I ain't never seen it, but they say if you see it you'll never live to tell anyone, so I suppose I don't want to see it."

"Where is it?"

"Dunno. Somewhere back in way off the river. You drop a stone down it, you won't ever hear it hit the bottom. It's like there ain't no bottom, just a top and a middle that never ends. People that look down it get sucked in. Like staring off a cliff too long it makes you want to jump in.

"You swear you can see the bottom plain as day looking back at you, like it was an arm's length away. It shines like the sun. The Indians say it's gold reflecting out of the hole. That was the lure, the gold. So the braves would climb down the hole to get that gold. They'd drop for hours but never get to the bottom. Even though it looked close enough to just reach out and grab. Sooner or later all of them, even the toughest, would lose their grip and fall. But the fall never killed them, because they never hit bottom. They died of fear or thirst or starvation but not the fall."

"That is a fairy tale," Tyler suggested.

"I sure hope so but you decide. Anyway, the story goes that some big hero of an Indian brave did reach the bottom once, I don't know how. Well, he ended up dying anyway. When he got down there all he found was a pool of water, reflecting the sunlight of the sky back up at him. That was the gold. And in the gold was the reflection of his face. The legend says it was the quiet down there that killed him. Being down there forever with no one but himself. Just himself and the quiet water and a warrior couldn't live with that.

"The medicine men tell of the endless hole that pulls men down, forward to their past, they say. It makes you think there's something worth having out in front of you but it's just your past coming back at you. You never catch up to it, never put it behind you. Some day it puts you down and the hole closes over. You go quietly. Everyone does."

Socrates waited for Tyler. It was slow in coming. "You think I'm caught in the Klondike hole?"

"I don't know for sure where you are, son. Maybe you don't either. That's all right, it weren't your doing."

"What wasn't my doing?"

"Leaving home. Your pa. All of it. I sometimes wonder if I didn't make a mistake letting you come. Maybe I should'a spanked you and sent you home instead of meddlin' with your life. Lord knows, I can be a real meddler sometimes."

"Listen here!" Tyler snapped, "When I met you on that train, I was as good as down in that hole of yours. But home? I would have jumped out the door first. Right then. No! That's not right either. I wouldn't have had the courage to do a thing." Tyler laughed, "Shit! I know. I'd still be in that boxcar riding to God knows where."

Socrates laughed with him. "It wasn't necessarily your fault, son. None of it is your fault. Maybe if you accept that it'll be easier to forget it."

"Socrates, I am forgetting a lot of it. Up here I'm everything I couldn't be back in Chicago. Here I know who I am. It's all black and white."

"Who are you, Tyler?"

"Who? I'll tell you who I am. I'm the man they call Timber Bull!" Then he winked, almost imperceptibly and grabbed another potato. It wasn't the remark of a young man experiencing the epiphany that marked the turn from adolescence to manhood, but it definitely was a wink.

Four

The rugged bed of the Bigfork River was running through the crags of the Klondike rocks. Within its steep banks raged a half mile of white water and froth. Dead snags marked the twisting corkscrew paths that threaded through the swiftly dropping elevation of the river. Granite boulders and slabs, in immovable defiance to the lashing white- foamed waters lurked just below the surface. They gave the water a glazed and smooth appearance but caught and held a log like a fly on sticky paper.

"That's it. That's the Muldoon Rapids. Worst stretch on the river, excepting The Falls, of course, but that's all set up with booms to get around it. Here it's just you the river and your God."

Tyler and Carl were standing by the bank, sharing the fascination of the turbulent water. A cold rain that had dumped sheets of water on them for the last four hours was just blowing clear and billows of mist were still dancing in the air. Logs were shooting through the rapids like spears, glancing off the rocks and leaping into the air, than piercing the water and submarining beneath the surface, until they struck another obstruction and became airborne again. Thousand pound projectiles adding their own fury to the raging slough.

"It looks dangerous."

"They've hung up a lot of boots along here, Bull. It's as bad as it comes. You see that white stuff there?" The surface was thick with foam, like pillows of soap scudding along with the current.

"Yeah?"

"When you get the water beating itself into those bubbles, then it's the worst. That's one way to tell. The other is by the empty places at the dinner table."

"Can you still handle it? Can you work out there?"

"No more. Used to, but no more. That's why I tend the rear. The rear is for old bulls and young ones." He laughed. "But listen, Bull, let the veterans take this rapids. You can't learn it so quick as that."

Just then Willie and his friends came racing through, riding through the flumes of Muldoon, shooting the narrow troughs of swift water. They stood well back on their logs, their long handled peavies held in front of them as balance poles. Their faces, streaming with water from the cold spray were etched with lines of intense concentration.

"They are tryin' to kill themselves, the young fools," Carl clucked. "Tryin' to give the rapids a new name."

"Who's name does it have now?"

"1 don't know who he was. Happened thirty or forty years ago. I think he vas a lumberjack name of Jacob Muldoon. Muldoon for sure, anyway. Jacob or Jake, I don't remember. Doesn't really matter."

"What did he do to get a rapids named after him?"

"Not much. Just drowned."

"Oh," Tyler said "1 don't suppose he was the last either."

"Not by a long shot. Come here," said Carl, tugging at Tyler's sleeve. "I'll show you someting."

They walked together down the tote path for a hundred yards, and stopped next to a small oak. He pointed into the branches. Hanging there was a pair of dried and shriveled boots, the soles split and curled, the spikes rusted and dulled. There was no way to guess how long they had been there; might have been forever. Tyler felt warm breath on his neck.

"Who's were they?"

"Muldoons, they say. He's buried right beneath us."

Tyler stepped back, and began searching the base of the tree for a headstone.

"No," Carl said. "Them boots are his headstone. They carried his body back from wherever the river gave it up and buried it here. The boots always mark the spot."

"What happens if they don't find the body?"

"I can't remember that happenin'. The river always gives them up after a spell. It plays with them and beats them up but it always gives 'em up. No matter how long. It is queer how it plays with them. Sometimes it tears the clothes right off people. Everthing but the boots. Just like the undertaker settin' up the body for the burying. 'Cept they don't look so good. You come out all swollen and stiff. You can't fold the arms over the chest. Have to cut them off sometimes and put them alongside the body. The skin is pale white, like the blood was sucked out with the life."

Tyler held up his hand, "That's enough, thank you, Carl." His eyes went back to the boots.

"If you look good, Tyler, you'll find about twenty pair around here."

Oregon Kid was entering the rapids close inshore on the near side of the river.

Deadfalls hung out from the bank and here and there a sentinal boulder stuck its shoulders out of the water. The river was running full of logs caught up in the churning white madness, rushing like lemmings to the calm pools beyond.

The Kid saw Carl and Tyler and pointed downstream where Willie and Boots were just coming up on the tote path.

"Tell those east coast crab suckers to put their bug eyes on this," he hollered as his log began to hit the boiling foam. The Kid was a handsome young man with long sandy hair and a well-trimmed beard. Like the others, he wore the uniform of the lumberjack; high-cut boots, loose woolen pants rolled high, black suspenders over a black and red checked shirt. He was hatless and his hair was flowing like the mane of an unbroken stallion running into a storm.

He was riding so far back that his heels hung out over the water. The front end was up bouncing in and out of the waves. He was surfing on the rollers, flying down the chute. His knees were bent slightly, his weight forward on his feet.

Skimming down the boiling water he was, to Tyler, the epitome of all the romance and lore of the lumberjack; a beautiful, poetic athlete carrying in his soul the song of manhood, in his chest the great pride that a man has when he has done something no one has ever done before or since.

"Look at that, Carl. Isn't that something?"

"I'm looking. I'm looking. Yeah, I'm looking to see where he will land on his butt."

The Tigers came up beside him. Willie curled his lip, sneering in mock derision at Oregon's show. "Hell, he wanted me to cheer for a little ride like that? That ain't nothing worth drinking over."

Tyler was about to say something when the Kid suddenly shifted his peavy and, lifting it high over his head, drove the point deep into the log under his feet. Then, to the astonishment of everyone, he leaped into the air and did a handstand on the end of the peavey. He hung there, his feet waving in the wind and like a rocket, he shot by them and disappeared downstream in the spray and wash.

"Holy mother of Christmas!" whistled Carl.

"Yeah," said Willie. "Tell me I didn't see that. I got to come all the way to Minnesota to see something like that? I don't believe it. I didn't see it. I don't see it I don't have to try it."

"You don't ever see a man ride upside down before?" Carl wondered.

"God no! I've heard of it. They say Dan Bosse could do it, but I ain't never seen it."

"Shoot, we all do it in Minnesota." Carl jabbered. "Only way to keep our shoes dry when we go to town on Saturday night."

"Oh, go on," said Boots.

"It's the truth I tell you."

"It's high grade b.s."

"Yah, that too."

Willie puffed out his chest, "Well I don't mean to brag, fellas but I was in the movies once." He looked serenely out over the water.

Try as he might not to encourage the arrogant man from Maine, Carl couldn't help himself. "What did they want you in the movies for?"

"A log rider, of course. They had a big time movie star that was afraid to get out on the river, so they offered me five dollars to ride a log. Cripes! Nearly a week's pay for doing what I do best! So I did the ride and they paid me. Then he offered me 10 dollars to fall off the log when I shot the rapids. I shot the rapids, all right, but I didn't fall. When that movie magnate asked why I stayed on the log, I said, 'Listen I've never fallen off a log in my life and I couldn't make myself do it just now. In fact, I don't think I could ever make myself fall off for less than twenty-five dollars.'"

"Twenty-five dollars!" Carl exclaimed. "Did you do it, then?"

"Nope. They thought I was holding them up so they got some guy who was good at falling." Willie looked downstream again, remembering the Kid perched on his peavey. "But that's a sight to remember. I gotta teach me to do that. It'd be worth a hundred to do that."

Tyler's feelings toward Willie warmed at the little man's childish admiration for his friend. Even more, he was nearly overcome with his own appreciation for the Kid. He knew he had just been witness to an incredibly impossible feat.

"Wonders will never cease, I guess," Willie added. "Next time I look, I'll probably see this Bull here coming through riding a log and carrying another on his shoulders." He poked Tyler in the belly and sauntered up the trail. Willie hit the drink five times that day trying to duplicate the Kid's feat but never did.

Five

That afternoon a jam formed in Muldoon Rapids. It started when a log, riding low in the water, squeezed beneath another, and was driven into a fissure between two boulders. Its free end, protruding upstream, driven by the water, rose out of the river and the giant jaw began to snag other logs that came down behind it. The jam grew rapidly towards the left bank, touched it and held firm. More logs were swept in behind the others and soon they numbered in the hundreds. Half the channel was closed, making the current in the remaining half double in ferocity.

The men battled courageously to break it off, but it was next to impossible to get at it until it reached the shore, and by then it was locked tight.

"It's a touchy one, all right," Socrates said from the wanigan. He was tied off above the entrance to the rapids. "A mean little sister. See there, Tyler, you can't tell what's going to happen to it. The rapids, being what they are anyway should be able to blow it right free. All that force, but it ain't doing it, so you don't know. You'd rather it just went ahead and jammed the whole river. I seen one of them down on the St. Croix. We had the boys at Dupont workin' double shift to get us enough sticks to blow it. But with a full jam you at least know what you got. This here kitten is like a shadow in the dark. You don't know what you got until it's jumping out at you. It could haul on ya. It could haul at any minute if the key log gives out."

"What's a key log?" Tyler asked.

"Key log. That's the one that starts the whole circus; the one that you have to get rid of to haul it. Trouble is, you can't ever be sure which one it is until it comes loose. By then it might be too late to get away. There's more than a few tree boots here that belonged to men that got caught in a jam that hauled without them getting free."

"Couldn't someone like Oregon or Willie do it?"

"Son, all those boots were worn by Willie's and Oregon Kids. The brave ones always go first. The cowards end up with their girls. It ain't right, but it's fact."

A number of men went to look over the situation. They went out onto the jam with their pikes and peavies and tried to clear it out. They managed to pry a number of logs off the undulating monster, but for every one that was freed, ten more drove in to take their place. Fearless as they were, the jam held, and none dared go out onto the tip of the wing where the key log held the jam solid. Rube, for the sake of safety, finally pulled them off.

"I can't understand it, the water should just blow it right out," Socrates surmised.

"Why don't you pour a little of your coffee over it," Spooner suggested, "and just burn it off?"

"Aw, shut your yap, before I make you drink some of the muck."

"Won't risk it until after I've fathered my children."

"Well, don't worry about that. The jungles are already full of monkeys." Socrates punctuated his remark by scratching his ribs like a gorilla.

"I didn't know you were so well traveled, boss," said Spooner, quickly retreating into the wanigan.

Around noon, Mike came back up river. Standing on the wanigan, wolfing down a sandwich, he looked over at the jam. To him it took but a moment's reflection. He turned to Tyler, the man who happened to be closest, and spoke between bites of his sandwich.

"Blow it, lad."

Tyler looked at Mike and hesitated before answering. "Yes sir," he said and went into the wanigan.

There were several cases of TNT. It stood near the door for handy use. Many of the river men carried a couple of sticks in their lunch kits for blowing out snags.

Dynamite was to a lumberjack what a hammer was to a carpenter; a tool of the trade, nothing to be treated carelessly but then, nothing to be feared either.

Tyler was removing the wet tarp from the cases when Willie came in behind him.

He watched Tyler long enough to see the slight trembling in his fingers as he worked. "Let me go, Bull," he asked.

Tyler straightened up. "No," he answered. "Mike sent me."

"I've done it before, a hundred times. It's no skin off my nose."

"Mike gave me the job."

"Why do you think he did that?" Willie asked.

Tyler reached down and began pulling sticks from the case. He held one up for a closer examination. "I think he wants to get me killed."

Willie snorted. "That's bullshit and you know it. You will get killed if you believe that. You were closest. He don't care who does it so long as it gets blown. It don't have to be you. He was just talking to the air. I've blown lots of jams and I teethed on a stick of glycerine." Willie put his hand on Tyler's shoulder, "Bull, there's no shame in letting someone give you a hand now and then."

Tyler looked at Willie, without fear or anger, and spoke in a low, measured voice, "Mike chose me. I'm going."

Willie shrugged his shoulders. "1 guess I knew that, Bull. I had to offer."

Tyler smiled, "Thanks Willie. You know, you aren't half as bad as you try to make out."

"And don't you ever let that get out. What am I saying? In an hour you won't be alive to say anything." Tyler shot him a look. "Kidding! I'm just joking you. You'll be fine. Just remember to cut your fuses long."

Mike came in the wanigan and saw Tyler wrap three sticks together with twine. "At least four," he said as he walked past on his way to the coffee pot.

"I was thinking six," Tyler said, starting a second bundle of three.

"Better yet," agreed Mike with a quiet nod. "If it saves a second trip, better yet. And cut the fuse long enough." Just so it don't catch you short, he thought to himself.

He watched Tyler finish wrapping and capping the sticks and went back outside. Tyler took the tied-off bundles and joined them together at the fuse ends. Reaching into a can hanging over the dynamite cases, he pulled out a dozen waterproofed matches. With an afterthought, he returned six and put the others in an empty Copenhagen tin and rubbed a coating of lard on it. He went over to the stove and poured himself a cup of coffee and sat down. He was alone with Socrates. The cook watched as Tyler poured down the hot liquid saw the tremor in his hand. He also was ready to take the job but said nothing.

Socrates got a cup for himself and sat down next to Tyler. Outside, the distant thunder announced the approach of another storm. Socrates took a deep swallow.

"Happens every day, Tyler."

"What does." Tyler set the cup down and turned away, feigning nonchalance.

"Hauling a jam."

"Uh-huh," Tyler nodded. Then he looked back at Socrates. "As long as you're worried about this, Soc, maybe you want to talk a little?"

"Just remember to cut your fuses long, three minutes or more, and keep one eye on your back door. Don't be in a hurry and remember, if it doesn't clear the first time we go back and blow it again. If the dynamite don't blow right away, leave it. We'll go back in half an hour. It's just trees out there, son. Nobody goes naked or hungry if we lose a little river time hauling that jam."

Tyler nodded and gathered up his gear. He went to the door and stopped. "You don't think this is part of Mike's toughness program, do you?"

"What? Naw! It's all just work to him."

"That's what Willie said."

"Willie knows. Tyler, take it as a compliment."

"Right. A compliment." Tyler started out the door, then stopped and came back.

"Socrates?"

"Yeah?"

"You got anything from your prayer book?"

"Uh, yeah, sure." He fumbled through his recollections. "They didn't have dynamite back then but I do think I can remember, ... Oh sure, I got one." He put his hand on the boy's shoulder, bowed his head and prayed, *"Merciful father, protect this man and take him into your care. Remember the words of your servant from so long ago when he prayed, 'Oh Lord God, remember me, I pray thee, and strengthen me, I pray thee, only this once, O God. Amen."*

"Amen," Tyler repeated, then added, "Socrates, who was this 'servant' who prayed to God?"

"You should know him, Tyler, he was a lot like you but a little more clean cut."

"Who?"

"Samson," Socrates answered with a grin.

Tyler came out on the back deck of the wanigan. The skiff was tied alongside and three hundred feet of coiled rope lay on the deck. Mike was waiting for him.

"Son, we're going to lower you down with the skiff and pull you back out the same way. When that fuse is lit, climb back in and we'll lift you off. Understand?"

"Yes sir." Tyler lowered himself into the boat. Mike handed him the oilcloth wrapped bundle of explosives and shoved him clear of the wanigan.

"If anything goes wrong," Mike shouted, "get ashore off the logs. If you can't do that jump off downstream. Remember, downstream."

Tyler waved in acknowledgement and then he was too far off for talk. Five men were tending the rope. The rapids took a gentle bend to the right and the skiff, if dropped in a straight line, would fall against the far shore. They let the line out fast, faster than the flow of the current to let Tyler paddle out across the current and catch the slight eddy on the far side.

The boat was just a wooden shell with a flat bottom and low sides that were scarcely a foot high. It danced and skipped over the water, the rapids tossing it about like a piece of paper on the wind. It was nearly impossible to keep the oars in the water with the rolling and pitching. Tyler was soaked with spray before he had gone a hundred feet. The storm hit then and big drops began spattering the water around him.

He slammed into the jam fifty feet from the end of the wing. The stem struck first, then the bow swung around and more water began washing in over the gunwales. He waved at the wanigan and they pulled in slack until the boat was hanging at the end of the rope like a pendant on a chain. Using the oar to fend off the logs, Tyler worked the skiff out toward the end of the wing, until he came directly beneath the monster that had started it all.

Tyler tied off the boat and bailed out the water. He reached for the dynamite bundle and the two poles in the bottom of the boat. Carrying them like spears, he worked his way over the jumbled logs. The logs were awash with water in some places. In others they had reared high off the surface of the river. Waves working beneath the jam created blowholes that shot spray into his face. He was surprised at how much it moved. Over a hundred feet long, the jam was slowly flexing up and down. It undulated like a huge stickle-backed serpent. Radiating out from the base, the spider webbing of logs were a mat like woven grass, worked by nature into a massive, grotesque fabric, the entire work supple and smooth when viewed from a distance.

"God, help me," he whispered like hundreds of men before him who had tried to blow a jam prayed that it didn't carry away prematurely. Ten minutes earlier he had hoped that it would break loose by itself. Now he prayed it wouldn't.

He climbed over the last obstruction and looked up at the key log. Following it down, Tyler saw a juncture where a dozen others were caught up crosswise to it. Below them he could see the water slapping the bark.

Stretching out, he pulled the dynamite alongside him and tied the bundle to the end of a pole. He worked the fuses out through the oil paper and, using his knife, made a fresh cut on the end of each. He pulled out the snuff can, took out three matches and peeled off the wax. He worked close to the chest to keep the rain off. He tried striking the first match against his nail, but his hands were too wet. Dropping it, he took the other two and struck them against each other. One of them sputtered and flared into life. Holding it alongside its mate and the other three from the tin, Tyler made a small torch. He gave a quick look back towards the boat and touched the matches to the fuse. The wrapping smoked and caught. The fire found the powder and it flared into life.

Tyler thrust the pole deep into the jam, gave it a final push and turned for the skiff. He was in the boat and waving to the tenders even before he cut the painter loose.

Tyler saw it coming ten feet before the impact; an old granddad log booming along in open water and heading straight for him. He grabbed the oar and tried to fend it off, but his paddle slipped off the bark without slowing it down. The log hit the bow dead center, shattering the fragile stem piece and laying open the hull. The haul rope tore free and the little skiff filled with water and buried itself in the waves.

Instinctively, Tyler dove for the haul rope. He had it in his fingers for a brief second, but the water tore the slippery line out of his grasp. Then he was swimming, trying to keep his head up in the turbulence.

In seconds, he was driven back into the jam. His legs were folded under him, the surging water sucking him under.

He grabbed frantically for a log and desperately tried to pull himself up, but the strength of the river was relentless. He was slipping off the bark and about to get sucked under when, suddenly the old log that sunk his boat hit the jam in front of him. It struck on end, hung there for a precious second, then slid in as the current caught it broadside. It bore down on Tyler, threatening to crush him against the jam.

He saw it in time, threw his arm out and pushed off, straining to boost himself up between the two logs. He rose clear to his thighs before the weight of the big log, driven by the pressure of the current, pinned him again. He threw his head back and screamed in frustration.

Twenty feet away the fuse was burning down. The flame was about to take him out after all; not because he dared come too close but because he failed to get far enough away. The cold water had sapped his strength and clouded his thinking. Hung up between the logs, his eyes fell into the narrow slit of water below him. Chips of bark and dead leaves were bobbing on the surface. They drifted about, creating patterns that before Tyler's delirious eyes slowly coalesced into shapes that triggered images in his head.

Suddenly he was there. Stankovich! The evil face blasted Tyler with curses for his betrayal. Tyler tried desperately to shake his head clear. The water moved and the pattern changed into his father's face It was a caricature of disappointment at his weakness now, and no less his villainous assault on the dead hero Graham. His mother, her heart cold and distant as it had always been, turned her face from his desperation and Graham screamed from his watery grave, beckoning Tyler to join him. Soon enough it would happen. The phantoms, their vengeance denied satisfaction these last months would now be satiated. The panorama of life had set all Tyler's demons upon him. They were on the hunt and his scent enflamed their nostrils. Their mouths salivated for the taste of his blood, their stomachs distended and hungry for his flesh. Toughness, in the end, was nothing against the weapons of nature.

The pressure on his legs was intense but bearable. That wouldn't kill him. Nor drowning. The dynamite, twenty feet away that would send lethal chunks of wood to tear his body apart and scatter his flesh across the river would be his death. Not even his boots would survive to decorate a tree. Tyler was to become nothing. The hole would close over him and he would be just another story bandied about in lumberjack saloons and bunkhouses.

*"Sure, boys, let me tell you how we stood dumb as
cattle and watched the Timber Bull get blasted to bits
when the Caldwell jamb hauled."*

"Caldwell? That happened up on Muldoon's Rapids?"

*"Naw. It's not called that any more. It's the Caldwell
Rapids now. Named after that kid from Chicago. They got
a law passed by the Minnesota Congress, in fact. They
hung a pair of bronze boots with his name on them."*

Was this the hole in the water or the hole in the Klondike? It
was one and the same after all. His future was death and before his
eyes he saw it being ushered in by the failings of his past. It was cold
and black. It was horrifying, so horrifying that he screamed with
rage at his puny efforts. After all the boasts and brags and show of
overpowering strength, he was reduced to nothing.

He saw Angel and Satan and Graham and all the demons and
saints that had torn him apart for so long. If they brought him no
strength, at least they cleared his delirium. His senses returned.

Then it began to flow into his body, into his arms. From a deep
well of resolve forged not from sinew but from the boy's soul it came.
With every fiber of his being he began to push against the relentless
force of the river, defying its power, challenging its own unthinking
certitude with a determination he had never felt before. And the
demons watched and waited, their teeth bloody and bared. But Tyler
had overcome them. If he would die, then he would die a man!

On the wanigan, they had watched in horror as the crushed boat
went down and saw Tyler nearly escape only to be caught between
the logs. Socrates had screamed and would have gone to help him
but Mike's restraining arms kept him from diving off the wanigan.
"What are you trying to do, you old fool?" Mike scolded him, "You
can't even swim."

"I'll run to him if I have to!"

"Only one man ever did that, Socrates, and they crucified Him.
Keep your head or we'll be losing you, too."

"No, we ain't going to lose him!" Socrates struggled in Mike's
arms. "Sweet, Holy Jesus," he prayed, "give the boy a chance."

They jumped off the wanigan and raced down the trail until
they were directly opposite the jam and stood there in the downpour, helpless and hopeless. No one was close enough to get out on

the jam, hurl the charge into the water and pull him free. Still, they screamed encouragement, unaware that he couldn't hear them over the clamor of the voices in his head.

Some of them had witnessed this scene before and loathed the finish that was about to come. The forces of nature were strong and inexorable. Once set in motion, they could crush out a life without conscience or mercy. To have it happen quickly, like a shot, was acceptable, but to stand and watch a man slowly die raged against nature. It moved those prayerless men to pray, and between each prayer they injected a curse for emphasis.

Then the log moved. Suspended over the cold, sobering water, Tyler was straining with such effort that sweat had broken out on his face, mixing with the spray of the river and cascading off his bearded chin. His hands were bare-knuckle white, the palms raw and bleeding, cut by the bark beneath them.

With strength beyond conscious human ability, he fought, and very nearly burst with the effort. He was no longer angry. He was disappointed in himself that he had been brought down with so little struggle. He had taken responsibility for both his entrapment and his escape. So now, when it was over, he struggled with greater determination than he ever had before. He moved it! The log swung out against the flood and then a little more. And more!

And Graham was back but this time he was encouraging and cheering. His father, too, and not as a stern and distant demon but a caring parent, afraid for his child. His mother turned, and smiled and held out her arms to him. And suddenly, by their grace, he was free and lifted himself clear!

He swung his lifeless legs onto the jam as the logs slammed together and the hole disappeared. The hole closed but Tyler still lived!

He struggled to his feet, gasping for breath. There was no time to stop the dynamite from going off. There was barely time to run and hope he could run far enough.

He started for the shore, stumbled and dragged himself over the logs, covered twenty feet, then thirty. From the right bank they lost sight of him behind the pile of logs.

"He's safe!" the Kid screamed.

"Not yet," Mike said. "Not with six sticks of dynamite at his feet."

Socrates looked at Sullivan. The boss' eyes were steady and unafraid. If there was any turmoil inside him, it didn't show. But

Mike's eyes were locked on the jam as hard and fast as a wolf on a kill. Whatever their past had been, the lad was still one of his.

"Maybe it's a wet fuse," Socrates hoped.

Then it blew. A blast, quick and sharp without the rolling thunder of a far off Explosion. It went off like the snap of a shattering tree. The concussion nearly knocked them down. The jam heaved up, rising higher and higher out of the river. Logs and pieces of logs flew out from the wing. They threw themselves to the ground as chunks of wood screamed over their heads. They slid over the mud, down the bank and into the water. They grabbed for tree roots and to each other.

The Oregon Kid was the first one back on his feet. He stared out over the water.

He was looking for Tyler, but saw nothing. "He's gone. No one could make it out of there."

"Not yet," Mike said again, even more emphatically than before. "Give him a chance." He stood up, the debris still raining down about them and began moving down the tote path.

"There she goes!" Willie yelled. "She's going to haul!"

The jam began to move over the water, the key log gone. As they broke loose, the logs began to flatten out. They floated free of each other and settled into the water, once more a fluid carpet of wood shooting Muldoon's Rapids.

Mike saw him first, but Socrates was quick to call it out. "There he is!" he screamed pounding his fists on Spooner's back.

"Well, I'll be. The son of a gun got out," Willie echoed.

Tyler was out in the middle of the logs, lying on his belly, clinging to a log.

"Is he dead or alive?"

"Can't tell. At least he ain't down in the water."

"He ain't moving," Socrates said. "He ain't moving!"

Rube agreed. "Well, if the blast didn't kill him, the rapids will. He sure can't make it down like that. If he can't stand up he'll roll for sure and be crushed."

"Well, he's not dead yet!" Oregon Kid chirped. "Look there!"

The Timber Bull was moving. Pushing off the log, he slowly worked himself onto his knees. He rolled onto his feet, gripping the log for balance and hanging on with torn and bloody hands. Then, with the entire crew screaming encouragement, Tyler straightened up, tall and far back on the log, and on bruised and rubbery legs, rode through Muldoon's Rapids. When he stepped ashore a minute later, he fell unconscious into the arms of Hungry Mike. Finally, he opened his eyes and looked weakly into Mike's.

"Was I tough enough," he groaned.

Stifling a choking laugh, Mike answered, "Aye, lad, tough enough for a dozen men. Tough as old shoe leather you were." Then he hugged him and they both knew why.

The Tigers later allowed as how they had never seen anyone survive anything like that before. Willie could remember his hero, the great Dan Bosse, doing something similar, but he acknowledged that Bosse had an otter for a mother. Socrates quoted endless passages from the Bible. Sullivan was more practical, pouring Tyler four fingers of whiskey and suggesting he ride the wanigan for two days while he recovered. Tyler protested vehemently, but in the end had no choice. The next morning he could barely stand, and couldn't walk at all. His legs were discolored from the crushing they took; his hands were cut and swollen and, if not for Socrates' reassurances, he would have sworn his arm was broken.

Socrates buttered Tyler's hands with carbolic salve and bound them with boiled cloths. He put his arm in a sling; the shoulder badly bruised from flying debris. With a needle and thread he stitched up a decent cut on his shoulder. When the men set out in the morning, Tyler morosely watched them leave.

"Don't be such a slump," Socrates said. You can sit here with me like a king in court and every time a man comes in to eat, tell again how you were holding the dynamite in your teeth when it went off. Add another stick every time you tell it."

So Tyler reluctantly took up the potato brush again. But rather than brag, he became quiet. The more the others hovered over him the less he seemed to talk about it. Instead of feeding his volatile young ego, Tyler's escape had left him sober and reflective. He told no one about the phantoms. Privately, he assured himself that they were nothing more than delirium brought on by the pain. But they kept returning to him again and again, especially at night. They were still marking time in his head, alongside the Klondike Hole and the drowning Angel.

There were demons yet to be exorcised, perhaps, as Socrates had insinuated, yet to be identified.

Six

"Mom! Mom! Walkin' on the river! It's walkin' on the river!" Six year old Joshua Tucker was jumping up and down on the river bank and waving at Socrates' wanigan as it cleared the bend in the Bigfork. For most of the day he had sat in the gravel, ever since the first of the logs and men had appeared on the water. Finally it had come, just as they said it would. A boat as big as a house. Why it was a house! Bigger than his house anyway! 'Walkin' on the river like they said it would.

Socrates spotted the skinny, barefooted boy and hollered back to Spooner in the Galley, "Break out the sweets, Spooner. We've got young'uns ahead."

He waved to Joshua. "Hey, boy! Go tell your ma and pa we're here," he called and began to work the raft ashore with the long sweep.

"Who's out there," Spooner said, poking his head out the door.

"Homesteaders," Socrates muttered. "Just some jug-headed homesteaders." Joshua was already running down the path to his family's cabin. This was far the most exciting thing he had seen since his folks had moved in. The funnest by far! He blurted out the news and was back at the landing even before the wanigan was tied off to the shore. A few minutes later his father, mother and a little sister, cuddled cautiously in her father's arms, joined him.

To Tyler they seemed to have been cast ashore not as land owning homesteaders, but as survivors of some shipwreck. He thought they resembled the Swiss Family Robinson minus their ingenuity, lucky charms and the treasures of a great beached sailing vessel.

The Tucker family was uniformly clad in rags. Their pants and shirts were all cut from the same cheap cloth. Joshua had outgrown his pants by six months, the frayed cuffs ending halfway between his knee and ankle. Except for his shirt, even the father appeared to have grown six inches since he was last measured for clothing. The father's shirt was a torn dress shirt as might be worn by a businessman in its better days. Two buttons held it closed at the front. The cuffs were rolled above the elbow. He had on a pair of scuffed and worn brogans.

Tyler wouldn't have recognized the mother as a woman at all except for her dress. Her face cried for relief. It was sad, gray and tired. The shadows and lines, the premature white in her straight and lifeless hair made her look old. Her hand-sewn dress was cut from the same gray cloth as the men. It bore only the faintest hint of style or definition. The demands of the family's situation had crushed the spirit out of her.

"Anton Tucker." The lanky man held out his hand to Socrates. "This is the missus," he said gesturing to the woman. She nodded, her eyes barely straying off the ground. The children weren't acknowledged at all. Socrates took care of the rest of the introductions, giving them sugar lumps in exchange for their names. The girl shyly identified herself as Rebecca and held up three fingers when he quizzed her about her age. He addressed the woman directly, taking her hand in his.

"Afternoon, ma'am. I'm Socrates, the cook of this outfit. This here is Tyler Caldwell. They call him the Timber Bull and this other feller," indicating his second cook, "Spooner, but he's got more bull in him than Tyler."

She nodded again, bashfully, but this time raised her head and her eyes looked into his with curiosity. "We certainly didn't expect to find a pretty woman like yourself so far back in it."

Jerking her hand away, she put it over her face, turned and ran back up the path.

Rebecca scrambled after her calling, "Mama, Mama."

"Please excuse my wife," Anton said. "She's been in pretty low spirits lately."

"It was a hard winter," Socrates sympathized. "Cold and storms like I never seen. It was enough to take the starch out of anyone."

Anton nodded. "It took the baby. Last week."

"Oh, no! I'm sorry," Socrates said, genuinely saddened. "Pneumonia?"

"I believe that was it."

"I'm awfully sorry," Socrates repeated. "She's a strong woman at that, isn't she?" Anton looked back for his departed wife. "Yes, she is. For a girl of twenty-four she has a well of fortitude."

Tyler and Spooner exchanged looks of disbelief. She could have passed for forty.

"Well!" said Anton turning to the path, "Come on up and visit, won't you? I can't offer much in the way of refinement, but I sure could do with whatever news you might have."

"How long have you been here?" Spooner asked.

"A long time. No, not really that long, but it seems long without the rest of the world around you."

"I know the feeling," Socrates agreed.

"Come up to the house, then?"

"Thank you," Socrates replied. "We'd be honored." He turned to Tyler. "Son, run and fetch the worm medicine from behind the flour bin, won't ya? And grab a sack of them cookies we made this morning." Tyler went back for the whiskey while Anton led the others up the trail.

He was a tall man, slender with a fragile look about him. His fine hands and long fingers seemed better suited for a piano keyboard than an ax handle. His hair, unlike his wife's, was still brown, straw-colored and thick. He had a ruddy complexion and seemed otherwise healthy but for the projecting cheekbones. He wore no beard. Anton walked with a loose-jointed rolling gait, like a man used to traveling on foot. He still had a flicker of life in his eyes, absurdly so to Socrates, when they came up to the cabin.

Their "house" was set in a clearing they had hacked out of the brush. It was close enough to the bottom-land to invite mosquitos in summer and faced northwest, open to the arctic blasts that swept northern Minnesota. It had attracted the mosquitos because of its convenience to the river and the minimum amount of clearing they had done to make it habitable. Socrates immediately saw it for the poor site it was. Farther back from the river, the land turned to a series of low rolling hills, mounds of dirt really, rising ten feet, then dropping into wet ash swales and rising again, evidence of old river channels. The closest good building site was at least five hundred feet back from the river, a distance the Tuckers had probably felt too far for security and comfort.

Anton built his house of everything the man and his wife could pull together from the land. Two sides were rough-hewn cedar logs, the bark still on them. They had chinked the cracks with mud and grass in a manner so crude that the dried weeds appeared to have been growing out of the walls. The front wall was a palisade of posts covered with pieces of cedar and poplar bark. The back was set directly into an embankment and had no walls at all. There were no windows. A small dugout alongside the cabin looked like the root cellar.

To the left of the shack was a lean-to shed of even poorer construction than the house. A Jersey cow, as thin and emaciated as the woman, peered out from beneath the sagging roof. A small corral surrounded several thousand square feet of dead saw grass, cattails and soggy manure.

Anton noticed Socrates looking at his cow. "She dried up last winter," he volunteered. "We ran out of sweet hay and had to feed her bark, swamp weed, anything to keep her alive. Cattails even. It's a wonder we aren't eating beefsteak. Of course, she'd probably taste like my shoes right now." He laughed self-consciously. Yet he seemed optimistic too, as if to say, it's all right, I can take it and some day you come back and see what we have here.

"She'll welcome some spring clover," Spooner said. Socrates was thinking that Anton was equally hard on all the women in his life.

He stroked his chin and muttered apologetically, "I was thinking of staking her out down on the river soon, but I can't take the time to watch her and the boy's too young. We'll see."

There were no other animals in sight.

Tyler came back with the jug and they sat on a log, resting their backs against the side of the house. The woman stood in the doorway, barring it as if she were defending her territory from these strangers. Her children clustered behind her but only until Tyler produced the sack of cookies, then they quickly deserted their mother for the company of the lumberjacks. When she saw Anton take the jug from Tyler, she abruptly turned and went inside, pushing the sagging door shut behind her.

Anton looked over his homestead and took a long pull from the jug, savoring the harsh, smoky taste he had gone so long without.

"Mmmm, God, that's good. It's been a long drought. I didn't bring but a little in with me and the colder it got the quicker it went." He took another drink and set the jug down between his feet. "I have a hundred sixty acres here," he bragged and with a sweep of his hand encompassed all the property down to the river and well back behind the shack. "I picked it up on a county homestead grant. We came up here last summer and another, what is it? Yes, another four months and I'll have established title. Not bad for a millenary clerk."

"Proved up," Spooner corrected. "Yes. That's what you call it up here. It's good land. It will make a good home."

Socrates winced.

"I got all the plans in my head how it's going to look. The house over there, toward the river; a new barn and granary right there." He nodded approvingly, indicating his satisfaction with the plan. "Yes, it'll be a showplace, alright."

Spooner cleared his throat. "1 don't mean to say anything disrespectful," he said, "but it looks like a woodpecker forty to me."

"Woodpecker forty, what's that?"

"Oh hush," Socrates hissed to the second cook. "What he means, Anton, is it looks a little rough. No trees to speak of. Mostly old snags and dead tops. The kind of place a woodpecker calls home. Not bad otherwise."

"The trees. Yes," Tucker agreed. "They were gone when we got here. I planned to spend the winter logging and sell it to folks like yourselves. The land agent said it was virgin land. It wasn't. It set us back some."

Socrates sucked on his pipe. "They were probably stolen. Happens all the time."

"Stolen?"

"Ten, fifteen years ago judging by the new growth. Some big company probably came through here on a drive and threw your trees in the river with the rest of it. Happened all the time years ago. You could have asked for another piece," he suggested.

"I thought of doing just that but then I figured, what the hell, Anton, you're going to be a farmer, not a logger. The trees are better off gone." Anton reached for the whiskey again. "Yes, better off gone."

So are you, thought Socrates, and changed the subject. "You came up last year? From where?"

"Cincinnati. I worked in a haberdashery like I said. The store had a fire and the owner gave it up. Times being what they are, I can't say I blame him. The wife is a schoolteacher ... or used to be." Anton laughed at his choice of words. "1 guess we're a couple of 'used to be's, huh? We thought she could find work teaching up here. It seems I have the only two children in this township. I was naive. A man grows up pretty fast up here, doesn't he?"

"Amen," Tyler said. "Grows up or gets out, right, Socrates?"

Socrates shot him a cautionary look.

"Anyway," Anton went on, "it was too late to plant, too early to hunt. Well, I hunted some so we'd have food. I had never shot a gun before, but I learned. We get fish from the river and the chickens attracted raccoons like you wouldn't believe. They aren't bad if you don't mind the greasiness. Seems we had more 'coons in the coop than chickens some nights. They finally finished off the chickens and left. But I finished a few of them, too." He laughed again. The whiskey was working on him. "The house. It's really something, isn't it? She says it's okay for now but I know it isn't. What can I do? Oh, and that damned cow. We bought it in Bemidji. She dried up right away. He knew she would." He curled his lip at the thought of the man who had swindled him.

"So I got to spend all winter scratching to keep her alive so we could breed her. Now I suppose she's the only cow in the township, too." They laughed politely, although Socreates knew it was probably the plain truth.

"Maybe I can mate her to a moose. You think?" He grabbed for the jug. "Mind if I have another little pop? It sure tastes good. Warms me up. Had a lot of work just to keep warm last winter."

"What are your plans," Tyler interrupted.

"Plans?"

"You know, what do you intend to do now?"

"Why, we're staying on, of course." His voice projected defiance and not a little resentment over Tyler's insinuation. "Neither the wife nor I will have any of it. Quitting? No sir." As if to reiterate his statement he added: "Over there by the barn, I already started turning over sod for a field." He pointed to a small patch of raw earth, brown and bristling with fibrous roots. "Oh, I know, the ground is full of rocks and roots but it will grow beans and potatoes. No sir, my family has always put down deep roots and stayed put. Father, grandfather, all the way back. We've been men of property and roots forever."

"Yes, it will grow potatoes," Socrates volunteered. "There's a lots of old shackers back in the woods that grow just those things. "But none of them are carrying the baggage of a wife and kids."

"Oh, yes, we are staying put. There's nothing else for it." Tucker's eyes went to the small rise behind the cabin where a little hand-fashioned cross stood watch over an equally pitiful grave. The fresh earth was ringed with stones and a bouquet of wilted Trillium lay on the mound. Socrates saw it and said a quick prayer for the child.

Tucker looked for his wife, unaware that she had long since disappeared into the dark cabin. "Roots! Ha!" he laughed. "I never saw dirt with so many damn roots in my life." The whiskey was well in him now. "Makes you wonder where they all come from. I think if you'd dig up a root and follow it to its end, you'd come up against a chestnut back in Pennsylvania."

It was funny but no one followed it up with a comment. He was making them uncomfortable. Socrates coughed and began playing with his pipe.

"Damn Cow!" Tucker cursed, oblivious to the children. "She dried up. My wife did, too. Weren't for the women going dry, who knows? The little tyke couldn't make it on what we were eating." He cleared his throat and wiped his eyes. "Got to the woman bad," he finished.

"Well," Socrates said, getting to his feet, "we've got chow to fix. Say, why don't you and your family come down to the wanigan for supper?"

Anton was staring at the ground, lost in his own thoughts.

"Mr. Tucker, are you coming to our place for dinner tonight?" Spooner repeated.

"Eh? Oh yes! Thank you. I'm sure we'll be pleased and honored to come." They stood up to leave. Amos kept his seat.

"Mr. Tucker," Socrates asked, "would you mind keeping the whiskey jug here?

Our boss don't go for whiskey on a drive."

Anton's eyes brightened. "Oh? Oh, sure! That's no trouble. I won't say a word."

He wagged a conspiratorial finger in front of his lips.

On the way back to the wanigan, Tyler spoke first. "He's killing them."

"Not him," Tyler. "The country."

"Sure, but he brought them into it. We're talking about little children and a woman who is obviously going crazy being here.

"That's pioneering, son. That's a job, too. It's a hard life. I just respect them for going after it."

"There should be a law against taking innocents like that up here."

"There is, Kid. It's called the law of common sense. Some folks don't seem to have any. I think that without it all you have to go by are your dreams and dreams are made up of ponies and palaces. Once you get to living your life on dreams, sooner or later you need the swift kick of reality on your ass to break you out of it. We all break it now and again. We all get the dreams kicked out of us eventually."

The night was mild so the crew ate around half a dozen campfires along the shore. Sullivan and his bosses dined in the wanigan with the Tucker family. Mrs. Tucker wore a different dress, cleaner than the other one. The material was far too light for that time of year, so she wore a shawl of a different material. Socrates sensed her discomfort and kept a healthy fire in the stove.

If the children were enchanted with the wanigan, three times the size of their shack and better appointed, they reveled in the stories told by Rube and the others. In no time at all, Joshua had left his place on the bench and crawled into Rube's lap, and Rube, no stranger to children and lonesome for his own, tenderly cradled the boy in his arms. Joshua asked a million questions and whenever his parents tried to shush him, Rube quietly waved off their protests.

"No need, no need. If a young lad can't get answers from the grownups, he just ends up finding them somewhere else."

After dinner the youngsters ran out to the campfires to hear more tales under the stars. Willie and the Oregon Kid were delighted at having a new audience. They turned the work of river driving into a drama the likes of which even lion taming could not compare.

Hungry Mike, to the amazement of his men, paid a suitor's attention to Anton's wife. He learned that she was also of Irish extraction, "Lace curtain, not shanty." she insisted. He allowed that a woman as pretty as her shouldn't be kept hidden away so far north but he was very grateful to have the pleasure of her company at his table. Socrates choked on his food three or four times during the meal at some of Mike's talk.

After dinner, they went outside to join the children.

"It's tall timber time, Soc," Willie coaxed, "and our throats are dry. You got any in you, old timer?"

Socrates had been a little touchy over Mike and Rube's domination of the dinner conversation and snapped at him. "Don't old-timer me, you green-gilled tenderfoot, or I'll throw you in a gunny sack and use you for an anchor for a couple of days. Fact is, yes, I've been saving one for just this spot because it's so special. So show a little respect for your elders if you wanna hear it." He dug out his pipe and relentlessly began to pack tobacco in the bowl.

"Are you going to tell us about Indians?" a wide-eyed Joshua asked.

"Why, bless your little heart. As bashful as I am, I do like to be encouraged. As a matter of fact, this is an Indian yarn."

"Shameful," Schnapsie muttered.

"I'll ignore that," the generous yarn spinner answered. He opened his mouth to speak but paused to stare into the flames of the campfire. A clear, white three-quarter moon floated high over their heads, random strands of cirrus clouds occasionally placing a veil over its glow. The night air drew them close about the fire. Socrates drew a deep breath, took a last drag on his pipe and began.

"This place here, young man, your father calls it Tucker's Landing, after your family. Well, that isn't really the name because, you see, it already has a name. See yonder there where that point of the bend sticks out there across the river? That's sacred ground to the Indians. A burial ground. Right over yonder. Years ago there used to be a Indian village. Chippewa. One of the finest, proudest breeds you'd ever want to know. Their chief was a man named Bustycagen. He was a powerful chief and his warriors were lean and plenty strong. They've made good top-loaders but weren't much for sawyers. Busty-cagan was even bigger than most white men. That's why he got to be the chief. But he stayed chief because he was so smart.

"This Bustycagen was a good friend of the white man. He trusted them and kept his people in line, like the Indian agents told him too. Other tribes went to war, but Old Busty toed the line and kept his hunting grounds. See, he could always tell which way the wind was blowing and a smart feller tries to keep the wind at his back. Well, Busty was like that.

"One time, the agent come up to see him and one of the young braves tried to kill him. Busty saved the agent's life. The man was pretty grateful, naturally, and wrote up a good report on Bustycagen and that made Uncle Sam grateful, too. Last thing Sam wanted was another Indian war.

"So Uncle Sam gave Bustycagen this whole township free and clear for his personal use. Thirty-six square miles to just one man.

Over there where his village stood was the center of the township so they gave it a name. Busty's Landing. So you see it already has a pretty good name. If you looked, you'd still find Indian signs there. The way the river changes course, you might even find some bones washed out from the graves. Busty was a Christian and buried all his people in the ground instead of Indian style. Busty's buried there, too, along with lots of arrowheads and the like. I've seen some of it. You get a chance, Joshua, you go look."

"Yeah! Gosh!" Joshua squealed at the prospect of hunting for bows and arrows and tomahawks. "Are there any scalps?"

"Scalps? Naw, I don't think there'd be much of a scalp left. That was a long time ago.

"Where did the Indians go?" Joshua asked, caught up in Socrates' spell.

"The Indian's don't own none of this any more. They sold it years ago for food and drink. Mostly booze. Most of them died from drinking or disease. White man's diseases. Some of them still live over at the Cass Lake reservation. They make 'em live like the white folk now. But Busty lived to see most of his woods cut down and the slash burned over. Someone wrote down what I'm going to say to you."

With that, Socrates produced a beaded headband from his pocket and put it on. He stood up and, stepping behind the log he was sitting on, knelt down and began to beat it like a tom-tom. Then he started chanting in a voice from deep in his chest that swelled up and poured forth the magical Indian language. His words hung in the clean night air and wrapped the company in their spell. And then he stopped only to start again, in English:

> *"Changing of the ways since early days*
> *on the shores of Bustycagan,*
> *When simple, indeed, were the red man's needs*
> *and there wasn't any logging.*
> *The river ran free and clean by fertile ridges*
> *where the pine tree stood in the solid woods,*
> *And there weren't any bridges.*
> *But the White man came to Busty's lodge*
> *and he drank his tea and he ate his fish,*
> *And they talked awhile with cunning guile,*

for gain was their only wish.
They built their camps on the Cagan shore,
and with sawyer, swamper and many more,
They cut and hacked until the pine was down,
lying dead on the forest ground.
And the river, now full of snags, like beggar's rags,
flowed by the barren ridges,
And now there were many bridges.
Many summers have passed,
Old Busty's eyes have lost their gleam.
His head is bowed and he dreams a dream,
of before the white man came to the shores of Bustycagan.
At night the young men sit and listen
To Busty's tales of yesteryear,
Of the white man and his logging;
while they drink their beer and they all chew Copenhagen."

Socrates' voice trailed off at the end. His audience was deathly still as the quiet sounds of frogs and owls and furry night creatures played about them far from the glow of the firelight.

"Gosh," Joshua said finally, "that's a great song. Did old Busty write it?" Socrates didn't answer because he hadn't heard the boy. He was far away, far in the past, speaking with the old Indian.

"No son," Hungry Mike said, putting his hand on Joshua's shoulder. "It was written by an old lumberjack named Duncan Ross. He wrote it about old Bustycagan."

"Why?"

"He knew him."

Tyler was staring into the blackness. He, too, had felt the draw of the rhythm, the momentum of time ebbing back and forth. He felt the land, changed but unchanging and only a little annoyed over the desecrations of humanity, yet also consecrated by the many who had walked upon it. He knew he was a part of it, not an observer but not in command either; just part of the changing guard. He was a piece of bark drifting on the Bigfork. Control? Strength? Power? No, he knew such things had no real value after all. Not Busty, nor he, nor even the remarkably adaptable Socrates and especially not the Tuckers. None of them would ever be measured with anything to approach the worth of a single star, tree or river. None of them had any more right to be here than a single drop of water from that beautiful river. No more than that, after all, were they. It saddened him that he had come to feel that he was the king and the trees were his subjects to be slaughtered and felled to fuel his ego. A new emotion was entering his heart. It was a feeling that he had never had before but it felt warm and comforting like a soothing balm on sore muscles. It was humility.

"I understand," he whispered to the sky.

Early the next morning, the crew pulled out. Anton and the children came down to the river to wave them off. Socrates had gifted them an embarrassing amount of canned goods, sugar and flour as well as much clothing. Anton graciously accepted the items on behalf of his wife and family.

"This will get us by until I get a crop in. I can't thank you enough."

"Maybe the next time through, you'll have us for a bar-b-que," Socrates chuckled.

"I might at that," Anton laughed, "1 might at that. God speed and keep you."

"And you, and yours," Socrates returned.

"What do you think," Tyler asked as they floated off, "Are they going to make a go of it?"

"Heck no! How the hell should I know?" Socrates snapped, "You ask me, all homesteaders are fools, 'specially the ones that can't tell a farm from a rock pile. He's sitting on a woodpecker rock pile and the fool can't even see it. You can see what he's pulling and you ask me if he'll make it? I'd lay money that they'll be gone by next spring."

"Well, don't bite my head off."

Socrates spat in the river and in his agitation dribbled most of the spit on his boot.

"Damn!" he blurted, and again, "Damn!"

Tyler broke into laughter and then, finally, so did Socrates and that brought back his normal disposition.

"It makes me mad to see those kids and that woman kept up here, is all."

"That's what I was saying last night and you didn't agree."

"Yes, you did. And you were right. There's a time to be a hero and a time to be prudent and that Anton Tucker don't know the difference."

"Can they survive where Bustycagan couldn't?"

"I know one thing they won't have to worry about that Busty did."

"What?"

"White men," Socrates snorted.

"Maybe they'll be here long after another old tradition is gone too," Tyler added. "And what'll that be, my boy?"

"Lumberjacks."

"That's for sure," chuckled Socrates. "We're all but gone now." He settled down for a minute and then steamed up again. "Hell no, they won't last. I just can't see it."

Nor did either of them see Amanda Tucker watch them from the cover of the alder brush, still wearing her party dress from the night before.

Amanda had brought the memory of Gertie flooding back to Socrates. Gertie, the strong one. Gertie, the willing one. How many times had she bailed him out and saved his ass from the scythe of the Grim Reaper?

It had done the same for Mike. Last night he had seen Tanjka again, for just a little while. Worn and wasted, pale and dying, as he last remembered the woman he had loved so long ago.. That was why he had insisted on escorting Amanda home alone, long after Anton had snuck off to finish the whiskey jug and the children had been put to sleep.

Seven

Tyler had been back on the river for two days. His hands were healed to where he could grip his peavey and the bruises on his legs, though still an ugly shade of purple, no longer seriously hindered his footing on the river. His mood was much better. His attitude had come full circle to where there was little that seemed to bother him anymore.

It was the twelfth Day of the drive. The logs had moved steadily through the stretch of the Bigfork below Muldoon's Rapids. Once out of the Klondike Rocks, the river widened and the land laid down beside it. There were more backwater areas, side sloughs and beaver-dug channels for the river to poke about in. Into these quiet pools the logs would wander. Like lazy cattle, they wandered off from the main current, slid behind a beaver lodge and hid, bobbing imperceptibly, coyishly among a mottled growth of matted pond lilies.

"It's like a Easter egg hunt," Snoose complained one morning. "Yesterday I crawled back behind an old blow down and so help me if I didn't find a log branded by the old Agassiz Logging Company. You know the old A.L. mark. They ain't cut for over ten years."

"That's nothin'," Schnapsie countered in the game of one-up-manship. "I got so far back off the river I bumped into a man said he was cutting for Agassiz!"

Tyler was back at the rear, tending out the balky logs. Again, there was no real shoreline to follow, just hummocks of muskeg marking the edges of the meandering waterline. They looked solid, but if one were to step on the wrong one, he would sink from sight, dumping the unsuspecting river man into waist deep water or even deeper muck. Men had died in this northern quicksand, sometimes by drowning, more often from embarrassment because they would rather drown than call to the others for help.

Tyler had just finished cleaning out a small pool filled with a mixture of logs and flotsam from the spring runoff. That done, he poled himself back into the current. Ahead of him, on the edge of the river channel, was a beaver lodge, so old it was covered with dry grass and small clumps of hazel brush. A willow had grown out at the waterline, inadvertently planted by a beaver years ago. It bent over into the water, its trunk and branches acting like a mycelial sweep for debris.

Two logs were washed up against the willow, jammed under its branches. Tyler worked up alongside the lodge. Stepping ashore, he clamped his peavey onto the first log. With a hard twist, he swung the outer end of the log cleanly into the clear. Then, grounding the peavey beneath the butt, he forced it off the mud of the lodge base and, giving it a final push, sent it surging back into the river.

The second log was more difficult. After a bit of wrestling, however, he also had this one on its way to the Rainey.

Tyler stepped back out of the mud and pulling his tobacco from a back pocket, sat down on a dry hummock of grass. He put a dip of snoose in his mouth, wiped the spillage with the back of his hand, and looked out over the river. There were some ducks, bluebills, over by the opposite shore, resting on their way north to let the winter retreat before them. A blue heron flew past him, its wings barely clearing the water as it followed the course of the river looking for something. Tyler thought, he's probably looking for the same thing I am, whatever that is.

The day was too nice and the sun too warm. To sit for another five minutes would have been an invitation to nap, an unpleasant position for anyone to be found in. Tyler got up and was about to jump onto his taxi log when he was attracted to something else beneath the willow. It was dark, scarcely more than a shadow and was moving slowly, bobbing just beneath the surface, buoyant and yet not so.

Drawn by a curiosity, Tyler moved closer to the willow and, leaning out over the branch, peered into the turgid water. It was fabric, red and checkered like a lumberjacks mackinaw. Thinking it to be exactly that, Tyler reached out with the end of his peavy and fished around until he had it hooked. Then, stepping back up the lodge, he pulled.

It held for a moment, rolling heavily under water. Then it ripped away. Tyler pitched backward onto the ground, the piece of sodden clothing shot out of the water and landed beneath his feet.

Socrates was rounding the bend and, seeing Tyler sitting on the lodge, yelled to him. "Hey there, lazy bones, you can't get any work done sitting on your ass!"

Tyler either didn't hear him or just didn't respond at first. But he wasn't on his ass for very long anyway. Scrambling to his feet, he dropped the peavey and back-peddled higher up on the lodge.

"Holy shit," he stammered. "It's an arm!" He looked about for help, saw Socrates for the first time and said it again, louder, "It's an arm! My God, come here! I found someone's arm."

From out on the river, Socrates saw the black shape lying in front of Bull, but couldn't make out what he was saying so Socrates grabbed the steering oar and went over to him.

"What in blazes are you crowing about?" he asked. "You being attacked by a beaver or what?" Spooner had come out on the deck to investigate the commotion. "He's touched," Socrates said to the second cook, poking a finger at his head.

"I caught him eating the food this morning," Spooner offered.

Tyler was pointing at the object in front of him. "Socrates, there's a body here! I just pulled an arm off it."

"Oh, oh," Socrates said. "Here, Spooner, tie us off as soon as we light. I'll see what's what."

"If it is a body, you see for both of us."

"Maybe you'd better dig out a pick and shovel while you're at it."

Spooner jumped from the wanigan and ran a line out to anchor the scow. Socrates came right behind him. He worked himself over to Tyler through the brush, came out on the lodge and bent down to examine the sodden material.

"It's an arm, all right," he pronounced, verifying the obvious. Fingers were sticking out from the sleeve, swollen and white, not unlike the surface of a marble statue. Even the ragged and shredded end that had torn away from the shoulder was bloodless. A clear fluid, either from the river or the body itself, was seeping from the wound. "Where's the rest of it?" Socrates asked, scratching his beard. "You didn't eat it, did you?"

Socrates smiled benignly at Tyler's look of disgust.

"Shutup, Socrates. It scared the piss out of me."

"I'll betcha it gave you the willies, huh? You ain't never seen nothing so gruesome, I bet. So where's the rest of it?" he repeated. "We oughta collect the poor fella if we can."

"Down there." Tyler pointed to the willow tree. Jarred from its hiding place by the peavy, the rest of the body had drifted nearly clear of the branches. It bobbed to the surface and was drifting, about to break out into the current. "There! It's starting to get away."

Socrates kicked the arm off the peavey and fished around with it until he hooked the dead man's belt.

"I've got him now," he grunted, hauling back. "Spooner, give me a hand." The reluctant Spooner pitched in and they brought the sodden body ashore and dragged it onto the lodge. It was amazingly clumsy and unwieldy. Unhooking the peavy, Socrates stuck the point under the corpse's chest and rolled it over. The neck was broken and didn't turn at first. It rotated slowly as if drawn by exhausted rubber bands. Finally it faced the sky and stared into the sun through life-less eyes.

The face was all busted up. The nose was gone as was all of the left cheek. The jaw was hanging from the skull by a few lacerated pieces of meat. It was about to fall off. A white furry mold had developed over the exposed skin surfaces. Several large black leeches were feasting on the remains. There was the sound of retching behind Socrates. Spooner.

"Oh, man," Tyler whispered. "What did that?"

"I'd guess a shotgun," Socrates replied. "It really chewed him up. Or maybe a pistol. Axe? Naw. A shotgun for sure. Whatever, he didn't die of old age. See here? Now the turtles have begun working on him too. If the water was any warmer he might have been eaten up by now, but that's a big meal for any guppy."

"Craig?" guessed Tyler.

"Craig," verified Socrates. "Over the winter sometime." Someone did him in and shoved him through the ice all right. He must have drifted this far and got back in here and the mold already got to working on him. Most of them I've seen aren't so ugly. Some of us actually do die of old age, you know."

"Who is it? You got any idea?"

"No idea. I don't know. Want to name him? It doesn't really matter once it comes to this, does it? This poor devil is past justice now, anyway."

Tyler stared at the shattered face; the shape of the forehead, the shreds of long dark hair, the glassy, washed out eyes. They were reduced to bleached marbles, possessing no more life than a stone. And yet there was a vague familiarity beneath it all. The way the eyes protruded from their sockets, the angular features of the long wrecked head. His eyes swept down over the body. The man had no shoes. Someone had stolen them. There were the marks of the turtles. They had eaten off the toes and part of each foot, the bones sticking out from their stubs.

A shiny object caught Tyler's eye. He picked up a stick and bending close to it, brushed away the mold and debris. It was a wedding band. Ole's!

The words came out in a hoarse whisper. "It's Stankovich!"

Socrates didn't hide his surprise. "No! It can't be! Stankovich?"

"Yes! It is. I'm sure it is!"

"How can you say that?" Socrates knew the old nemesis as well as anyone and he couldn't recognize him from the torn face. "There's no way of knowing, son. It could be him or one of a hundred other guys."

"Socrates, he's wearing the ring he stole from Ole! Look here!" Tyler pried up the ring finger for Socrates to examine. The old mentor couldn't identify the ring for sure but he had no reason to doubt Tyler.

"Well, I'll be damned!" he agreed, "So, it's the old Horseman, himself. Now he's a seahorse but looking worse for the wear." Then Socrates looked hard at Tyler. He had accepted the boy's identification of the body and was searching not for a judgment of death but of life. What was he feeling at this moment in the presence of the man who had represented so much that tormented him? Tyler read Socrates' mind and his answer was quick in coming.

"He's dead."

Socrates pressed the matter nevertheless. "Is he? Is he really dead or just changed?"

Spooner let out a nervous laugh.

Tyler looked again at the rotting body, then turned away and sat down. Socrates waited for an answer and when none was given, he ventured deeper.

"Tyler, is he dead to you?"

"Well, what in the hell else could he be?"

"I'll suggest something. He could still be a cancer eating your insides out. He could be that. A tumor, or boil or cyst. A pounding in your brain. A knot in your gut. How the hell should I know? But there it is. A tumor can be cut away, but it leaves a scar too. I'm asking you; is there a scar tearing at you yet? Tyler, I've fished maybe a dozen or more men from this river. Half were murderers and half were just murdered. When they've gone through the ice and floated around for a while, they all end up the same; in some foul backwater eddy. So terrible to smell even the brush wolves pass them by."

Socrates got up and went around to Stankovich's feet. He was ankle deep in the water. "This one's done, Tyler. Whoever killed him, well, maybe he'll be coming down next week. But this one's done with. Don't keep his memory alive with a bellyful of hate."

Tyler wouldn't look at Socrates.

"Do you hear me?" the old man whispered. "Tyler, look at me."

"I don't hate him anymore," Tyler answered quietly. "Is that what you want to hear. It's done with."

"Oh? You said the next time you saw him, you'd cut out his heart. Have you forgotten that? You have a knife. There's his heart!"

"I didn't mean it." Tyler's voice was barely audible.

"Didn't mean it? Oh, you meant it," Socrates pressed. "I know you did because I was there once. I recognized the talk. You meant it so much it's been burned on your face for the last two months.

"It's gone, I tell you!"

"I've seen it at table, in your work, in your talk. You hated him so much it spilled over onto everything else that touched you. You have to finish it here and leave it here! You have to decide, is this the man you hate or is it someone else?"

"You're crazy! I don't hate anyone!"

"Sullivan?"

"No! I . . . not anymore." He was confused.

"Who then? Your old man? Me? Who?"

Tyler backpedaled away from Socrates. "No one, dammit! Listen! I don't hate anyone! It's done with."

But Socrates was like a hound on a meaty bone. "Tyler! Leave it here or stay here with it!"

"It's gone, I tell you!" Tyler was screaming.

"Finish it, Tyler! Finish with this man and go on living. Whoever and whatever you hate, leave it here."

Spooner shook his head. "You are a crazy pair. The both of you."

"Yes! Yes!" Tyler said, "Spooner's right, maybe *you're* the crazy one. Why should I listen to you? You never even wanted me here."

"Finish it!" Socrates shrieked. Rising up out of the river he came to stand over Tyler. "Finish with this man and go on living! Finish it! Who? Tell me!"

Tyler leaped to his feet and grabbed the old man. He held him off, shaking the boney shoulders in his powerful hands.

Spooner tried to step between them but Socrates stopped him. "Finish with it, now, boy!" Though he was choking, Socrates was still relentless. "Let it out, dammit! Let it out! Who do you hate so much?"

Tyler was killing him. Socrates' face was purple, his voice began to trail off, his arms had fallen off Tyler and were flailing at his side. And then, just as suddenly, the Timber Bull stopped. He stared in wonder at the old cook. His hardness softened and his eyes filled with tears. He pulled Socrates to him and embraced him in a way he had never held, or been held, by anyone before. And then he began to cry. He shook convulsively, racked with sobs. He cried like a baby and Socrates held him like one, rubbing his face and stroking his hair.

"It's me! It's me, isn't it? I'm sorry I'm so sorry. Oh, God, it's me," he cried over and over.

"I know," Socrates said. "And I am sorry you came to this. Now, it's finished. Now you know. Now you can set it right." He shook convulsively, wracked with sobs. He cried like a baby and Socrates held him like one, rubbing his face and stroking his hair. He held the boy, soothing him, calming him, as a father holds his son. And when it was over, they sat together on the old beaver lodge for the better part of half an hour; Tyler, Socrates, and Spooner who had not the vaguest idea of what was going on.

After a long while, Tyler bent over the body. He drew his knife out and, cutting off the finger, retrieved Ole's wedding band.

They took a pick and shovel, chopped through the mud and sticks of the lodge until they opened the chamber inside. Then they rolled in the body and covered it over.

Socrates bowed his head and prayed, "Lord, show what kindness you can spare on this lost soul and guide the living back to the straight paths of your righteousness. Remember your own words and think of this man: '*I will send a great flood and I will blot out this man who had defiled me in his iniquity and I will make new the face of the earth and all its inhabitants. Amen.*"

"Amen," echoed the others.

They returned to their labors, put the wanigan back on the river and left that place. There were no corked boots to mark the grave of the man who called himself Stankovich. He left no legacy except the part he had played in Tyler's own death and rebirth. When evening came, Tyler lay down and slept, a peaceful, dreamless sleep, the first in many months. He had finally made peace with his family and himself. He was ready to become the person he was destined for.

Eight

Socrates swore Spooner to secrecy but he related the entire story to Mike Sullivan who only nodded at the outcome, satisfied that Stankovich had finally come to justice of a kind.

As for Tyler, his coming of age, his purging of the demons of his youth was complete. Socrates, who had never totally relished his job even in the worst of times, now reluctantly acknowledged that his mentoring time was over. If the near tragedy of the jamb had sobered him and rekindled an awareness of his vulnerability, finishing with Stankovich had cleansed him. It reminded him that vulnerability could be a good thing as well as a weakness. He had also learned a valuable lesson: that the person we can hate the most is oneself. He had learned that few emotions can be as comforting as humility.

"Look at that," Willie moaned one morning after they had been visited by a late frost. A thin layer of skim ice had formed behind the wanigan. "The river froze up on us again!"

"Well, we'll just bust her open, then," Tyler said as he snatched up the Tiger and threw him ten feet through the air. In a gesture of added playfulness, he jumped in behind Willie and called for a bar of soap.

On the fifteenth day, they were about to cross the Sturgeon River, a smaller tributary of the Bigfork. Sullivan planned to run straight past the Sturgeon, picking up the extra flowage and keep going until he reached the sluice booms at Big Falls, another two days ahead..

The news Boots brought back up the tote path abruptly changed his plans. Boots had been riding the front with his comrades when something happened to send him running back in such a rush he had taken off his shoes to make better time.

Mike had just sat down to test the edibility of a large quarter of salt pork when Boots came running up.

He stopped in front of Sullivan and waited impatiently while Mike worked over a mouthful of food. Mike smiled kindly as he chewed and swallowed. "Boots. Hello."

"It ain't good, Mr. Sullivan," Boots was still panting.

"Bad news? What of it, Boots?" He saw the driver was winded. "Here, sit here and catch your breath. Was someone hurt?" Mike asked with rising apprehension. Boots shook his head.

"Well, speak man. What is it?"

"Oh! The boom, Mike!" he blurted.

"What boom, Boots? We don't have a boom on the river."

"I know that, Mike. But someone did. It's catching all our timber and brought us up short."

"The hell you say!" Mike stood up. "Who would put a boom over the Bigfork at the head of my drive?!"

"That's all I know, sir."

"Above or below the Sturgeon?" Mike demanded.

"That a good sized creek comes off the left bank?"

"That's it. So?"

"Above, Mr. Sullivan. She's blocked above."

"Did you cut it open, then?"

"No sir." He hurried to add, "It's fitted with chains. We had no saws or axes."

"Then take a saw and cut it open."

"Still can't, Mr. Sullivan."

"Well, dammit, Boots, why can't you cut it open?" the exasperated Sullivan insisted. "Is St. Michael himself guarding that blessed boom!"

"Sumpthin' like that, Mike. There're men on each end and one in the middle. They have rifles. They said they'd shoot our ass off if we set foot on it."

Mike slammed his fist into the table, sat back down and threw his face and his voice in supplication to the heavens.

"Saatala!" The word went forth across the river and deep into the woods and echoed back like the cry of a man who had been wounded beyond all endurance.

Rudy Saatala. A Finlander of impressive proportions and obstinate ways. He was an independent, bullheaded, bragging, swaggering, swearing, shouting, spitting reincarnation of Goliath himself.

Rudy owned nothing and owed nothing to nobody. His home was Effie, a watering hole five miles north of Bigfork. He knew the Koochiching area like a wolf knew his territory and, like a wolf, he put his scent on every landmark in the county. If he coveted it, he had to possess it. All winter he had been working out of a camp up near the head of the Sturgeon at the northern end of Pine Island. If the normal boss was the highest and last authority in a camp, than Rudy ran his camp like a feudal lord.

Mike had known Saatala since boyhood. Their families were highly regarded in their own townships and on those rare occasions when fate would cause trails to cross, the tension between them would hang like a cloud of mosquitoes in June.

Some of the greatest donnybrooks ever fought north of Grand Rapids were between the Sullivans and Saatalas, with Mike and Rudy standing firm in the middle, defending their familial breastworks. They were considered equals, contemporaries in most ways even though Rudy was, by five years, Mike's elder.

Physically they were like night and day. Both were big men, but the bigness moved in different directions on them. Mike was a husky two hundred and fifty pounds spread over a six foot frame. Rudy, on the other hand, was a classic Finlander. He was six feet four inches tall and carried nearly two hundred and thirty pounds on his graceful frame. He was clean-shaven, for vanity's sake, except for a great handlebar moustache, also for vanity's sake. His head was adorned with flowing locks of black hair that only recently had begun showing traces of gray. His manner was aristocratic, his temperament dictatorial. He knew only two ways of running things; his and all the others. And he never had time to listen to the others.

Mike admired most Finlanders. They were exceptional lumberjacks and Mike was proud to have them on his crew. It took no more than thick timber and greasy food to keep them happy. He never knew a Finn who hadn't made it in the world whatever the hardship. They could work their way out of poverty and into prosperity faster than any people he ever knew.

Out of the woods, the Finlanders were no less in control. They carved out farms, built towns and brought civilization to a northern wilderness. They were of strict Lutheran persuasion and prided themselves on their rigid righteousness. However, let loose amongst the trees, they would revert to the habits of their Viking forbears.

Every man strove to be the "Bull of the Woods." The Finns boasted of great tracts of north woods laid waste by the wide-ranging battles that occurred sporadically throughout the logging season. Rudy had never lost a contest and was so established in his authority he was contested no longer. He was the supreme, uncontested, Bull of the Woods.

Mike and Rudy had met only once in a situation where pride and stature were at stake. It was at a lumberjack jamboree in Grand Rapids twenty years ago. Saatala was the perennial champion and went out of his way to advertise that fact. His trumpeting forewarned every town he entered, every bar he burst into.

"Here comes Rudy! The Bull of the Woods! There are none so mean, none so strong, none so big as ever bested Rudy Saatala!"

Mike had never competed head to head with anyone in his life. He had grown up on a small farm outside Bemidji, honed his skills in the winter logging camps and summer fields. Thanks to hard work and good genetics, he developed into an incredibly powerful, young man. Word of his bear-like strength and prowess with an axe did not go unnoticed by the logging fraternity. He, too, acquired a reputation, although through third parties rather than by his own bragging.

Rudy was aware of this great bear cub from Bemidji but held him in no regard. Why should he? Mike was not a Finlander. Nor was he a braggart. As long as a man never put a challenge to Rudy's supremacy, he would remain a nonentity. If anything, he saw Sullivan as just another whetstone upon which to sharpen his knife.

Sullivan had gone to the jamboree purely in search of women and drink but was talked into entering half a dozen contests by virtue of his cronies' boasting. When Saatala saw Mike's name on the entry boards, he saw an opportunity to add another notch to his own name and lost no time in getting the word out.

"So they let cub bears into the contest, eh?" he goaded. "Well then, it'll be up to the men of Grand Rapids to put them in their place. I, Rudolph Saatala, am the greatest woodsman in Minnesota; in the world, perhaps. Who knows, eh? I will crush this potato packer and send him back to his berry patches. Rudy Saatala swears to it."

To which Mike countered, "Who is this Rudy fellow, anyway? He talks like a jackass my Uncle Patrick once owned?"

Approaching the final tally, Mike had won every qualifying event he had entered, none in direct confrontation with the braggart, Saatala. Little by little, the competition was eliminated. The championship match pitted the four remaining challengers in the one man crosscut. Mike and Rudy, stood side by side to attack a twenty-four inch pine logs.

Rudy waved to his cheering admirers and took up his saw. It was custom ground and filed, with a brass bound handle. Mike, empty handed, took his place alongside him and, turning to the crowd, politely asked to borrow a blade from someone. He had brought none of his own. A middle-aged pulp cutter with a bushy beard stepped forward.

"Take this'un, young feller, she knows where the bottom of the log is and cuts true."

"That's kind of you," responded Mike. "Who might I thank for this fine looking blade?"

"My friends call me Socrates."

"Thank you, Socrates. My friends call me Mike."

"You're welcome, Mike."

"Enough hearts and flowers," Rudy shouted, "Its time to sort out the men from the boys."

"Keep it in your pants, big shot." Socrates was not then acquainted with the scriptures.

At the gun, they tore into their work. Sawdust poured from the cuts like water from a faucet. The saws were a blur of motion, the rhythm like a fine tuned polka band. Muscles bulged on the massive arms as they forced the teeth deeper and deeper into the wood. Each stroke seemed to take another inch off the logs. Mike looked neither left or right. He was a study in concentration. Rudy had started well, but halfway through he began to feel the burning. His arms were on fire. He knew the time to bear down, fight through the pain and finish the job with neither feeling nor strength left in his body was now. He knew the course well because he had contested many times before and won them all. He was confident, the pride of his family. His reputation was at stake. Now he would break the back of the usurper Mike Sullivan.

Then, just when the pain began to spread through his shoulders and pile up in great knots on his back, he heard it. It came clear and easy as a man might do it while on a Sunday stroll. Mike was whistling 'Coming Through The Rye'!

Rudy took his concentration from the log just long enough to glance over at Sullivan and, in that instant, bound up his saw so fiercely he snapped the handle off in his hands. Mike kept cruising, his song picked up by the crowd. He finished twelve seconds ahead of the second man. Rudy didn't finish at all and was disqualified. He cursed his luck and in the face of an offered handshake he cursed Mike.

"You stupid, Mick," he shouted. "The devil take you, you cheat!"

"You cut good with that fancy saw, Rudy, but the metal was no good. Use Swedish steel, not Finnish. Remember that. Swedish steel and Irish luck!"

That night Saatala and six of his friends drunkenly confronted Mike and his companions outside the Red Rooster bar and a brawl erupted in the darkened street. There were only three Finlanders standing when the constables finally broke it up. Sullivan was as bloodied as the others, his forte not being in blocking another's blows, but in returning them two-fold. The police escorted them to opposite sides of the city limits and considered the matter settled.

But the incident festered in Rudy's gut for years. As for Mike, he was drunk when he hit town and drunk when he left and scarcely remembered the escapade except for the prize money and a big silver axe-head buckle he still wore on his belt. As they matured, both men were conscious of the bad blood between them, but only one of them meant to do something about it.

"I'll talk to him," Mike said matter of factly. "He has no right to block the river unless he has it full of his own logs. He knows that. It's just part of his old grudge. Yes," he repeated on his way down the trail, "I'll talk to him."

"Better luck talking to a stone," Socrates muttered. "Spooner, my boy, cast off those lines and shove off. We don't want to miss the action."

"1 don't know Saatala," Spooner said, "but he sounds like a real ass."

"Oh no, not at all" Socrates corrected. "He's as affable as a puppy, so long as you have your foot on his throat when you're petting him."

"I will do no talking, Sullivan, not to you nor to anyone! Especially not to you!"

Rudy was across the river from Mike, yet his powerful voice carried easily.

"Saatala!" Mike's voice was equally powerful and just as full of determination.

"You have no legal right to block my passage. I see no logs in the river!"

"No? Well, you shall see a river of logs very soon. And right goes with the might, Mr. Sullivan." Rudy punctuated his remarks with a gesture at his three rifle-toting guards.

Mike made another attempt. "My logs are already filling this boom of yours and your timber has yet to show! Let us pass and be gone! It will cost you no time!"

"I will not do that, Sullivan! I have twenty thousand pieces back up the Sturgeon! We will be into the Bigfork at first light and it will take you a whole day to pass through. I will not lose the time here and what it costs me at Big Falls."

Sullivan had expended his patience. "You do not forget do you! I bested you once when we were children and made you eat your bragging words and you still do not forget! Like a child yet you behave! If you had left your woman's bed a week earlier and hired some men who want to work instead of coddling children, you would have been in the Falls by now! What you have done is wrong!"

Saatala took the rifle from the man next to him and pointed it at Mike. He fired and the water erupted at Sullivan's feet. "I won't warn you again. Bind your tongue and your men or I'll not hold back my crew!"

Undeterred, Mike roared back, "I'll not begin it. My conscience will be clear, whatever happens!" Without waiting for another rejoinder, he started to leave with his people. Then he noticed the man guarding the near end of the boom. He was barely twenty years old.

"I know you," Sullivan said, looking the young man over.

"My father has a farm near Black duck."

"Yes, we helped rebuild your barn when the lightening took it. You are a Finlander, are you not?"

"We are all Finlanders, working for Mr. Saatala. My name is Rudy."

"Like the master. Do you support him and what he says?"

"He pays us."

"Enough to shoot at me and my men with your rifle there? Your neighbors?"

A thoughtful pause. "I don't know. I have only shot game."

"Remember, Rudy," Mike said as he started back up the path. "Remember the difference."

He was striding fast; Willie, Boots and the Oregon Kid hurrying to keep pace behind him.

"Bind my men, he says! That man is as stubborn as a mule but has the memory of an elephant. Bind my tongue, he says! I have never seen a sharper tongue. They have no need for saws and axes, the way they cut with their sharp tongues. And then he shoots at me! Well, we shall see!"

He stopped and looked to the sun. It's blaze was already turning from golden yellow to orange through a shroud of spruce trees. "In one hour it will be dark. Then we will blow it up."

Willie was shivering. He was neck deep in the cold water, drifting with a log and holding on by a nail driven into the side. Only his head, covered with a black cap, showed above the surface. Socrates had mixed lampblack with lard and painted his face. He was smeared with another thick coating of lard over which he wore two layers of woolen underwear. If he were to lose his grip on the nail, the sodden underwear would pull him under fast. On top of the log, wrapped in a waterproof leather bag, lay the dynamite. In a coffee can smoldered a handful of live coals.

Willie had eagerly volunteered for the job, claiming to be smaller, quicker and a better swimmer than anyone in the crew. The argument was rhetorical. Mike gave him the work because he was handy. But Willie had made himself handy because it seemed like a great adventure, the stuff of stories and brags.

The sky was low, black, starless and perfect for a man who did not wish to be observed. The log was just one of many still working their way into the boom. Already thousands of logs had backed up behind it and he could get no closer than two hundred feet from the front.

Taking the dynamite, he snaked his way over the field of timber. Ten minutes later, he was back in the water. Barely fifty feet ahead and off to his right was the middle guard. The man was sitting in a boat tied to the boom. His rifle was lying next to him. In his hand was a pipe. He was facing away from Willie. His fly was open.

The Bangor Tiger made his way forward to the end of a log, past it, down the length of another and, eventually reached the boom.

The constant grinding of the logs on each other covered what little noise he was making.

Placing the dynamite on top of a boom log, he ducked under it, coming up on the downstream side. Willie unwrapped the end of the fuse and cleaned it with his knife. Then, opening the coffee can, he tipped it on its side and tapped the coals to the front. Blowing them to life, he put fuse to coal. It sputtered into life.

The plan had been to swim away and come ashore downstream of the boom. That would have meant stripping off the underwear and getting even colder than he was. Besides, Willie knew the value of a tall tale and never passed along the chance to create or embellish one.

So, pulling himself onto the boom, he tiptoed towards the guard until he was right along side of him. The man had sat down and was nodding, half-asleep. Willie spoke to him.

"Say, partner, If you're going to guard this boom, you'll have to do a better job than that."

"What?" The man lurched to his feet, nearly falling over backward in the process. Rolling forward, he tipped trying to pick up the rifle and sprawled out of the skiff and onto the logs. The rifle fell out of his hands and would have dropped into the river if Willie hadn't caught it. The guard was in eminent danger of sliding through the logs, but Willie reached out and, grabbing him by the collar, helped him to his feet.

The guard stared at his strange intruder. In the dark, with the lampblack, Willie had no face. He was dripping water. The weight of it had stretched his long johns so much that the seat was down to his knees. And now he was holding the rifle!

The guard threw up his hands. "What are you?" he demanded. "Who?"

"Willie," Willie said. "Who are you?"

"Ivar. You are on my boom."

"This is a nice boom," Willie offered, "but you are using it to corral another man's logs. That's what they call rustling, isn't it?"

"I do not know what you are saying?"

"Out west they shoot rustlers and when you come from Maine like me, this is out west. So I think," Willie rationalized, "I should shoot you. Okay?" Willie punctuated his remarks by poking the barrel into the man's ribs.

The Finn understood the part about shooting all right and stretched his hands even higher. "No! No!"

"What are you reaching for?" Willie asked, gesturing at the man's arms.

"You have my rifle."

Willie looked down at the carbine. "Oh. Is this yours? Damn! I must have left mine back at camp." Here, take it, but don't drop it again. Your boss can't afford to go buying you a new gun every day."

Ivar took the rifle with one hand, his other still in the air. He slowly brought both to the gun and almost reluctantly pointed it at Willie, unsure if he was friend, foe or phantom.

"You cannot be out here," he cautioned. "Mr. Saatala said no vun but me can be out here. Leave now."

"I'm just leaving. Is this the way?" Willie pointed to the shore.

"Yah. 'Dat's right. You go now."

Willie took half a dozen steps and, almost as an afterthought, turned back to Ivar. "Say, Ivar, I think you had better leave too."

"Oh?" Ivar was suspiciously fingering the rifle. "Why you t'ink so?"

"I t'ink so because there' s dynamite back there just about ready to go off. You might get squished."

Ivar looked behind him and saw the sparkling fuse not forty feet away.

"Yumpin' Yimminy!" he cried, starting towards it. He took four steps, then thought the better of it. He stopped and turned back towards the boat. Tossing in the rifle, he jumped in behind it, and wrestled with the knot tying it off to the boom. It was wet and unyielding. He looked pleadingly to Willie for a knife, but Willie was gone. Without hesitation, Ivar jumped back onto the boom and raced Willie to shore.

The three of them, Willie, Ivar and Rudy, the shore guard, watched the great flash of power. The force of the blast lifted a fifty-foot length of the boom on the crest of a water spout before dropping it in a shower of broken pieces.

"Holy smokes," Rudy said, pointing an accusing finger at Ivar, "You did that with your smoking pipe, I suppose?"

Ivar was shaking his head in despair. "I did not do that. I did not do that," he kept repeating over and over.

Willie thanked them both and disappeared in the dark. The logs, now unbound, surged down river.

There was nothing for the incensed Saatala to do but throw a second boom across the Sturgeon to keep his own logs from being swept away by Hungry Mike's.

They ran past the blown boom all that night and into the next morning, under the stares of the sullen and resentful Finlanders. By noon, Tyler, Carl and Paddy were drawing up with the rear. Two of the Finlanders watched them as they came working down the shore. A number of logs had gathered at the remnants of the broken boom, and as Paddy and Tyler were clearing them, the Finns closed in.

The taller of the two, spoiling for a fight, began to belabor them in Finnish.

"What's he saying," Paddy asked the shorter one.

"He say's those logs are Saatala's."

"He's wrong," Paddy answered. "They have our brand on them."

The other Finn translated, waited for a response and interpreted, "My friend says these logs have no brand."

Paddy spat a stream of tobacco juice on the gray bark. "They do now," he muttered and rolled in another one.

The bigger man was cowed by Paddy's disregard for his intimidation and moved over to Tyler. Again he spoke. They waited for the smaller one.

"He says he wants to break your nose."

Tyler rolled out the last log before answering. "Tell your friend," he addressed the short one, "the logs are gone. There is nothing left to fight over."

This was duly reported as was the mean Finn's response. "He says you are a coward. You are afraid to fight him."

"Oh, oh," Paddy muttered, hitching his pants. "Here we go again."

But Tyler ignored the challenge and, stepping out onto the last log, began working it into deeper water. He stood there looking at the Finns for a moment. "Tell him," he finally answered, "he is right. I am a coward."

Again the exchange and the reply, "You are too big to be a coward."

Tyler shrugged as if to say, have it however you want.

Paddy said to the English speaking Finn, "Wait until I'm gone, then tell your friend that if he had fought with my friend, my friend would have buried him in the mud up to his knees. Head first. And also tell him, his nose reminds me of the hook on the end of my peavey." He followed Tyler and Carl out on the river.

Behind them they heard the exchange of Finnish and the big man began jumping around in a rage.

At that moment Rudy came out onto the riverbank with his foreman. The straw-boss had one of the rifles.

"Are those Sullivan's men?" he demanded.

The smaller Finn shook his head affirmatively.

"Give me the gun," Saatala said, reaching for the rifle.

Paddy was thirty yards away, moving slowly with the current. Saatala chambered a round and brought the rifle to his shoulder. Laying his cheek on the stock, he put the front bead on Paddy's back and centered it in the rear groove. He held on his target and slowly tightened on the trigger.

At that moment Paddy turned his head. Their eyes met over the gun barrel for just that second, then there was a roar and the rifle jerked in Rudy's hands. The bullet hit the log at the waterline six inches below Paddy's left foot. Paddy looked down at the water and back at Saatala.

"I could have killed you, then," Rudy shouted. "Someday I will."

Paddy stared at him, memorizing the face. He was prepared to put ashore and take on all four men and the rifle if need be. Tyler was a hundred feet ahead, watching. Paddy calmly recharged his chew, tightened his jaw and narrowed his eyes until they were nearly closed.

"I accept your apology, gov'nor," he said tersely as he slowly drifted out of Saatala's range. "Until we meet again."

Nine

*B*ig Falls was created during the last ice age ten thousand years ago. A granite shelf had heaved, cracked, settled, and over many thousands of years wore into a ledge over which the river tumbled 18 feet to its lower bed. Beneath the falls, broken boulders formed a shallow, rocky trap for any form of flotsam that passed over it.

To get by the falls, the logging companies built a sluiceway along the right bank. From the sluice way a long gathering boom extended back up the river and stretched across to the opposite bank. Any log coming downstream would be intercepted and channeled by this boom down to the sluice-way. Up to four gates could be manned simultaneously depending on the amount of river traffic. To finance the upkeep of this equipment a toll of one cent a log was levied on the driving company. Independent loggers, such as Saatala, paid another penny a log premium.

It took Sullivan six hours to clear the Big Falls gates and it was accomplished with only one minor incident. Old Toad had fallen to the rear while Socrates treated a gash on his leg. Hurrying to catch up with the others he took a nap at the same time by hooking a ride on a schoolmarm; a log with a big crook in it so it wouldn't roll in the water. For a man who could find repose in a mosquito-carpeted swamp, a schoolmarm floating downriver in April was close to feather bed comfort. He curled up in the crook and drifted off. Toad was sleeping so soundly that he almost got swept through the gates. At the last minute, the shouting woke him up and he escaped death by leaping up and grabbing the sluice gate lever.

The wanigans were hauled out by teams of oxen, portaged on roller logs to a landing below the falls and re-floated.

The tail-men were three miles down river when the first of Saatala's crew appeared above the boom. They had been driven hard, worked around the clock by an angry Saatala. He hurried up to the sluice boss.

"I am Rudy Saatala," he said. "Do you know me?"

"Of course," replied the boss, "I was here last year when you ran that cedar drive."

"I do not remember you," Rudy said. "Where is Sullivan?"

"Mike? You just missed him. He went out not three hours ago."

"I must catch him."

"You send a messenger down the trail, you can catch up with him by noon."

"No, man!" the exasperated Saatala shouted, "It's my logs I want to catch him with! Send them through!"

"My men are worn out. We just finished sluicing Sullivan."

"My crew is tired, too!" Saatala shouted. "What of it?"

"I think we could let your logs gather for half a day and sluice them all at once."

"Sluice them now! As they come!"

"If we do that, you'll end up with your drive scattered the length of the river."

"I don't care what you say, I want my logs over your dam now."

The boss, although considerably smaller than Saatala, eyed him with contempt. "I don't think I will oblige you, Mr. Saatala."

Rudy grabbed the sluice boss by the neck and squeezed. "Then open your boom, by God, and I'll run them over the falls!"

"You'll grind them to cordwood if you do that," the boss gasped, swaying in Rudy's grasp.

"But I will have the satisfaction of seeing you tied hand and foot to the first log! Will you now give me passage?"

In the end, the Sluice boss saw the wisdom of Saatala's suggestion and turned over the gates to him. Rudy cleared the falls with his own tired men doing the sluicing, then he tongue-lashed them back onto the logs.

A day later Mike passed through Linford. Socrates opened his kitchen to the small troop of tattered children that stood on the banks, but there was no stopover for the exchange of news.

Two days beyond Linford, the first logs hit the catch boom on the Rainy River. The drive was rafted up and passed over to a tugboat that took the timbers in tow and hauled them down river to the Itascan mills in International Falls.

Mike gave his men a day off, paid them, and marched south with those that weren't staying on in town.

It had taken nineteen days to come down the Bigfork. It would take three to hike back to Craig. In the course of the drive an estimated five hundred logs had been lost by sinking or jamming beneath the surface. They had made passage over twenty sets of rapids of varying difficulty, overcame one major jam, and hauled a dozen smaller but annoying ones.

Mike figured the rest of the journey would be easy.

Ten

The trail back to Craig had been cut out years before. It was built wide enough for the carts that carried the wanigan pieces back upriver and had been improved over the years to haul goods between International Falls and camps to the south. Several times it cut close to the wandering Bigfork, but generally ran straight as an arrow in flight. It was as though the men who swamped it out knew there was no time to be lost in getting back to the blowout that awaited the weary lumberjacks.

Springing out, the return to civilization, did wonders to alleviate the aches and pains of a hard winter's work. The thought of warm beds and cold whiskey was attractive enough that they could tolerate the hardtack rations and sleeping on the ground for the three nights on the trail.

The men were antsy with anticipation. Their stories grew more ribald, the boasting more vocal. By the third night, however, as the night wore on and the cloudy sky created a mood of somberness, the talk turned to home and to partings. That night, Socrates called on one of his favorite stories; not his actually, but Old Toad's. He thought it might have some meaning for Tyler.

"Toad?" he asked as they sat around the fire.

"Yeah?"

"Why don't you tell us about your home?"

"I don't have one, Socrates. There's just me and my sisters. You know that."

"The one you had, Toad. Tell Tyler about them. He might something learn from it."

Acquiescing to Socrate's request, Toad straightened up and cleared his throat. He stretched his arms out as if reaching back into the past and the story gradually fixed in his mind ready to be played out as he had played it out for himself so many times before. Suddenly he was a child again and he spoke as it happened, long ago.

"'Papa was coming.' My mother would always sit by the kitchen window of our cabin in Birchview and listen for his return. It was a scene repeated many times during the winter.

"The horses have bells on their collars, but sometimes when it was very cold, we heard the clinking of the heel chains and the creaking and crunching of the runners as the loaded sleigh slipped over the frozen snow.

"My father cut spruce pulp in the early summer. It was called the stripping season because the bark could be easily removed with an old wooden wedge made from an axe handle. All you had to do was start on top of the eight-foot piece, pry the bark loose and give it a healthy yank. Even as a nine-year old I helped with the barking.

"My father did his hauling in the wintertime. During the winter months when the swamps were frozen, they iced the Rainy River to carry a team of horses and two or three cords of pulpwood. In early fall or spring we tested to make sure that the ice is strong enough. A man walked with a double bit ax and struck a heavy blow on the ice. If water didn't show in the cut, it was safe. Walking ahead of the team, he repeated the ax swinging every thirty or forty feet.

"The wood was taken across the Rainy River to Barwich, Ontario. My father made one trip a day to Canada. Then he loaded up another sleigh and brought it back to the homestead to make an early start in the morning. He parked the sleigh on poles to keep them off the snow.

"It was this last trip of the day and my mother was watching and listening at the window. I was nine and had the cows to milk and feed. We had three brown Swiss of good stock, and some chickens and geese. But we lived off the pulp cutting. We had a contract with the mill in Barwich. They bought a load a day all winter. If we missed a load they might cancel the contract and award it to another man. We were so poor that without the contract from the mill we could not keep the farm. Even so, we were very poor and the work was hard especially for father.

"Mother heard the clinking of the heel chains as the sleigh came up to the yard. The team knew the routine so well. It stopped the sleigh right on the poles and waited for dinner.

"Mother was looking out the window and saw the sleigh, but no papa. Still she got up and started to put the food on the table.

"'Come, Children,' she said. 'Papa will be in any minute now. Sit down for prayer.' We hurried to the basin beneath the cistern pump and washed our hands in the warm water mother poured into it. There is only a sliver of soap left on the soap plate and my little sister rolled it into a ball and threw it at me. We were still laughing as we took our places at the table. We sat there waiting for papa. Finally mama got worried.

"'Arthur,' she said to me, 'go and help your father. His dinner is getting cold.' Our dinner was turnips and venison, but mama was very proud of her table and liked to serve hot meals. I was hungry for the meal. She made bread pudding with raisins for dessert.

"'Yes, mama,' I said and went to the hooks by the door. I put on my coat and boots, cap and mittens, and went into the yard. It was very cold now. The sun had set and a wind was starting. The horses welcomed me because they were hungry and tired. I thought papa was close by so I started to unharness the team to help him but even after I put them in the barn and fed them, he had still not come up. I thought that maybe he dropped something on the road and went back for it.

"On our sleigh the reins were long and reached to the back so papa could walk in the tracks of the runners and stay warm. I walked around the sleigh to see what might be the trouble. The shotgun was lying on the sleigh. Papa carried it with him to shoot game, not for fear of wild animals. He was afraid of nothing. On a sunny day he brought home fat little grouse for the table. I pulled it out by the barrel. The hammers were forward. It had been fired. I hurried back to the house.

"'Mama!' I shouted as I ran in. Mama!

"'Mercy, child,' she cried in alarm. 'Don't startle me so.'

"'Mama,' I hurry on. 'Papa is not in the barn or anywhere and his shotgun has fired. It was on the sleigh.'"

"Mama was very frightened now. There were seven children in the house and I was the oldest. Mama was very frightened because I told her about the shotgun.

"'I am going to look for papa,' I say and pulled my mittens back on.

"'No!' She was very frightened. 'Arthur, stay in the house with the children! I will go look.' She tried to grab me but I ran back outside. I ran for a mile into the woods. It was dark and very cold and very still. My boots on the hard snow and my breathing were the only sounds. They seemed very loud in the dark woods. I think I must have run forever. It frightened me. And then I found him. He was lying on the ground. Something had made the gun go off and he was hit in the chest. The snow was red for thirty feet behind him where he had crawled or maybe the team dragged him before he dropped the reins.

"'Oh, papa!' I cried. I turned him over and saw the blood on his chest. His eyes were open and looked at me for help, but they did not cry out, for he was dead.

"'Oh, papa!' I cried again and laid on top of him. His blood was on my face and hands and coat. I tried to warm him, thinking that I could make him wake up. I was only a child and did not understand. I called to papa and shook him. I kissed him but my tears were freezing on his face. He was already very cold. In time, I understood. I placed his hands together on his chest but they kept falling off. Papa looked so strange laying there in the woods no longer my strong papa. I could not leave him like this but finally I did.

"I ran back home. Mama was in the kitchen. When she saw the blood on me she covered her face with her hands and trembled. She was waiting for me to say something but I was afraid to say it. Finally she asked, 'Is he hurt, Arthur?'

"I could not stop the sobbing. 'Yes!' I cried and ran to her arms. 'Oh, Mama. Oh, Mama.' Then she knew that he was dead. Because I found him I felt responsible. I felt bad that I left him alone in the woods. 'I'm sorry,' I cried."

"Mama, too, cried for a long time and then became very strong, like papa always was. She gave me a hot roll and sent me to the neighbors for help. Men came and carried papa out of the woods and brought him to the church right away so the younger children would not see him dead in the house.

"The next morning I drove the team over the Rainy River. The team would not follow me as they did papa so I could not test the ice. We crossed safely anyway. Still we lost the contract because they thought a nine-year old boy could not load and haul three cords of wood each day. Our life was very hard before but now was worse.

"Mama could not take the loneliness and her mind went. She was sent to the sanitarium but killed herself in the spring. We were sent to foster homes. The day they split us up was the last day we saw each other for thirty years. The grownups said it was better if we thought of our new homes as our real ones but since they split us apart I have had no home.

"Our farm was sold after mother died and a year later I ran away and went out on my own. It has been that way ever since."

Socrates touched Toad on the shoulder when he story was over but said nothing. The other listeners sat quietly with their eyes averted.

Tyler leaned over to Socrates and whispered in his ear. "That story was for me wasn't it?"

"No," Socrates said. His eyes glistened wet in the light of the campfire. "It was for me."

Eleven

When they broke out of the woods outside Craig, they walked into a fraternity of a thousand men who were already crowding the bars and spilling out onto the sidewalks. They were lying on the boardwalks and falling out the windows. Craig was flat out bursting at its flimsy seams with humanity. The streets were awash with men, most of them drunk, many of them fighting, some of them unconscious. Circles of lumberjacks were gathered everywhere around jugs of whiskey, singing and dancing through the day. At night the partying continued without letup. They tramped up and down the street, sidestepping the brawlers and tripping over the fallen men. They were springing out, the money burning holes in their pockets and being converted into pleasure and fun as fast as the cash boxes could take it in.

Down the street came Sullivan's men, a swagger in their walk and pride in their talk. They whooped and hollered their way through town, elbowing through the drunken revelers and shouting creative obscenities. Street hounds joined in the chorus. Bar men rubbed their sweaty palms in greedy glee and broke out more of the cheap rotgut. The women in the whore-houses dashed a layer of rice powder over their breasts and readied for another onslaught.

In twos and threes and fours they scattered into the tarpaper saloons and settled in for the long drunk.

The Four Horsemen had never been rebuilt. The rubble from the fire was settled even with the muddy ground and only the barrel stove stood against the forest backdrop.

Tyler and Paddy passed by without even a sideways glance though both privately noted its passing.

They paused in front of the Best Chance Bar but Paddy stopped Caldwell from going in.

"What's your hurry, Timber Bull, or are you the bull of the barrooms now, too?" he said. "What are you talking about, Paddy? We've waited a long time. Let's get at it."

"Well, you'll not be forgetting your manners now, would you, Bull?" Paddy said with an admonishing look. He nodded to indicate the Bangor Tigers who were eagerly pressing them from behind.

"Oh, yeah! Sure!" Tyler agreed. Turning to Willie, he said, "Do you boys have any special traditions back in Maine regarding who you drink with and how?"

"Hell," Willie snorted, "I'll drink with anyone just so they carry their share of the tab. I'll even drink with you weed cutters if you promise not to slobber."

"I thought as much," Paddy agreed. "In Minnesota we have a tradition that new comers to our sod are given the courtesy of opening the festivities."

"You don't say? First in, first up to the bar and first drunk, huh?"

"Absolutely, and since you are the guests of honor, why don't you Maine boys take the lead?"

"Fine words," Willie replied. He was just a little suspicious. "You really mean them or is Bull here going to pick me up again and use me to open the door?"

"He means it," Tyler encouraged, "and no hard feelings over the past. You are the three finest river men that ever wet their boots in the Bigfork and Paddy and I will defend that claim to anyone."

"Well, thanks. That's generous of you," Willie said, accepting their handshakes. He hadn't time to embellish his acceptance speech further as he was thrown into the bar. Following up immediately, Paddy stuck his head in and hollered, "Timberr!" close on Willie's heels.

Thirty men lunged for the free booze as a bouncer caught up Willie and marched him to the bar. It was a bar like all the bars in town; smoky and musty, dark and noisy. It was full of lumberjacks with all their smells and sounds. They were drinking, playing cards, wrestling in the sawdust on the floor and kicking over the make-shift spittoons. The walls were lined with sleeping jacks, some of them propped into a sitting position. The rest sprawled out in such a way as to create a nuisance for the others. The noise was deafening. Between the bragging, singing, swearing and arguing it was impossible for a man to make himself understood without pressing his mouth right up to the other's ear.

A number of whiskey jugs from which the men were constantly drawing stood on the bar. Beer was being put away so fast that the bartenders had emptied the kegs into an open tub and were dipping the mugs in it. Tyler and the boys sat down, unlaced their boots and joined in.

In two hours, all five of them were sitting on the floor, drunk to their gills. Four empty booze bottles were scattered around them. Most of it they had drunk but a lot of it went into the mouths of passing strangers.

"I think it's time I went looking for some companionship!" Willie shouted. "Boots, 'Stache, what do you boys think?

Their silent nods were taken as assent.

"Bull, are you ready?"

"For what?" Tyler mumbled, "You wanna get out of here?"

"No, no, no, Bull. Suds and soft women," Willie corrected him, holding up three fingers. "How about it? Maybe you're too young. Maybe you're not young enough," he laughed.

"Too young?" Paddy said, rising to the challenge. "We're never too young. Another month in those trees and we might have been too old. I'm game. Bull, are you game?"

"I'm game."

"We're game, Willie. If I can just get these old legs propped up under me." They hugged the wall and lurched to their feet. "Just don't blame me if the ladies only have eyes for me and my devilish smile."

"What are you talking about?" Willie bragged, "I could spend six hours honing my face on a grindstone and still make you look like a poor cousin to a warthog."

Throwing their arms around each other they made their way out the door and across the street to Pretty Peggy's.

"Whew! We're gamey all right," Tyler sniffed as they undressed in the backyard of Peggy's. A bathhouse had been set up to protect her girls from the foul smelling lumberjacks.

"Lye soap or lilac, boys? One or the other," said Turk, the old toothless bath attendant. "I don't care but no one goes near the ladies smelling like the cracks between their toes or their butts for that matter."

Three big wooden tubs stood out in the open air. A sheet metal stove with a tank of steaming water set on top was roaring next to the tubs. Behind them stood a water tower of sorts that was filled from the river much the same way as a watering tank. A web of pipes and faucets kept the tubs warm and reasonably clean for bathing.

"The finest fuckin' bathhouse north of Effie," chortled Turk. He looked to be ninety-five if a day and claimed to be Peggy's secret lover. He had a foul mouth and abrasive manner, with a penchant for pouring scalding water on his patrons.

"I bet it's the only bathhouse north of Effie," Willie shot back, "and I don't even know where Effie is."

"Well, if you knew where Effie was, you'd still be standing here naked in my yard, you little twit. You're just hoping one of the girls peeks out the window and takes a look, aren't you?"

"No harm in window shopping."

"There is if it causes her to pack up and leave town because you've got a dick smaller than a bottle cork."

"Finished?"

"No, but it's a good beginning. If you got a hankering, the next tub is twenty miles and a spit through the woods and spit is what they fill it with. You can go there if you want to take a chance the wolves don't lick you clean first."

"This will do," Tyler pronounced.

"Damn right it will, young fella. Now shut yore yaps and get in."

They climbed in, two to a tub, took the bar of lye soap and the horse brushes and sanded off the dirt and dead skin.

"Mercy," Paddy said, "there's more crud on this old body then there are rings on a pine. This was a good idea."

Tyler settled back in the soothing warm water. "It sure was. Ow! Hey you!" he screamed as Turk doused him with the hot bucket.

"Hee, hee," Turk giggled. "Like scalding hogs at the butchers."

"Don't remind me of butchers, Laddie," said Paddy. "I know a devil of a butcher."

While the young men washed the scales from their bodies, the older roosters were still back at the Best Chance. Socrates, Schnaps, Snoose, Spooner and a few others sat around, downing straight shots and dipping pickled pork hocks out of a two-gallon crock set in the middle of the table. They started off as any sprung-out jacks might, puffing their chests, drinking their whiskey and looking around as if to say, "Look at us all you pretenders, we're the best there ever was and still is! We just come down the Bigfork with a bag of whoop and holler stories to tell." And they told many for the price of a drink. But eventually the stories ran dry.

When the depressant in the alcohol began to take its toll, Socrates got maudlin. "This is it for me, boys. I'm packing it in," he announced abruptly.

"What'a'ya mean," Snoose stammered. "We ain't even been in but one joint so far."

"I'm not talking about now, you fool. I'm saying this is my last camp. After this trip I'm out of the woods for good. I'm hanging it up."

"Good!" Snoose said, "Now we can get us a real cook." He looked at Socrates as if he was expecting him to break out in his mirthful laugh.

"I mean it, boys."

Schnapsie was shocked. "Soc, how can you say that? The camps are your life, same as for us."

"Was my life. Always will be a part of. But I been thinking a spell on it. It's time to face up to my problems."

"You don't any problems, Soc," Spooner insisted, reaching for another chunk of sour pork. "That's why you always go out and find someone else's to work on."

"Sure," Schnaps added. "Why if it weren't for you digging into every body's troubles, camp would get intolerable boring, Soc."

Socrates ignored Schnaps and answered Spooner. "I didn't have 'em because I'd never let 'em catch up with me. Fact is, Spoonie, I've been running away from trouble all my life. Just like young Bull, there. Gertie was the last one I lit out on, right when she was about to get steamrollered by some crooked cops. I'm going back there and settle down. Maybe I can get used to hot water and cool sheets after all, Schnaps." Socrates turned to his old comrade in arms. "I don't have to be in a tree camp to find trouble. Troubles land on me like apples fall from trees. Cities are full of 'em."

"You gonna be a hotel man, then?" Schnaps wondered.

"Maybe. I could help fix that place up right nice; maybe even make a little money."

"Still let us stay there?"

"Hell, no. Said I wanta make a little money. If I have my way, we won't even let you on the island." He stopped and stared at his glass, then he picked up his whiskey and held it in the manner of a toast. He looked around the table. "Damn right, you can stay there," he mumbled. "Anytime you want. For as long as you want. I'll miss you all."

"Well, thanks," said Schnapsie. "That makes me feel a little better."

"A little better," Snoose agreed.

Thirty minutes later, the guys got out of the tubs.

"Wowie!" Willie said looking over his scrawny body, "I look just like one of those boiled lobsters back in Maine! I'm as white as that wax store manikin that Torkie fell in love with last year."

"Poor, Torkie," said Boots. "A good pair of spectacles could have kept him out of the slammer. But he had his vanity." Boots punctuated his remark by framing his face in his hands.

They dressed fast, climbing into fresh-brushed pants, shirts and long johns washed and dried over hot rocks. Then they went into Peggy's parlor and sat down. Peggy, herself, came in a moment later. She was wearing a red satin dress with white lace that run under snow-white breasts that threatened to pour out over it. Her hair was a mass of blonde curls and she had biceps as large as most of the men on Mike's crew. "We're filled up at the moment, boys, but we'll fit you in soon as possible. In the meantime, mind your manners and say your prayers. There's bad whiskey and good donuts on the sideboard. Help yourself. It's on the house."

"First class!" Willie yelled.

"Always, sugar," Peggy answered with a wink. "Mike's boys always get first class. Say," she added, "you're not from around here, are you?"

"No, ma'am. Me and my friends here are from Maine. Boots and Moustache. We're Bangor Tigers, ma'am."

"Then you've come to the right place, hot stuff. We're gonna haul your ashes proper." She winked again and bustled out of the room.

"Hey, she's a pistol! Old enough to be my ma, but who's to say how ma should spend her Saturday nights, eh?" Willie laughed.

Peggy's was one of only six buildings in Craig boasting a foundation. Three were warehouses owned by logging companies. The other two were cat-houses like hers. But hers was the largest and the only two-story "hotel" in town. She had six rooms up and three down plus the parlor and her own quarters. Her women were durable, if not particularly beautiful. Most of them came up from St. Louis or Omaha. As Peggy said, "I'll have none of those phony Chicago floozies banging men in my house. They go through a man's pants when he's asleep, whether he's in them or not. No Minnesota women either. All they do is sit in their rooms and read the King James Bible. I never met a good Lutheran prostitute. Give me a fallen Catholic or God fearing Baptist, any day."

She was fair and honest when dealing with honest people, but would spit in your face if you called her a softhearted woman.

"I'm a bad woman and that's all that I am, Jack," she'd say, "but listen to this; I'm the best at what I do. You can brag to your wife after you've spent the night with Pretty Peggy, if you still want to go back to her. So shake that log out of your pants, if that's what it is and let's get down to business."

She knew her place because she had defined it. And like the women she learned on in Chicago, she knew how to bare her claws and defend her sandbox.

"I'll tell you about Peggy's mean streak," Socrates had reminisced one night in camp. "Peggy had a good thing going soon after she landed in Craig. She had the best house, prettiest girls, if that's what you'd call those bull-riding Cajuns she brought up from 'Loosiana'. She had good looks, her drinks weren't watered and the sheets got washed at least once a week.

"But one day, these two pointy-shoed pimps came up from Chicago. In a big touring car. They were sitting in the car but the car was sitting on a flatcar on the rails. They drove it right off the flat car and parked it in front of a cheap shack they had built. They were sleazy enough to be Italians. The place they set up was such a shack it wouldn't appeal to the rats. If they'd folded before they started it'd be good riddance. Cold, leaky and sheets the color and smell of pee. Well, excuse me if it offends your senses, I'm just saying how it was.

"But they brought with them a dark woman, a mulatto. She was light brown but real pretty; not fat like a mammy. And she could strut her stuff! She wore a red silk dress and red patent leather shoes. She didn't need no corset either. Not like those other heifers you see here. When she walked down the street, from the back she looked like two cats wrestling in a gunny sack.

"She was a dazzler. She had the walk and look of royalty, like she would have been a queen back in the Congo somewhere. And she knew what she was selling the way she rolled her eyes at you. And her skin! She only bathed in milk. Every week two cans of it come in on the Gut and Liver just so she could soak her little behind in the stuff. No kidding! It was supposed to make her pretty brown skin soft as a baby's butt. Naturally, everyone wanted to feel that for himself. And on top of all that, they say she knew tricks that hadn't been seen since the British run the French out of Canada.

"Well, business fell off for Peggy and those pimps weren't too nice about it, either. In fact, they bragged that soon Peggy would be making the beds in this other woman's house. Talk like that reminded Peggy of the Chicago days and she wasn't going to sit still for it.

"So, Peggy got some men friends together to fix those gigolos. One night someone made a big cross and set fire to it in front of their joint. Supposed to make them think it was those KKK boys from down south. They did, too! But then things got out of hand and they took the two scumbags and tarred and feathered them and then beat up the mulatto pretty good too. They were gone by morning. Likely just headed back to Chicago. Left the car parked and covered with snow. Couldn't get it out, anyway, in the winter. I think it ended up in the river. It was such a pretty car. I'll never ride in a pretty car like that.

Peggy showed some mercy on the mulatto and took her in long enough to heal up and she left Craig at about the same time as Gertie. Yeah, Merlatta is her name. If you think you saw her at Gertie's, maybe you did. But I'm no gossip. Anyway, that's Pretty Peggy for you."

It wasn't a hour before Peggy had cleared two upstairs and the three downstairs rooms. She sent Paddy and Tyler up in the adjoining rooms.

"You two get comfortable," she ordered. "It'll be fifteen minutes, sugars, while my girls freshen up and have a bite to eat. They've been too busy to stop for meals."

"Take your time, my beauty," Paddy sang. "I have no place to go but heaven."

"Heaven is where Peggy will send you, honey. Just don't expect me to talk you through the pearly gates, because I've got no pull on the inside."

"No fear, Pretty Peggy," Paddy said. "Sure as God is an Irishman, He looks after his folk from the emerald isle." He threw off his boots, dropped his suspenders, and lay back on the broken-backed feather bed. Then he saw the connecting door to Tyler's room.

"Bull," he cried, bursting in on Tyler, "Ain't this a hellava place?"

Tyler was stripped to his underwear, stareing out the window. "It sure is, Paddy, but I don't want to visit right now." Paddy obediently backed out of the room and closed the door, then immediately reopened it.

"So come and visit me then," he offered. "We'll send for another bottle and have a party with the colleens."

"I'm worn out. Honest," Tyler yawned. "Party on your own, Piggy. I just want to get laid and go to sleep."

"I'll do that," agreed the amiable Irishman, again shutting the door.

"But," the door opened again, "if you hear wild music coming from here, come and join in. It'll be me and my leprechaun mates holding forth."

"I will. I will," Tyler promised.

Even now the footsteps of six extra large Finnish leprechauns were pounding up the stairs.

Eager to catch up with Sullivan's men in Craig, they had double-timed back along the tote road and got to Craig five hours after the others.

After fifteen minutes of slugging whiskey at the Best Chance Saloon, they had smoke rolling out of their ears. Someone asked them where they come from and they said the Rainy, off a log drive. Another asked where their camp was and they said up the Sturgeon River. Another said were they the ones that Hungry Mike had suckered out of the right-of-way and they busted the noses of all three of the inquisitive fools. Then they brought one around to ask him where Sullivan's yellow crew was hiding?"

Socrates and his buddies were hiding right there in the corner, listening to the tirades and praying for invisibility.

Not figuring Socrates and the others to be river drivers, the wrecked jack could only remember the bragging of Willie and Paddy. He spat out his floating teeth and blurted, "Five of them are over at Pretty Peggy's. They went for women."

The Finns stormed out of the bar, knocking Snoose off his chair in the process. "I should'a popped him one," growled Snoose after the Finlanders had left.

"Yeah," Schnaps counseled, "but it's hard to fight with your pants full of poop, ain't it? Let it lay."

"I'm lettin'. I'm lettin'."

Rudy Saatala had passed by the "Best Chance" and walked over to Sad-Eyed Sam's. Mike was there, putting down chow with his left hand and Wild Turkey with his right. Rudy stepped over the bench and sat down across from him. He was spoiling for a fight, and if Mike had accommodated him at all, it would have been there and then. Instead, Mike looked over the bottle that he held to his lips, took along pull and put it back on the table. The lack of either fear or surprise in Mike's attitude threw Rudy off balance for a moment.

"Rudy. Last time I saw you, you were squinting over a rifle. You look even uglier over the far end of a bottle."

"You stole my water, Mike. You blew up my boom and stole my water."

"First in is first down, Rudy. That's the rule and that's the law. If it's water you want, get it from the waiter." For all the food and liquor he had put down, Mike was still in control of himself.

"It's not water I'm after now, Sullivan," he said. Men wandered in to watch the growling between the two wood's bosses. There were soon forty or fifty men gathered around the room and more coming all the time.

"I'll take a share of your bottle and we'll settle up like men."

Mike took another bite of his ham sandwich and chewed it pensively. "I heard you took target practice at one of my men. I won't drink with a man who shoots at innocent folks. If it's whiskey you want, Rudy, you can get that from the waiter, also."

By not rising to Rudy's taunts, Mike was making a fool of Rudy. The veins were beginning to stand out on Rudy's neck and moisture was glistening from his forehead. Now he must either call Mike out or get up and sneak out the door. He was backed into a corner and pride demanded that not happen. Saatala reached for the bottle of whiskey. Mike's hand shot out and closed over his.

"So then," Rudy said, "we'll have it out now."

Mike swallowed, wrenched the bottle from Rudy's grasp and took another drink. He looked at the contents through the brown glass. A smile began to play over Mike's face.

"I'll tell you what, Rudy." He waved the bottle at the assembled audience. "Tell you what we'll do. We wrestle for it. You win and you get the bottle. See? There is the start of a good drunk still in her. I win, and I walk you down the street with a lead rope around your neck. Just like the big cow you are acting like. And you have to moo like one, too."

Rudy stood up, intent on striking Sullivan. The spectators spread out. Mike held up his hand and spoke again.

"You win and you get the bottle, and you lead me through town in my long handles. That's my last, best, and final offer."

It was an offer Saatala might have refused if it wasn't for his pig-headed pride. It was fair and then some so only cowardice could explain not agreeing to it. Besides, he had such an anger boiling up inside him that no one would beat him this day. He settled back onto the bench, rolled up his shirt sleeve and braced his elbow on the table.

"No," Mike shook his head. "Not here. We'll go outside."

Sullivan swept away the dishes, picked up the table and carried it through the crowd and out into the middle of the street. Others followed with the benches. The big men sat down again and braced their right arms on the table. Their hands joined, Rudy's long fingers enveloping Mike's shorter, thicker ones.

Their eyes met and locked. The bravado disappeared and smiles dissolved into clenched teeth and angry stares. Fingers tightened, forearms swelled, and the contest was on. For five minutes neither man moved the other off the vertical. Nor did either show any sign of yielding.

Time passed. Ten minutes, fifteen. The sun stood still. The crowd was quick to ante up money, eager to bet on the outcome and soon the table was piled with bills and silver. With the passing of time, the wages were doubled then redoubled, and still the combatants sat like rocks, their arms locked in trembling inertia; Prometheus and Hercules straining to break free from each other's bonds. A lifetime of hatred was wrapped up in the match and it could not be quickly decided. In the end it might decide nothing at all, for hatred does not so easily dissipate.

Just after Paddy had closed the door to Tyler's room for the last time, there was a knock on his door. He had been amusing himself by trying to dance an Irish jig on one foot while he picked his toes with one hand and drank from his whiskey bottle with the other. He stopped his singing.

"Sure, and that will be my lucky Colleen, now," he crooned, walking over to the door. He didn't quite get there. The door blew in, shattered by the boots of the husky Finlanders.

Paddy wasn't so drunk that he couldn't distinguish between a rice-powdered woman and a full bearded man, nor could he mistake the blood hunger in their eyes for the look of amour. He braced himself for first man, swinging the bottle up against his head. The Finn collapsed as shards of glass fell from his liquor soaked scalp.

"Bull!" Paddy shouted. "Get in here!" That was all the warning he was permitted. Paddy tagged the second one with a good shot to the ear and even had time to finish him off with a solid right to the bridge of his nose.

The Irishman was grinning, enjoying the exchange of camaraderie with these playful strangers. He took a step back to get lined up on another target, but that was it. He was buried in an avalanche of bodies as the rest of the Finns stepped over their fallen comrades and charged into the room. They dragged him to his feet and two men pinned him while the others rained blows on him. Paddy finally freed himself by biting off the ear lobe of the man who had handcuffed his right arm.

"Bull!" He screamed. "I could use a bit of help."

Paddy smacked the man on his left in the groin and, swinging in wild abandon, danced free in a circle of hovering attackers.

"Now you cowardly assassins. Bull! Let's have you one at a time like gentlemen, shall we? Bull, where are you? Come on, you louts!" And one at a time they came at him, swinging from the heels, landing a few and missing some, too. For his own part Paddy was holding up, although the strength was ebbing from his arms as fast as the blood flowed from his face. The tide was slowly turning to the favor of Saatala's crew.

Tyler had fallen fast asleep.

Back at the Best Chance, they were still talking about the abrasive Finlanders. "What 'ya think?" Snoose wondered. "Should we go over and lend the boys a hand?"

Socrates and Schnapsie looked at him as if he'd lost his mind. "Talk him out of it, won't ya," Schnaps said.

"Absolutely." Socrates was three sheets to the wind and raising a fourth. But even so, he recognized the absurdity of Snoose's idea. "Let me think for a second here. Oh yes, how about this? *'Don't plot against your neighbor; he is trusting in you. Don't get into needless fights. Don't envy violent men. Don't copy their ways, for such men are an abomination to the Lord.'* Proverbs something or other."

"I sure don't want to be no abomination," Schnaps seconded.

"Ah shoot, Socrates. How come you can always come up with a quote to back up what you want to do, but not the other guy's?" Snoose was spoiling for a fight.

"Selective reading, careful pruning and adjusting the words to suit the need, my friend." Socrates put his hands alongside his head and slowly rubbed his temples. He shut his eyes and grimaced slightly. "Besides," he softly added, "I don't feel up to any rough-housing tonight. I'm kinda tired, you know?"

"That's right," Schnaps agreed. "We're all kinda tired. 'Cept for this young lion here. You go ahead Snoose and have mine, too."

"Aw, cripe. You guys can all go to hell for all I care." Still, Snoose laughed at the foolishness of his own suggestion.

Mike and Rudy were still locked in combat at Sad-Eyed Sam's. By now, stakes filled the table, a pile to either side of the men. The greater margin of bets was placed on Mike, but not by much. There was some concern that he had ruined his training with the food he had wolfed down since he hit town. Rudy, on the other hand, was mean, angry and hungry. He had drunk just enough liquor to stoke the fire in his belly but not enough to make him weak.

"Come on, Mike," one of his supporters encouraged. "Put him away so I can buy me a drink."

"Bust him up, Rudy. Remember what he did to you on the Sturgeon," countered a blonde Scandinavian logger.

Neither Mike nor Saatala gave any indication that they heard the bantering. Their eyes were still locked on each other's. The tension on the arms had not relaxed since the start of the contest; their veins standing out like roots bursting through the sod. Their breathing was deep and steady, the intensity still undiminished.

"Twenty minutes," intoned a fat little clerk counting off the time on his pocket watch.

Supporters of each man had dipped bar rags in ice water and were sponging off their champions.

About that time Paddy came to visit Tyler again. Two of the howling Finns had locked his arms and, in trying to drive him into the wall, misjudged by two feet and sent him flying through the connecting door. He came to rest across the foot of Tyler's bed, amid pieces of the splintered door.

Tyler bolted upright. "What'd I say about staying out of here?" he threatened.

"Holy mother of St. Patrick, man," Paddy cried. He had cuts above his eyes and was bleeding from both corners of his mouth and one ear. There was a note of concern in his voice. "Were you unconscious or what? Buckle your pants and pucker up, Bull, we're getting company!"

The 'company' came through the door fast on the heels of Paddy's warning. The Finns, hungry for revenge, smelled the kill. The odds were now two to four. Paddy had managed to fling one man out a window and cold-cocked another with a pitcher.

Bull and Paddy fought back to back to protect each other's rear. Tyler was still fresh and, if his drunkenness kept him from landing many solid blows, it also let him take a few without going down. He drove another Finn out of the room when the man made a rush for him just as Tyler bent over to pull up his trousers. The Finn flew over his back, crashed through the window off the porch roof and came to rest on the street twenty feet from Mike and Rudy. The sight and sounds of falling bodies generated more fighting outside and the street filled with screaming, struggling men.

Seconds later Willie, Boots and Moustache kicked in Tylers' door, the last one still on it's hinges, and threw themselves into the fray. Interrupted from their lovemaking, the three brought a new sense of adventure to the fracas. Willie quickly established control over the situation.

"There Boots! That one! No! No, you idiot, the guy with the black suspenders! 'Stache, get the man with the handlebars. Wait! This one first!" he screamed as he was wrapped up in a Finn's arms. The Tigers handled themselves well, thanks to a proper New England upbringing and Willie's propensity for staging every event for future retelling. Their boots were wrecking havoc on the taller Finns' legs. The tide turned in favor of Sullivan's crew.

Seeking a respite, Paddy and Tyler broke off from the others, crept back to Paddy's room and collapsed on the bed. A moment later, Peggy "just about had enough of this free advertising", and walked into the melee with a lead pipe and a pistol. She shot a hole in the ceiling, bringing down a good chunk of plaster, and rammed the pipe into Boots' belly. The fight ended as abruptly as it had started, the Finns not unhappy to disengage with their pride.

"I'll shoot any man still here in ten seconds," she bellowed, but the bordello would have emptied anyway because a lumberjack came in yelling about the arm-wrestling going on between Mike and Rudy. Finns and Tigers, alike, they hitched up their pants and scrambled out of the house.

Behind Peggy had come the women intended for Bull and Paddy. Poking through the debris, they finally located them under the bedspread in the adjoining room. Unable to rouse the two, they pronounced them done for the night and rummaging through their pockets, extracted the proper pay along with a generous tip for the trouble. Propping the doors back in place, they left to attend to other business.

Socrates and his buddies also heard the news about the marathon contest and hurried over to Sam's. They forced their way through the crowd to the edge of the inner ring of spectators.

"Forty-five minutes," intoned the timekeeper, "and no advantage."

Indeed, the two arms were still standing as straight as a pine. The exhausted muscles throbbed against the glisten of sweat and trembled against each other.

"Ain't no one ever gonna win this one," declared a front-rower.

"Oh yeah, snarled Socrates, spitting his works at the man, "Hungry Mike's the winner any time he wants."

"Yeah?"

"You bet!"

"Table's open old man. Put your money where your mouth is." Socrates reached down and pulled out his roll. He still had over three hundred and fifty dollars to his name. Ten minutes earlier he had figured on using the cash to help get Gertie's boarding house set up on a paying basis. Now, he was being challenged to back his man or get out of the game.

"Why don't you bet it all, you old fart," the young lumberjack said, goading Socrates on.

Socrates looked at his stake and then at Hungry Mike. His boss's eyes never left Saatala. He gave no indication at all that he knew the old cook was there. There, thought Socrates, sits the best friend a guy could ever want. He knew that but for Hungry Mike Sullivan he would have been begging the streets of Minneapolis with his brother years ago. Yeah, he thought, here was the kind of man you'd bet your life on, much less your stake.

"Hell, yes, you assholes," he shouted above the cheering, "I'm putting three hundred and fifty dollars on Mike Sullivan! Any takers?" But takers were few, since most of the betting money was already in the game. Only fifty dollars found its way to the table.

Then, it happened. Mike's arm moved off center by nearly two inches. Rudy's own hand moved into the top position over Mike's. A slow smile spread across Rudy's face. Men stepped forward, reaching into their pockets.

"What do you say now, old man," came the young jack again "Your money still ready to back the Irishman ?"

Socrates didn't blink. "All you got and more on trust, you little shit."

The young jack reached in his pocket and brought out his own stake. With the help of his friends, he covered the rest of Socrates' three hundred. "Bet made and witnessed," said the jack.

"Made and witnessed," Socrates agreed. He turned back to the action at the table just as Mike's arm slowly moved back to dead center. The smile disappeared from Rudy's face. The advantage was lost and so was the exuberance of Rudy's backers. Now the faint smile belonged to Socrates.

At one hour Willie and the Tigers had pressed their way into the crowd and put their own money on Mike. The Finns came over with them, a truce of sorts being declared. They emptied their pockets for Rudy, the man who never settled for less than first place. The biggest of them lifted Willie on his shoulders so he could see over the crowd to "tell us when Rudy puts him down."

"I hope you can hold me up because it won't be in your life-time," the bashful Willie boasted. "Nor in your son's son's either." Time passed slowly. At one hour and twenty minutes, Rudy's entire body was screaming in agony. But as terrible as he was hurting, he guessed that Mike had to be feeling the same. Rudy made a decision. This was the time to commit it all, lock, stock and barrel. He was determined to drive Mike back off center. He had done it once and only a Herculean effort on the part of Sullivan had saved him. Another push and this damned black Irishman was done for.

Saatala threw everything he had into it. It started from the toes, flowed up his legs, his buttocks rising, illegally, an inch off the bench for greater leverage. He rotated his shoulder, bringing it behind his arm, driving into it with his full weight. He grunted, and swore. He called on his father, mother, God's chosen and God's damned. He swore at Mike, Mike's parentage, his ancestry and his progeny. He cursed to heaven the power of Sullivan's arm and blessed his own. He prayed, pleaded, swore and begged. He ground off the edges of his teeth, the chips floating about in his spittle and oozing from the corners of his mouth. Rudy gave his very soul to that one supreme effort. And for all that, he moved Mike's arm less than half an inch.

Half an inch and Mike held. He had taken Rudy's best and now it was his turn. The veins on Rudy's face were bursting. The whites of his eyes burned cherry red. The blood spread across his temples and cheeks. Mike eyes bored into Saatala's and in them he saw Rudy's defeat. And Mike could have offered a draw there and gone back to his drinking. But Hungry Mike was not in the mood for pity and he had never settled for a draw on anything in his life. Victor or vanquished, one way or the other, Mike believed in bringing things to a proper conclusion.

Now, as he looked into Rudy's eyes, Mike felt the same frustration he had felt with Stankovich. Only three times in his life, including now, had he faced off against Saatala. In fact, he was the only man Sullivan ever had to defend his honor in front of his men and strangers. Would it never end with this man who could not be at peace with other men? Mike was angry that his dinner and the celebration of a successful camp had been so interrupted. But most of all, he was determined not to fail his men. He was doing it for his lumberjacks. Otherwise he would not have done what he did.

Then they heard it. Softly at first, then louder as the crowd grew hushed to catch the melody. For many in front of Sad-eyed Sam's that night had been in Grand Rapids years earlier to witness their first confrontation and recognized the tune. Mike was softly singing, "Coming through the Rye."

Rudy stared at him in disbelief. With a look of calm, relaxed determination Mike began to move Rudy's arm. Back to center it came and then over. Slowly, but steadily, Mike tipped him over. Rudy's eyes broke from Mike and went to his failing arm. He doubled his effort. He cursed and prayed and screamed again. And then it broke. It snapped with a crack that penetrated the cheering and silenced the onlookers. It cracked like a rifle shot and swept over the stunned lumberjacks like a lightening bolt.

Mike had broken Rudy's arm! The hand bent over and flopped onto the table and one last time Rudy's scream rent the fabric of the air. His face drained of color, and Rudy passed out.

Mike relaxed his grip and Rudy fell backward off the bench. Men rushed to his side, picked him up, and lifted him onto the table. The winners swept forward to collect their bets, digging under the stricken logging king in their exuberance. Mike stood up, patted Rudy gently on the shoulder, and went into the kitchen. Sam was waiting with a pot roast.

"If you had done him any quicker, Mike, she wouldn't have been done," laughed Sam. "What a show! I sold five hundred dollars in whiskey and food! I should split it with you. Horseradish?"

"Yes, thanks." Mike grinned in pleasure at Sam's joy and sat down to the aromatic roast. "You wouldn't have any minced pie to go with this would you, Sam?" he asked. "I haven't had a good minced pie in ages."

Socrates came in a few minutes later, sat down across from Mike and silently watched him eat. He so loved this hulking Irishman, so constant and unchanging.

"Does it compare with my own roast, Mike?"

Mike washed down a bite and nodding, wiped his mouth. "It seems so long ago, doesn't it, that you borrowed me a saw and I bested Saatala. A saw was all you had then. Again tonight you wagered everything you had on old Hungry Mike."

"You didn't need my backing, Mike. You had him beat anyway."

"Maybe," Mike nodded. "Maybe. I do not understand the temperament of that man. Such pride and all it led to was a wooden splint and a long trip to the surgeons. But you, Socrates, I thank you for your trust. And now," he said changing the subject, "seven hundred dollars in your pocket. That's enough money, a man could drink himself to death ten times over."

"Oh, no. Not me, Mike. Maybe before, but I have plans with this money. Here," Socrates said, handing over the wad of bills. "Here's all but ten. It's safe with you. I'd get rolled in two minutes and then I'd just end up back in some dirty camp next winter."

The words and the tone in which they were spoken did not escape Sullivan. "Is this the last, then? Are you leaving old Mike for some soft featherbed?"

"It is. I've told the others, too. I'm putting away the apron the same as I put away the saw years ago. I'm done. Stick with Spoonie. He's a good young kid."

Mike looked at him and slowly nodded. He understood. "They were good years, Socrates." There was no need for further words. He took the money and slipped it under his shirt. "I'll keep it until you ask for it."

"Uh, uh. Until we're back in Deer River. Not before, no matter how hard I might beg. Agreed?"

"Whatever."

"Deer River."

"Agreed."

"If you excuse me now, I've a few choice words to belabor the men of this sorry town with. It's my last celebration, you know."

Sullivan's boys were so concerned that everyone knew that they were Mike's men and the Finns were Saatala's that they started another fight to get their point across. They began by beating up on each other with the exception of Willie and his new friend, Dansk, the big Finlander. The two picked on a camp of Germans from over on the Littlefork. It didn't much matter because in a matter of minutes, everybody in town was fighting everybody else without prejudice or bias.

The fight had a certain resilience to it. It swelled at times, engulfing hundreds of men. After awhile the alcohol and fight dissipated and it would shrink to just a few as the others wondered off looking for more drink. Refueled, they would wander back out onto the street, pushing and pulling, mauling each other like big playful puppies. Henceforth, men claimed the streets of Craig that night were paved with teeth and sleeping lumberjacks.

By midnight, Socrates, Seifert, Snoose and Schnaps were sitting in a bar again. They had been out in the rough and tumble with the others and were taking a breather. The night was wearing on with little sign of letup. Presently a bunch of Finlanders stomped in and, still in the spirit, called "Timberr!" Seven of them bought rounds and they began telling stories.

"Now listen to them blowhards," Socrates said, "not a true word in the whole bunch."

Just then one of them, older and not as handsome as Finns were apt to be, began his brag. He stood on a chair in the middle of the room and began to regale the crowd about how he was the reincarnation of Paul Bunyon himself.

"I, by god, am the best damned ax man ever to cut a swath through the timber, and you know why, don'tcha? It may be that I am Paul Bunyon, himself, come back to lead you pore dumb rabbits out of the wilderness. When I be done up here, this forest will be nothing but a church lawn!" He began laughing at his own inanity and fell to the floor. The other Finns, reflecting the derision of the crowd, poured out their beer and whiskey on him.

Suddenly the quiet Seifert was on the chair. He stood there a moment with a look of uncertainty, then pointed at the Finn and yelled, "Hey you hog-faced blowhard!"

The Finn looked up at him as if he were a Sunday school preacher. "Yes. Yes, vat are you saying?"

"You talked about reincarnation as if our lives are blessed by it, but only I, the noble Seifert, know the true meaning of re-in-car-na-tion." He said the word slowly, hammering on all five syllables like he was driving a nail.

Socrates and the others were going crazy over Seifert's audacity.

"Look," Socrates cried, "Seifert's gone loco! He's round the bend and taking water." He yelled at Seifert, "Get down, you fool, before they drag you down!"

Seifert ignored him. "I heard it a long time ago," he continued, "in an Indian village far up in the Cree country. We was sitting around a fire one night; me, a fat old medicine man and a very mysterious white man who may have been a hundred years old, maybe two hundred. And say, do you want to hear this or not, Mr. Bunyan?"

The Finns were standing slack-jawed and mute over the presence that the quiet Seifert was exerting. They dumbly nodded.

"Okay, boys." He cleared his throat noisily and spat a big wad of tobacco six feet Into a spittoon. Then he started.

> *"I've been a traveler all my life*
> *Never burdened by man or wife.*
> *Tho' I've wandered from Texas to Nome,*
> *I've never been more than a step from home*
> *All that I have and all that I am is carried*
> *In my cranium.*
> *So I guess I'm a philosopher of sorts*
> *Not the kind that rants and snorts*
> *But just a man who takes a look at life*
> *And makes no claims, preaches or cavorts.*
> *But I've seen some things that bother me*
> *Preposterous things that shouldn't be*
> *That make me laugh and make me grin*
> *But none more so than the baboon Finn.*
> *He's tall and slender, of dubious gender*
> *He likes to brag with a brain that lags,*
> *his mouth.*
> *I just come down the Bigfork River,*
> *Carryin' a peavey and ridin' a sliver.*

And in all that time upon that streamlet
I never saw a Finn get his toenails wet.
They like to talk and boast and strut
But I'm thinkin' now, you know what
They are cowards in their guts
With cupcakes where there should be nuts."

The bar broke up in gales of laughter; the men dancing and singing the last line over and over again. The Finn picked himself slowly off the ground. In a blurry-eyed voice he demanded, "Who in the hell do you think you are telling a joke on us?"

"Well," Seifert drawled, "Ain't you the bunch of dumb muskrats that got cut off by Hungry Mike Sullivan who just busted up your best man? Broke your boom and his strong right arm?"

"Who are you, anyway?" the lumberjack demanded.

By now there wasn't a man left sitting. "Well it's the truth, by God, you dumb, blind, braggart, because we're the gol-darned boys what done it!"

Seifert disappeared beneath the sea of men.

"Quick, grab him," Schnapsie said. He climbed on a table and dove into the throng. The fight engulfed the bar and flowed back out onto the street. The donneybrook went on for another hour until the passion finally ebbed. Then they all stumbled back into the bars to drink together and finally pass out.

Snoose and Schnaps hauled Seifert out of the pile and quietly snuck off with Socrates to one of the cat houses noted for its big Nordic women. They tried to squeeze into one of the packed rooms but, business being as brisk as it was, none of the woman would have them. They spent an hour drinking on the madam's hospitality, singing their songs: The Little Brown Bulls, The Crow Wing Drive and the Festive Lumberjack. It was well past midnight when Socrates led a chorus in his crackling voice:

"I've been round the world a bit and seen beasts great and small.
The one I mean to tell about for darin' beats them all.
He leaves the woods with his bristles raised, the full length of his
  back.
He's known by men of science as the festive lumberjack.
He's a wild, rip snortin' devil ever time he comes to town.

He's a porky, he's a moose cat, to busy to set down.
But when his silver's registered, and his drinks is coming few,
He's then as tame as other jacks that's met their Waterloo.
That's met their waterloo."

It was two in the morning when they wandered out to a stable behind the house and lay down in the hay, and went to sleep.

Three hours before sun up, Socrates wakened them with a loud cry. He was coughing and grasping for breath. Seifert sat up and hurried over to him. The old man's body was locked up; his arms extended rigid at his side. His eyes were closed. He was trying to breathe, but couldn't. His face was red and swollen, and radiated the pain that had hold of him. His chest was heaving uncontrollably.

"Socrates! Socrates!" Seifert grabbed his arms and shook him. "You're dreaming! Wake up, man, wake up!" But Socrates didn't wake up because he couldn't and then Seifert knew it wasn't a dream.

The others woke up to his shouting.

"What's goin' on," Schnapsie asked from over in the corner. "You still fighting?"

"Schnaps! Help me! Soc is real sick.", Schnapsie got up fast and hurried over. He looked Socrates over quickly and grabbed Seiferts arm. "Quick! Go get Mike," he ordered. "Tell him ... tell Mike, Soc is real sick."

Seifert hesitated. He stared in disbelief at Schnapsie. Then he looked back to Socrates and believed. He jumped up and ran out. Schnapsie roused Snoose and, together, they took hold of Socrates and cradled him tight, trying to stop the convulsions. But they looked at each other with the look of knowing. Socrates was having a stroke.

By the time Seifert returned with Mike, Socrates was still. He lay in their arms, the tightness gone, his body relaxed. Mike knelt down and felt for a pulse. There was none. He gently closed Socrates' eyes, and turned to the others.

"It's okay," he whispered, patting Schnapsie on the shoulder. "He's gone now. It's over." Tenderly he put his arms under the body and picked him up. For a man that had been so tough and wiry he felt so light.

Sullivan carried him over to Peggy's house. He found her standing in the parlor.

She looked at Socrates.

"Is he . . . ."

Mike nodded.

"How?"

"He just wore out, Peg. Died in his sleep. I need a room."

Peggy went to clear a downstairs room. A few minutes later, Paddy and Tyler came running in. They saw Mike, with Socrates. The old man's head was tilted back over Mike's arm. His mouth was open, the arms hung loose and lifeless. Snoose stood off to the side with Schnapsie, the little camp fool, clutching Schnaps' arm. His head rested on Schnapsie's shoulder. He was whimpering. Schnapsie was crying, too. Peggy came out of the bedroom.

"You can bring him in now, Mike."

"Wait!" Tyler came over to them. "What happened?" He looked at Mike. Mike shook his head.

"He's gone, Tyler."

Tyler was thunderstruck. "God! No! No! Who? Who did this? I'll kill him!"

"Snoose took Tyler's arm. "Wasn't no one," he said. "He died just now when we was sleeping, Tyler. Socrates died in his sleep. It weren't no one. He died and never said a word."

Tyler's eyes flew through the group. Their faces were empty, hopeless. Mike tried to step around him.

"Wait!" Tyler said, "Where are you taking him?"

"In there," Mike said gesturing towards the bedroom door. "I'll lay him in there and stay with him."

But Tyler was adamant. "No! I'll do it. Please. Mike, please." He gently took Socrates from Sullivan.

Mike gave up his cook's body to Tyler who cradled him in his arms, tucking the old gray head into the crook of his shoulder. He carried Socrates into the bedroom and laid him down on a feather comforter.

Mike turned to Peggy. "I'll have a bottle if you have one in the house, Peggy."

Wordlessly, she produced the whiskey and gave it to him. Mike followed Tyler into the bedroom. They sat together, cried together, and through the long night, kept another vigil for one of Hungry Mike's men.

In the quiet hours Tyler came to tell Mike about Socrates and what the old man had done for him. He told him about the father who had driven him out and the old cook who had taken him in and fathered him. Mike listened and in the honesty of the telling, finally related his own secret.

All his life he had known he was destined to be a logger. God had ordained it when He gave Mike his great body. He was born with the strength of two men and an unyielding tolerance for cold and hardship. There was a time when it might have been different.

When Mike won the lumberjack championship from Saatala a two-hundred dollar cash prize went with the silver buckle. Folks around there thought it odd that Mike would use the money to enroll at the University of Minnesota. But it wasn't his doing. It was his mother's. It had always been her dream that one of her children should go on and receive the kind of education that she had only dreamt about. Her only other child, a daughter, married early and started to raise a brood of her own. To get her way with Michael, she used the strongest means possible. Dying with pneumonia, she extracted from him a deathbed promise that he would try school.

He put up at the dorm on the Forestry School campus and enrolled. Within two weeks he was aching to quit. On the third, he met Tanjka Kolaczyk. Tanjka was two years younger than Mike and ten years more experienced. She was a crazy, happy, wild Hungarian gypsy with long, raven-black hair, large hazel eyes and laughter that could charm a stump into singing.

In Mike she saw a handsome, bashful hunk of a man, charming in his backwoods manner, endearing in his sensitivity. She contrived to meet him. Leaving the library with an impossible load of books one evening, Tanjka asked him to help her and by the time they reached her apartment, he was enchanted with her.

Not that she was such an innocent maiden but certainly enough so that when he obliged her first invitation to kiss her, the shiver of excitement that ran down her spine was real. And when they finally went down to the riverbank and made love, her wild nature burst forth and her fire enslaved him.

Mike fell so completely in love, there was room for nothing other than Tanjka and his classes, which he took seriously because she demanded it of him.

By summer break, Mike was ready to propose marriage. Tanjka insisted they wait. She enjoyed her freedom, her studies, and her work at the small Cedar Avenue café. It provided her with enough money to enjoy her free-spirited lifestyle.

Mike yearned to steal her from the city and bring her back to Bemidji. He had an incredible nesting urge; promised her a cabin in the woods, warm quilts and quiet summer evenings serenaded by the calling of the loon. But Tanjka was adamant, so, rather than jeopardize their relationship, Mike capitulated.

She stayed in the city while he returned home to help with the summer work. They wrote every day, she about her love, he about his north-country; even about the cows which he suddenly found to be beautiful and poetic. Each night, before falling asleep, he placed himself in her arms. Every morning he awoke to her smile. Every day was spent with the memory of her laughter. And then he would write again to thank her for these gifts.

His friends thought he was crazy. What had happened to this big roguish woodsman-farmer who rarely talked of women and was so timid around them. Even his father volunteered that she must be quite a looker and Mike would blush and suggest that she was a lot like his mother.

Fall came and Mike couldn't wait to board the train back to Minneapolis. It was still a week before classes, but Tanjka's letters had stopped coming and this scared him. He chattered like a squirrel with the amused conductor all the way to St. Paul. At the depot he shouldered his duffel bag and loped the mile and a half down to her apartment building. She wasn't there. Neighbors told him she had been gone for almost a week. Mike dropped his gear and ran over to the cafe where the embarrassed owner put his arm around Mike's shoulder and told him that Tanjka was ill and in the hospital.

At the hospital he forced his way into the quarantine ward where she lay with scarlet fever. She was in a coma by then. He sat with her and held her hand and sponged her face with a cool cloth. For eighteen hours he stayed at her side and threatened to kill anyone who tried to remove him. In the end the staff took compassion and left him alone. And in the end, Tanjka died.

She had no relatives, always insisting that was the truth. Mike used to laugh at this but now he saw it was so. He took his tuition money and paid for her funeral. He and a half-dozen friends gathered to say goodbye to her young Bohemian spirit and then it was over.

He returned to the farm. His father died in an accident that winter and the next summer Mike signed over the farm to his sister. That fall he went into the woods and his heart never came out again. Forever after, in the face of every man he lost, he saw Tanjka. Death would always be the only adversary Mike Sullivan could never best.

Twelve

*T*yler and Mike stayed with Socrates until morning. Word of his death had gotten around Craig and a large and sober group of men waited outside Peggy's with the patience that men have when forces beyond their understanding have taken control of them.

At eleven, Socrates was consigned to a rough pine box and carried out of Peggy's by six of Sullivan's finest men. They marched in silence down to the river.

Paddy and Seifert had dug a grave on a willowed bank of the Bigfork where Socrates could lie and look to his river and his forests forever. Five hundred men whom Socrates had known, befriended, laughed and lived with attended the service.

Standing by the grave, Mike handed Socrates' Bible to Tyler. "Please read something," he asked.

Tyler took the book. It fell open to a passage Socrates had once marked. In a hesitant voice, Tyler began:

> "'Once upon a time the trees decided to elect a king.
> First they asked the olive tree, but it refused.
> Should I quit producing the olive oil that blesses God and man,
> Just to wave to and fro over the other trees, it said?
> Then they said to the fig tree, you be our king!
> But the fig tree also refused.
> Shall I quit producing sweetness and fruit
> Just to lift my head above all the other trees, it asked?
> Then they said to the grapevine, you reign over us!
> But the grapevine replied,
> Shall I quit producing the wine that cheers God and man,
> Just to be mightier than all the other trees?

No, I would rather be no more than what God has decided for me, for that is enough.'"

Tyler closed the book. Tears streamed down his face but he didn't care. There was more he wanted to say even though he knew it would never be enough. He composed himself for a moment and then spoke directly to the body that was Socrates. And his words were not unlike another scripture passage.

"You took me out of my country and delivered me into a wilderness. And in that wilderness I found myself. You took a boy into your woods and patiently let him grow. You were a father to me the whole while, a brother to all, all your life. You are a king uncrowned, Socrates." Having said this, Tyler turned away and wept.

There were many men crying now, crying without tears but with much sorrow as men do for another man they loved. They lowered the old cook into the grave and covered it over, then laid a pavement of rocks over it. They erected a clean white cross of peeled tamarack and from it Schnapsie hung a pair of boots as befitting a river man. For the rest of that day, there were no drunks, no fights in Craig. But there were many stories told and retold of Socrates, the old lumberjack who could read.

It was a quiet crew that boarded the Gut and Liver that afternoon. Only once did Schnaps and Snoose try to break the somber atmosphere.

"Say," Schnapsie said, "weren't those women some lookers, though?"

"Especially that Gretchen and Heidi," Snoose said referring to a pair of identical Nordic twins.

"They sure looked enough alike to be twins, didn't they?"

"Oh boy, "especially Heidi," Snoose agreed.

But the spark of humor failed to catch and they fell silent until the silence gave way to conversations and reflections on life and such.

By six that afternoon, they had passed through Deer River. Tyler had spent the entire ride staring out at the landscape. The great forest had been left behind for another half year, maybe for all time. In his heart was an aching loneliness. He was sorry for words said and unsaid and emotions gone unexpressed. There were other moments when he imagined the last few months as one long rumbling trip on the Gut and Liver; a fantasy ride from which he had never disembarked. It was composed of fables and legends, stories of men who never existed and never could. But, in the end, the pain kept bringing him back to reality. Alone he had boarded a train and alone he would leave it.

The sun was low and glowing cherry red when they reached Grand Rapids, seven months after shipping out for the woods.

As soon as they arrived, men began making plans to scatter. A freight train bound for the west was coaling in the yard and a number of the boys were determined to make the wheat fields for spring planting. Tyler stood on the dock in front of the station and watched them ready their gear.

The Oregon Kid came over and grabbed him by the shoulder. "Bull." he said excitedly, "Come on and ride with us. Paddy's coming and so are the Tigers. We'd make a great team, you know; really give lumberjacks a bad name out there."

"Thanks," Tyler said, "I don't think so. I have some things I've got to do first."

"We're heading for Dakota; Montana, maybe. If there isn't work, I promised to take them out to the Pacific. You ever been there? No? Well, listen, you won't believe it." The Kid stopped when he saw the look in Tyler's eyes. He wasn't there anymore nor in Montana or Oregon. He was lost somewhere in his own thoughts.

"Tyler," Oregon asked, quietly this time, "Tyler, please come with us."

Tyler let him into his thoughts. "I got to see some people first, Kid. Thanks, anyway "

Quiet Seifert drew up to him. "Son, you ought to see the place. Just to get away. If a fella is ever going to love the land, it's out there. No trees to cover it up. No hills to hide the size of it. It's right there, right in your face. It gets on your hands."

"That's right," the Kid agreed, enthusiastic again. "There's so much and there. Here in Minnesota, in the timber, you can see maybe ten minutes. Out here it's two days." He was referring to distance in terms of time needed to walk it as a man on foot was apt to do. "Before you're done, you gotta go west. You gotta."

"Sure, Kid," Tyler said, glad that they were letting him off like this. "Before I'm done I will. With you. Before I'm done I'll see a lot of things. There's some things I've already done that I've got to straighten out."

The Kid understood. "Going home?"

"For awhile." Then, to change the subject, "You? Are you coming back in the fall?"

"Me? Sure, I wouldn't miss it. I want to be here when the last tree falls. You know how it gets in your blood."

"Yes," Tyler said. "It does get in your blood." But he was thinking of Socrates and the plans he had made. Schnapsie had told him how Socrates was going to hang it up and go back to Gertie. Gertie had to be told. His mother and father had to be told, too. They had to know that he was all right. He had to know how they felt. Not that it mattered so much anymore, because he knew that whatever happened at home he would be okay now. He had to tell them about Socrates even if they didn't understand.

The Oregon Kid broke back into his thoughts. "How about you, Bull? Coming back? The beast will need a partner. You could save another man's life." He was asking if they would ever meet again.

Tyler looked at him with fondness. "1 hope so, Kid. I can't say now." There were so many questions yet. "You know."

"Sure," the Kid soothed. "I know." The others had already moved off. The whistle on the Westbound blew and the train started to pull out.

The Kid thrust out his hand and Tyler gripped it strongly and held it. "Got to go," the Kid finally said. Tyler reluctantly let go.

Paddy moved in front of him. "Goodbye, Bull," he smiled. "May the good Lord hold you in the palm of his hand until we meet again." Tyler smiled back and awkwardly stuck out his hand. Paddy ignored it and they embraced.

"You're a hellava lumberjack," Paddy said.

"As are you," Tyler returned. "Both of us. We're the best there ever was, aren't we." It was not meant as a question. They grimaced and laughed, remembering the misadventures they had suffered.

Paddy and the Oregon Kid ran to catch the train. Tyler watched them cross the open set of tracks and climb onto one of the boxcars. Another train, eastbound, came through and, for a time obscured them. Still, Tyler looked to where the train would be.

Tears were running down his cheeks again. He felt like he was at a funeral. "And may the good Lord keep you all in his hands, too," he prayed.

When the eastbound freight cleared the station, he saw them again. They were up on the roof of the car. Paddy the Pig was waving to him, calling to him one last time to come with them. The Bangor Tigers were standing next to him, waving. Seifert and Toad were sitting on the roof, Indian fashion, Seifert's quiet eyes looking west. The Oregon Kid was at the back of the car. He whooped to Tyler and, bending over, did a handstand. He lifted one arm and waved goodbye. The Tigers grabbed his legs and playfully hung him over the side of the car.

Tyler laughed and waved. He kept his hand in the air until they were nearly out of sight, until Mike Sullivan came up behind him.

"You're not leaving with the others, then?"

"No," Tyler answered. He didn't turn so Mike wouldn't see him crying. "No, I have some things to take care of."

"That's good," Mike said, "Always finish up one job before you start another." He watched the receding train with Tyler for a time and then asked him the same question the Kid had. "Will you be coming back next year, Tyler?"

Tyler shrugged. "Mike, I don't know. I want to. I plan to." He started to say more, stopped, then added lamely, "But I don't know."

"You don't have to," Mike said. "I know how that is." Then he added, "If you do come back, work for me. It's time Rube stayed home with his children. I think you could be my wood's boss." Then he laughed. "Unless you want to saw with the Timber Beast again."

Tyler wiped his face and looked at Sullivan. Four months ago, he would have crawled to hear that type of compliment; would never have dreamed he would hear it from Mike's mouth. Now he shouldered it easily, accepting it as naturally as he now accepted his own maturation.

"Maybe Saatala will need a good right hand, huh?" Tyler countered. "Maybe I should hire out to him."

"No, No!" Mike chuckled at the notion. "Rudy will be his own man again by next year. One arm or two, it won't matter. Tyler, if you come back, you work for Hungry Mike. Fair enough?"

Tyler joined Mike in the laughter and it felt good.

"It will be an honor to have that position."

"You earned it."

"I don't think I would have survived the first month at another camp."

"You would have survived, Tyler. Do you know why? Because you are of good stock, Tyler of Chicago. Your father gave you that."

"Yes. I suppose he did, after all." Then he added, "And my mother, too."

"Aye, and your mother, too. They put something strong and good in you that just took a while to come out. They did that for you." Sullivan considered the matter for a moment and then went on. "Will you be passing through Minneapolis?"

"I expect so. To tell Gertie."

"I thought so. There is something I have to get to her." Mike took out the seven hundred dollars.

"I heard that you won this for Socrates," Tyler said.

"Maybe I did. Then, maybe Socrates helped me to win it. Those things happen like that."

"I wish Paddy and I had been there to see it."

"You were there, Tyler. All my boys were there," he winked.

"Why don't you give it to her, yourself, Mike?" Tyler asked.

Mike looked at the money and considered the question and its implications. He looked at Tyler. "I haven't been down there since Tanjka. It would be hard."

"You just told me to finish one job before starting another, Mike. I'm in no position to give advice but it seems."

Mike cut him off. "You're right. I should go." He paused. "I think I owe it to Socrates."

"We could ride down together," Tyler suggested.

"Yes," Mike said. "That would be nice. And we can discuss your new wages. Maybe," he added, with a twinkle in his eye, "I will go on to Chicago with you. I would like to see that big city again."

"Holy shit," Tyler cried, suddenly a child again. "Would you do that? My parents won't believe it. Let's do that! Tomorrow morning."

It was agreed. Sullivan said his good byes and moved off into the crowd. Today, he still had to close the camp account at Itascan Lumber's Grand Rapids office and draw his foreman's pay for the winter. He would then take ten dollars of it, make a huge meal at the hotel restaurant, get a quart of Old Crow and go to his room.

Tyler looked at his turkey. How small and foreign it looked to him now. It contained all the souvenirs of his winter. His heavy clothing, the corked boots, some wooden trinkets he had whittled in camp, the ugly football the Kid had bequeathed to him, and Socrates' Bible. In his pocket was a hundred and forty dollars. He picked up the sack and threw it over his shoulder. He looked around. There was no one left at the depot. From a camp of a hundred people, it had dwindled to just himself.

Walking downtown he passed in front of a barbershop. Through the reflection in the glass he examined a face he didn't recognize. Coupled with his luxuriant head of hair, he would have made a handsome mountain man. There was just a little facial skin showing on the cheeks around his striking blue eyes. Once soft, smooth and white, it had turned into a leathered shade of brown. Behind him a mother walked by with her child. As they moved past, Tyler could hear her speak to him. "Yes, dear, that man is a lumberjack, just like your father was."

Inside the shop the owner was getting ready to close up. He looked up and saw Tyler. He caught Tyler's eye and, picking up a razor, made a shaving motion. Tyler ran his hand over his beard. It would be an impressive thing to take home to his parents. What the hell, he thought as he walked into the shop. They'll never believe any of it, anyway.

A half-hour later he was on Lake Street smelling of lilac cologne. His pace was strong and confident and he knew exactly where he was going. When he reached the end of the street, he turned right onto the lane and walked up to the little, green-shuttered cottage. He hesitated at the gate, then opened it and went up to the front door and knocked. He heard foot-steps, saw the knob turn and the door open.

"Reverend Houghton!"

"Hello? Yes, I'm Reverend Houghton. Have we met before?"

"Jennifer's father?"

Houghton's parental instincts sharpened. "I have a daughter named Jennifer."

He watched Tyler with interest. "Are you a friend of Jennifer's?"

Tyler tried to regain his composure. "Ahh, sir, I've come to call on your daughter. With your permission. And her's, of course. If she will see me, that is!" He stopped himself.

A bemused Reverend continued to stare at him.

"We met in Duluth last fall, sir. She was returning from school then."

"Oh, yes," Houghton said, nodding his head slowly. "I believe ..." He was scrutinizing Tyler carefully, trying to place the familiar voice. Finally he pointed at Tyler. "Aren't you one of the boys from Sullivan's camp? Yes, you're the one they call Bull, aren't you? Timber Bull?"

Tyler's reply was controlled and even. "No sir. I was in that camp. I know the man you're referring to. Timber Bull is dead. We buried him on the Bigfork."

"How did he die," Houghton asked. There was suspicion in his voice.

"He fell in a hole, sir; in the river. He couldn't get out. It closed over him and he was gone."

Houghton shook his head. "How terrible! Another man gone. Were you there?"

"Yes sir. I was right there with him. At the last instant I got out. The Bull didn't make it."

"I'm sorry. I remember he was a troubled soul. I hope he found the Lord before it happened."

"He did sir," answered Tyler. "I'm sure he did. He had changed a lot over the winter. He was a good friend of Socrates and learned a lot from him."

"Oh, Socrates. The dear man." The sorrow was written on Houghton's face. "I just heard this afternoon. I wish I could have been there."

"He went in his sleep," Tyler said. "He won't be forgotten."

"Well! Yes," the Reverend agreed. "Maybe that's better for this Bull, that he made his peace in time. Socrates, he was always at peace. I shall remember them both in my prayers. Now, who did you say you were, then?"

Tyler took a deep breath. "My name is Tyler Caldwell, sir. Until last fall I was a student at Northwestern University in Chicago but I took a year off for work and travel. I thought a year in the camps would do me some good."

"Really! That must have been quite a challenge. Of course, Caldwell! Yes, come in Tyler. I do remember. Jennifer has talked of you on several occasions. She'll be pleased to see you. She hadn't expected you to come back, you know." Then Reverend Amos Houghton stepped back to admit Tyler and the young man entered his home.

The End

CPSIA information can be obtained
at www.ICGtesting.com
Printed in the USA
JSHW011923170323

3909950001B/6

9 780984 965410